High Kill

Praise for *HIGH KILL:*

"The author has captured the culture and realities of so many communities in Appalachia. As I read chapter to chapter, I could picture the cases I have prosecuted over the years and the faces of the animals from these cases. Though disturbing at times, this book will keep the reader engaged and wanting more."
Gillian Deegan, Virginia Prosecutor

"*High Kill* is all the things you expect in a good mystery novel - and much, much more. It's also a look at a major problem in Southwest Virginia - rampant animal abuse, often aided and sometimes committed by the very Animal Control Officers who are paid to investigate it. And a look at the heart of Appalachia, with its Mountain Mafia of corrupt local officials, poverty and drugs. The journalist heroine chasing a serial murderer runs smack into the nexus of animal and human abuse. Fast-paced and well-written, it echoes all-too-common headlines in today's papers."
Terry Anderson, former war correspondent and hostage, author: Den of Lions

"Ryan's ... prose is textured and lived-in, particularly when describing the settings and people of Randall County...on the whole, the author manages to move beyond crime novel clichés and expose the deeper ills of the society in which her tale is set."
Kirkus Reviews

High Kill
Diane Ryan

Tanglebranch Manor
A Division of Steemhouse Publishing

This is a work of fiction. All of the characters, organizations, and events portrayed in this novel are either products of the author's imagination or are used fictitiously.

HIGH KILL

A Tanglebranch Manor book
Published by Steemhouse Publishing, LLC
North Tazewell, VA 24630
info@steemhousepublishing.com.

www.steemhousepublishing.com

ISBN 978-1-7336040-0-0 (paperback)
ISBN 978-1-7336040-1-7 (ebook)

First Edition April 2019

Cover design and rendered artwork by Gary Mucklow, 2019 ©
Additional effects: Michel Quievreux and Diane Ryan
Photographic elements: Abstractor/under license from Shutterstock.com

ACKNOWLEDGMENTS

This novel would not have been possible without the support of an extended family of writers, editors, and animal welfare professionals. Trying to name them all would be an exercise in futility, but I will mention several special contributors.

Eileen McAfee has spent a portion of her life researching and documenting abuse in municipal animal shelters. She's the author of the Final Report on Abuse at the Russell County Animal Shelter in 2016, as well as the Wise County Report on Criminal Acts by ACO Arwood in 2018. The current improving conditions for animals in the Commonwealth of Virginia are due at least in part to her unfailing commitment to this cause.

Marcia Landau has been a staunch supporter of my rescue efforts in Southwest Virginia and an avid fan of this novel since its earliest drafts. Without her, it would not exist. Marcia, we did it! We finally made this happen. You are my soul sister and confidante, and I only hope I can bring even a fraction of the joy to your life that you bring to mine.

Several of my friends at the Internet Writers Workshop were indispensable in developing this novel from a technical standpoint. Carol Kean, Bob White, T. Francis Sharp, Michelle Riccio, Mark Kilfoil, Mark Piper, and Parker Rimes—I will never forget what you contributed to my early efforts. Your belief in my strange little manuscript is what kept me going long before I understood the scope of its purpose.

Last but not least I must thank the editorial and executive staff of Steemhouse Publishing. What you all came together to make happen is nothing short of miraculous. I predict you'll leave an enduring legacy not only on the Steem blockchain but for mainstream publishing as well. I love all of you dearly and look forward to many, many more years of us working alongside each other as professionals and friends.

Thank you, Gary Mucklow, for the phenomenal 3D rendering you did for the cover. It only took forty-seven tries. Or was it forty-eight?

Michel Quievreux—dieu merci pour Krakow! The hours you put into this project are what saved it. Every page of this book bears your influence.

Jayna Locke, Patti May, Reba McNeill—what a wonderful editing team you are! Daniel Thompson-Yvetot and Caleb Lail—this is the product of all your hard work and commitment to making our Triangle dream a reality.

I'm grateful to all of you.

HIGH KILL

CHAPTER ONE

Veterinarians had to kill things. Eric Blevins got it. Students became doctors one necropsy at a time. If he'd started Tech that fall like he planned, they'd have had him cutting up a lot of dead animals before they ever let him lay a hand on the live ones.

But there weren't any veterinarians on the mountain tonight. Just killers.

The dogs had a coon up a tree. Old Strut was barking short, and Eric could see a spotlight shining high on the ridge. Then another light with a smaller beam turned away and started moving down the hill. Junior Rasnick's head lamp, bobbing and bouncing along the path.

Eric waited beside the pickup trucks on flat ground below, curious. It wasn't like Junior to leave the hunt. He figured he'd hear the reason soon enough. And eventually there came Junior, crashing through the underbrush. Might as well have been a three-legged rhinoceros for all the noise he made.

"They must've got him," Eric said when Junior got a little closer. "I know that bark."

"Eh, fuck," Junior said. "You seen Rosie?"

Eric blinked. "No. She not up there?"

"Hell, no. Took off after a goddamned rabbit 'bout the time Strut went on the track." Junior pulled a beer from the cooler in his truck bed and drank half of it in one gulp. "She turns up, throw her in the box. I'm headed down the holler to see if she went that way."

Eric watched Junior move off with the shuffling, stiff-legged gait of a man who'd spent most of his life underground. Hips, back, knees—a body gave out early in the mines. Junior carried his rifle away from his side for ballast, making him look twice as wide as he actually was under the bulky Carhartt. Eric remembered him being a lot bigger before the roof bolts gave out in Low Fork No. 3 and Junior lay there for two days until they got the rocks moved. But that was years ago. Could be Eric's memory was as faulty as Rosie's tracking sense.

On the ridge, the spotlight bounced off the limbs of a naked hardwood, probably the big maple that hogged the outcropping. Eric had stood at the base of it many times, staring up the massive trunk. He'd seen plenty of coon taken out of that tree over the years. But the brutality got to him. Its effect was cumulative. At some point, he finally saw one more mangled gray body than he wanted to see in flashbacks when his head hit the pillow that night.

His Grandpap figured it out, but he never said anything. Lately, he just told Eric to watch the truck while they went up the mountain, especially if they left a dog in the box. Those Gillespies one holler over had a habit of taking what didn't belong to them, and a good-hunting hound would keep them in pills for the next six months even if they couldn't sell him with papers.

Killing for sport didn't put food on the table. Grandpap didn't eat the coon they took. It wasn't about meat or pelts or nuisance pests. It wasn't even about the trophies. It was all about the dogs—making them crazy for the hunt. And six months out of the year, the hunt was something Eric could get into. He'd have been right there with them on the ridge from April to September. But come firearms season when you took what you treed, he'd just guard the truck. And he'd never say anything, and nobody would ask. The coons would die, and he'd see them brought back torn to pieces, but by God he wouldn't have to watch while it happened.

He heard her a few seconds before he saw her coming out of the dark, trotting along the old logging road with her tongue dragging. Rosie had no doubt run the ridge from there to kingdom come, tracking junk game she probably never caught. She came straight to him and dropped to her belly, rolling partway onto her side with her front leg curled in submission. Pretty clear she wasn't looking for praise. Probably begging him not to boot her in the gut—likely what she'd get if Junior had been close enough to kick her.

"Come on, girl." Eric reached for her collar. "Let's get you in the truck."

She heaved herself onto the tailgate and padded into the dog box. Flopped down on the cool aluminum and just lay there, panting.

Eric shut the door of the box. Should be about over, this hunt. Law said they had to be out of the woods by two, and it was well past midnight. He checked his watch. Closer to one, actually. Old Strut was still at the tree, carrying on. And now the pup had the scent, so his bawl carried down the mountain along with Strut's.

Somebody would shoot this one down. Pup was too green to go home without fur in his mouth. Eric understood the logic. It was the doing he couldn't quite follow through with. Sure enough, the shot rang out clean and sharp, and seconds after, sounds of carnage. Guttural, primitive—growls and snarls and, mercifully, silence from the coon. Hopefully he was dead when he hit the ground.

Eric busied himself cleaning old napkins from the glove compartment of his Grandpap's Silverado. From there, he could keep an eye on Rosie recovering in Junior's dog box, and see the lights start to make their way down the mountain. The bright one out front was Grandpap. Behind him, Junior's oldest boy Josh bobbled along with a puny little glint of something that Eric could only see when the beam was pointed directly at him. Cell phone flashlight? Probably.

Junior must have been watching the lights, too, because he showed back up about the same time the others did. Eric shut the glove box and climbed out of the truck.

"And there she is." Junior stared at Rosie in the dog box. "Worthless piece of shit."

Eric pointed the opposite direction in the holler than Junior had gone looking for her. "Came from over that way."

"How long's she been back?"

"Since right after you left."

Junior muttered something Eric didn't try to interpret and slung open the dog box. He grabbed Rosie by the collar and dragged her out.

Eric's Grandpap had reached the truck. He opened the door and lay his rifle on the seat. Behind him, Josh was using the coon carcass as a tug toy, locked in a battle with the pup. One glimpse of fluffy ringed tail and bloody, popped eyeballs was enough. Eric focused his attention ahead, on Junior and Rosie.

Junior clipped a leash to the big Walker hound's collar and jumped her off the tailgate. He led her to a skinny locust tree a few feet away and tied her to its trunk. Broke his single-shot open and loaded a cartridge.

Eric's heart rate jumped. "What are you doing?"

"I ain't feeding that idiot," Junior said. "Not even worth selling."

Rosie wagged her tail. Slowly, in a wide arc.

"You're going to shoot her?" Eric squinted, hoping he'd misunderstood.

"Well, I'm not going to marry her."

Grandpap took a few steps toward Junior and pressed the backs of his fingers into the bulky padding of Junior's Carhartt sleeve. "Not in front of my grandboy."

Junior glared at him, eyeball to eyeball, man to man. Neither said anything for a long few seconds.

"Just turn her loose," Grandpap said. "You're far enough away from your house. She won't go home."

Eric clamped his teeth together. *Don't say a word. Not one word.* His cheeks felt hot. Jaw ached. *Fuck you, Junior, you ignorant bastard.* There was enough rope in the tool box to tie Junior to that goddamned tree and draw a bead on him same way he planned to draw down on Rosie. Eric had half a mind to do it.

"Your grandboy's a pussy?" Junior spit tobacco into a nearby bush. "That's what this is about?"

"You ain't shooting a dog in front of him. That's all."

"Well tell him to turn around while I do it. He ain't got eyes in the back of his head."

"I'll take her home with me," Eric said.

His Grandpap pointed a gnarled, work-stained finger toward Eric's face. "Shut your mouth. You stay out of it."

"But—"

"You heard me, boy."

Junior laughed and took another spit. "Next thing you know he'll be crying over the coon."

On the other side of the truck, Josh snickered. It was just loud enough to hear over the pup, whining and scratching to get back out of the dog box where Josh had put him.

"Let her go," Grandpap said, towering over Junior by at least six inches. "Or I'm going to shove that rifle up your ass."

Junior shot a look at Eric that would have withered tomatoes on the vine and unbuckled the wide leather collar from Rosie's neck. She ran right back to the truck and hopped on the tailgate.

"Jesus fucking—" Junior didn't finish the sentence. He grabbed Rosie by the hind legs and jerked her to the ground. She landed in a heap but didn't complain, just lumbered back up again and wagged her tail.

Junior slammed the tailgate harder than necessary. "I'm gone."

And he was. His boy Josh caught up with him right after he got the truck turned around and hopped in while Junior was still rolling.

Junior pulled out of the clearing and missed clipping Rosie's front shoulder by inches. She ran alongside the truck until they disappeared at the fork, and Eric supposed she kept running alongside it all the way to the road because she didn't come back.

Grandpap picked up the dead coon and tossed it in the truck bed. He pointed toward the cab. "Get in."

"But what about—"

"Get in the damn truck."

"But—"

"You need to learn when to leave it alone, boy."

That look. Eric had seen it his whole life and knew what it meant. It meant the conversation was over and if he kept pushing it would result in a backhand. He clenched his teeth and hauled himself into the truck. His cheeks burned like he'd already been slapped, hot against the crisp November air. He knew his place, knew better than run his mouth. But damn if he didn't want to. Damn if he didn't want to say exactly what he thought about Junior Rasnick and his fucked up way of doing things.

They met Rosie about an eighth of a mile from the hardtop. She was backtracking, nose to the ground, trotting along with her tail high. When she saw them she gave a little prance sideways, a big goofy hound smile on her face. Still just a pup, nowhere near finished. Eric sat forward, lowering his window as they got close to her.

"Put that window back up." Grandpap didn't slow the truck. "Ain't none of your business. Just let it be."

Eric stared hard at him. Didn't say a word, but thought aplenty. He checked the mirror. Rosie loped along beside the truck, keeping pace. She didn't seem anxious, just happy to be in sight of people she trusted. Not for long. Life as she'd known it was ending. Just as soon as the truck tires hit pavement, Rosie would be left behind, on her own, and catching the rabbits she chased would be a matter of survival, not sport. The last glimpse Eric caught of her in the mirror, she was still galloping behind them on the shoulder of Highway 12, a tri-colored speck fading to nothingness as the black night settled between them.

Eric didn't figure he'd be much for sleeping once he got home, and he was right. No matter that half an hour after they rolled into the yard, Grandpap was snoring in the recliner with one boot off and the other unlaced, a half-full pint of bourbon on the end table beside him. Eric took a long pull off the bottle himself before he slipped back out the door. He whistled for Popper, and the grizzled old Blue Tick came crawling out from beneath the underpinning of the chicken hutch.

"Let's go, boy," he said. "I got a job for you."

Eric put his dilapidated Ford Escort in neutral and pushed it to the end of the driveway, something he'd gotten good at his senior year. Either he never woke anybody up sneaking out or neither of his grandparents cared. Tonight might be a different story, because his Grandpap would know exactly what he was up to. As it stood, he didn't know what the hell he was going to do with Rosie if he found her. Leaving her in those woods again was not an option he'd consider.

Popper rode shotgun all the way to the turnoff. He sat in the front seat like a real somebody, facing forward, looking as serious and somber as Eric felt. His floppy jowls wiggled with the movement of the car, long black ears dangling well below his jaw. With the inexplicable insight some dogs have, he'd sensed the gravity of their mission and conducted himself accordingly. Eric knew Popper had forgotten more about treeing coon than most dogs would learn in their lifetime. But tonight he'd help flush Rosie out of her hiding place, if she'd found one. Maybe then Eric could relax and get some sleep. That was out of the question otherwise.

Eric didn't waste time. He drove to the clearing where the trucks had parked earlier, rolled his windows down, and called for Rosie. He avoided the ruts that could catch an axle and leave him stranded. Condensation swirled in the Escort's high beams, tiny particles of moisture that gathered like a silent mob in the still hours before dawn.

Odd being back there, seeing the dead grass flattened and the tire tracks they'd made just a short while ago, when the clearing rang with the bawling of coonhounds and terse voices. The ridge lay blanketed under a layer of fog that hugged the Clinch, and when it came, it always settled just before daylight like smoke roiling on the ground. Easy to get lost in low visibility, so he'd stay in the car. But Rosie could find him, fog or not. He just had to be there in case she was looking.

He let Popper out before they started back down the holler, and the old dog loped along in the Escort's low beams as they eased down the logging road. Eric whistled, called, gave the horn a few short beeps. So far, no Rosie. Just darkness, Popper's tail waving in the headlights in front of him, and fog dropping a few more inches every minute.

Then Popper doubled back. His gait had changed. So had his stance. His nose came up and he was taking information from the air now, not the ground. He tracked sharply north, in the direction of the river. And disappeared over a lip of rock and down a grade that ended in a bog.

Eric and his Grandpap had hunted that land for years. He worried for Rosie, if she had somehow found herself on soft ground at the bottom of the hill. Couple years back, the neighbors had lost cattle in that muck when they escaped across downed strands of barbed wire. Eric had been part of the rescue party sent to haul them out with a tractor, but it was too late by the time they got a road cut.

"Shit," he muttered, and braked to see what would happen next.

Somewhere several hundred feet down the hill, Popper let out a series of low whuffs, not his treeing bawl, and not anything Eric understood from Popper's seven-year run as the best wide hunter in Southwest Virginia. Then he yipped, a sound Eric had never heard him make on the trail. Less than a minute later, he appeared over the rise and just stood there, looking at Eric like he couldn't figure out why he was being ignored.

God damn it.

He might as well go caving without a rope, as take off down that embankment with fog rolling in. But in the absence of rope, he'd settle for a hound with a good nose. He checked his cell phone to make sure he had battery and signal. Grabbed a leash from the back floorboard where he always kept one just in case and fumbled around until he found the big handheld spotlight he never left home without. Switched it on—good. Strong beam, wouldn't fade on him any time soon.

"Come here," he told Popper. The dog hesitated, then obediently picked his way to Eric. Once the leash was clipped, Eric let Popper guide him down the hill.

The grade leveled off into the bog, about half an acre in the bend of the river that flooded often and was no doubt full of artesian wells. The footing was shit. Eric did manage to find ground he could walk on, but one misstep and he'd lose a boot, or worse.

"Rosie!" he called, hoping for movement, a whimper, a bark, anything that would give him a direction. "Rosie! Let's go, girl. Let's go home."

Silence. Except a low whine from Popper.

Eric stopped calling and looked at his dog. Popper was telling him something—what? There was no game on the ground there or in a tree, or if it was, Popper ignored it. This was something else. Something that had Popper on edge—anxious, not eager. Eric let the leash fall slack, holding only the loop.

"All right then," he said. "Show me."

Popper seemed confused for a moment, then he moved off in the direction of the river, with Eric in tow. Rains had been heavy for the last month, but the water had receded and the entire bog lay covered in muddy brown scum.

Because of the monochrome of dried mud, the flash of blue Eric caught in his spotlight beam got his attention. He shone the beam along the ground and could see paw prints leading in that direction. Popper had been over there, had sniffed all around that piece of ground. Blue. A familiar blue. Eric should know what he was looking at, but didn't—yet. It was a bright shade, something manmade. Plastic. Yeah, that made sense. One of those blue poly drums like the soap for an automated car wash came in.

Rosie probably wasn't in the drum. But something was. The top had come partway off and hung by a busted silicone seal, one edge of it wedged in the muck. Whatever lay inside the barrel had Popper as upset as Eric had ever seen him.

"Okay," Eric said. "I believe you. You say I need to go, so I'll go."

He followed the paw prints Popper had left earlier, figuring the dog wouldn't walk on unstable ground. Easy does it, one inch at a time. Test the ground before committing to each step. So far so good. Didn't seem like he'd get mired up but no use taking stupid chances.

Right there at the barrel, he noticed the smell. A deer carcass? It was early in the season to find gut piles and offal from field dressing with that degree of rot. Temperatures had been cool, so he figured whatever this stinker turned out to be, it had been in the barrel at least a month. And if it washed downstream in the flood waters, no telling where it came from.

He couldn't see into the barrel without bending down, putting himself on Popper's level. That didn't seem appealing, so he nudged the barrel with the toe of one boot. It was heavy, partially filled with water and whatever, but once he kicked it loose from the wild grape vine holding it, the barrel plunked flat into the mud and didn't roll. Eric gave the broken lid a quick tug. It came off in his hand. He tossed it aside and aimed the spotlight beam into the hole.

At first all he could make out were ribs. Maybe a deer, more or less the right size, still covered in tissue that looked almost freeze dried—but didn't smell that way. Everything but the bones was that same shade of muddy monochrome. Except on one of the forelimbs, just above a joint that would correspond with the human wrist—something greenish. Putrefaction? Ink?

A tattoo?

He could just make out the shape of a cross. A Celtic-looking cross, with elaborate shading and some kind of writing beneath it. Everything below the carpal joint was hidden underneath the leg bones, the body tucked and packaged into that barrel with no regard to proper alignment. Eric's stomach started to heave. No way he was looking at what he thought he was looking at.

Then he saw the skull.

It wasn't apparent at first, lolled off to the side and covered in muck. But as Eric revealed more of it with the spotlight beam, he saw empty eye sockets, matted hair of no distinguishable color, and teeth in a jaw that hung slack. One of the lower molars had a silver filling.

Eric didn't make it three steps before he puked. He retched until it hurt, hanging on to the pinprick of light at the center of his blackening vision, knowing if he went down in that bog he could easily end up like the body in the barrel, and it might be a long, long time before anybody thought to look for him there.

(Key of G)
It's like driving down a road that goes to nowhere
And I can't read a single goddamned sign
I don't know if I've ever been real enough
Or if I was just a waste of time.

It's like rain keeps falling but the ground is dry
When the sun don't bother showing up to shine.
I don't know why you couldn't just lie to me
And say you needed just a little time.

Can't you just go, let me breathe a while
You can't catch me if I don't fall
See, I don't bleed and I don't cry
I'm not who you thought I am at all.

---Erik Evans, 2001

CHAPTER TWO

The James River rolled its way under Richmond's I-95 bridge, millions of muddy gallons carrying silt and coal ash and whatever organic pollutants it could pick up on its journey to the sea. Traffic on the bridge was moving, but slowly. Stuck in the northbound fast lane, Taylor Beckett watched the quiet, inexorable flow take the bend southward and continue toward Chesapeake Bay. Deceptively calm, murky, and the color of liquid earth, the dark water kept a lot of secrets.

The Capitol District hid somewhere to her left, behind a retaining wall and several tall buildings. To her right Union Hill, where so much history lived. She'd been all over this city in the past three years, interviewing, researching, and digging for ratings gold. Sometimes she found it. Most of the time she didn't.

On Mayo Island, an oversized billboard promised a sixty-million-dollar jackpot for Powerball. Modest prize, by nearly every standard these days. Taylor tapped her fingers on the steering wheel. She'd never bought a ticket. Not much confidence in luck. Tip her off about a rigged draw, though ... now that might give her ethics a real stretch while she decided what to do about it.

Traffic inched toward the heart of the city, Taylor and all the thousands of drivers and passengers caught in the same construction snarl.

Depending on her frame of mind, a traffic jam could be either curse or cure. She welcomed this one, since today she wasn't homesick for her desk, but infinitely more drawn to the congestion and the smog and the cracked concrete than she was to the controlled chaos of a newsroom. Everything felt more real out here. She felt more real. She stayed closer to her thoughts on the street, closer to every reason she'd decided to report the news rather than make it. She had no desire to be on the other side of somebody else's coverage ever again.

She switched from Sirius to FM and listened to the final strains of something by Def Leppard. A little too eighties for her taste, but she let the dial sit where it landed on WKLR. The classic rock station could be diverse when it wanted to. They'd lose her with anything released after 2005, but she was good until then. Music had stopped when her life did. It took many years and a lot of miles before she dared to touch the radio again.

North of the coliseum, the afternoon traffic thinned and her drive to the station hit warp speed. She parked in WRCH's back lot far sooner than she'd hoped. The convenience store robbery in Colonial Heights hadn't taken long to cover—seventy dollars out of the till, robber waving something around under a towel that may or may not have been a gun, security footage in the hands of police. She'd driven her own car, ditched her cameraman before they even left the station. Yeah, he'd probably complain. Again. And she might hear from the broadcasters' union. Again. She'd taken less than a minute of film herself with a handheld. So much simpler that way most of the time, especially if she wasn't interviewing or doing a live feed from the scene. She pulled the SD card from her camera and went straight to her desk, an afternoon of laptop editing ahead of her before she gave any copy to the anchors.

"Hey."

The voice grabbed her attention just as she plopped into her chair. She looked up. Charles Carter, politics and current affairs, at her service.

"Oh, hey." She waited until he made it all the way to her. Then asked, "What are you doing here? I thought you were covering the Senate Ag Committee."

"Adjourned until tomorrow." He pushed a stack of binders, her stapler, and two dirty coffee mugs aside to perch half his ass on the edge of her desk. "So who dunnit? In Colonial Heights?"

Taylor stared at the screen while her laptop booted. "PD'll probably release a name by the time we go to air. Everything I have will be yesterday's news."

He smiled, but kept his mouth firmly closed. Gave a little nod, and pulled a folder from under his arm. Held it toward her, dark fingers clamped hard on the manila cover. "So check this out."

Taylor blinked. Stared at the folder, considered taking it from him, and laced her hands on the desk instead. "What is it?"

He flapped it at her. "Body number three. Randall County. They're giving this to Vanessa."

She glared at him and snatched the file from his hand.

He grinned. "That's my girl."

"I'm not your girl."

"But you know you want to be."

She gave him her fiercest stink-eye. "Randall County—where exactly is that? Three miles east of Hillbilly Hell?"

"Southwest part of the state. Near the Tennessee line."

"I know that," she snapped. Then, "Why Vanessa?"

Charles shrugged. "Maybe she waved her pom poms just right and Hennessey liked it."

"Yeah. Or maybe she waved a little pussy at him instead."

Vanessa Chambers. Hal Hennessey. Reporter and assignment editor—wouldn't be the first time. Taylor just wasn't sure she believed it, even if she had been quick to think in that direction. More likely, Vanessa just happened to be standing by the water cooler when Hennessey chose to put a crew on something six hours outside their coverage area.

Vanessa Chambers. *Way to go, Hennessey.*

Taylor opened the file and scanned the items it contained. Couldn't focus, and closed it again. Didn't remember a single word she'd just read.

Vanessa Chambers. *Shit.*

Not even two years out of Emerson, an eight-month internship at CNN—hired off a resume and a three-minute demo reel. But she was cute. Oh yes, definitely cute. Strawberry blond, and size four would hang on her like a circus tent.

"Hmm," Taylor said thoughtfully. "Wonder if she gives head."

"Ah, now. You know that trash talk don't work on me." Charles gave a short laugh. "I'm impervious to you."

She cocked a brow. "Oh, big word. Did you need a dictionary for that one?"

"Maybe I did, but I borrowed it off your desk."

Impossible to keep going with it at that point. She cracked up, pinching the bridge of her nose between two fingers. "God help me."

"Now look at the file, Beckett. Tell me you couldn't do something with that."

She looked again at the information in the folder. Not much—AP ticker about three dead bodies in Southwest Virginia, all shoved in blue poly drums, sealed with silicone, and dumped in the woods. All male, late teens or early twenties. Somebody's moonshine gig gone bad, probably. Or dope. Always dope in that part of the state. Then a couple stories from a paper out of Bristol, no photos of the victims, just a laundry list of details. She looked up at Charles and shrugged.

"What am I supposed to be seeing here?" she asked. "Whatever it is, I'm missing it."

"It's what you're not seeing," he said. "Not even my kind of news, but I'll bet I could spend half an hour online and flesh out a better story than anything in that folder. These are three kids, Beckett. People. They left footprints where they walked. And all they get is four inches on page three?"

She had to admit, the coverage did seem a little thin.

"Doesn't that at least make you curious?" he asked.

Maybe. A teeny bit. Then again, Charles Carter had missed his calling as a skip tracer. Or a CIA spook. He always made her nervous—the kind of shit he found about people with a Tor browser and a few clicks of the mouse? No telling what he could dig up about her if he ever thought to look.

"So, what do you want me to do?" she asked. "Hennessey's already given this to Gidget."

"Yeah, but she's still out on that tax evasion thing over in Newport News. He hasn't talked to her about it yet. He can still change his mind. So, I want you to go in there and tell him you need Kavanagh and Perry, a car, and a budget. Then I want you to take your ass to Randall County and find out what's going on.

Time to wake up, Beckett. You're not getting any younger. You think you're just going to coast into an anchor chair because of shit you reported ten years ago—I got news for you. 'Gidgets' like Vanessa Chambers are going to beat you to it while you're out taking cell phone video of gas stations."

She stared at him. Tried to decide if she should slap him on the right cheek or the left. Would a handprint even show up on skin that dark? Maybe she'd dot his eyes. Black men most definitely got shiners. Or she could just knock his teeth down his throat and be done with it.

"You're an asshole, Charles. Did you know that?"

"And you're a cantankerous, foul-mouthed, entitled white bitch. But I love you anyway. And so does Hennessey. If you tell him you're going to bring him back a different story than that one off the wire, he'll trust you to do it. But if you just sit on your ass and let Vanessa have it—then I don't know, Taylor. I guess that's the point I'll really start to worry."

Taylor. Shit. Why did he have to go and play the "friend" card?

Underneath her desk, she kicked her trash can. "God damn it."

"If you turn that over," he said. "I'm not cleaning it up."

She rolled her eyes. "It was a handheld. Not a cell phone."

"What?"

"The gas station video."

"Okay. If you say so."

She gave her head a small shake and closed the folder. Got up, and headed toward Hennessey's office.

Before she made it too far, though, she turned and pointed a finger at Charles. "Just let it be on record that I'm doing this under duress."

He laughed, brilliant white smile throwing sunbeams all over the room. "Duly noted."

(Key of F)
If my fortune cookie's right
Then I don't have no damn foresight
And I can't drag myself in from the rain.
Sorry for the second guess
So I'll confess that you know best
And chalk it up that I'm not on my game.

I wonder if you ever knew
All the shit that I would do
When you would slam that door and lock me out.
Should have stayed and talked this through
You know that I'll still wait for you
And while I do, babe, you still knock me out.

Switch-track ahead and don't you stop it
Show me an exit sign
Give me an off-ramp, a fast lane.
Switch track or die, I'm gettin' off it
I need a way out, a way off this train.

Well, I'm a boy who loved a girl
Who loved herself and loved the world
Who loved his love but didn't love him back.
And you're a bitch who blew my mind
You keep me workin' overtime
You push, you pull, yeah, girl you got the knack.
                                   ---Erik Evans, 2002

CHAPTER THREE

Taylor stared at the back of Stu Perry's ponytailed head. In the front passenger seat of the car, he made a big show of examining the tiled walls and concrete ceiling of the East River Mountain Tunnel as they drove through it. Behind the wheel, Nigel Kavanagh hadn't taken his eyes off the road for the last quarter of a mile. Taylor wondered if he had even blinked.

"So what do you think it would take to bring this mountain down on top of us?" Perry asked.

"No idea," she said. "But don't be putting that idea out to the universe."

"Me saying it won't make it happen." Half-turned in his seat, Perry squinted at Taylor. "I'm just postulating."

"Postulate on your own time." Kavanagh didn't look at Perry as he spoke. "Right now just worry about where the hell we're going. You're navigating. So navigate."

"Fine," Perry groused. "Keep driving. Straight. Don't turn. Or bad things will happen."

At that, Kavanagh shot Perry a quick sideways glance. "I mean when we get through the tunnel, you asshat. Not while we're in it."

"Both of you shut up." In the back seat, Taylor looked at the map on her phone, which hadn't lost signal underground. Repeaters, maybe? Mounted in the tunnel? "Immediately after we're clear, take the exit toward Bluefield."

"So we're almost there, then?" Kavanagh's gaze met hers in the rearview mirror, but only briefly before it snapped back to the road in front of them.

"Still about an hour away," she said.

"Where the hell are we going?" Perry grumbled. "And has anybody ever come back from there?"

Hennessey had put his foot down this time. Taylor would not cover the story alone. But for this piece—this location—that was fine. Perry was okay behind the camera, and as segment producer, Kavanagh was good in a pinch. At just over six feet, however, and an easy two-hundred-eighty pounds, Kavanagh was even better in case of emergency. He was non-violent. Mostly. But Taylor had seen him toss a rowdy protester with one hand, in 2014 when rioting and looting did not break out in DC, at least not on the corner where they'd set up.

The I-77 exit ramp dumped them onto a four-lane with almost no other cars in sight. After a couple miles, the road funneled them around a tight curve and underneath a modern-looking overpass. They rode in silence for a few miles, until they passed a state line marker announcing that Virginia was for lovers.

"Wait…." She looked at the map on her phone. "We had to go to West Virginia to get back to Virginia? Where did that happen?"

"Halfway through the tunnel," Kavanagh said. "It straddles the state line. Take a breath, Beckett. Your passport's current, right?"

For the next half-hour they rode mostly without conversation, in the shadow of a mountain that loomed parallel to the four-lane like an ancient sentry standing guard. It created a mental barrier as well as a physical one. They'd crossed an entire range between the I-77 tunnels, leaving behind a busier, brighter world that included major metropolitan areas like Roanoke and Lynchburg. From here all the way to Tennessee lay the forgotten miles of Southwest Virginia, notorious for poverty, prescription drug abuse, and inherent mistrust of outsiders. Taylor noted the proximal decrease of chain stores and recognizable branding, the gradual transition from welcoming and accommodating to a world with the shutters drawn. Private and commercial properties grew smaller, less well-maintained. Many billboards stood empty, no message at all.

"We need gas," Kavanagh said. "Anything nearby?"

Perry looked at him. "You're just now realizing this? Now that we're out here in the damn jungle?"

Taylor consulted her phone. "Several gas stations just ahead. I think we'll be fine without military extraction."

"What about food?" Perry said. "Please tell me there's food."

Minutes later, Kavanagh killed the engine beneath the weathered canopy of a convenience store. Taylor thought about staying in the car, then thought about how far they might have to drive before the next public restroom. She got out and stretched, sampling the breeze in a series of sniffs. Nice. Car exhaust and gas fumes. So much for clean mountain air.

Women's restroom—a door that closed with a bolt latch, a sink barely hanging on the wall with a roll of brown paper towels beside the faucets, and a sign on the back of the plywood stall door that read, "hold handle down to flush." Really? People needed instructions for that? Taylor hovered. No way she'd put her ass on that seat. Howard Hughes might have been a germaphobe, but at least he didn't die of a staph infection.

That done, Taylor browsed the cooler for liquid refreshment and found the usual selection—Pepsi and Coke products, a bevy of energy drinks, and Pure Leaf Tea. What a nice surprise. Even lemon flavor, which she liked. She grabbed a bottle and browsed for a snack, bypassing the candy bars for something with a bit more substance. Trail mix, maybe. Nuts were full of protein, right? And she needed protein to fend off … what? What was that sense of unease, like she was being watched?

She peeped over the top shelf of the display rack, through all the little single-serving packages of Planters—cashier behind the counter with a name tag, a man in a dirty blue shirt with reflective strips sewn on, and a woman in a denim skirt with hair so long she could probably sit on it. That was her surveillance team. They took turns staring, discreetly, never for more than a few seconds at a time. Body language was non-confrontational, and when the man in the dirty shirt caught her looking back, he smiled. A couple of teeth missing, the rest stained with tobacco.

At least she hoped it was tobacco.

Nobody spoke to her. Now they weren't even looking at her. Forget the snack. She stood in line behind the woman with long hair. The cashier spoke perfunctorily, no pleasantries. When Taylor stepped up for her turn at the register, all conversation ceased. Just punch, punch, punch the buttons and a somber gaze that was not unfriendly yet undeniably austere. Taylor paid with exact change, grabbed her drink off the counter, and race-walked to the door.

At the car, she met Kavanagh's eye as he finished cleaning the windshield. "Take the magnets off," she said. "Put them in the trunk."

"What?"

"The WRCH magnets—take them off the doors and put them in the trunk."

"Why?"

"Because if we want anybody here to talk to us, we can't come in with a bullhorn announcing that we're from off the rez."

"We're not doing that."

"Trust me—we are. Just do it, for fuck's sake."

Stu opened his door and stepped out to rest a forearm on the roof of the car. "If I take the damn things off myself, will you let us eat?"

"Jesus." Taylor grabbed the magnet from her side of the car and tossed it in the back seat ahead of her.

Kavanaugh shoved the squeegee back into its holder mounted by the pump and jerked the station ID off the driver's side. He took his place behind the wheel and handed the magnet to Taylor. She put it with the other one facedown on the floorboard. Not quite as well-hidden as they'd be in the trunk, but close enough.

Back in the car, they turned west on the four-lane. Taylor consulted her phone, then leaned forward and showed Stu her screen. "Chinese, Mexican, assorted heart-attacks-in-a-sack, and pizza, five miles ahead."

Twenty minutes later, they parked in front of a Mexican restaurant with their Chinese takeout and divvied up the contents of four bags. Taylor used the time to go over her notes, occasionally sipping a spoonful of egg drop soup and nibbling on the deep-fried pieces of whatever that came with it. She didn't share Stu's insatiable appetite, nor Kavanaugh's tolerance for grease. But when in Rome—well, she'd make do.

"Here." Stu reached backward between the front seats as far as his shoulder would rotate. "Have one."

Taylor glanced up. Fortune cookie—no thanks. She'd sworn off those and any tripe messages they contained years ago. "You eat it. I'm good."

Not that she totally discounted the whole fortune thing. Maybe it held a shade of truth—sometimes. At least once, even though it hurt to remember.

"What's yours?" her college roommate had asked all those years ago, leaning across the table for a peek at Taylor's fortune. "Mine says, 'land is always on the mind of a flying bird.' What the hell does that even mean?"

Taylor folded the tiny slip of paper in half and shoved it in her pocket. "It says I have rice in my teeth."

Karmen Fernandez looked at her with a blank expression for a second before making a face. "Bullshit. Wait...really?"

Taylor laughed but didn't feed Karmen's curiosity further. "Where is it you said we have to go first—before study group?"

"To my uncle's bar. My dad sent him three hundred bucks to give me, and I need it."

"You said something about a guy."

Karmen rolled her eyes. "There's always a guy, Taylor. Always."

No shit.

"Some dude with the band," Karmen said. "Uncle Luis keeps wanting to introduce us. I think he's supposed to be there tonight."

"Band?"

"Bunch of wankers call themselves Mellow Jennie. Doesn't really sound like a band I'd want to see."

"It's a name...kind of a stupid name...but so is Third Eye Blind. And you'd go see them."

"Damn right I would." Karmen started clearing their table, shoving empty food wrappers into one of the paper soup containers. "So, let's go. Time's wasting."

Taylor finished the last bite of her egg roll and swallowed it with melted ice she slurped from the bottom of her cup. Her fingertips slipped into her pocket for the fortune cookie message, so she could toss it on the pile of trash Karmen had ready for the garbage can. But she hesitated, unsure why. It was just a scrap of paper, mass-produced and widely distributed. It meant nothing. Still, though—it niggled at her.

You are someone great men will write songs about.

On their way to meet guys in a band, no less.

Taylor let the fortune hide in her pocket and followed Karmen out of the restaurant.

Decades later, in the back seat behind Kavanaugh and Perry, Taylor put the lid on her soup and placed it back in one of the paper sacks. Some decisions still haunted. Best there be no reminders of them, ever.

(Key of G)
I'll never be the star, the main headliner
Not one of the movers and shakers making rain.
But I play my songs and people sing along
So I get more things right than I get wrong.
I'm not a man who wears his heart on a chain
I don't need more notches to stay on my game.
But I don't want to lose a chance to make you happy
Cause I know a good thing when I see it coming at me.

Hey, this is me, and now I've got you in sight.
You're where I go from here, and it all starts tonight.
Where were you while I've been living my life
You're where I go from here, and it all starts tonight.

I never knew I had such a big sum missing
I should have seen my numbers did not make sense.
If life is equation, I've been backward all along
Reversed every column, and added it all wrong.

This time, I'm not wrong.

---Erik Evans, 2003

CHAPTER FOUR

The Randall County Sheriff's Office might have been a school at one point. Taylor's suspicion about that had to do with the old roll-out windows on the upper floors, and the gymnasium with the collapsible bleachers she could glimpse through open double doors at the end of the long main hallway. Whatever the case, all traces of such history had been scrubbed from the front entrance and vestibule, now equipped with metal detectors, bulletproof glass, and magnetic card readers for ID badges. She waited there with Kavanagh and Perry, making use of the chairs set in a row along one wall.

"Taylor Beckett?"

She stood, recognizing the Sheriff from online photographs and videos of press conferences.

"Terry Hastings." He extended his right hand.

His handshake was practiced, grip firm, palms not quite calloused but far from soft. He met her gaze levelly, blue eyes clear and steady. Nothing in the room competed for his attention. She imagined that people had voted for him based on that handshake alone. Consummate politician—but sincere? Hard to tell.

"We can go in my office if you want," he said. "Coffee's fresh."

Taylor smiled. "Thank you. Sounds good."

Perry and Kavanagh stayed put, well-practiced in their roles. Both were reading—Perry, something on his phone, and Kavanagh, something from the pile of magazines on a table in the corner. Taylor fell in step behind Sheriff Hastings, sticking close when he buzzed them through the second set of bulletproof doors with a quick swipe of his ID card.

"We haven't been in this building long," he said as they walked. "Fewer stairs than the top floor of the courthouse where we used to be, so you won't hear me complain."

She smiled and nodded. And observed.

Not quite the stereotype, this guy. Youngish—mid-forties—his thick black hair flecked with silver. He moved like a former athlete. Running back in college? Maybe his thing was baseball. Track? She would have pegged him as a high school athletics coach a lot faster than she would have guessed county sheriff. Did that work to his advantage or disadvantage? He certainly seemed comfortable in his own skin.

"So what can I do for you today?" He showed her into a room large enough for his desk, a micro-kitchen, and a full-sized conference table. He pulled a chair back and motioned for her to sit.

"This is just an introduction." She made herself comfortable on the leather seat. "Couple of stories off the wire—just wondering who I should reach out to. You seemed obvious."

He nodded once, then turned to a small coffee maker tucked into the corner of a short credenza. Not a Keurig. Plain coffee, fresh, and it smelled strong. "Cream and sugar?"

"Black, thank you."

He filled two mugs bearing the Sheriff's Department logo and carried them to the table. He handed her one and took a seat across from her. "I make it stout. Let me know if you change your mind about that cream."

Disarming, this man. But she sensed that, like his handshake, it was a practiced skill.

"Are you local?" she asked, curiosity getting the best of her. "To the area—to Southwest Virginia?"

"I am, yes. Fourth generation. Parents born and raised here in Randall County." He pronounced it "Ran'all," with no audible "d." "So were their parents, and grandparents before them. Hastings were here before the mines." He took a cautious sip of his steaming coffee. "Although I did spend a few years in Knoxville. University of Tennessee—Forensics."

She blinked and said the first thing that hit her brain. "The Body Farm."

He nodded. "Yes."

"How interesting."

"Oh, yeah. Very. I ended up diverting into law enforcement instead after I graduated, but the background's been useful more than once."

"No doubt."

"So how can I help you? You said something about stories off the wire?"

"Yes." She nodded. "Altizer, Dillow, and Hess. The blue barrels."

His brows twitched at her mention of the barrels, but his expression reverted instantly to neutral. And stayed that way. "Our three recent homicide victims."

"Three different fatal mechanisms," she said. "But each of the bodies was found stuffed in a blue plastic drum. Are you officially linking them yet?"

He smiled with his mouth closed. "How about this—how about I give you everything we've already released about each of those cases. They're active investigations. There are things we aren't going to tell you, on or off record. But we have a good working relationship with local press. I see no reason we can't extend that to include your agency as well."

"Thank you." Taylor smiled, hoping she nailed the charm as effortlessly as he did.

"We have a public relations team tracking news stories if they involve our cases or our deputies, and they keep digital copies of all the articles. Everything from major news outlets to Facebook, Instagram, and Twitter."

She blinked. "Really?"

"Oh, yes. We're active on social media. It's an excellent tool for law enforcement. We locate quite a few fugitives by posting wants on Facebook. We even have an app—a tip line—for mobile devices. You should check it out."

"I will." And she would. Most definitely. But that wouldn't be her story, no matter how many human-interest rabbits Hastings deployed for her to chase. "So can I get a copy of your press file— 'everything you've already released' about these cases? That would be a good place for me to start."

His eyes narrowed. But then he nodded, acknowledging her request. "I'll put a packet together for you." He took one more sip of his coffee before he nudged the cup aside and stood. "If you'll wait out front, I'll get it to you in just a few minutes."

Fine by her. Taylor considered it a win. He'd told her exactly nothing, but an awful lot at the same time. They'd taken each other's temperature across that table, and that was as good a starting point as any.

⁕

Strangled, suffocated, and gassed—three similar but different ways to die, one method of disposal. Just another day at the office for a psycho with an imagination.

Taylor pushed the pile of clippings and printouts toward the center of the table. Arms over her head, fingers laced, she stretched until her back popped, using the moment to sneak a glance at Kavanagh and Perry. With her on the outdoor patio of their bed and breakfast, they sat hunched over their half of the file Hastings had given her at the sheriff's office, brazenly doing the work of an investigative reporting team. Cameras and other equipment sat forgotten in their rooms.

Wonder what the broadcasters' union would have to say about *that.*

"This isn't so bad, for a B&B in the jungle." She looked around the half-hidden side yard off the edge of the patio, at the shade cast by a ridge that rose abruptly from the terrain behind them, and the deep green of spring grass that stood no chance of being bleached by the sun. Ever. "Beats the Super 8."

Perry glanced up. "Yeah, but for another thirty minutes of drive time you could be at the Martha Washington. Bet they have wi-fi."

She lowered her arms and just sat there for a moment. Wi-fi would be handy as hell.

"What's up with these names?" Perry asked, squinting at one of the printouts. "Like 'Honaker.' Is that something regional? I never heard that in New Mexico. Or Oregon. Just here."

Kavanagh shrugged but didn't look up from the report in his hand.

"What about Quesenberry?" Perry frowned. "That's another one I keep seeing. Anything like a huckleberry, or some shit you bake in a pie?"

Kavanagh stared at him. "Try eating a 'Sprayberry' and see how far you get."

32

"Halle Berry." Perry grinned. "Can I eat that?"

"Oh, for God's sake." Taylor slapped a palm hard on the table. "So what are we thinking? Killer test-driving each m.o. to see what fits?"

Kavanagh scratched his head. "Early victims. Playing around with methods. That would be my guess."

Taylor pulled one news story from the file. It was a scanned copy of a front-page newspaper article, bearing a date from the fall of last year, when they found the first body.

"Hey, Kavanagh," she said, speed-reading the article. "The first vic—the one in the swamp—Altizer, right? Dylan Altizer?"

"I think so, yeah." Kavanagh didn't look up, back to studying the paper he held. "Actually, a definite yes. That's what I have here—the press release after they IDed him."

Perry shuffled some papers on the table in front of him. "These were stacked chronologically. Would it help if we sorted them by victim? I've got one here from Topix, people talking about the kid who found the Altizer body."

Taylor blinked. "A kid found him?"

"Well, teenager. Nineteen, I think. Or there and abouts."

"So what are they saying on Topix?" she asked.

"Basically, that he's a pussy. This one jackass says he was coon hunting with him earlier that night and he got all jacked up over somebody shooting a dog."

Taylor frowned. "Too many pronouns. Who got jacked up? Who shot the dog?"

"One of the hunters shot the dog. And this kid, Erik Evans...."

Taylor was sure Perry kept talking. But she didn't hear anything else. Because he couldn't possibly have said what she thought he did.

That name.

No way in hell.

Darks spots started at the edges of her vision and plowed inward. She gripped the edge of the table with both hands to stop the patio from spinning.

"Wait," she said, not caring who she interrupted. "What was that name again?"

Perry scowled at her. "Eric Blevins. Why? Ring a bell?"

Yes, but not in a way that would make sense if she tried to explain it.

Breathe in. Breathe out. Slowly. Don't hyperventilate.

"No. Just—" *Speak. Say the words. It's not that hard. Focus.* "Somebody get me his contact info. I want to talk to him."

Jesus. This was the last damn thing she needed. She had good reason for working alone whenever she could—it was way too hard trying to hide the crazy when shit like that happened.

Taylor could go for months without trouble. Then the least little thing—a word, a song, a name—could trip her up and send her sprawling. Always best when she didn't have an audience.

Kavanagh and Perry had taken the car and gone hunting for beer. The bed and breakfast was dry, no alcohol served. Dinner had been hot roast beef sandwiches with chips—Taylor and her crew were the only guests, apparently not important enough to fire up the kitchen for a full meal. After forcing half of hers down and tossing the rest, she'd come back to the patio, since it was quiet and reasonably secluded.

She looked up at the sky, squinting. Overhead, it shimmered blue and bright. But there in the shadow of that damn mountain, dusk dark had come early. No direct sun, no light and no warmth. Thank God she'd packed a sweater.

Why in the hell did that kid's name have to sound like—

Taylor drew her feet into the oversized lawn chair and wrapped her arms around her knees. The memories would come whether she wanted them to or not. At least she had some privacy here on the patio. At least there was that.

"I asked you three times—are you ready to go?"

Taylor gave her head a hard shake. *Go away, Karmen. Go away, Chicago.*

Not a chance. Might as well settle in for the ride.

As real as if she were actually standing there, Karmen Fernandez stared at Taylor across her uncle's bartop, waiting on a response. "I asked you three times—are you ready to go?"

Taylor pinned her attention on Karmen instead of the guys doing sound checks on the dive's tiny stage. Not easy—the guys were much more interesting.

"Sure," Taylor lied. "Any time you are."

Across the bar, Karmen tucked a wad of bills into her pocket. Money from Karmen's dad in Venezuela, delivered by her Uncle Luiz.

Taylor glanced back toward the stage.

That dude meant it—whatever he was telling his guitar. And they were definitely talking, the man and his dark red acoustic. He had it amped, complete with a stomp box to give the notes a dirty sound, and he was playing the feedback Hendrix-style. Taylor couldn't stop watching.

And then he sang a few lines, lips close to the mike and his eyes shut. *"It's like driving down a road that goes to nowhere, and I can't read a single goddamned sign."*

Probably her age or close to it, with dark blond hair poking from underneath a knit cap. Shadows around his eyes, painted there by genetics rather than exhaustion, gave him a haunted look even when he smiled. And he did smile, at no one in particular, when he slapped a palm across the strings to silence them.

"I think you got it," he said into the mike, offering someone across the room a thumbs-up. "Sounds good up here."

He pulled the strap over his head and set the guitar on a stand near the amp.

From her spot near the wall of taps, Karmen hadn't moved for at least a full minute. Taylor didn't bother wondering why. She studied Karmen as the guitar player took the steps two at a time and headed their way. Ah, yes. Karmen—lovely Latina girl with big black eyes and long dark hair—posture erect, shoulders back. Chin up. Standing a little hipshot, thumbs hooked in the waistband of her jeans. Pretty. Even sexy. Taylor just stood there, feeling utterly unable to compete.

Mr. Guitar leaned both elbows on the bar. Tats here and there, one on the inside of his left forearm that was some sort of inscription. Leather bands and a string of wooden beads looped around the opposite wrist. He motioned for Luiz, who had just stepped out of the storeroom wheeling a large CO_2 tank on a dolly. The two men greeted each other, and Luiz parked the dolly beside the bar. Without being asked, he poured something dark and foamy from the tap and set it in front of the guitar player.

Luiz took Karmen by the arm. "Evans," he said. "This is my niece I been telling you about. This is Karmen. And Karmen, meet Erik. I may have mentioned him?"

Karmen beamed. "Yeah, I think so."

The guitar player—now ostensibly Erik Evans—offered Karmen a warm smile and brief handshake. Taylor watched, grateful that no one seemed likely to call upon her for conversation.

Then Erik looked straight at her. Extended the same hand, his gaze intense and dark as it sought hers.

"Karmen's friend," he said simply.

Jesus, lord. *Move, damn it.* Taylor forced her arm to unlock, forced her elbow to bend. Forced her right hand into his, even though at the last instant it seemed to float there on its own.

She nodded.

It was a millisecond. One beat too long to go unnoticed. But he didn't release her hand immediately. Just looked at her. And Taylor looked back.

"Staying for the show?" He finally let go of her hand.

She shot a glance at Karmen.

Karmen smiled, oblivious to whatever was jumping back and forth between Taylor and Erik Evans. "Sure. That okay with you, Tay?"

Of course it was okay. Wouldn't have mattered if it hadn't been. But again, all Taylor could do was nod.

So fast it made her dizzy, Taylor snapped back. Back to the patio, back to the table. Back to the dim light and the chilly evening and the roast beef sandwich rolling uneasily in her stomach.

Good God. Would it ever end?

As memories went, that one wasn't so bad. It was just a name, after all—with a very unfortunate rhyme.

She pulled the sweater tightly around her and rested her head against the back of the chair. Maybe she should call it a day and go to bed, just to be on the safe side. The Blevins kid would keep 'til morning. She sat there for another couple minutes, then got up and found her room.

CHAPTER FIVE

Always something about girls—the way they looked, the way they moved, the way they smelled—then all it took was one whiff of whatever it was that Haley Asbury washed her hair in, and Eric lost every word in his otherwise respectable vocabulary. Good thing she was a talker, or they never would have hooked up after the homecoming game his senior year. Eighteen months later and she still sent him spinning, out of his head, like now, lying underneath him in the bed of his work truck, bare legs wrapped around him and fingers tangled in his hair.

God—those first minutes after it was over—nothing else mattered. Just the wet and warm and sweet of her body, butter in his veins, hovering on the edge of oblivion with his face buried in the side of her neck. They could have been parked beside the Eagle Heights water tank or sinking to the bottom of the ocean, and Eric wouldn't have cared. Just skin on skin, tangles of her long blond hair on his cheek, the feeling that she *saw* him, *knew* him, understood what made his body work and his mind stop running circles around everything he wanted but couldn't have—that's what kept him going. Kept him from drowning in the failures, from drowning in the putrid water rising higher by the second, filling the blue barrel they floated in and taking away all the air that just moments ago seemed limitless—

Eric pushed himself off her and rolled sideways, first on his back blinking up at the sky, but then he sat up, struggling to breathe. For a few seconds all he could do was gasp, open-mouthed, fighting for oxygen like it was in short supply. The dream tickled the edges of his consciousness,lingering there even with his eyes wide open. He could still smell the rot. Six months since that awful night in the bog, and he hadn't buried the memory, even though Dylan Altizer's family had finally gotten to bury their son.

He ran a hand through his hair. Let a breath out slowly. *Act normal.* No sense freaking Haley out. She didn't know about the dreams. Nobody did.

"Doze off?" She rested one hand against his back.

He nodded. "Forgot where I was for a minute." Then he tossed a grin over his shoulder, taking in the sight of her lying where he left her ... *how* he left her. "See what you do to me?"

She poked him in the kidney and he gave the obligatory flinch, then squeezed one of her small kneecaps between his fingers until she howled and kicked his hand loose. Their routine, their ritual, knowing each touch that was welcomed and all that were unbearable—neither was exactly ticklish but certain things were off limits, sort of. She was funny about her knees. Something he could always have fun with, when the mood struck.

He eased backward onto his side and stretched out next to her. "You're going to get caught skipping one of these days."

"It's just Ag." She frowned. "You'll have me back in time for Biology."

It was gentle, the breeze that walked up his bare legs and ruffled the hair on his arms. She felt it too, and he could tell. The smooth, pale skin of her breasts broke out in gooseflesh. No way he could resist running his fingers over that. He followed his hands with his mouth, tasting her one more time before they had to cover everything up with clothes and get back to everyday life.

"Just don't let your grade slip," he said.

"Okay, Daddy. I won't."

He shot her a look. "That's disgusting—right now, when we're doing *this.*"

"Well, that's who you sound like—*don't let your grade slip.* It's not going to. Ag ain't nothing. Shit. I'm dating an old man. Got a county job and a county truck, and now he thinks he's gonna tell me what to do with my grades."

At least she was smiling when she said it.

He cocked an eyebrow. "I didn't hear you complaining about this county truck a few minutes ago."

"What do grades matter anyway?" She shook her head. "Straight As won't make me a better wife."

"No, but they'll sure help you get into a good school."

"I told you—I'm going to Southwest. They don't give a shit about your GPA as long as you get that diploma. Or GED. Hell, I could quit high school right now and still start the nursing program next fall."

"Grades matter, Haley. Even at a community college."

"Your four-point-oh didn't get you into Tech, did it?"

He stared at her. "Yes, it did, actually."

Fuck.

There went the mood.

"I showed you the acceptance letter," he said. "But I blew my goddamned knee out last game, remember? Bye-bye scholarship. And you know as well as I do that my grandparents can't afford that kind of tuition."

She sat up and started gathering her clothes. "Yeah, I remember. Vet school—you and your big talk."

The jingle of his cell phone saved him from saying something he'd have to apologize for later. He looked at the number. Bobby Cordle, the other guy out reading water meters that day. Lunch was over. Back to work.

"Yeah," he answered simply, succeeding after three useless attempts to swipe the green button.

"Hey, we need you on Baugh's Ridge. Big Mack's out doing cut-offs and somebody chained a dog on one of the meters."

Eric blinked. "They did what?"

"Big-ass dog, too. Mean as shit."

"What do you want me to do about it?"

"You're the dog guy," Bobby said. "Pretty sure you can think of something."

The dog guy. Eric didn't even bother with a retort. Grandpap was *the dog guy*—he'd been raising coonhounds since before Eric was born. Yet somehow Eric got stuck with the title. Oh, well. He could have been called worse.

"Be there in about twenty," he said. "Gotta make a stop first, then I'm on the way."

Haley didn't talk much as he drove her back to the high school. Eric pulled into the side lot right there in front of God and everybody. He always did. She never got in trouble for cutting class, and having taken four years of Ag under the same teacher, he doubted she ever would. She kissed him sweetly on the mouth, let it linger for a bit before she broke away and climbed out of the truck. After she was gone he ran the tip of his tongue over his bottom lip. Something strawberry with a trace of mint, and Haley. He'd taste her and smell her for the rest of the afternoon, and that was fine. Better than fine. Just how he liked it, and how he wanted things to stay.

Baugh's Ridge was an old mining camp, houses lined up side by side, separated by narrow strips of yard and an occasional dilapidated fence. The houses themselves looked worse for wear, with sagging porches and trash piles and coal dust embedded at least four generations deep in the soil. They all sat close to the road, leaving little room for anybody to park. With the ass end of his pickup halfway across the driving lane, Eric stopped on the narrow shoulder and stepped out, feeling stickiness high on his thighs that reminded him of Haley. Of what they'd just been doing. Hard not to smile at the thought, but everybody was looking at him, so he put on his best bored Public Service Authority face and grabbed the yellow Dollar General bag off the passenger seat.

"What the fuck did you do, Blevins?" Bobby propped an elbow on the bedrail of the other PSA Ford, the one that matched Eric's except it was a lighter shade of blue. "Go shopping?"

Eric reached into the bag and pulled out a pack of hot dogs. "Told you I had a stop to make."

On the other side of Bobby's pickup, a low bark. Dog had a deep voice, and didn't sound like a hound. Eric pried a hot dog from the pack and broke off one end.

"Anybody in the house?" he asked.

A third PSA employee, the one from maintenance doing the cut-offs, hauled his bulk from a white F250 parked in the road one house up. Mack Bowling, with a meter wrench in his hand. "No. Bastards know what today is. We cut 'em off last month, too. 'Cept then they had a broke-down SUV parked on the meter. Front tire setting right on top of the cover. Had to get the law out here to make 'em push it off."

Eric laughed. Leave it to a bunch of pillheads—ingenuity at being ignorant.

"Okay," he said. "Show me your killer."

The dog was pretty much what Eric expected. Intact male, shorthaired and stocky, with a big head and powerful jaws. Brindle with a patch of white on his chest and four white legs. He wagged his tail stiffly, front paws planted and weight shifted forward, mouth closed between barks.

"Think he means it?" Bobby asked from a distance away.

"Why don't you come over here and find out?" Eric tossed the end of the hot dog between those large front paws.

"Fuckin' pitbull," Bobby said.

"Yeah," Eric said. "Right. But the only difference between a pitbull and any other dog is how they bite. If he doesn't bite, there's no difference. He's just a dog."

The chain was anchored in a way that allowed the dog access to the front porch as well as the meter. So Eric started walking toward the house, keeping himself well out of reach. He dropped a couple more bites of hot dog on the ground and the pit snuffled them up, still giving an occasional gruff bark, but looking at Eric with more interest now than suspicion. Near the steps, Eric squatted. He tossed another bite of hot dog. The big brindle ate it. Then another, even closer. And another, right at the limit of how far the chain would reach.

"Reckon they fight him?" Bobby asked.

Eric shook his head. "He bows up too quick on people for that. Fighting dogs can't be aggressive toward people. Too much risk for the handlers."

The pit still wagged his tail stiffly, but his weight was balanced squarely over all four paws now, and he'd started panting. Mouth open, tongue lolling. Good sign.

Bobby unfolded his arms. The movement, subtle though it was, earned him a glance from the pitbull. "Ever seen one of those dogfights, like, for real?"

Eric didn't look up, keeping his attention on the dog. Direct eye contact, but gentle. Non-threatening. Reassuring. "Nope. Don't want to, either." He placed another chunk of hot dog directly in front of him. "Here, boy. You gotta come get it."

The pit edged closer. Opened his mouth, closed it. Licked his nose. Drooled.

"You gotta give something to get something," Eric said quietly, still engaging the dog in soft eye contact. "Nothing's free."

Think he understands what you're saying?" Bobby asked.

"He understands more than you think." Eric broke off another piece of hot dog and just held it. "What's your name, boy? Diesel? Axel? Brutus?" He rattled off some of the most overused tough-dog names and watched for a response. Nothing. "What about Frankie? Since you'll sell your soul for an Eckrich Frank."

Bobby laughed. "You ain't got a lick of sense, Blevins."

"Come here, Frankie. I think we can be friends." Eric held up the hot dog bite in his fingers. "Look. We can even eat dinner together." He popped the hot dog in his mouth and chewed. Slowly, so Frankie could watch.

Frankie's tail wagged. With more sincerity this time, and such force it moved his brindle butt from side to side. He licked his nose again, and after a second or two, slobbered up the hot dog bite still lying on the ground at the far reach of the chain.

Eric duck-walked a little closer. Placed another hot dog bite between them. Frankie inhaled it.

"Okay," Eric said. "This time we're going to do this like two rational adults. I take a bite, you take a bite. That's how it works." He ate another piece of hot dog. Cold, nasty, but the psychology was effective. Frankie leaned far forward and took the next bite directly from his hand.

"Goddamned dog whisperer," Bobby muttered.

"No," Eric kept his tone even and light. "You just gotta understand what motivates them."

"Which is?"

Eric didn't bother answering. Food, prey drive, play drive. Dogs were pretty simple. But not as simple as folks like Bobby Cordle. No sense wasting his breath on any explanations.

"Big Mack's going to need you at the meter," Eric said. "Go over there and stand by. I'll tell you when I think it's safe."

Bobby went without protest, sufficiently motivated by the chance to feel important. Eric allowed himself a silent chuckle and fed Frankie another bite of hot dog.

"People are dumbasses," he told the dog in confidence. "Just remember that and you'll do okay."

Frankie sniffed his fingers. Licked them. Eric stroked him under the chin, then rubbed the massive jowls and gave him a good scratch behind the ears. Frankie stood there, panting. Whined. Ate another piece of hot dog.

"Go for it," Eric said loudly enough for Bobby and Big Mack to hear. And pried another hot dog from the pack.

It didn't take long. Frankie was still chasing bits of meat through the grass when Eric heard the meter cover thunk back into place.

"Thank you," Mack said.

"Goddamned dog whisperer," Bobby said again.

Eric stood slowly and gave the dog another pat on the head. He walked back toward his truck, Frankie padding slowly beside him as far as the chain would let him.

"Hey, I been meaning to ask," Bobby said once they'd all stepped off the property. "Did you talk to that reporter?"

Eric frowned. "What reporter?"

"One from Richmond, the woman."

"I don't know anything about that." Eric wiped his hands on a napkin from the Ford's glove box.

"My sister ran into her yesterday, at the gas station. Thought maybe they were just passing through, but then somebody saw 'em out front of the Sheriff's Office. Reckon they're here about those killings?"

"Why would she want to talk to me?" Eric shut the passenger door and walked around the front of the truck. "I don't know anything."

Bobby shrugged. "You know as much as anybody does. I mean, you found the first body."

Eric's face turned to stone. He felt it as it happened, couldn't convince forty-three muscles to smile, or seventeen to frown, or however many the latest Facebook meme said it took. He didn't chance a look at Bobby. Just kept his eyes fixed forward, on the truck's door handle as he opened it, and on the passenger seat where he tossed the empty Dollar General bag and hot dog wrapper.

"Call me if you need anything else," he said, and slid behind the wheel.

Reporter?

He started the engine and drove forward, looking for a place to turn around.

From Richmond?

Eh, probably nothing. No reporter had ever wanted to talk to him about anything. Especially one from Richmond.

He backed into one of the wider driveways that didn't have a vehicle blocking it and sat there for a minute. Thought about Haley. Wondered if her Biology class was about to let out. He glanced at his phone in the truck's console, half-hoping for a text message.

It showed a missed call. 804 area code.

Richmond.

(Key of G)
It's a thought
It's a feeling for a while
That we try to fight and do our best to understand.
It's a wall
That we never meant to build
So we tear it down and do the best we can.

What if maybe it's all leading somewhere good
If it's moving like it should
We won't have to fight our way back out.
What if one day we look back the way we came
And we like the change we made
No doubt.

Now I know
What it's like to just wake up
And realize the road you're on just leads you down.
So you stop
And you force yourself to turn around.
And what's behind you catches up without a sound.
                    ---Erik Evans, 2003

CHAPTER SIX

"I want to figure this kid out fast." Taylor didn't look up from her cell phone screen as she spoke. On it, personal information she shouldn't have but did, fruit of the guerilla-style background search Charles Carter had initiated from Richmond. "On paper, Blevins is nothing but mixed signals. Graduated four-point-oh. Athlete. Popular kid, right? Not sure about that."

On the patio outside the bed and breakfast, Perry and Kavanagh stared at her with blank expressions.

Taylor pretended they were paying attention and switched her screen to a PDF of Charles's ThinkPad notes. "Other than basic honors, no real academic awards. No scholarship. Lives with his grandparents. Grandfather unemployed for the last twenty years, grandmother is a lunchroom cook at the middle school. Absent mother and father. Dad did a stretch at Coffeewood for manufacturing back in the early two-thousands. Mom has been missing in action since he was two. Our boy went straight to work after he graduated, full time. Doesn't engage much on social media. No criminal record, not even a traffic ticket." She thought for a minute. "Talking to him on the phone earlier—just a vibe, so I'm not sure why I think this, but he might respond better with less testosterone in the air. Can we do a code word?"

Perry gave a slow nod, grinning. "I have a suggestion."

Taylor shot him a look. "Let me guess. Halle Berry."

"No." Perry's grin got a little bigger. "Just tell us to get lost."

"Subtle," she said. "I'm going for subtle."

"Headache," Kavanagh said.

Taylor squinted at him. "Huh?"

"Say your head hurts. No Excedrin in your handbag. I got some in the room. I leave to go get it, Stu goes after a soft drink to wash it down. We stay gone."

Stu. Taylor cocked a brow at Perry. He didn't look like a "Stu." He looked like a ... well, an Angus. Or a Bruno.

"I can text you," she said. "If you need to come back."

The bed and breakfast had been their best option to meet, since Eric Blevins hadn't seemed comfortable with the idea of talking to them in a public place. That sent a frisson of unease up Taylor's backbone, but she wasn't sure why. On the phone, the kid didn't seem secretive. Or devious. Just uncertain, and cautious. He talked slow, took his time answering all her questions. Didn't come across as a four-point-oh. But high school transcripts didn't usually lie.

Car tires on gravel got everybody's attention. Blevins, and he was right on time. Older model subcompact, red. Dull paint, one wheel cover missing on the side she could see. He got out, and Taylor sat forward in her seat, instantly on the hunt for anything other than his too-familiar name that might detonate one of her triggers.

Pretty obvious he didn't see them, not at first. He just stood there for a minute, sizing up the place with a guarded expression. Good-looking kid—medium height, built for the football team with wide shoulders and the athletic stance of a runner. Tailback, if she remembered right. Dark brown hair, straight, hanging in his eyes. Cheekbones and skin tone that suggested Native in the mix somewhere. At least he wasn't rangy and blond, with eyes that looked black from a distance but were actually a deep indigo. She had no idea what color Eric Blevins' eyes might be. And she didn't care, as long as they weren't the same blue from her memories.

She stood slowly, heeding a bizarre intuition that sudden movement would spook him.

"Eric." She waved. "We're over here."

They locked eyes, and he started walking their direction. A hedgerow of forsythia loomed between them, shedding faded yellow blooms all over the ground and offering the patio a bit of privacy. He pushed some willowy branches out of his way and stepped around, gaze flitting from her to Kavanagh and Perry, and back again.

"Hi." He stopped walking.

She offered her warmest professional smile. "Eric, this is Nigel Kavanagh and Stu Perry. They're my crew."

Once more, his eyes darted from her to the two men. But he didn't greet anyone out loud, just nodded once in acknowledgment.

Taylor made a mental assessment of his clothing. Gray hoodie—right for the season there in the mountains, and Levis. Nothing fancy. Lace-up hiking boots, probably steel toes, most likely required for his job. He was a no-frills kind of kid. No piercings, no visible ink, and no jewelry. Eyes—a nice, safe brown.

Inside her, something unclenched. Not her Erik. Nothing like him. Today would not be difficult. No Nightmare on Memory Lane to spend the next six months recovering from.

"Come on," she said. "Have a seat. Would you like some coffee? A soft drink?"

"I had a pop on the way over," he said. "I'm good, but thank you."

Her seat at the table faced the gravel lot, placing her back against the clapboard wall of the house. Kavanagh occupied the three o'clock position, and Perry didn't sit at all. He stood by the edge of the patio, smoking a cigarette and flicking ashes into the forsythia. When Taylor sat, Eric followed her lead. He picked the chair at nine o'clock, putting him almost immediately at her elbow, but with the width of the table between him and Kavanagh.

She rubbed her forehead lightly. "Mmm," she said. "Can't shake this headache. Sorry if I seem a little out of sorts."

Perry crushed his cigarette butt under the toe of one loafer. "Want me to get you a Dr. Pepper to, uh ... uhm ...."

Taylor could only blink. Leave it to Perry.

Kavanagh cleared his throat. "I have some Excedrin in the room. Want one?"

"Maybe two," she said, and looked pointedly at Perry. "And yes, I'll take that Dr. Pepper."

Several long beats of silence passed after Kavanagh and Perry left. Taylor and Eric just sat there. They didn't move, didn't speak, didn't look at each other.

Then Eric shifted in his chair. Slouched a little, rested his palms on his knees. "Guess you figure you don't need your bodyguards."

Nothing slow about his speech now.

Taylor's eyes narrowed. Canny little shit.

"Cameraman," she said finally. "And segment producer. Not bodyguards."

He smiled, mouth closed. The look on his face was apologetic. "I didn't mean anything by that."

"Sure you did," she said quickly. "But that's fine. Now that you're on to me, can we forego any more bullshit and just talk?"

One dark brow twitched. "Sure."

"I came here not sure if I'd get a story," she said. "I figured whatever we took back with us wouldn't be 'film at eleven' kind of stuff. But I have to admit, I did think we'd find a little neater package. Now, the longer I'm here, the more questions I have. I don't think this is as straightforward as somebody wants us to believe. What do you think?"

"Nothing, really," he said. "I still don't know why you want to talk to me."

"Your name's all over the police report." She placed the tip of one forefinger on a folder marked "Altizer." "From that first body. Yet I can't find any article or coverage that suggests the media spoke with you at all. To me that seems unusual."

Eric shrugged. "It's because I didn't have anything to tell."

"I understand you were coon hunting earlier that night in the same general area."

He nodded.

Jesus. This was going to be like pulling teeth.

Okay. Time to strike a match and see what caught fire.

"Who shot the dog?" she asked.

His expression sharpened. Hardened. His gaze quit wandering around the patio and zeroed in on her. "What? Nobody shot a dog."

"Somebody on Topix says one of the hunters killed a hound that night."

Tension gathered around his eyes. "What does that have to do with anything?"

"I'm not sure," she said. "Probably nothing. But it's odd. Just thought I'd ask."

"It's not odd. Not around here. A dog don't do the job, it serves no purpose. Hunters kill 'em all the time. Leave 'em in the woods. Trade 'em, dump 'em, whatever. Nobody shot a dog that night, because my Grandpap threatened to beat some ass if they did. So they just left her. And I went back looking for her. That's when I found the barrel."

Much better. She knew he had it in him, and now he was talking. Like she'd kicked a stone loose in the dam, and back pressure was doing the rest.

"Did you ever find the dog?"

He took a deep breath, and it hitched for a moment before he blew it back out. "Yeah. Couple days later. She was splattered all over Highway 12. Got into it with a coal truck, probably."

Taylor cringed. It wasn't part of her act. "That's awful."

"People here," he said. "They don't give a shit. A dog's just property. Me—well, I've always wanted to be a vet. Got accepted at Virginia Tech. But I lost my scholarship when I busted my knee, so there wasn't no way in hell I could go."

Taylor blinked. Not the conversation she'd expected to have.

"There's always a way," she said. "Especially for somebody with a decent GPA. Student loans—did you consider that?"

"Grandpap said no. Said I'd be in debt for the rest of my life, and he sure as hell wasn't going to sign for anything to help me get in over my head."

"He didn't have to. You could—" Shit. Wasn't even worth finishing the sentence. She'd read somewhere that the local high school dropout rate there in Southwest Virginia was one in four. The fact that he had a diploma at all was cause to celebrate.

"Okay." She'd hoped to redirect the conversation, but had herded it straight into a pen with her own snarling frustration instead. "Listen—I'm going to shoot straight with you. I'm at a loss. My friends and I just spent the last twenty-four hours wading through bullshit your county sheriff gave me to read. I've never seen such so much nothing in all my life. I called the Commonwealth's Attorney, sent emails, tried every number listed for county administration. Not one callback or reply. Where do you go for information in this town? I mean, even the newspapers—you've got three people killed in some pretty sadistic ways, shoved in barrels like garbage and dumped over the hill. And the headline in your local rag this week is about some bubba who put a gate across a PSA access road? Really?"

Eric laughed out loud. The transformation was striking—from taut, pinched features to a huge smile with perfect, white teeth, dimples, and eyes that shone with intelligence and good humor.

Taylor stared. And felt pretty sure she was seeing the real Eric Blevins for the first time.

"Oh, wait." Jesus. Could she *be* any more obtuse? "You work for the PSA."

"Yeah." He nodded, and the smile disappeared. "I know all about that gate. And the property on the other side of it. About the water tank we're wanting to put back there, and the fact that the county owns enough acreage at that elevation to put a gravity system in at least two different locations that don't involve taking that man's land."

Taylor frowned. "Taking his land?"

"Yeah. Eminent domain."

She blinked. "Wow. I guess I just didn't read far enough. I scanned the first few paragraphs and lost interest."

"Of course you did. You were supposed to." He leaned forward with his elbows on his knees. "I figure they have to cover the story, if they want to sell papers. But Heflin knows how to bury it, way down, on purpose, so most people never see it."

"Heflin? Who's that?"

"Sonny Heflin. Big newsman around town."

Taylor scribbled the name down. "How old are you, Eric?" She looked up from her notes.

"Nineteen."

"How do you know all this stuff—about eminent domain, and newsmen throwing a story?"

A flash of that big smile again, and this time it left behind a residual grin, or maybe a smirk. "I work for the PSA, remember? Worse than a bunch of women in a beauty shop."

Shit—God help her. The worse she jacked up this interview, the better a subject he made.

"So what's your theory about local media?" she asked. "Because what you're describing sounds a lot like bias."

Judging from the lack of hesitation before his answer, he didn't even have to think about it. "Board of Supervisors controls that paper. They don't want it printed," he said. "It don't get printed. If that's what you mean by 'bias,' then yeah. I guess you're right."

Taylor rubbed her forehead. That pretend headache she'd developed earlier had started to feel uncomfortably real. "Eric, have you ever been anywhere else? Farther than Roanoke or Bristol?"

"I went to New York City once, with Upward Bound." His mouth twitched, an almost-smile. "I actually liked it. Wasn't nearly as crazy as I thought it would be. We got to see the nine-eleven memorial. Man—that was something."

She frowned. "Upward Bound?"

"It's an outreach program from different colleges, like Tech. It's for high school students whose parents didn't get a degree. You spend part of your summer on campus, and they take you on trips, show you how the other half lives. I loved it."

"Wow." That outreach program—it needed talking about. But right then, all she could think about was how articulate he could be.

"You don't talk the same," she said. "Here with me, as you did earlier on the phone."

"I talk like whoever I'm around." He drummed his fingers on his knees. "If I say things in front of you like I do at home, you'll think I'm just another dumbass from the holler. But if I use words longer than four letters around the guys at work, they give me a hard time."

Taylor shook her head with empathy, not envying this kid the life he lived. "So tell me about the first body. How you found it."

"Tromping around the woods, and there it was—this big-ass blue barrel. Dog acted funny about it, so I looked inside. Couldn't tell much really—just bones and ... brown yuck. I knew what it was, though."

"So what did you do?"

"I got the fuck up out of there. Went back out to the road and called the law. They came. It was a circus. I left. The end."

"Mm hmm." Taylor's eyes narrowed. "Do you ever wonder who did it?"

"We all wonder who did it."

"Did you know Dylan Altizer? Before he was killed, I mean?"

Eric shrugged. "He was a year behind me in school, but a different county. We're Double A, so I never played him on the field."

"Meaning you went to a larger school."

"Yeah."

"Did you know the other two victims?"

Eric shook his head. "They weren't from here."

"Right. Dillow was from Johnson City, and Hess from Roanoke. What do you think they had in common?"

"They were guys, around my age. That's pretty much it, far as I know."

"Did they all play football?"

He gave her a sideways look. "You think it has something to do with that?"

"Not really. I'm just fishing."

"I don't know about the other two," he said. "News didn't say."

"News didn't say much of anything, from what I've seen."

His eyes smiled, even though his face didn't. "Right."

Despite her best efforts, Taylor's own poker face went to shit. "Is local TV news just as bought-off as print media around here?"

"I don't know," he said. "I don't watch it."

She got her smile under control before she said anything else. Not much to smile about anyway. If they really had been playing poker, the kid won that round. "I guess that's all," she said. "Unless you have something else to tell me."

"Can I go now?" he asked.

"Yeah. You could have gone at any time. I just thought there for a minute we were having a good conversation."

"We were." He stood and pushed his chair under the table. "But we can speculate all day long, and it still ain't news. I really don't know anything that will help you with your story."

Maybe not. But she wasn't so sure.

"Will you take my card?" she asked, tugging it from her zippered binder on the table. "And call me if you think of anything?"

"Sure." He dug in his back pocket and produced a wallet. Into the wallet went the card, and just like that, the conversation was over. He went back the way he came, around the forsythia, and Taylor just sat there staring at the folders.

(Key of G)
It's okay if we don't talk
If we just sit here and catch our breath
It ain't like we jump fences every day.
But I'll bet you have to wonder
If the greener side is the better place to land.
Well, I hit hard enough that I can't say.

What I know is I don't want to be here with somebody else
And I want to keep you all to myself
And how do I tell if we are feeling it both the same
Jump quietly
Fall on me
Gentle as the rain.

---Erik Evans, 2003

CHAPTER SEVEN

On the veranda outside Richmond's Bealle Terrace Restaurant, Taylor traced the margin of Michael Dillow's autopsy report with the tip of one index finger. It held information she hadn't known, but no real surprises. And that was disappointing, in ways she hadn't yet put into words.

"Hennessey's giving you some rope." Across the table, Charles Carter took a drink of his water. "He trusts your instincts, but you gotta admit—two days, three staff members, a bed and breakfast, eighteen meals, and four tanks of gas ... and you come back with newspaper clippings and thirty minutes of footage shot from the shoulder of a public road. He may be starting to regret not putting Vanessa on this like he wanted to in the first place."

A dozen sourpuss retorts floated through her mind, but she just wasn't in the mood for that. A good cry, maybe, if she hadn't kicked the habit ten years ago.

"I know," she said. "But it's ... I don't know how to explain it. That whole part of the state—the clannishness—I wasn't prepared. At all. You hear stories about the poverty, and the drug abuse. The poor healthcare, and the high school drop-out rates. But until you stand there, and they're looking at you like they all know the joke and you're the punch line—it's hostile. A closed society. You need a native guide just to drive some of those streets. You can't approach people. You can't ask questions. I left two dozen messages all over town for people who ought to welcome the chance for a little regional exposure. Nope. Except for Blevins, not a single callback. Charles, these aren't poor, underprivileged people that society just forgot about. They shut a lot of doors themselves, and they don't want them opened back up."

Charles grabbed a pumpernickel roll from the basket between them and broke it in half, his hands nearly the same shade of brown as the crust. "Not too friendly, huh?"

"It's more than that." She sighed. "It's a different world. A foreign culture. And it isn't thriving, but I don't think they care."

"That's pretty harsh, Taylor. You don't want to be caught saying that to the humanitarian crowd."

"I'm not saying it to them," she said pointedly. "I'm saying it to you."

"Okay." He nodded. "I hear you."

She looked through the latticed veranda railing at the gardens below, at the evenly mowed blanket of grass that ended at the James, and the roses grouped by color beside the stone wall separating lawn from river.

"Even nature's on a different schedule there," she said. "The forsythia's still in bloom. Bradford Pear—shit, those came and went three weeks ago here. And I didn't see any roses."

"So what are you going to do?" He slathered a generous pat of butter on the inside of his freshly halved roll.

She shrugged. "Still thinking."

He held one half of the roll toward her and waggled it back and forth until she looked at it. "Try a bite. These little bastards are delicious."

"Too many carbs," she said, then took the roll from him anyway. "But fuck it. That does look good."

He laughed.

"I think the answer is going to be in the question," she said after a bit. "But I have to figure out which question hasn't been asked yet."

Charles broke another roll in half. "So you got two of the families to sign for release of the autopsy report to you. But not the third one."

She silently read again the cause of death written on Dillow's paperwork. Asphyxiation. Mechanism: smothering. Manner: homicide. "The first one, actually—first body. Dylan Altizer's family didn't want to talk to me. Just wanted to be left alone."

"Do you blame them?"

58

She looked up. "Yeah, I do, actually. I'd like to think if Dylan was my loved one, I'd be cooperating with anybody in the world who showed an interest in finding his killer."

"So that's what you're doing—finding his killer, not reporting the news."

"That's not what I meant," she shot back. "Investigative journalism. It's a thing."

"Okay." He sounded conciliatory. "You're right. It is. Take a breath, Beckett."

The autopsy findings for Cody Hess were similar. Cause of death: asphyxiation. Mechanism: carbon monoxide poisoning. Manner of death: homicide. Social media squawk and at least one news agency seemed to agree that Altizer had been strangled to death. Assuming that was true, she didn't need to hold the official document in her hand to know how the cause, manner, and mechanism would read.

"A lot of things parallel in these cases," she said. "But the mechanism ... that's tripping me up. Why would the killer keep changing it?"

Charles shrugged. "Experimentation? Convenience? I don't know. Could be a lot of reasons."

"One print article says Altizer had evidence of bruising in what was left of his throat tissue. Crushed hyoid. So I called the guy in Bristol who initially reported that, and he confirmed. He got the intel before the investigation went dark. Dillow and Hess hadn't been in the barrels as long when they turned up. There was still a plastic bag over Dillow's head, duct-taped around his neck. With Hess, there were telltale markers of high carbon monoxide levels. This is all significant," she said. "I just can't put my finger on why."

"Hmm," Charles said. "Can I see that?" He reached for Dillow's autopsy report.

Taylor gave it to him without hesitation.

"It's a de-escalation pattern," he said after a moment. "Think about it—Altizer was choked to death. That's a very physical, hands-on kind of thing. Rage, or passion. Kind of makes you wonder if our guy actually meant to kill him or if it was just an altercation that went south."

Interesting. A possibility she hadn't considered.

"This guy," he said, pointing to the report. "Plastic bag over his head. Less violent and physically taxing than bare-handed throttling, but still isn't quite a method our killer feels comfortable with. He leaves the bag on because he's too squeamish to take it off. By the time he gets to Hess, he's had time to think about this. To plan. So once our victim is immobilized, the killer gases him. No muss, no fuss. Put the lid on the barrel and haul it off somewhere. Mission accomplished."

"Oh, my God," Taylor said. "That makes sense."

"Thing is, we don't know if gassing is going to make him happy, either. If there's a next victim, I think we can look for the mechanism to be even cleaner, more efficient. There is a learning curve here, but it's pretty shallow."

"There were signs of sexual assault with Dillow and Hess," Taylor said. "Perianal bruising, and they collected some foreign DNA from Hess. No CODIS match, but at least they have it."

"Huh." Charles sat there for a moment, eyes narrowed. "So now I'm wondering if the whole Altizer thing was pillow-biting gone wrong, not just an altercation."

"Holy shit."

"Which leads us to another question—do we think the primary motive is sexual?" Charles wiped his hands on his napkin. "Or does he just get off on what he's doing to them?"

Taylor shook her head, at a loss. "Who the fuck knows. But I damn sure intend to keep asking questions."

Twelve years and eight hundred miles in the past, Chicago created a monster that still lived in Taylor's every day present. It burrowed tunnels through her soul, sent memories shooting down the tracks of her heart like the L she used to take all over the city with Karmen.

Until.

Studying for midterms back in 2003, all the lines of empty words running together on the page—Taylor couldn't remember if stratification was more heavily influenced by kinship or caste. Both? Surely one weighted the scale more heavily than the other. Did it matter? Did she care? What the hell was she going to do with a degree in sociology anyway?

Noise erupted from the other side of the room. Karmen, on a tear, cursing in Spanish and throwing stuff. A crash and the tinkling of small broken things. Not the makeup basket! Oh, no. Taylor would never figure out which eyeshadow applicators were hers and which were Karmen's now.

Taylor shoved herself off the bed and went to inspect the damage.

"Those earrings!" Karmen ripped all the covers off her bunk and tossed them on the floor. "The hoops with the other hoops inside. Have you seen them?"

"Not since you let Nikki borrow them."

Karmen stared at her. "Nikki," she echoed. "Oh, fuck. That's right."

"Why do you need them? Where are you going? It's Tuesday night."

"Uncle Luiz called me," Karmen said. "MJ is playing the bar tonight. Me and some friends are going down."

MJ. Mellow Jennie. The hot guitar player—ah. Okay.

But, shit. Seems like she would have at least rated an invitation.

Taylor frowned. "Ever think I might want to go, too?"

Karmen shrugged. "Sure. I don't care—come with. But Vicki and Kess are on their way here now. And you're—" She didn't finish the sentence, just pointed palm-up to Taylor's stretch pants and oversized sweatshirt.

"Give me five minutes," Taylor said. "And I'll surprise you."

Four minutes and thirty seconds later, Taylor had zipped her best pair of knee boots over her black leggings and traded the sweatshirt for a long cable-knit sweater. Not a stitch of makeup—no time—but the bar was dark anyway, and who was she kidding? Mr. Guitar wouldn't notice her beside Karmen Fernandez even if she dumped five pounds of Smashbox on her face. What man would?

Karmen, wearing a glittery cropped blazer over flared jeans, looked at her and gave a tight smile. Didn't say a word about Taylor's fashion sense.

A short hop on the L and half an hour later the four of them walked in the front door of Uncle Luiz's bar. He served them immediately, at a tall, round-topped table near the stage. No band yet, but their instruments were already in place. Taylor would know that dark red acoustic anywhere.

Drinks were on the house. By the time the show started, Taylor had torn through several bottles of Smirnoff Ice and didn't trust herself to do much talking. So she just listened, to the music, to Karmen brag about having the lead singer's number in her phone, to the guitars, the drums, the lyrics. To Erik Evans' voice. How he held a note, supported it, conserved each breath. How he handled intervals, and how *on* the note he was, every single time.

Well, I'm a boy who loved a girl
Who loved herself and loved the world
Who loved his love but didn't love him back.

Original stuff. She felt sure of it.

She'd had vocal training since she was fourteen. Never much of a singer, but learning to breathe properly, project, and moderate pitch helped her speaking voice tremendously. And damned if she didn't recognize something in his technique.

See the small defenseless songster—thirds. *Child, tho' your way seems long*—seconds. Drills she would never forget.

And I don't know if I've ever been real enough
Or if I was just a waste of time.

Jesus, lord. How big of a nincompoop would one have to be to break *that* man's heart?

By the time Erik's band finished the first set, four malts had worked their way through her system. Restrooms were located at the back of the bar, separated from the main stage by a long wall where people gathered to wait their turns with the porcelain. She waited hers, standing in line with other mortals while her eyeballs started to float.

And out of the men's room walked Erik Evans, tall and lanky and every bit as imposing as the rock star he hadn't yet become.

He saw her and stopped in his tracks.

"Karmen's friend." He smiled. "I met you a couple weeks ago."

She nodded, made a fair effort of smiling back, but knew any attempt to speak would be completely pointless.

"Glad to see you here," he said.

Sure. Just like he was probably glad to see Karmen, standing at the foot of the stage gyrating her hips and wiggling to the beat of every song he played.

Something. Just. Say. *Something.*

"Vaccai."

He blinked. "What?"

"I hear Vaccai in your intervals."

Oh, my God. Stupidest thing to say *ever.*

But he grinned, a lazy, lopsided grin that made it all the way to his eyes. "Actually, yes. You do."

"You're classically trained," she said, stunned that they were actually having this wackadoodle conversation.

"I wouldn't say that," he said, holding his position in the crowd while foot traffic milled all around him. "Vaccai is everyman's operatic. I took voice for a little while. Figured I needed to, if I wanted to have one at all in ten years." He hesitated, and tipped his head a little sideways. "*Manca sollecita, Più dell'ùsato.*"

Oh, yeah. Now this was a game she could play. "*Ancorchè s'agiti, con lieve fiato.*"

"You sing?" he asked.

"Not if I can help it."

He laughed out loud. "Oh, come on, now."

"My parents wanted me to. Hoped I could. But I have the passaggio from hell. Even Vaccai couldn't help me with that."

His laugh idled down to a chuckle, but his eyes never stopped smiling. "I gotta go. We're up again. But who knows—maybe I'll catch you after the show."

(Key of A)
See us climbing like a rocket too far from the ground
At the edge of rhyme or reason, I don't wanna come down
You got me where you want me, doesn't matter how
Because I'm in for a penny and I'm in for a pound.

What we started, are we gonna ever finish?
Is it gonna be another dead-end spin
Where you are is where I want to be
We both know why but we don't know when.

You know the stakes
Know your mind, that's what it takes.

One, two, three and you're alone with me
Just us now and are we gonna be
Crazy as we wanted when we had a choice
We've made it now so we'll just see.

We know what we've done
Bullet ain't gonna fit back in that gun.

---Erik Evans, 2003

CHAPTER EIGHT

By the following afternoon, Taylor had amassed a collection of info about every registered sex offender within fifty miles of Randall County. The Commonwealth of Virginia had its own public database, and one of the national watchdog groups had an interactive map posted online. It showed little flags at the addresses where offenders lived. The most reliable indicator of future behavior was past behavior. Good to see this rule of thumb taken so seriously.

Through an online search, she also found a sexual harassment claim filed by a former animal shelter employee and a multi-million-dollar lawsuit against the Randall County school system. Apparently, they had hired a sexual predator and allowed him unrestricted contact with elementary school students. Several complaints had been lodged about him. That gave her pause. Randall County authorities didn't investigate reports of sexual abuse perpetrated against children enrolled in their school system? Or did they just not care?

One by one, she went through the list of offenders and cross-referenced their registry information with their other criminal convictions. She looked at age, physical health, gender of the victim when provided, and whether or not the crimes were violent. She ruled out statutory rape cases where it appeared the minors were consenting but just too young, and ruled out women. For the moment, she ruled out anyone who was married based on statistical probability. She'd come back to that and rethink it if she had to.

By the time she went home that evening, her brain was spinning with all the details she'd packed into it. A glass of wine would taste good but numb little. She needed something with a punch, or a kick, or a sledgehammer. Something to make her forget. Unless

Townshend was right and there really ain't no way out, however much booze.

You are someone great men will write songs about. Fucking fortune cookie. Okay, so it was a coincidence that one random inscription on a worthless scrap of paper sort of got it right. Because Taylor had been someone a great man wrote songs about—for at least five minutes.

Well, maybe two years. But that was the extent of her run as a muse.

I never knew I had such a big sum missing
I should have seen my numbers did not make sense.

Yeah, you had your columns backward, alright. Oh, Erik. Why did you have to play it safe? The numbers most certainly did not make sense. And what was so safe about that?

Good lord. Just too much.

Makers Mark. She had that in the cupboard. Cask strength, too, even if it wasn't a full bottle.

So get up and go get it.

Done.

Had to stop this crazy train of thoughts and memories picking up speed inside her head. She was a lifetime away from it all now, twelve years and eight hundred miles, right? But still the images and words floated through her mind—jackhammered through her mind—screaming wouldn't help. Tried that already. Just made her throat sore. Crying wouldn't help. Not that she had any tears left. Time to drench herself in bourbon—thank you for that mental picture, Townshend—Taylor tipped up the bottle and chugged.

A while later, when she could tell her ass was actually in contact with the floor again, she sat in front of her sofa holding the empty bottle with both hands, picking at the trademark red wax stuck to its neck. This was no way to live, from memory to memory, so terrified of an emotional ambush that she couldn't even interview a witness without first making sure his name was the only thing he had in common with the man she would love until the day she died.

You are someone great men will write songs about.

Yeah, right. Maybe "Tequila Makes Her Clothes Fall Off," or "Bitch."

She plunked the empty bottle onto her coffee table. Glass against glass—she'd set it down too hard but nothing broke. Motor skills, yeah. They'd gone bye-bye.

She still had the pictures. Couldn't look at them, but couldn't burn them, either. Maybe just one peek. It had been so long since she'd seen his face that she couldn't really remember what he looked like anymore. She used her coffee table to help push herself up, but never made it to her feet. Stopped on her knees, reeling, and decided to just crawl. All the way to the wall of cabinets and shelves across the room, where books and keepsakes and knickknacks lived, some on display and some hidden so far down and underneath the detritus of a disorganized life that she should have forgotten them, yet somehow never did.

Boxes, envelopes, and folders of pictures that all felt familiar in her hands—she remembered them all. Remembered treasuring them. Remembered the day she could no longer face them. She knew exactly where to find the best pictures of him. On her knees, careful not to scatter everything, and there he was, smiling for the camera, ageless in pixels, immortal. His face—now it all came flooding back—skin with golden undertones, small, faint birthmark on one cheek, shadowy eyes—okay, no. This wasn't going to work. Box it all back up, shove it under the other stuff, push it as far back in the storage compartment as she could. Out of sight, out of mind. Just get it gone.

She tottered upright, using the cabinetry for balance. Six or seven steps to the sofa—one thing about living in a loft was the open space—but she didn't feel right. She felt sideways. The room spun. Okay, not good. This was—falling now. Couldn't stop it. Falling— coffee table—very loud. Glass everywhere. But it didn't hurt. Nothing hurt. Not even her heart. Taylor closed her eyes and let sleep take it from there.

Dream as if you'll live forever.

That was the inscription on Erik Evans' left forearm, inked by the careful hand of an artist with a really good eye for kerning.

He and the drummer had joined Karmen's group at the corner booth, where Luiz moved them to accommodate everyone. Erik dutifully took a seat beside Karmen. The drummer sat squished between Vicki and Kess, which left Taylor on the end, on the outside edge of the seat. Four girls, two guys. It seemed pretty clear that she'd be going back to the dorm alone that night.

Nobody at the table talked about Vaccai. She was the only dipshit who'd done that. And now Erik wouldn't even look at her, but instead kept his attention fixed on Karmen. Of course he did. Karmen had that effect on men.

Just before midnight, Taylor decided she'd had enough. Her buzz was long gone, replaced by a swimmy-headed, achy, almost sick feeling. Food would help, but the kitchen had closed at eleven. Back at the dorm, a half-full box of Ritz crackers beckoned to her from the closet on her side of the room. Time to heed their call.

She didn't make an ordeal of it, just leaned over and quietly explained to Karmen that she would see her later. And slipped out, making one last stop by the ladies room before pushing her way through the double front doors and onto the street.

Erik Evans stepped out of the alley beside the bar and just stood there, hands in the pockets of his coat.

In her surprise, Taylor nearly stumbled, but at the last second managed to keep it together and not look like an idiot. Well, any more like an idiot than she already did.

She stopped walking. "Do you have a twin? Because I could have sworn I just left you in there at the table."

"Back doors serve a noble purpose," he said without cracking a smile. "They double as escape hatches."

Even at that hour, Chicago wasn't asleep. Traffic moved on the streets, storefronts glowed from light within, and sour steam rose from the underground. Taylor opened her mouth to say something, then forgot what it was. So she just stood there, feeling stupid, listening to horns honk in the distance.

"You hungry?" he asked. "There's an all-night diner about two blocks from here. My treat."

Mouth hanging open—hopefully not too far but she couldn't really tell. Shut it fast. A glance over her shoulder to make sure Karmen hadn't sent a search party. And still no words formed. But the diner sounded great. Food—wasn't that why she'd left?

So she nodded, and simply fell in step beside him when he started walking.

Such a long stride—she felt like Ginger trying to keep up with Black Beauty. He kept his hands in his pockets, moving briskly. Good grief. She might actually have to trot to keep up with him.

"You and Karmen," he said. "The two of you really good friends, or what?"

"If you slow down a little, I might be able to talk."

He cut his speed by half. "Sorry. This better?"

"Yeah." Taylor considered all the ways she might tackle his question about Karmen. And decided simple truth was best. "She and I are roommates at the dorm. We hang out some. Share a makeup basket. That sort of thing."

"She reminds me of my ex," he said.

Taylor blinked. "You mean, the girl who loved herself and loved the world and whatever and whatever and didn't love you back?"

He laughed. "Yeah. That one."

"I knew it! I knew you wrote that song."

"I write most of our stuff," he said. "We do ... well, maybe three covers. The rest of it's original."

"Are you the only songwriter in the band?"

"Tillman writes some—he's on keyboard. The one we did tonight, about the truck stop? That's his."

"Yeah, I remember that one. Guy gets kicked out of the car by some girl and then meets a lot lizard."

He stopped walking and just shook his head, but at least his eyes were twinkling. "So that's what you got out of it, huh?"

She faced him on the sidewalk, finally able to smile at the ridiculous shit she seemed determined to say. "I don't know. I guess maybe I wasn't really paying attention."

"It's about how one minute you think your whole life is destined to be just one long series of bullshit moves, then everything changes. You meet that one person who makes all the difference."

"Oh." She nodded like she understood completely. Erik's music, yes. Tillman's song, with all its talk about short skirts and patent leather boots—not so much. "Okay."

"You know," Erik scratched his head, looking uncomfortable. "I sorta jumped the fence—coming out here to try and catch you before you left. Luiz wanted me to meet Karmen. She's okay—I'm sure she's a nice girl, but I'm not interested in her. And it's probably going to cause some friction if I'm interested in you instead."

Taylor sighed. "Probably."

"That bar's our best gig. And some of the guys—well, they're really serious about this. Me? I've got a day job. I do okay. I just hope we can handle this with some discretion."

Oooh, second thoughts. One stupid comment too many. She really, really shouldn't have said that about the lot lizard.

Wait ... day job?

"So what do you do?" she asked. "Your job, I mean."

"CPA. I work for Heinburg & Associates, on the Backstrom account."

"A CPA," she echoed. "Like—a number cruncher?"

He nodded. "Yeah. It's my fourth year with the firm—I did internship there before I graduated. Foot in the door and all that."

"You—" Heaven help her. She didn't have a clue what to say. So she stuttered. "Your ...." She pointed to the ink on his forearm. "That."

He made a move like he was tugging shirt sleeves. "Suits." He pretended to straighten a tie. "And these things. Nobody sees my ink. Nobody gives a shit about it anyway. Not as long as I do the work, and do it better than anybody else they could hire."

Jesus, lord. A freaking white collar professional, moonlighting as a rock star. Wonder what he did with all that crazy, tousled blond hair when he was at work? "What's the Backstrom account?"

"Our biggest client," he said. "It's a design engineering firm— they're global, but their main office is here in Chicago."

"So that's a big deal." For once, the right words came out sounding the way she intended. Very serious, and respectful of what he'd accomplished.

He nodded. "Yes. For me it is. But for the guys—they just want to play music. And Luiz's bar is the best venue on this side of town for the crowds we draw."

Shit. She owed Karmen no great loyalty. More than one guy Taylor had her eye on had ended up in Karmen's bed. She'd never pressed the issue, because any man that easy to pick off couldn't have shared her level of interest anyway. But this? This was a whole different animal. No way would she be responsible for Mellow Jennie losing their gig. Shit, shit, shit."Maybe we should hit that diner another time," she said. "You get yourself untangled from the whole Karmen mess, and then who knows."

Idiot. Stupid, dumb fucking do-gooder conscience.

He looked at her for a long moment, not moving, not saying anything. Then, "You're probably right."

So there it was. And there it ended. Can't put the bullet back in that gun.

"Thank you, though." She smiled wistfully. "I'll probably regret it for the rest of my life that I said no to you."

"Taylor."

A voice, cutting through the fog in her head. But she wouldn't wake up. Not yet. Just wanted to sleep.

"Taylor." More insistent this time, accompanied by a hard shake.

She opened her eyes.

Charles Carter loomed directly above, his handsome, dark face only inches from hers.

"Taylor, wake up now. You're hurt. We gotta get you seen about."

"What?" She squinted. Couldn't focus.

"You fell and hurt yourself. I think you need some stitches."

So caring, that Charles. Concerned. A good friend.

"Mmm."

"Did you drink that whole bottle of Makers Mark? I mean, should I be worried about alcohol poisoning here?"

"Wasn't full," she mumbled.

"Come on, Taylor. Sit up. Can you do that for me?"

Probably not. But she'd try.

Oh, boy. The room sure could spin.

And all that blood—was it hers? Or did she finally make good on a threat and kill somebody?

Broken coffee table. Where did all the glass go? Her arm hurt like hell. She glanced down. Just below her elbow, a large shard protruded from her skin, rivulets of dried blood making macabre patterns on both sides. She reached for it.

"No—no, no, no." Charles grabbed her hand. "Don't do that." He leaned her carefully back against the sofa. "Let me just ... I'm going to call an ambulance. Just sit tight."

She watched him dial, not caring. Not feeling much of anything, except intense burning in her arm where the glass poked out of it.

"How'd you get in?" she asked.

"You gave me a key, remember? Last year. So I could check on everything while you were in Denver for that conference."

"Nine-one-one. What's your emergency?"

Taylor could hear it plain as day, the operator's voice. Did Charles have the phone on speaker or was the volume turned up that loud?

"We need some help," he said, and offered a short explanation.

Taylor listened as he gave the address. Then she frowned. "Why are you even here?"

He put his hand over the bottom half of his phone and whispered loudly, "Because you called me."

She whispered back, "No, I didn't."

"Yes, you did." He pointed to her own phone, lying on the sofa near her. It was blood-covered and left red streaks all over the pale cream upholstery.

"Daaaaaamn," she mumbled. "I don't even remember."

"Listen woman, you need to be still." Once he hung up with nine-one-one, Charles grabbed her arms and held them higher than the level of her heart. He sat on the floor facing her, one long leg braced across hers because there wasn't anywhere else to put it. "Just quit moving. You're making it bleed again."

She stared at him, blinking slowly, eyelids made of lead. "You're a good friend."

"Just looking out for you, Taylor. Just looking out."

"I'm not a good friend to you," she said.

"Hush, now. Don't talk like that. Just sit here with me. Paramedics are on their way."

"But I lie to you every day," she mumbled. "I just bring you down. Paper clown." She laughed at the Townshend reference, but the sound felt thick and distorted in her throat. "My name's not even Beckett."

She slumped forward, too weak to sit up any more. The last thing she felt was the rough yarn of Carter's sweater against her cheek as she passed out against his shoulder.

(Key of A''')*
So you take a step
And you walk on solid ground
You think you're doing fine.
There ain't nothing else you need.
And the broken glass is the last thing on your mind
But that's what makes you bleed.

I could never be your someone else
I could never be the reason why
I don't want to be the worst mistake you made
Don't want to be the reason that you lie.
I don't want to be the bad excuse
Just another ordinary fail
Walking light through shards of broken dreams
Talking like a cautionary tale.

Where is all this heading now? Should we just assume the worst?
Or could we just step outside our glass house, would that be a first?
If I said just watch your step, careful of the shattered dreams
Move in circles, back and forth, and never saying what we mean.

---Erik Evans, 2003

CHAPTER NINE

Another dirty morning in the city, with smog hanging low and humidity drawing pollution into droplets of condensation that trailed down dusty car windows. It made even honest sweat feel nasty. Taylor squinted against the glare of a sun that hung just above eye level, grateful for the pain meds that took care of both the hangover and the sting of her crosshatched forearms.

In the passenger seat of Charles's sporty little Volt, she inspected the bottle of pills from the hospital pharmacy. "Street value of this?" she said. "About two-forty." She rattled the twelve oxycontin tablets against the plastic. "Need some cash? Short hop over to Ran'all County and they'll be lining up to take 'em off your hands."

Charles laughed. "Coal miner's cocaine."

She almost smiled, but didn't feel quite up to it yet. "Hillbilly heroin."

Charles eased toward the main flow of traffic in front of the hospital, craning his neck hard to the left to look for an opening.

"Never could figure out how somebody who can't buy milk for their baby can still feed that habit," he said once they were merged into the line of cars.

She took the lid off and peeped inside. The pills looked harmless, almost like aspirin tablets. "Only thing I can figure is that it works like a co-op. Sally uses part of her disability check to buy this bottle. Right?" She held it up. "She sells six, keeps six. Except she tacks on a little more to what she sells, maybe thirty dollars a pill rather than the twenty she bought in at. So she's only out sixty bucks. And she can probably sacrifice that for the high."

"Or maybe she says fuck your big city pills and just goes to get another tooth pulled. She's on disability, right? Medicare pays for the prescription and everything she sells is profit."

"That's what I would do," Taylor said, keeping tongue firmly in cheek as she twisted the lid back on the bottle. "So what if you can't chew or smile right, as long as you can't feel your face."

Charles nodded, grinning. "Exactly."

Taylor looked at the pill bottle. "I did some research on this. West Virginia is going after some of the big pharmaceutical companies hard. We're talking billions. Restitution and whatnot."

"Yeah, I think I read something about that."

"Article in the Post?"

"Maybe."

"Apparently West Virginia has the highest opiate overdose rate in the nation, something to the tune of seventeen hundred overdose deaths in a five-year period. And get this—during that same window, almost eight hundred million doses of opioids were shipped into West Virginia by the companies named in the lawsuit."

Charles whistled. "Jesus. Big, *big* money." Then he frowned. "That's West Virginia, though. Is it connected?"

"One of the top four counties named in this suit borders Southwest Virginia on the northern edge. McDowell. And another from the top ten—Mercer—borders it to the east. Addiction doesn't follow dots on the map. Neither does greed. If it's happening on one side of the state line, it's happening on the other."

"Think it has something to do with the barrel murders?"

Taylor shrugged. "Probably not directly. If Big Pharma is ordering mob hits, they probably aren't targeting some of their best customers." She put the pill bottle in her handbag. "But drugs are going to come up in this somehow. The victims turn out to be pillheads. The killer has an addiction." She paused. "The killer has enough dirt on enough dealers in that town that he can do whatever the hell he wants and not have to worry about somebody squealing."

Charles nodded. "Ah. Hmm."

"I just wish I could figure out what angle the Sheriff is working."

Charles glanced sideways at her. "He's the Sheriff. He's working the Sheriff angle."

Taylor rolled her eyes. "Not what I meant."

"Then say what you mean. Stop talking in circles."

Move in circles, back and forth, and never saying what we mean.

She stared at him. Felt something inside her surge, then recede.

Don't flip shit on him, Taylor. They're just words. The kind that everybody says.

If Charles noticed her sudden anxiety, he gave no indication. "Are you thinking he's dirty? Or incompetent? Or just not the right man to head up an investigation like this?"

Taylor shook her head. Partly to clear it, partly to communicate. "He's smart. A forward thinker." She glanced down at her hands in her lap. Trembling. She balled them into fists. "I believe he's doing the best he can with this investigation, probably a better job than some of his contemporaries from that region. I don't think he has a good suspect, and he's not defensive, like he's protecting someone. But my gut also says he's a player. He has something to lose. He needs to solve this case, but it can't get messy. Too many people watching."

"Sum up your first impression of him in fifty words or less."

No problem. She could beat that by half. "He's a puppet master. He knows exactly which strings to pull."

"Very interesting." He drove on without saying anything else, until they came to the next stoplight. "You hungry?"

"Yeah, a little."

He pulled into a shopping center on the other side of the intersection. Years of working together had given them quite a bit of insight into what the other would consider edible and what to avoid at all costs. Fast casual always seemed fine with Charles as long as he could order whole wheat and flatbread. Taylor had much less discriminating tastes when it came to food, but she'd draw the line at a double quarter pounder with cheese. It wasn't really a compromise when he nosed the hybrid into a parking space in front of a chain bakery cafe known for clean ingredients and a healthy menu.

"The Italian half sub," she said before he could ask. "And the big salad. Vinaigrette. See if they have any Pure Leaf in the cooler. Lemon, preferably."

"You're not going in?"

"Nope. I'm still too high, and I look like Frankenstein."

"You going to be able to handle all that in the car?"

"Yes. Because you're going to bring back plenty of napkins."

Charles had a hand on the door handle, but he stopped and just looked at her with a ghost of a grin. "You have this giving-orders-to-the-black-boy thing down cold, don't you?"

She nodded. "Yeah, and be sure you get me some extra crumbles for the salad or I'll make you go back in for them."

His grin morphed into a full-blown laugh as she talked. He just sat there shaking his head for a moment, then he unfolded his long frame and got out. "Back in a minute." He slammed the door and headed for the entrance.

While he was gone Taylor inspected her injuries in the sunlight. More than fifty stitches across a dozen wounds that had needed closing, most of them not deep but long and gaping. She had cuts on her forearms, cuts on her chest, cuts on her face. She clearly wouldn't be doing any on-air work for a while.

The hospital had kept her overnight for observation. The large glass shard near her elbow had lodged against an artery, and before they removed it in the E.R., the hospital put a surgical team on standby. She didn't remember much about Charles showing up at her loft the night before, but she remembered him stopping her from pulling that shard out of her arm. Probably saved her life, or at least a whole lot of blood.

He was back in minutes, carrying two sacks of food, a lemon Pure Leaf Tea, and bottled water. With a bit of a wince, she reached across the car and released the door, giving it a little shove so he could hook it with a knee and open it all the way.

"Make sure your crumbles are in the bag before I sit down," he said.

Taylor checked, and they were. Then she looked at him. "You wouldn't really go back in there just because I told you to, would you?"

"Nope." He got in and shut the door. "I'd go because I'm just a nice guy like that." He pulled a wad of napkins from his bag and handed her half of them. "I think they put all of these in with my food. I must look like I make a hell of a mess."

Taylor laughed.

They ate in silence for a while, windows cracked so the sounds of the city could play like a soundtrack around them. Noise, all of it, but familiar and reassuring. Life goes on. No matter what happens at the individual level, the collective continues.

Taylor took a deep breath. She owed Charles something—a thank you—some small indication that what he'd done for her meant something. Because it did. But sentimentality? Not her strong point. Not anymore, anyway.

"Thank you," she said softly. "For last night. For coming to help me, for staying at the hospital—you didn't have to do any of that."

His shoulders hitched upward, then back down. He didn't look at her. "You'd have done the same thing for me."

Maybe. Taylor wasn't sure she would have. And that was not something she wanted to admit.

"So what was that all about, anyway?" he asked after taking a long drink of water.

How to answer? Taylor couldn't imagine what she could possibly say that would make sense. So she said nothing.

"Okay." He nodded. "Tell me this much, then—is it likely to happen again?"

When he didn't look directly at her, she stared at the side of his face. "That bottle of Makers Mark had been sitting in my cupboard for three months. At least. I take a nip of one thing or another almost every night. But have I ever had to call you and ask for help? Before this?"

He shook his head. "No."

"Okay, then. There you have it. Last night was a one-off. I got carried away. Just too much on my mind. It was a mistake."

He finished his panini and shoved all his trash into the empty sack. "This thing with Randall County has you in a spin, doesn't it?"

Again, she shrugged. "I don't know. Maybe. Something does. It could be that. Or—" *Or what?* She wouldn't keep going with the thought. Because it would only lead her back to Chicago, and that was where all the monsters lived.

"Is there anything I can do to help?"

She thought for a minute. "You're already doing it."

"No, I mean with the story."

"That's what I'm talking about." She offered him a half-smile. "All that info you dug up about the Blevins kid—really, Charles? I don't even want to know."

He laughed.

"I may need you to do something like that again."

"Sure," he said. "Just say the word." He found an unused toothpick in the console and tore off the plastic wrap. "I think Hennessey would sign off on me going with you next time, if you want me to."

"Hah," she said. "Right. You'd stick out like a sore thumb wrapped in a Clean Energy Band-aid."

He gave a theatrical flinch. "Ooooh. Ouch. Man. Didn't see that coming."

She looked at him hard. "What? You would."

"And you a racist ho."

Taylor laughed. "Hey, you wouldn't see me signing up to cover Pakistan."

"We don't send reporters to Pakistan. A little outside our coverage area."

"So is Southwest Virginia."

"You realize you're comparing it to a third-world country, right?"

"Spoken by someone who's never actually been there."

He sat still for a moment before he replied, chewing on the toothpick. "You're telling me there really ain't no brothas over there?"

"I'm sure there are, but I didn't see any."

"You're shitting me. There for two days and you didn't see a single black person?"

"No. I didn't. And it wasn't on my agenda to go looking for any."

"That's a story in itself."

"Then have fun covering it. It's not my story. You can have it."

"Hmph." Another moment passed, then he looked at her sideways. "A Clean Energy Band-aid? Really?"

"Never actually seen one, but I guarantee if somebody ever made them, they wouldn't sell for shit west of Wytheville."

"Give us fossil fuels or give us death."

She thought about some of the slogans and propaganda she'd seen in Randall County. "Friends of Coal" bumper stickers. Black and white vector images plastered on the back windows of pickup trucks—a coal miner on his hands and knees, headlamp shining in front of him, crawling along underneath the words "Family Tradition."

Taylor sighed. "Did you know a green energy provider approached one of the counties over there about putting wind turbines on East River Mountain? Board of Supervisors hated the idea. Green energy, in coal country? Oh, the scandal. They worked the landowners into a frenzy—no wind farm was going to come into that county and destroy the pristine beauty of 'their' mountain. So the county passed a tall-structure ordinance, supervisors kept their seats in the next election, and there went twenty-five million dollars in revenue they could have generated from the wind farm."

"Wind farms aren't as environmentally friendly as they seem, though."

"Neither is coal mining. But they don't have a problem with that."

"Okay," he said, and seemed to measure his words. "But here's the thing—I'm not trying to tell you your business. I know you. Have known you for years. I know how you talk, and how you think. But you might want to be careful with all the negativity. You go over there, you come back, and I haven't heard you say one positive thing about that part of the state. That's not going to play well when it comes time to air, and you know it. So just ... keep that in mind."

Taylor flopped her head back against the seat. "I know. You're right." She paused, thinking. "There are some good people in Southwest Virginia. Really upright, hard-working folks. Like that kid—Eric Blevins. But there's an overlay of something else, something downright insidious. Blevins is gifted in so many ways, but he'll waste to nothing if he stays in that world. A four-point-oh, out there reading meters. And for Randall County, that's a good job. Some little girl's going to see that and grab on tight—she'll make sure she's pregnant in four months, so they can be married in six. Because that's as far as she can think ahead, and he'll never see it coming."

"Positive, Taylor. You're trying to find something positive."

She groaned. "Fuck it. What if there isn't anything?"

"There is." Charles reached down and cranked the car. "You just have to keep looking."

CHAPTER TEN

From where he parked his Escort near the chickens, Eric could see the crawlspace door hanging open underneath the front porch. That portal to hell was the only access to the musty underbelly of the house, and its gaping maw could mean just one thing—something else broke and Grandpap was under there trying to fix it.

Eric's old hound Popper dragged himself from beneath the chicken hutch with a stretch and a yawn. Nobody begrudged him that sleeping hole, because as long as Popper's speckled hide stayed in it, there wasn't a fox or a coon or a possum alive could make a meal out of any chicken on the roost. Eric wouldn't have run him out anyway. The dog had earned the right to sleep wherever he wanted. Hell, Eric would have brought that big old Blue Tic right into the house with him and let him have half the bed, if it was up to him. But it wasn't. Gram got the final say on that. The only animals allowed past her doorway were field dressed, cleaned, plucked, or packaged, and ready for the slow cooker.

"Hey, boy." Eric stopped long enough to give Popper a pat on the head. The hound made a noise that split the difference between groan and whine and leaned full tilt into the ear rub that came next.

Eric glanced around while he petted the dog. Ridgelines in every direction, and between them, almost a hundred acres of prime woodland shot through with easements. Grandpap had racked up when the gas wells came through. About the only part left untouched was the lot where the house sat, just a few yards from the rubble of the old log cabin.

He'd never known any home but this. The house had been built back in the forties by his great grandfather, on land first settled by his Cherokee ancestors after they hid in the mountains instead of marching west like the government told them to. He'd paid attention in U.S. History when the teacher talked about the Scots-Irish migrating to Appalachia a hundred years before the Trail of Tears, about the culture they brought with them, about their clashes with the Native tribes. Well, maybe they did fight with the Indians over land and game and just about everything else, but his family was proof that at least one Cherokee and one Scotch-Irish hillbilly got along real well.

Popper followed him as far as the porch steps but didn't bother climbing them. There had been a time when, banished from the house or not, the hound would have pushed his luck as far as he could. Right to the door, in fact, and sprawled on the welcome mat. But this last winter had been hard on him. Cold and damp took its toll on those old bones. These days Popper all but creaked when he walked, and sometimes the steps were just too much. Eric watched him amble back to the chicken house and slide beneath the underpinning, tail and pads of his back paws the last parts of him to disappear.

"Take them boots off," Gram called from the kitchen. "Don't come tracking your dirt in here." She poked her head around the doorframe and frowned when she saw Eric. "Oh. I thought you was Hoyt."

Nope. Not his Grandpap. But—he was wearing boots. Eric glanced down at his feet. "Want me to take mine off, too?"

"I reckon, if you been tromping around out there in the mud with him." She turned back to the jars lined up on her countertop, Ball and Mason, cleaned and boiled and turned upside down on towels to drain. "You just get home?"

Eric didn't crack a smile. "Nope. I been standing in the yard for the past two hours wondering what Grandpap's doing."

Gram didn't acknowledge the sarcasm. "I washed up all them jars that was out in the barn and backed up the sink. He run the snake and hit tree roots. I think he's going to end up replacing the whole line."

He frowned. "All the way to the septic?"

Hinges on the screen door gave a squeak. Grandpap came in from the porch, where he'd left his brogans sitting by the door. "Well, you ain't going to tie in PVC with cast iron, 'less you know something I don't." In his white sock feet, he padded to the sink and worked his way down to one knee, peering through the open cabinet doors at the P-trap. "Get you some coveralls, boy. I need help."

Eric didn't say anything. Just stared at the back of Grandpap's head.

Haley. She was on her way to meet him at Burger King. He'd only come home for a change of clothes. But what the hell did that matter when Grandpap had big plans for him to do something else.

Eric took his phone out of his pocket and sent Haley a text.

In his room, he pulled tan coveralls on over his jeans and PSA t-shirt. About the time he got them zipped, his cell phone beeped. He grabbed it off the edge of the dresser and read Haley's reply.

"Halfway there already," she'd texted back. "This is bullshit."

He agreed. But saying no to Grandpap when work needed to be done would be the shot heard round the world. Haley might get pissy, but Grandpap got mean. Especially if he wound up halfway down a fifth of bourbon. Even Gram might not be able to stay out of his way then.

In the kitchen, Grandpap had already disconnected the P-trap and taken it outside to flush with the hose. Back in with it now, he lay it on one of Gram's towels and set the emptied bucket back underneath the stub from the sink drain.

"Why don't you just hire this done?" Eric crossed his arms and leaned against the countertop, waiting for orders. "I'll pay for it."

Grandpap barely made eye contact before his attention went back to the sink drain. "Boy, I ain't never paid somebody for work I can do myself." He dropped to one knee and peered underneath the cabinet. Wiggled the length of drain pipe the P-trap had connected to, and frowned. "I'll use the angle grinder in here, but you need to take the sawzall under the house. Ain't no use setting the place afar."

Afar. Afire. Same difference.

Did he sound like that, too, when he talked?

Eric rubbed his eyes. Every house in Appalachia had a basement, except theirs. Just the thought of crawling around on that hard dirt made his bad knee hurt.

He shifted his weight to the other leg. "Grandpap," he said. "Let me take care of this. I work. I can afford to call a plumber."

"Yeah, you work, all right." Grandpap scowled but didn't look up. "Big money."

A hundred things Eric could have said in reply, and not one of them worth the clusterfuck it would cause. He chewed the inside of his cheek until he tasted blood. Then he let the screen door slam a little harder than he should have on his way out to the porch.

In the back yard, several lengths of PVC drain pipe lay where Grandpap had dragged them from the barn. Not even a last-minute trip to Lowes would get him out of this mess. Looked like that damn crawlspace door would be the only tight fit he had to look forward to the whole rest of the evening.

"Not like you actually fucking stood me up or anything," Haley bitched at him over the phone. "Asshole. I don't think you have any right to tell me I can't go to the farm."

By "farm" she meant one of the in-crowd hangouts, an actual farm with a barn where liquor bottles nested in the haystacks and a perpetual haze of pot smoke hung in the air. Eric had been there, but he was never in a hurry to go back. Just not his scene, although it was where he and Haley had finally hooked up on a horse blanket after homecoming his senior year.

"I think I have every right," he said. "I mean, are we together, or not? I don't like the idea of you being there without me. Too much can happen."

"You don't trust me?"

"It's not you I don't trust." He shifted his leg on top of the bedcovers, holding the icepack tight against his knee. Damn thing throbbed like an ear ache.

"I can handle myself."

"I know you can." He willed patience into his voice that he didn't feel. "I just don't think it's a good idea."

"You should have told your Grandpap to suck it." A dinging sound in the background—her car, key in the ignition. "That's what you should have done."

"It's family," he said. "I can't just leave him here to do all this stuff by himself. I drink water out of that sink, too."

The car engine started. "You're so full of shit, Eric. You won't stand up to him because you're afraid of him. It's obvious."

Eric's cheeks burned. God, she could piss him off so bad sometimes.

"I gotta go," she said. "I'll call you tomorrow."

"Wait." He checked the connection. Call ended. "God damn it." He threw the phone down on the bed.

Shit. He had half a mind to go to the farm anyway and drag her ass out of there. Then he pictured the scene that was likely to cause and thought better of it.

Fuck, his knee hurt.

Grandpap kept a bottle of pinks in the medicine cabinet for his occasional bouts with kidney stones. Surely he wouldn't miss just one.

Eric left the ice pack on his comforter and hobbled down the hall to the bathroom. Quietly, he opened the medicine cabinet. *Don't let the pills rattle.* Oxycodone, ten milligrams. He slid one out with the tip of a forefinger and swallowed it dry. Set the bottle back the way he'd found it and shut the mirrored door. Stared at his reflection for a moment, hating the red splotches on his cheeks that advertised his frustration like neon. Fuck that. He limped into the kitchen, trying to walk normal so Gram wouldn't put two and two together and go count pills.

He reached into the refrigerator for a can of pop.

"Put that back and get you some water," Gram said from the pantry, switching off the light on her way out. "Right here at bedtime—all that sugar'll rot your teeth."

Jesus. Was he twelve? Eric hesitated, allowing himself to wonder just for a moment what she'd do if he ignored her.

He sighed and set the can back in the fridge.

"I never gave you fruit juice in your baby bottle," she said. "Wouldn't let that sorry excuse you had for a mama do it, either. And you never had to have no teeth pulled. Grew in all straight and white. Makes a difference, what you let a kid suck on when they're little."

She shut the pantry door, all five feet of her with a long, gray braid down the middle of her back.

It wasn't her beliefs that kept her from getting a haircut. Gram hadn't set foot in a church since Eric had been old enough to know what a church was. Well, maybe a funeral or two. But if she lost that braid, Grandpap would shit cinder blocks. A woman's hair was her glory, he'd say, quoting a Bible he never read. A Bible he *couldn't* read. Grandpap could barely sign his name. No use for schoolin', not in his day. Yeah, times had changed, but any man keep his nose in a book when he should have been working wasn't much of a man in Grandpap's eyes.

Eric took a glass from the cupboard and ran it full of tap water. From a well, since the PSA lines didn't make it that far up the holler.

"I didn't give your daddy fruit juice, either," she said. "Or sodey pop. And he had a mouth full of teeth 'til he got half of 'em knocked out in lockup."

Selective memory—yeah, sure could come in handy for a good case of denial. The way Eric recalled it, his daddy already had a few gaps in his smile before he got sent up—the meth had rotted him down to nothing long before then.

He didn't point that out. Just nodded at Gram and finished his water. Set the glass in the sink and walked back to his bedroom, praying she wouldn't notice the hitch in his stride.

Funny, how his mind worked when he was asleep. He could still think, sometimes, especially in dreams like this one. So he should have been able to control the scene. Order the events. Have some say in what happened next. But he couldn't. And he didn't. He was just along for the ride. It didn't seem right, but what could he do? Just keep walking, putting one foot in front of the other, until he finally figured out what he was there to see.

Eric should have recognized the building. The parking lot. The garage bay with the door up. The white room full of blue barrels, all new and waiting to serve a purpose. But he didn't. He didn't recognize any of it. He'd been there before, but it was a different "there"—this was a projection, not a memory. His own rendering of some reality he'd experienced but somehow forgotten.

Rosie was there, too, Junior Rasnick's dead Walker Hound. She'd sidle up just close enough to him to make him think he could touch her, then she was off and running with her nose to the ground, chasing rabbits in her imagination. She looked just like he remembered her, minus the flat head and guts spilled all over

Highway 12. Damn, that had been hard to see. Even harder to clean up. He'd dragged what was left of her to the shoulder, then come back later with a shovel and made it all go away.

Here, though, she still looked like herself. Acted like herself, too—short attention span, big goofy grin on her face. Everything around her was white—the walls, the floor, the ceiling. Not like any building he'd ever been in. And she knew her way around it. She led him down hallways and through doors he hadn't even known were there. He followed, certain he was supposed to.

And then she disappeared.

He stopped walking, understanding with a jolt that he had no idea how to get back to where he started. She'd led him so far in that he'd lost all sense of direction. He stood there for a long moment, searching for some way to orient himself in all the whiteness. He would have given anything for a splash of color, some break in the monotony of all that pale. What Rosie gave him instead was a sound, a yelp, somewhere far in the distance, and it sounded like she was in pain.

He turned another corner and he was back in the room with all the blue barrels. Not good. This time, one sat on a platform raised off the floor about two feet. It put the top of the barrel just below eye level. Dear God, no—he did not want to look inside. But he knew he had to. That's why he was here. He needed to see this.

Grow a pair, Blevins.

He forced himself to move. One step at a time, toward the barrel. Something he just had to do, like it or not. He steeled himself and peeped inside.

Yep, Rosie was there. Just like he expected. No surprise. And she was dead—good and dead—with a cable around her neck attached to a broken stick. That didn't make sense. None of this made sense. He just wanted to wake up. Wanted to forget this whole dream. Wanted to forget Rosie, and everything that had anything to do with a goddamned blue barrel. Wake up. Time ... to ... wake ... up.

Eric jerked upright, tossing covers aside, gasping for air. Sat there in a cold sweat, just like always. But this time the dream stayed with him, cloying like a bad scent, oozing from his mind and out through the pores of his skin. Holy shit, it seemed so real. Much more so than usual. And what could he blame it on? The goddamned oxy, probably. Well, from now on his knee would just have to fucking hurt. Better a little physical pain than whacked-out nightmares about a bunch of crazy shit he hadn't caused and couldn't do a damn thing about.

(Key of A)
So tears fall
Drops of lonely, bitter hate
Call it what you want to
It's not rain.
Feed on anger
Say it gives a better edge.
Numb it if you want to
It's just pain.

Wide awake but tell me you've been dreaming
Quote the facts and call it true believing.

If two plus two is one
Then that's where the truth dies
I am already done
With these lies.

You called it right
Called me down, called my bluff
You were just the spotter
I held the gun.

Instead of thinking we should just keep walking
I went back and that's when you stopped talking.
*   ---Erik Evans, 2003*

CHAPTER ELEVEN

Damn buzzing, beeping, whatever the hell that noise was—it had no business in the newsroom. Was their teleprompter on the fritz? Jesus Christ, that was loud enough for the microphones to pick up. Didn't anybody care? And shit—there it went again. What the absolute fuck? Why wasn't anybody doing anything about it?

Taylor's eyes popped open in the darkness. The sound stage from her dream cut to black like someone killed power to an internal feed. She lay there for a moment, blinking. Damn. Couldn't even get away from work when she was asleep. Maybe she needed a vacation.

The buzzing again, near her head and very insistent. Taylor sat up. Shit! Her phone on the nightstand, vibrating and chirping to the tune of the Avengers theme song. She squinted at the window. No light peeking through the curtains. She turned her squint toward the clock. Five-thirty. Who the hell was calling her so early?

She picked up the phone and looked at it. 276 area code. Southwest Virginia? She swiped to answer.

"H'llo?"

"Taylor Beckett?" A strong male voice, slightly familiar.

"Mm hmm." She rubbed her eyes. "Yes. This is Taylor."

"Terry Hastings, from Randall County. I thought you would want to know—we found another one last night."

"Another what? Oh!" Wide awake now, no caffeine needed. "Another barrel?"

"I told you I'd give you the same courtesy I give our local news," he said. "I'm letting everybody know—I'll be doing a press conference at noon. If you can get here, please do. Sheriff's office, first floor, in the old cafeteria."

"Oh, uh ... I—" Shit, shit, shit. Five hours away. Yeah, she might make it, if she went in her pajamas and drove triple digits. "Sheriff Hastings, I'm in Richmond."

"If you can catch a commuter flight, we have a couple airports nearby. "There's one in—"

"I'm on it." So what if she cut him off. He was talking way too slowly to let him finish the sentence. "See you at noon."

She muttered something that sounded like "goodbye" so it wouldn't seem like she hung up on him and immediately searched for Kavanagh's number in her contacts.

"Mmph," was Kavanagh's only greeting.

"Get hold of Perry," she said. "We're heading out as soon as I can book a flight. Randall County—they've got another one."

A second or two passed as he processed her words. "Hennessey," was all he said in response.

"He's my next call," she assured him. "You were my first. Don't you feel special?"

She hung up with Kavanagh and woke her boss. "We're going back to coal country," she informed him. "Victim number four. Apparently, they found him last night."

Hennessey sounded like he'd gargled with blasting grit. "Him?"

"I assume, yes. All the other victims have been male. Killer seems to have a 'type.' "

"You've been doing this long enough to know you can't make assumptions like that." Hennessey cleared his throat. "Just go. Get it done."

Three hours later, Taylor and her crew sat wedged in the cabin of a Cessna Skyhawk, somewhere high over the Roanoke Valley. She and Kavanagh had let Perry have the front passenger seat, since his legs were longest. The domed roof of the Skyhawk pressed low over her head, windows crowded in from the sides. She sat very still and kept her focus on the notepad that contained all her questions. She definitely had a few.

By ten-thirty, they'd taxied to a stop at a tiny hometown airport—just a landing strip, really—and picked up the rental car waiting for them in the lot. It was a Dodge Caravan, but felt like a Greyhound coach compared to the Skyhawk. In the middle row, framed on both sides by huge panel doors that could make both sides of the van slide backward at the touch of a button, Taylor stretched her legs as far as she could and slouched in her seat like a teenager on a school bus.

With Kavanagh at the wheel, they left the airport and drove almost three miles down a mountain to reach civilization. Taylor had spent so much time that morning focused only on what lay directly in front of her that to sit back, take a deep breath, and look around seemed almost unnatural. How nice it felt to just exist for a minute. To just stare out the window, notice the world outside, and its beauty. And there *was* beauty, the way the land rolled and grass grew high up the mountainsides, a lush, green carpet that looked like velour from a distance. Above it, tree-covered ridges touched the sky, their smooth lines occasionally interrupted by an outcropping of rock, sheer-faced cliffs rising at such an angle from time-worn hills that she wondered if any human had actually ever set foot on them.

On impulse, she lowered her window long enough to frame up a shot with her phone and snapped a picture. Checked it for clarity—yep, that was a good one. She found Charles in her contacts list and sent it to him.

"You told me to find something positive," she typed. "This."

Less than a minute later, her phone chimed.

"Told you it was there," he wrote.

"Right. I just had to look."

A few seconds passed before her phone chimed again. "I can almost see why they think windmills are ugly."

"But trash piles, junk cars, dilapidated houses, and strip mines are gosh-darn lovely."

A longer pause this time. Then, "You are hopeless."

She laughed quietly and put her phone away, letting him have the last word.

In town, Kavanagh found the Sheriff's Office with little trouble, the route familiar after their last trip. They'd made it from the airport in half an hour, leaving them plenty of time to lug the camera equipment into the building, find the old cafeteria, and set up at the large folding table closest to the lectern. Perry and Kavanagh busied themselves with tripods and whatnot, keeping gear contained to just a few squares of low-pile industrial carpet. Taylor spent most of the time reviewing her notes and wondering why the three of them were the only people in the room.

At five minutes before noon, everyone showed up at once. Sonny Heflin—she recognized him from the hours she'd spent poring over Google Image returns for all the Randall County native media personalities—editor of two weekly newsprint publications and owner of the byline for the PSA gate story. Behind him, anonymous reporters who may have been from any of the regional papers. And then a small murmuration of perky young women carrying handheld digital video cameras. Ah—the local TV personalities had arrived. They all looked at her, and at Perry's JVC with its fancy lens hood and fuzzy boom mike. Took obvious notice of Kavanagh's equipment bags on the floor with the WRCH logo and network affiliation printed brightly on each side. A couple of them offered tight smiles—for Taylor and each other—but like starlings in flight, they moved in tandem to execute a very efficient setup of tripods down the long row of tables at the back of the room.

Oops. Was there an unwritten rule about where cameras were supposed to go? Or a written one, for that matter? Had she and her crew taken someone's seat?

Better question—did she care?

A glance at Kavanagh and Perry told her they either hadn't noticed or didn't give a shit. Probably the latter. Their expressions remained carefully neutral, posture relaxed. Kavanagh had plopped his ass in a seat at the end of the table, waiting patiently with one arm draped across the back of the empty chair beside him. Perry stood between the wall and the camera, quietly observant without a fidget or a twitch. The consummate professional—if he had ever entertained a salacious thought about Halle Berry or anyone else he wanted to eat like a pie, it wasn't evident in his demeanor now.

Sheriff Hastings breezed into the room at exactly one minute before noon, flanked by uniformed deputies and two state police officers. They gathered around the lectern, unsmiling and officious. Hastings frowned down at his notes, bags under his eyes and skin pasty, evidence of a long night stamped on his features.

The tallest deputy lowered what Taylor had assumed to be a projector screen. It was wide enough to cover most of the white wall behind the group of officers. Not a projector screen at all, but a light gray background bearing the Sheriff's Department logo. Overhead, a row of canister lights switched on, their glow muted and warm. It had never entered Taylor's mind to peep behind the table set longways in front of the lectern, covered by a dark cloth with the words "Protect and Serve" printed near the fringe. Apparently that little setup hid a reflector. What resulted was a near-perfect clamshell lighting effect that erased the dark shadows on Hastings' face as effectively as Photoshop.

At the view screen of his camera, Perry pulled back and frowned. Then he gave a small shake of his head and tweaked his shot. Taylor caught Kavanagh's eye. His brows ticked upward, almost imperceptibly. He looked back at her, saying nothing, but communicating volumes.

"Good afternoon," Hastings said into the lectern's mike. "Thank you all for coming. Just before eight o'clock last night, nine-one-one dispatch received a call requesting officer assistance on Old Sandlick Road. The caller stated their dog had returned home carrying what appeared to be human bones in its mouth. The responding officer confirmed this once he arrived on scene. We initiated a grid search of the Garden Hill area that ended around two a.m. with the discovery of human remains.

"The body was sent to the state medical examiner in Roanoke this morning. We should have autopsy results in a few days. Upon initial observation, the remains appear to be those of a young adult male. Identification has not been made at this time. Decomposition was advanced. However, dentition was intact. Based on several factors, we believe we will make a positive I.D. off that."

He looked up from his notes. "I'll take your questions." He pointed to someone over Taylor's right shoulder. "Rebecca."

Taylor turned to see one of the TV reporters brighten in response to being called. "Do you think this is connected to the three unsolved murders you're currently investigating?"

Hastings didn't blink. "It's too early to say for sure."

Another reporter took a turn. "Did you find a blue barrel at the scene?"

A muscle in the side of Hastings' face twitched. "We did recover a blue poly drum about fifty feet from the remains, yes."

At any other press conference, the room would have erupted in at least a buzz, if not a roar. Here, everyone went silent, Writing, typing, making notes in some form, but nobody asked the next question.

Taylor raised a hand.

"Miss Beckett." Hastings pointed to her.

"Altizer and Hess were both from Virginia. Dillow was from Johnson City, Tennessee. Has the FBI been involved in this investigation at all so far?"

Hastings stared at her. His mouth thinned into a hard line. "Dillow was originally from Johnson City, yes. But the most current driver's license issued to him bore an Abingdon address. We have no reason to believe any of these young men were transported across state lines." He straightened and stood a little taller, fingers clamped around the sides of the lectern. "The State Police have been working with us on these cases."

Fair enough.

She nodded. "Thank you."

He pointed to someone else along the back table. "Nita."

"Are you ready to call these serial murders now?" Nita asked.

Taylor turned for a quick glance at Nita. Older, not fresh out of high school the way the others looked. Still a little too wide-eyed for Taylor's liking, but at least she put the burning question out there.

Behind the lectern, Hastings motioned at one of the deputies. The younger man left his place in the line of officers flanking the Sheriff and approached with his hands clasped behind his back. He leaned forward so Hastings could say something in his ear, then nodded and picked his way toward the edge of the room.

"We definitely see a pattern," Hastings said to Nita. "It's undeniable. But to label it as 'serial' would be premature at this time. We have no evidence to show that the same person committed all four crimes."

Really? Taylor fought the urge to smack herself on the forehead, since she couldn't smack him.

Taylor glanced over to see the deputy who'd just left Hastings picking his way to her through the empty chairs.

He came close enough to lean across the table and whisper in her ear. "Hastings said he'll give you an interview after the press conference. Just meet him in his office."

Taylor said nothing. Just caught the deputy's eye to acknowledge she'd heard, and turned her attention back to the front of the room.

Privileged? The chosen one? Hell, no. She'd just been told to shut the fuck up. Not the first time in her career, but damn. He was the one who called her at five a.m. to tell her about this bullshit conference.

The next question fired from the back of the room was about other evidence at the scene. Five seconds into Hastings' reply, she could tell he didn't intend to be forthcoming. So she tuned him out. She could watch the video later. More important was spending the next few minutes trying to figure out if she was going to play his little game or not.

(Key of F)
Time has come for me to decide
I get what you have implied
And I don't want to take sides
But here I am at a crossroad.
I thought I might turn around
Go up the way I came down
But it's some damn shaky ground
And I am redlining, overload.

But I'm ready now to make up my mind
I'm not wasting any more of our time

On the line now
Taking what is mine now
Marking every message read
Hearing what my heart said.
You make the leap now
Close your eyes and jump now
Marking every message read
Hearing what my heart said.

---Erik Evans, 2003

CHAPTER TWELVE

Taylor left the cafeteria before the tedious Q & A ground to a stop. Her guys would cover it. She had to think.

She walked alone down the long, tiled hallway toward Hastings' office, admiring the woodwork on the old lockers left in place along the walls. Good choice. She would have left it all in place, too. Not quite ornate but far from simple—based on what she knew about hardwoods, the locker framework and doors had been hewn from American chestnut. That meant the building was turn of the century, updated through the years but never gutted for renovation. Lots of history in that place. Lots of history in that town. A lot of water under the bridge that never quite managed to flow past the other side.

Hastings' secretary bustled about in the receiving area just off the main hallway across from his office. His door stood open. Taylor stopped walking, unsure what to do.

"You can go on in and wait for him, honey." The secretary smiled. "He messaged and said you might be on your way here."

He messaged. Social media guru. Good old Sheriff Hastings. Taylor thanked her and stepped into his private workspace.

Wonderful security he had. But then again, did he need it? All the bulletproof glass and metal detectors were in the vestibule, to make that big impression for visitors who might have sketchy ideas. Here, the mood relaxed. More doors open than shut. A big oak desk at the back of his office, conference table nearby, all obsessively neat with no documents or any type of work product in sight. The file cabinets were surely locked. So were the desk drawers. Not that she had the slightest interest in testing them. But he was a "place for everything and everything in its place" kind of man, and that was important. All the sensitive things under lock and key, but everything else completely accessible. Interesting. Knowing this about him would help her understand what he was after, and how far he might go to get it.

His coffeemaker sat dark and cold on the credenza. How would he feel about somebody else tinkering with it? Only one way to find out. Taylor ran some water in the pot from his mini-sink and added enough grounds to the filter cup to satisfy most people's definition of "strong." Then she took a seat in one of the wingback chairs in front of his desk and waited for it to brew.

She had just poured herself the first cup when he walked through the doorway. Seemed logical to grab another cup from the rack and pour him some as well. She met him with it halfway to his desk.

"Keep your enemies closer," she said, not quite having to force the smile as she handed the coffee mug to him.

He took the mug. "You're not my enemy, Miss Beckett. And I'm not yours."

"In that case," she said. "Call me Taylor."

"Okay." He took a careful sip. "Taylor, you make good coffee."

He set the folder of notes he carried on the corner of his desk. With his free hand, he motioned to the general area of his face. "What happened here?"

For a second she just stared at him, wondering what he meant. Then she got it—her stitches had come out a couple days ago, but the cuts on her chin still showed through no matter how much makeup she packed on top of them.

"Chasing a subject through Best Plaza—I really wanted that interview. He went through the glass wall and I went after him. What are a few stitches in the name of journalism."

Hastings laughed out loud. "Good one."

She made a face. "Actually, I fell and broke my coffee table. At home. It was embarrassing and ridiculous."

He laughed again. Carrying his coffee mug, he stepped around the corner of his desk and sat in the big leather chair behind it. "My wife makes a poultice out of pine sap that would be good for those cuts. It increases the blood flow and whatnot—speeds healing. And it feels damn good. Tingles a little bit. Want me to see if she has any made up?"

Taylor shrugged. "Sure."

Why not.

He typed something into his phone. Really? He was asking his wife about pine sap poultice? Taylor felt her brows creep upward. Did her best to look impassive, but figured she probably failed pretty miserably at it.

Hastings set his phone on the desk and pulled a keyring out of his pocket. He unlocked the drawers on his right side and put the keys back in his pocket.

"I appreciate you coming today," he said. "And in answer to your question—yes. The feds have been in touch."

"In touch? What do you mean by that?"

"I mean two similar deaths could be a coincidence. Three, not so much. Let's just say they're monitoring the situation. And after what we found last night, I'm expecting another phone call from their resident office in Bristol just any minute."

"Is that a good thing or a bad thing?"

He laughed. "I'll see the glass half-full as long as I possibly can."

"Optimism is always nice." Taylor had seen him in action. She knew that was all the answer she'd get.

"I have a lot of respect for you as a journalist," he said. "I understand you were a recipient of the Livingston Award a few years back—that 2009 story about the engineering racket in Chicago?"

Taylor blinked. He'd done his homework. "Yes."

"Some of those guys went away for a long time, thanks to you." He took another sip of coffee. "Do you remember a Lieutenant Weber?"

Wow. She hadn't heard that name in years. "Of course. He was over the task force."

"That's right. Well, he has his own district now. Captain Weber—have you been in touch with him lately?"

She shook her head. "I haven't talked to anyone from Chicago in a long time."

"I gave him a call a few days ago. Just ... on a hunch. Talked to him about you, asked him if you're a team player. I know the two of you worked pretty closely seven or eight years ago. See, I'd entertained the idea of calling you before we found this new victim— because you never followed up, never aired anything after your trip over here. That surprised me. I thought you were a little harder-hitting than that."

Taylor wrapped both hands around her mug and cradled it in her lap. "Oh, I'll knock the hell out of something if I see a clear target. But with this—I didn't feel like I had a story. Or at least not *the* story. I think the real news is bigger than four dead boys."

He nodded slowly. "Well, Weber said I want you on this. And he told me you can be trusted. So I'm going to make a leap of faith here. But in return, can you guarantee that you won't go to air with anything before you talk to me about it?"

Unbelievable. Just fucking unreal, the set of balls on this man. Was this the way he trained the local press? Taught them to clap like seals when he wanted, and be silent as butterflies when that suited him better?

His phone beeped. He tapped out a text reply and set it down again. Then he pulled a thin stack of files from one of the drawers he'd unlocked. From one folder he took four eight-by-ten photos and placed them on his desk, in a row, turned so they wouldn't be upside down for her.

Taylor leaned forward. Jesus Christ. Morgue photos. Now *this*—this was going somewhere.

"I'm out on a limb here," he said. "But now you gotta give me something. This conversation, even if you agree to nothing else—it needs to be off the record. Can we do that?"

She didn't hesitate. "Absolutely."

"Okay, then." He gave her a long, intense look. Then he pointed to the photo on the far left. "Our latest." Then the next one over. "Dylan Altizer." And then the next. "Michael Dillow." Finally, the one on the right. "Cody Hess."

Strange, putting faces to those names. Or maybe not faces—Dillow and Hess still had a few pounds of flesh, but nothing recognizable. Just puffy and putrid, covered with adipocere, dark fluids oozing from every orifice. Altizer's body was dessicated, like he'd spent a few days in a dehydrator. His corpse had the appearance of a mummy, with leathered skin tented over bones, hollow eye sockets and an open jaw. Clumps of light brown hair clung to the scalp and looked as brittle as steel wool. The spots with no hair were simply exposed bone, grungy white in contrast to the dull, muddy brown scum that coated the rest of the body.

Taylor took a deep breath. Exhaled slowly. That's what the Blevins kid had seen in the woods? At night? Alone? Good lord—a wonder he didn't lose every marble he had.

Coping with the horror of violent death was a learned skill. Even Taylor still flinched at the worst of it sometimes, though not nearly as much as she used to. She'd had no choice but find ways to cope. Either that or lose her mind.

The unidentified victim was partially skeletonized, strung together with dried sinew. Several pieces of him appeared to be missing. He'd been reassembled on a stainless steel table, minus a femur, most of his ribs, one entire arm, and many small bones from his feet and hands. Mercifully, his head was still attached to his torso. At least there was that.

Taylor squinted and looked closer. Around his neck—what was it? Tattered pieces of duct tape?

"This one," she said, pointing to the photo of the skeleton. "Any sign of manual strangulation—crushed hyoid, broken bones—anything to suggest a struggle?"

Hastings shook his head but didn't say anything.

"Okay, well—" She looked down at her coffee and frowned. "Then I think these are out of order." She moved Altizer and the newest victim like tiles of a slide puzzle until they'd swapped places in the lineup. "He's still your first victim," she said, touching the photo of Altizer. "You know that, right?"

Slowly, with narrowed eyes, Hastings nodded.

"I can't explain why this body—" She pointed to the new find. "Is in worse shape. But he died after Altizer. I'd bet money on it."

Coffee mug abandoned on a plastic coaster beside his blotter, Hastings sat back with his fingers tight around the chair arms. "You wouldn't lose."

Of course. Knoxville. The Body Farm. Hastings could probably interpret information from those corpses as well as the Medical Examiner.

He frowned. "I want you to tell me why you think so."

"De-escalating violence," Taylor said. "Altizer's murder may even have been accidental. At least not premeditated. It was an in-the-moment kind of thing—the choking. But once he crossed that line, your killer found out he liked it. Got off on it." She thought for a few seconds. "Any indication that Altizer was sexually assaulted?

His family wouldn't release the autopsy findings to me. But I have Dillow and Hess, and I know about the perianal bruising."

Hastings looked at her for a long moment before he spoke. "Altizer was inconclusive for that."

"Well, whatever the case—after Altizer, the killer started thinking ahead. Next time, he was prepared. The latest body and Dillow were both bagged. Suffocated. Right? With stuff he had to acquire and bring to the scene?"

He nodded.

"But Hess died from carbon monoxide poisoning. Killer hooked a hose to his car and shoved the other end in the barrel. Or something to that effect. Probably didn't take long."

Again, Hastings nodded.

"He's not experimenting with methods," she said. "He's improving with practice. Getting more efficient. Pretty soon he'll figure out how to kill them without lifting a finger." Taylor pointed to the photos. "Can I take those with me? Or copies of them?"

Hastings rubbed his eyes. "Ordinarily, no. But after that phone call to Chicago—they said I should give you whatever you need. So you can have these. But you'd better be every bit as discreet as Weber says you are."

"You have my word." She scooped the photos into a pile and dropped them into the manila envelope that Hastings held open for her. "If I had to guess, I'd say you know exactly why the second victim decomposed faster than the first."

"I think I have a pretty good idea." He fastened the clasp on the envelope and handed it to her across the desk. "Altizer was reported missing in January of last year. It was a cold winter. Lot of nights the temperature didn't get out of the teens. The barrel was probably airtight for most of that time. I don't believe the lid came loose until the force of the floodwater broke the seal. Then you have a body encased in mud—you get a little bit of preservative effect. Until the temperatures start climbing, and active decomp starts.

"This latest one, though—I figure he was killed last summer. Instead of cold, you have some pretty extreme heat building up in that barrel at a critical time. It's possible that the pressure of all those gasses is what broke the seal. Hard to say for sure. But you can imagine the insect activity. The animal scavengers. Surprising we have as much of the remains left as we do."

"You mentioned something about dentition," Taylor said. "What's up with that?"

"This guy had a lot of work done. Couple of bridges, acrylic veneers, and three implants. They have batch numbers."

"Ah."

"I'm no forensic odontologist," Hastings said. "But it looks like the kind of reconstructive work somebody might have done after rehab."

"Meth mouth."

"Exactly."

Taylor finished her coffee and set the cup on the floor beside her. "So, are you getting any trace evidence off the bodies? Besides the foreign DNA from Hess?"

"Not really. But that little bit of DNA will be enough, if we ever have a viable suspect."

"No match through CODIS?"

"Not so far."

"What about the barrels? What are they telling you?"

He shrugged. "Nothing, really. They're what's called 'open top' barrels, not like the ones that chemicals or soap or degreaser comes in. They have a removable lid, not just the bung holes. Anybody can buy them—kind of expensive, but not hard to get your hands on. We had all these tested to see what they may have originally contained, but no results on any of them. Looks like they were all new. Unused."

"Well, the only other question I planned to ask is about the boys themselves—were missing person reports filed on all of them?"

"Yes. But before you even go down that road, think about it. You have the one from this general area—Altizer—but then you have Abingdon and Roanoke. Who's going to put it together, that all of these missing people from different counties are connected? Our killer has either been very careful or very lucky. He's never hunted the same ground twice. I don't know how he's choosing his victims, but he's doing it wisely. I mean, look at it—he killed four people *that we know of* before anybody even realized we have a serial."

"So, you *are* calling it a serial."

"Not to the press."

Taylor cleared her throat. "Uhm—uh ... hello?"

"But see, you're going to do the right thing," he said. "And that makes it a little different."

A knock on the frame of his open door caused Taylor to turn in her chair. Hastings' secretary stood behind her with a small jar in her hand.

"Your wife dropped this off just now," she said to her boss.

Hastings pointed to Taylor. "It's hers."

The secretary took a few extra steps into the room to place the jar in Taylor's hand.

"Thank you, Goldie," Hastings said.

His secretary nodded and left them alone again.

Taylor studied the thing in her hand, a four-ounce canning jar with a cute little diamond bas relief pattern stamped in the glass. "Is this ...?"

"Pine sap poultice. For your face. You can use it like a cream. And you don't need much. A little dab two or three times a day—you'll notice a difference pretty quick."

Taylor opened the lid and sniffed. Oh, goodness—fresh pine—nice. She wouldn't mind having that scent in a candle or twelve sitting around her loft.

She gave Hastings a sideways look. "Why are you doing this?"

"Because I know it works," he said. "I've used it myself, plenty of times."

"No, not the poultice. The conversation. The photos."

He propped his elbows on his blotter and laced his hands together. "Oh, I definitely have my reasons. Better believe I have an agenda. But it's not at your expense."

She didn't say anything, but she didn't break her gaze. Didn't waver. Just waited to see if he'd continue.

He did. "This town is a fishbowl. Lot of guppies swimming around in circles, bumping into each other. Nate Bostick, our Commonwealth's Attorney, was a criminal defense lawyer for fifteen years before he got elected. The CA before him—Johnny Willis—didn't run for another term and went into private practice instead ... in the same firm where Bostick spent fifteen years defending the folks Willis tried to prosecute. Same office, in fact. Same desk. The chairman of our Board of Supervisors sits on the Industrial Development Authority board, the Coalfield Economic Development Authority board, and the PSA board. The PSA Administrator is married to our Magistrate. It doesn't take much of a misstep to stomp all over some very connected toes.

"So here's the problem. My investigators have a lot of questions that need to be asked. And a bunch of folks aren't going to like it when we knock on their door. I've been racking my brain trying to figure out how to play both ends against the middle. I need to solve this case, but I don't need to piss off half the voters in the county."

He steepled his two index fingers and rested them against his mouth. Looked thoughtful for a moment, then laced his fingers back with the others and exhaled slowly. "I'll run for Sheriff again next term. My wife owns a business in town—she does massage and infrared therapy, sells some of her organics. Does pretty well. Caters to a certain crowd, if you know what I mean." He met Taylor's gaze with a cocked eyebrow. "I have a girl at the high school and my son's in middle school. They're good kids. I'm proud of them."

Another pause.

"Thing about a fishbowl," he said. "It doesn't take much to get the ecosystem out of balance, make one guppy start chewing on another one. I have four dead bodies floating around and they're stinking up the water pretty good. There's some guppies looking at other guppies kind of sideways right now. Well, they can look at me all they want. But I got a family. And I know how things work in this town."

How to answer that? Taylor had no idea. She just listened, let him fill the silence.

"So here's what I'm thinking." He lowered his forearms until they rested flat on the desk. "You need a story. You won the Livingston, and then I don't know what the hell you've done for the past seven years. You sure haven't been living up to the hype. You're a damn good journalist, but you've been coasting. Well, I'll make a deal with you. You carry my water up this hill, and I'll give you an all-access pass. You go to air with nothing that you don't run past me first, but you have my word that I'll stay out of your way while you're rooting up that next award."

Taylor stared at him, speechless.

He stared back. He didn't blink.

She did.

(Key of D)
Forecast calls for sun but it don't feel right
Clouds overrun the sky
Breath of spring today
Tomorrow the cold wind
Freezes us back again

Hopeful conversation walks such a fine line
Turns on the thinnest dime
Losing sight of purpose
Was never the better plan
We do the best we can.

Break it down, cut to the chase
We're not wrong, just out of place
Sell your soul to keep your faith
Our dreams don't lie
Dreams don't lie.

It's a spinning compass
It's a broken wheel
We should see it but we don't
We should feel it but we won't.

.

Even now, you're on my mind
Don't know how we let this slide
So much hope gets lost in time
Our dreams don't lie.
Our dreams don't die.

---Erik Evans, 2003

CHAPTER THIRTEEN

The funny thing about selling one's soul—at first it felt like a win, regardless of the eventual outcome. At least that had always been Taylor's experience. This time, not so much. It just felt like a big question mark.

She sat in the van while Perry and Kavanagh went into Hardees. Apparently, they were starving. Again. She could eat, but not that. Maybe if she conserved energy as much as possible, she could live off her fat stores long enough to find a Subway.

Leaving the Caravan's sliding doors open made her feel too exposed. So she settled for a lowered window. She used the time to inspect the pine sap poultice made by Hastings' wife. He'd said she could use it like a cream, which meant she could use it without a compress. She opened the jar and sniffed again. Still nice.

Taylor wasn't a skeptic when it came to herbs and the medicinal use of plants. She wasn't a hard sell about the potential therapeutic benefit of pine sap. What fascinated her about the stuff was where it came from. *Hastings' wife.* She'd never stopped to consider him as a whole person, just as the embodiment of his job. But if he had a wife, that meant someone loved him as a human being and a man, not just as a public servant. He'd spoken of his wife quite warmly, and texted back and forth with her so casually that Taylor had to assume they kept a running dialogue all day long. How this affected her opinion of Hastings she wasn't entirely sure. Not yet. Had observing all of that impacted her on a subconscious level, made her more willing to trust him? He'd admitted his ambition without apology. This could have made him seem shallow and egocentric. Instead, he just came across as savvy and capable of grasping the bigger picture.

A truck pulled into the parking space beside her. It idled there for a moment, then the engine shut off. Someone spoke her name.

"Miss Beckett."

Eric Blevins, behind the wheel of a dark blue Ford pickup with the PSA logo on the door, wearing a highlighter-yellow traffic vest.

She blinked in surprise. "Hi, Eric."

Small towns. In Richmond, the odds against randomly encountering a familiar face on the street were astronomical. In a county where the entire population numbered fewer than forty thousand, those odds got a little better. Obviously.

"I wondered if you'd come back," he said across both their opened windows. "With that fourth body and all."

"News travels fast." She smiled. Not a horrible thing, running into him like this. "I went to the press conference earlier. They're really piling up—the victims."

"Yeah." He nodded. Then he pointed toward Hardees. "Your Secret Service guys grabbing lunch?" His broad smile lit up the darkened interior of the county truck. "They left you kind of open out here, didn't they?"

Taylor laughed. "Top secret mission. Ears only. Sorry. My lips are sealed."

His grin faltered. "What happened to your face?"

She held up her forearms, showing him the scars there, too. "An invasion of raccoons at Scuffletown Park. They'd already taken the walkways and were holding the squirrels hostage when we got there. We had no choice but go in."

The blank look he gave her at the mention of raccoons gave way to a chuckle. "You ain't right," he said, shaking his head.

She let him finish laughing and then told him about the coffee table.

"I have a question," she said after that. "Old Sandlick Road—do you know where that is? I can't pull it up on GPS."

He nodded. "Where they found number four, right?"

"Yep. Think you could take us to it?"

He draped his left wrist over the steering wheel. "Uhmm—yeah. Okay."

"Up for a joyride after work? I mean, if you don't have plans."

"I don't. And sure—that'd be fine." He looked at the Caravan. "We taking your wheels? 'Cause mine won't hold everybody."

"Fine with me."

He frowned. "That's a rental, right?"

"Yes. We flew in this morning. This was at the airport waiting for us."

"Well, you need to take that one back and get something with Virginia plates."

"What? Why?"

He smirked. "How do you think I knew you were here?"

Taylor just looked at him.

"Folks at the office got all excited," he said. "Going on about this news crew from Maryland. One of them said some blond reporter was sitting in front of Hardees. I figured it was probably you."

She pointed down, indicating the van. "This has Maryland plates? I didn't even look."

"Yeah. You're not exactly incognito."

"So what's going to happen if we drive around with Maryland plates? The locals show up with pitchforks and disappear us down a mine shaft somewhere?"

Eric looked out his windshield. Taylor followed his gaze. Perry and Kavanagh were coming out the door, bags in hand.

"No," he said. "It'll just be uncomfortable as hell."

"Okay." She sighed. "I still have your number. Is it okay if I give you a call around four-thirty?"

"Yep. I get off at four. So that sounds good."

Eric started his engine and backed out of the parking space, raising one hand to wave at Kavanagh and Perry before he drove out of the parking lot and down the street.

"What's happening at four-thirty?" Kavanagh asked.

"He's going to show us the dump site," she said. Damn, those hamburgers smelled good. Maybe she could choke down a slab of greasy, grain-fed beef, just this once. "Old Sandlick Road."

"Not me," Kavanagh said. "I got a ton of shit to do at home this afternoon."

"Me, either." Perry dug in his bag. "Sorry, Beckett. I can't do it today."

Kavanagh examined a foil-wrapped hamburger that looked six inches tall. "The pilot said he'd hang around the airport 'til three. I'm going back with him. My ass'll be sitting in Richmond by four-thirty."

All it would take was a call to Hennessey, and she'd have her crew for as long as she wanted them. But Taylor dismissed the idea as soon as it formed. She'd need them later—no sense pissing them off now.

"Fine," she said. "But I'm staying. I'll take you to the airport and keep the van. I want to see what this kid can show me."

Since it was so late in the day, the only vehicle with Virginia plates that the rental company had left at that location was a Dodge Ram. Taylor didn't need seats for a whole crew, so that make and model worked for her. The manager impressed her with his willingness to accommodate. More hassle for him, no real benefit. His lot wasn't even "sitting fat" with cars. Was he a local or a transplant? He could have been any college kid from anywhere— well-dressed, no twang, and clearly motivated to work. Whatever the case, she'd be sure to drop that branch a five-star review on Yelp when she got home that night.

Taylor couldn't explain the change in her mood. Something about fully committing to this story had liberated her. She was all-in with Hastings. Couldn't unmake that decision. She'd sent her crew home, stayed behind to scour the trenches and see how much dirt she could turn. It had been years since she felt this engaged with her own reporting. Years since she'd felt this optimistic. And she liked Eric Blevins. Genuinely. Looked forward to spending the afternoon letting him play tour guide, showing her the view from inside a culture that was utterly impenetrable otherwise.

He met her at Walmart. Parked his battered little car at the lower end of the parking lot and climbed in beside her, eyeing the interior of the new Ram with appreciation.

"Sweet." Eric nodded his approval. "I'm going to buy one of these for me someday."

"Think so, huh? Then get your ass back in school," Taylor said. "Take your Gen Ed courses at the community college. Those credits will transfer. It's a hell of a lot cheaper that way."

"I thought about trade school. Maybe welding. The mines are always hiring for that. Welders, cutters—"

She stared at him. "Do you hear yourself? Do ... you ... *hear* ... yourself? Fucking four-point-oh talking about working in the mines."

"School counselor said they need people like me at Vo-Tech. That they'd help me figure out how to pay for classes. That was before I graduated, but I feel sure they'll still work with me."

Taylor had put the truck in drive, but when he said that, she put it right back in park. " 'They' being who? The vocational school?"

He nodded.

"God damn it, Eric—listen to what you're saying. Are you telling me that this school system lets Vo-Tech actively recruit kids who are on an academic path?"

He shrugged. "They had some statistics about job availabilities over the next ten years. Apparently, skilled labor is going to be more in demand than white collar work."

"Jesus H fucking Christ." She let go of the steering wheel and shook her head in disbelief. "Are you serious?"

He stared at her.

"Eric—that's bullshit. Somebody needs to ... those idiots need to lose their fucking jobs. I agree we need skilled labor in this country. I won't for a minute dispute that. But high school guidance counselors sending college prep kids into certificate programs because the vocational school needs students?" She sounded harsh, even to her own ears. But God damn—she'd never heard anything so outrageous in her life. "Wonder who gets the kickback from enrollment?"

Smiling, full-of-life Eric had fled. In his place, statue-Eric, wearing a mask of neutrality, posture and movements benign and nonthreatening.

Shit.

She sure as fuck should have seen that coming. Violence in the home—Eric was a peacemaker. He'd spent his whole life in a domestic minefield, learning how to not trip the wires. How to carry himself, what expression to wear, how to look no one directly in the eye when things got tense.

Taylor rubbed her face. Hard.

"I'm sorry," she said. "I have a strong personality. I say what I think, with very colorful language. But you don't have to shut down, Eric. Go ahead and call me on my shit. Tell me I'm out of line. I don't pout up or cry like a little girl. I just drink too much Makers Mark and fall face-first through my coffee table."

There it was—a hint of that electric smile, although it was aimed at the floor, not her. He poked one of the dashboard vents with one finger and nodded.

"Okay," she said. "Where am I going?"

He gave her directions out of the superstore parking lot that took them past the edge of town and straight into the hills. At first the road just grew narrower, but then the pavement started to crumble. Soon it fell away altogether, and they were driving on gravel.

"What the hell?" She slowed down. "Where'd the road go?"

"Under your tires," he said. "This is Old Sandlick."

"No wonder I can't find it on GPS."

"A lot of these gravel roads show up on Google Maps," he said. "No idea why this one don't."

Taylor's fingers tightened on the steering wheel. The truck seemed ridiculously oversized—dwarfing the single travel lane, its deep treads slipping on the uneven roadbed. She slowed even more and sat forward in her seat, reminding herself to breathe.

"Oh, shit." She tapped the brake. Ahead, a car approached. Not an exceptionally large car, a sedan of some sort, but it loomed huge in a lane not wide enough for two vehicles to safely pass.

"Take it easy," he said. "Ain't no big deal. Just hug the shoulder. You'll be all right."

"There is no shoulder," she snapped.

"Sure there is. Put your front tire over in the ditch a little ways. It's dry right now, ain't no mud—this is a four-wheel drive. You got Goodyear GS-As on here. Don't worry about getting stuck."

The other car passed without slowing down. Gray dust rose in its wake.

"Oh, my *God*," Taylor complained.

"Breathe," Eric said. "Just drive like you own it."

"Own what?" She allowed herself a quick glance in his direction. "The truck? The road? The seat up my ass?"

He laughed. "The whole world."

"How bad will you wreck us if I let you drive?" she asked.

"I've never had a wreck. Been in one, but I wasn't driving."

The rental company had a policy—no drivers under twenty-one. Fuck that, and to hell with manager-of-the-year. Taylor stopped the truck in the middle of the next straight stretch of road and got out.

She tapped the passenger window and Eric lowered it.

"Get out," she said. "Go around. You're driving."

"Hell, yeah." He nearly knocked her over when he opened the door.

Safely buckled in the passenger seat, Taylor finally took an easy breath. Eric took control of the Dodge as naturally as if he'd been born with it attached to his ass.

Country Boys Can Survive. Hear, hear, Hank Williams, Jr.

Vaguely, Taylor remembered passing a few houses after the road turned to gravel. But she hadn't seen one in miles. She looked at Eric with a frown. "So according to the press release this morning, a homeowner called nine-one-one saying their dog came home with human bones in its mouth. All fine and good—but where are the homes?"

He pointed directly ahead. "Up here. This is just a dead stretch. We came in from the four-lane. Garden Hill comes in from the other side of the mountain. I think that's where they found him."

Sure enough, within the next mile, homes reappeared. Unlike the faded farmhouses and sagging barns at the other end of the road, these were mostly singlewide trailers. Some had no siding on much of the exterior, just particle board weathered to a dingy gray, or Tyvek insulation panels. Mounds of garbage moldered in nearly every yard, much of it loose and scattered across the ground. Pickup trucks with flat tires held dozens of black plastic trash bags, fat with waste, piled in their beds as high as the cab. And animals—Taylor cringed at the sight of hounds anchored to doghouses, everything within reach of their chains utterly barren of grass. Puppies running everywhere, even in the road, cats mingling among them. Game chickens in little pens with barrels for shelter—cockfight, anyone?—and horses with every rib showing grazing on dirt.

Taylor held a hand over her mouth and watched it all pass outside her window, trying to imagine how so many people lived in this degree of squalor, completely invisible to mainstream America and never so much as pinging the world's humanitarian radar. She'd made a snarky comment to Charles about this earlier—dilapidated houses and trash piles. Now, seeing it up close for the first time, whatever stereotype she'd referenced grew pale in comparison to the real thing.

"Up here's where the first responders staged," he said, pointing to a small open field with grass still flattened by vehicle tires. "I have no idea which house made the call."

"How do you know about the first responders?"

"People talk. There's a dude in maintenance lives over here somewhere. He was telling me about it this afternoon."

Past that group of singlewides, between two bends in the road, no sign of civilization could be seen at all. No other structures crowded the roadside. Instead, the forest closed in, towering hardwoods and some kind of sprawling bushes with dark green, waxy leaves.

She pointed to them. "What are those?"

"Mountain laurel."

"Oh, gosh—they're gorgeous. Do they just grow wild?"

"Yep." He eased the pickup off the road onto a widened spot of the shoulder. Put the transmission in park, but didn't kill the engine. He pointed out her window. "Look down there."

Taylor made herself taller in the seat so she could see more of the hillside that fell away from the shoulder only a few feet from where they sat. The bottom was obscured by the angle of the grade— just too steep for the base of the cliff to be visible.

"I can't really see," she said. "What is it?"

"The Clinch."

"What?"

"Clinch River. A fork of it, anyway."

"Dylan Altizer was found near a river, too, wasn't he?"

"Yep. Another branch of this one. But I don't think the guy's dumping them in the water. The Clinch is still kind of small up this way. I mean, you could sink a barrel, but it won't stay sunk. Water gets up, shit comes off the riverbed and gets caught up in trees on the bank."

"Well, maybe that's exactly what happened."

"If he's local he'd know better than dump in the river. But I still think the floods last spring were a problem. If I had to guess, I'd say he pulled up right here, unloaded the barrel, and rolled it off this ridge. It was fine 'til the water got up. I mean, can you see anything laying on the ground at the bottom? Nope. Pretty well hid. But those houses are downstream from here. You get a big rush of floodwater, and guess where all the trash at the bottom of this mountain's going to end up."

She sat back and leaned her head against the headrest. "Interesting." She thought about it for a bit. Then, "Can you show me where you found Altizer?"

He scratched a spot above his eye. "Well—yeah. But probably have to be tomorrow. It's going to get dark on us today."

Tomorrow. She hadn't thought that far ahead.

"If you're still in town," he added.

"I can be," she said. "For that."

"Tomorrow when I get off work, then? Like we did today?"

"Sure." She gave him her most genuine smile. "Sounds like a plan."

(Key of A)
Here we are
Daring trouble to come find us
Hide and seek
My safest place is with you
Let it keep
Let it all come crashing inward
We will stand
I will be here when the bitter tears recede.

One step at a time
We're moving forward
Can't stop to look down
Can't afford to wait
We're strange allies
But moving forward
Moving forward
Just the same.

---Erik Evans, 2003

CHAPTER FOURTEEN

Holiday Inn had built a new Express on the four-lane near Walmart, and they had Wi-Fi. So Taylor took full advantage. She'd checked in the day before, after dropping Kavanagh and Perry at the airport. No complaints about the room—she'd gone to bed before nine and slept straight through until morning.

After a late breakfast, she spent time poring over the photos she got from Sheriff Hastings, comparing them with pictures taken when Altizer, Dillow, and Hess were alive. She spread all the photos out on the long table beneath the wall-mounted flat screen, side by side, in two rows. Autopsy photos across the bottom, snapshots of them when they were living, breathing people above. A conspicuous gap over the latest find.

What did those four boys have in common? What made them attractive to the killer? Not physical characteristics, at least nothing obvious. Dylan Altizer had been tall and thin, light brown hair streaked with natural blond, blue eyes, a goatee. Several piercings and tattoos. Michael Dillow was also tall, but beefy. Maybe even a little soft around the middle. Dark hair, dark eyes. Clean shaven. Didn't look like the body mod type. Cody Hess had been short and stocky, brown hair, athletic. Seemed like he could have put up one hell of a fight—so why didn't he?

Fight. Maybe the fight was gone out of everybody in Appalachia.

Eric Blevins had talked about being a welder in the mines. Were the high school counselors in that district really funneling their brightest minds into certificate programs instead of college? It had to be some kind of numbers game. Maybe certain funding was dependent on enrollment. Maybe the vocational school was fighting to keep its doors open and dipping into the college prep pool was the only way to guarantee the minimum number of students for whatever grant program they depended on. But at the expense of their young doctors and lawyers and—well, yes, veterinarians? It seemed ludicrous. Instead of showing Eric how to find the money to pay for vet school after his injury knocked him out of a scholarship, his counselor had suggested a welding course. In what universe ...? Taylor couldn't even imagine.

Somebody knocked on the door. Taylor straightened and, for a moment, thought about ignoring it. Because really—who? Nobody knew she was there, much less which room number.

Oh, wait. One person did, because she'd told him.

She got up and went to look through the peephole. Eric Blevins stood in the hallway wearing that damn highlighter-yellow traffic vest.

She opened the door and let him in.

"I've been trying to call you," he said.

"My phone never rang."

Then she thought about it. She hadn't had a text message or social media notification all morning, either.

Her phone lay on the nightstand where she'd left it to charge. She picked it up and swiped the screen. Nothing. She looked at the charger. No light.

"Well, shit," she said.

"Try a different outlet." Eric pointed to a receptacle over the table where all the photos were spread.

Taylor froze.

He stood there for a moment, not moving, staring at the photos. Then, "Oh, man."

Taylor made a lunge to block his view. Started to reach for the photos to sweep them all into a pile, but stopped when Eric pointed to Altizer's desiccated corpse.

"Oh yeah, I definitely remember that guy." His words sounded too casual, too light. They didn't match the look on his face, which grew taut, then guarded.

Jesus, lord—what a rookie move, forgetting those photos were there. Letting Eric see them. *Not very discreet, Beckett.*

Hastings would shit.

But as she watched, Eric's expression changed again. A keen, analytical edge settled on it, and stayed. Intensified. Taylor didn't touch the photos. Just let them lie there, and let him look.

She unplugged the charger and tried it in the outlet over the table. Green light came on, phone's screen lit up with the Android picture of an empty battery. It also indicated the phone was now receiving a charge. She left it on the table above the pictures, moving very slowly, trying to read the look on Eric's face without distracting him.

"I was trying to let you know I'd be late getting here this afternoon." He didn't look up from the photos. Took a step closer to the table, and leaned down for more intense inspection. "At least five or five-thirty. But we should still have enough daylight. They had a big leak in town today—had to dig up part of the road. Put me out there flagging. I got behind on reads and need to make it up. Good overtime, though."

"Flagging?"

"Yeah." He gave her a quick glance. "Traffic."

"Ah." Taylor thought of all the road construction she'd driven through, all the flaggers she'd never given a passing glance. How many people drove right past Eric Blevins today? Annoyed, harried, unaware of the kindness and intelligence behind his brown eyes. Unaware that his eyes were even brown. Unaware that he had a way with animals, a gift for gauging people and sizing up a situation, and dreamed of being a vet.

She swallowed hard. "Eric, how old was your mother when she had you?"

That got his attention. He looked up and stared at her for a couple seconds before he said anything. "Uh—seventeen. I think."

"So technically, I could be your mother."

"I guess so."

"Had I been your mother when that high school counselor failed to show you all the ways you could get money for college besides football scholarships, I would have handed somebody's ass to them at the next school board meeting. Look at me."

He frowned. "I am."

"No. I mean *really* look at me." She did the V-sign with one hand, pointing back and forth between his eyes and hers. "Don't even think about Vo-Tech. I don't want to hear you mention welding again. We're going to find you some grant money, student loans, whatever it takes to get you into some Gen Ed classes this fall. Do you hear me?"

He almost shrugged, but choked it down until it was just a twitch. "Why do you even care?"

"Hell if I know." Might as well be honest. "But I am professionally, morally, and ethically offended by the idea of you being a welder. Or a flagger. Or anything else that doesn't require a post-graduate education. Mark my words—if you defy me in this, I will personally beat your ass."

He didn't crack a smile. "I almost think you could do it, too."

"Oh, I could," she assured him. "Try me."

Finally, a smile. Even a tiny laugh. And he turned back to the pictures.

She let him study them, moving thoughtfully from one to the next, no indication at all that he was horrified, sickened, or even bothered. Like that part of him had switched off, completely eclipsed by a hunger for understanding, a need to know exactly what he was seeing, and why. She got it completely. It had taken her years to cultivate that skill, but critical thinking under pressure depended heavily on it. And Eric was a natural.

"What's this?" he asked after he'd been poring over the photos for several minutes. "Right here. On his neck."

He pointed to the photo of Dillow's bloated body. To an area just under his jaw, where the skin was abraded and discolored.

"The autopsy report mentioned duct tape," she said. "He was found with a plastic bag over his head. Manner of death—he suffocated."

Eric rubbed his eyes. "Jesus." Then he picked the photo up and held it directly under the light mounted to the hotel room wall. "But this—" He pointed to the discoloration. "Duct tape doesn't explain why he's bruised right there. It's a thin line. See? And there's more than one of them. Like stripes. Almost like—" He stopped talking. Gave his head a small shake. "I don't know what I'm talking about." He placed the photo back on the table and turned to face her. "Are you good with five-thirty?"

"Eric, what were you going to say?"

"Just some stupid shit." He blew it off with a scowl. "Watching too many episodes of CSI, or something."

132

Taylor could have pushed it. But she knew from experience how quickly he could shut down, so she let it go. "Five-thirty's fine. Meet me here?"

He nodded. "Yeah. I'll let you know if something else comes up. Just keep your phone charged. Right?"

She smiled. "Right. Go read your meters. See you in a few hours."

Until this trip, Taylor had never bought clothing from Walmart. But here she was, Day Two in Faded Glory, and she hadn't broken out in hives or caught on fire. When she flew into town, she hadn't been prepared to stay. But a chance to learn about the area from a native tour guide was just too rich to pass up.

Eric got there a little before five-thirty, and this time she handed him the keys before they made it to the parking lot. She'd been impressed with his driving chops, on the dirt road and on the highway. He wasn't a slow driver, not overly cautious, but far from reckless. Capable. Confident. All the things he'd need to survive in the competitive world that existed on the other side of these mountains—if the feudal world between them didn't destroy him first.

"You hungry?" he asked. "I am. I say we grab something in a bag and go."

"In a bag," she said. "Yeah, about that—I've had a hell of a time finding anything worth eating. It's all fast food. How do people even survive here?"

Behind the wheel, he shrugged. "I don't know. We just do."

"You know that life expectancy is shorter in this part of the region than anywhere else in the country, right?" She watched him for a response. "And a study from 2006 shows that ten percent of the nation's nursing home population lives in Appalachia. Think that may have something to do with bad eating habits?"

"Probably. And the dope. And the mines. And the tooth decay." He gave her a pointed look. "Periodontal disease affects about seventy-five percent of middle-aged dogs. About fifteen percent of those with late-stage disease have heart problems, like endocarditis. It's caused when bacteria around affected gums gets in the bloodstream and irritates their arteries. You have to think the same thing's true with people, too."

Taylor stared at him. Couldn't say a word. Goddamned little wise-ass. He did that on purpose to shut her up. Game, set, match.

Finally, she just shook her head and sighed. What else could she do?

He went through the drive-thru at Burger King and ordered a hamburger meal for himself, grilled chicken salad for her. It'd be a real challenge to eat that in a vehicle, but she'd give it a go. He'd almost paid for it before she could stop him.

"Let WRCH pick up the tab," she said. "Save your money for school."

A few miles out of town, they passed the entrance to the county's big industrial park, elegantly named "Rosewood." Taylor had researched it, learned the development was less than six years old, and stood empty—all five hundred acres of it. The land was cleared, roads laid in, water and sewer lines installed and operational. Yet no businesses—not one—had signed a lease. Further digging had revealed the project was funded by a ten-million-dollar economic development grant. But instead of attracting businesses that would provide jobs for the local unskilled labor force, the county insisted on placing so many restrictions that only "upscale" companies need apply.

"What do you know about that?" she asked, pointing to the rock bridge that marked the entrance to the park, flanked on one side by an empty guardhouse.

"I know it's a fucking joke," Eric said. "And I know there's an orchard on the very back side of it that my Gram asked me to bring her some baking apples from when they start dropping."

"You've been in there?"

"Oh, yeah. We have lines in there. And an easement for the Eagle Heights water tank."

"Why do you think the county placed such prohibitive restrictions on it?"

"Being snobs, I guess. Hell if I know. Hell if anybody knows." He made a face. "Trindell wanted to put a manufacturing plant there. They make heavy mining equipment. We're talking easily three hundred jobs. But their proposal included metal-sided buildings. Nope, can't have those. Can't have all that ugly-ass equipment sitting around outside, either. So Trindell withdrew and built a plant in Montgomery County."

"Wow." Taylor put the lid on her half-eaten salad. "That's insane."

"You want to know why we don't have fancy restaurants here?" he asked. "The kind where you can find healthy food?" He didn't wait for her to answer. "Because most of them serve alcohol. Here in Randall County, you can't serve alcohol within sight of a church. And I read somewhere that there's four churches per square mile. I don't doubt it. Steeples everywhere."

"Is that a county ordinance?" she asked.

"Yeah. I mean, it could be voted down, but the Tabbies would riot."

"Tabbies?"

"Tabernacle. You've seen the long hair and dresses, right?"

Taylor's mind flashed back to the first trip she'd made there, in a car with Kavanagh and Perry. The convenience store, the woman with hair down the middle of her back. The stares. "Yeah, I think so."

"They'd have a fit if somebody tried to kill that ordinance. They'd have every elected official in Randall County shitting their pants. It'd be worse than the zoning mess."

"What zoning mess?"

He glanced at her, but quickly turned back to the road. "Oh, lord. They had to change the venue for the Board of Supervisors meeting that month, so many people showed up to yell. More than six hundred. Plus the president of Farm Bureau. They were hot."

"So what were they trying to do with the zoning?"

"Stupid shit like farmers having to operate their business within certain hours. UPS and FedEx only being able to make a set number of deliveries to each home. Home businesses having to limit their customers. You could only have so many cars in your driveway. Trees and bushes had to be a certain size. And if you couldn't meet the code, you got fined. Crazy shit. Property owners came un-fucking-glued."

"Well, I guess they did." Taylor shook her head in disbelief. "What were they trying to accomplish?"

"We'll never know because they scrapped the whole thing. Thank God. Most folks in the county think the Board of Supervisors and some developer were ass-fucking each other over the land. Trying to run all the farmers off so they could scoop up the acreage for a song and build more shit we don't need. Somebody was going to get rich, but it wouldn't be the people who live here. They'd just get displaced. Eminent domain all over again, just pretending to be something else."

"Who was the engineering firm?" she asked. "Do you know?"

"For Rosewood?" He shifted in his seat, propped his left arm on the window ledge. "Yeah. Same engineering firm the county always uses—Jackson & Howell, out of Bristol."

"Tennessee?"

He shook his head. "No. Virginia side."

"What do you mean—same firm the county always uses? Don't they put those jobs out for bid?"

"Yeah, but J&H always wins."

"One thing a lot of people don't think about," she said. "Is that design firms get their cut off the top. They get paid before anybody else—whether a project is finished, or not. You mentioned developers—well, if there had been a developer behind the Rosewood deal and the zoning, they're screwed at this point. But the architects and building design engineers ... they're sitting pretty right now. Couldn't care less if any industry ever builds on that piece of land or not."

"You're right," he said after a moment. "I never thought about that. But how would the scam work?"

"It depends on the players. But you could have a piece of land with issues that make it undevelopable—for geological reasons, whatever. Pay off whoever it is you need to keep that quiet, bring in the design engineers, put a plan on paper, get grant money to build. The design firm makes their cut, the planning commission gets their kickback, and who gives a shit if the project ever sees completion. Everybody's making money, and that's the important thing, right?"

"You've seen that happen?"

Boy, had she ever. "That, and worse. The money's not as big for a design firm as it would be for the developer over the long term. But it can still be enough to kill for, especially when somebody starts making noise like they're going to expose it."

Eric took his eyes off the road and looked at her with wide eyes. "You think that has something to do with the murders?"

Taylor took a deep breath, blew it out slowly. Pointed to the road in front of them so he'd face forward again. "Not directly, no. But I think that sort of corruption can contribute to an environment."

Eric snuck a couple of sideways glances at her as she kept talking.

"The whole bodies in the barrels thing," she said. "That feels more homegrown. It's one person, acting on psychotic urges. But watching the way this community responds to those crimes—it's like watching mushrooms grow in cow shit. You just have the right climate for it. The right nutrients in the soil. And you have an infrastructure that's totally unprepared to deal with something like that."

Outside her window, land rolled by—hills and valleys and rocks and grass. She watched it, saw houses without color, generations of hope exploited for so long that now it was just gone.

"That's my story," she said quietly, fueled by resolve. "That's the one I'm here to get. And I have a feeling it's not going to be pretty. So maybe you should give it some thought, after today, if you can afford to be involved. I can use you. Won't lie about that. But at what cost?"

He didn't answer at first. Just drove, and gave nothing away with his expression.

"Okay," he said after a too-long moment. "I'll let you know."

CHAPTER FIFTEEN

Another work week, lunchtime, and Eric pulled the largest of two hamburgers from the paper sack sitting beside him on the picnic table. He folded the wrapper back to expose half of his Baconator, looked at all the grease dribbling down and puddling in the foil, and frowned. Ten percent of the nation's nursing home population? Really? Okay. That meant he had a while to clean up his eating habits. He took the biggest bite he could fit into his mouth.

Haley's yellow Cobalt cruised past the old caboose at the park entrance and nosed into the spot beside his county truck. Spring Break—free to meet for lunch right there in the open. She shut the engine off and got out, long blond hair whipping in ropes around her face. The wind was up, gusting through the valley over Lake Barrett, swirling around Haley like it wanted to crawl underneath those flapping shirttails and pop a few buttons.

She folded her arms around herself to batten down her clothes and climbed onto the picnic table beside him. Legs—miles of them. Wrapped in denim, and she wore her Wranglers tight.

He handed her the bag, which he'd managed to grab before it got blown clear back to Wendy's. "I got you the junior with bacon."

She took the bag but didn't look inside it. Just folded the top into a tighter wad and set it between them. "Not hungry."

Uh-oh.

Eric studied her profile. Haley's face had character—a nose that grew just a little crooked after one of her Daddy's half-sheared lambs bucked up in the chute and busted her in the face with its head. Big blue eyes, a full mouth that always tasted like strawberries and mint.

Today, her features looked tight. She'd barely given him a glance since driving up, and that struck an odd note. They never got all lovey-dovey with each other, except in private. Public displays—not their thing. She'd wrestle much quicker than she'd cuddle. But today something was bothering her. No doubt about it.

He picked up Hayley's drink from the table beside him and offered it to her. "How about this? Want your pop?"

She took it from him and played with the straw.

Okay. So, moody it was, then. He went back to eating his hamburger.

Her straw squeaked against the cup's plastic lid. "I heard you was riding around with that news reporter yesterday."

The bite in his mouth got a little tougher to chew. He worked on it for a few more seconds, swallowed hard, and washed it down with a long drink.

"Is that what has you all worked up?" Hell, if that's what was bugging her, didn't seem like it would take much to put her mind at ease. "She could be my mother, Haley. Not like you have anything to worry about."

She still didn't look at him. Wiggled the straw, dangled the cup between her knees. "She ask a lot of questions?"

"What do you think?" He looked at his burger, thought about taking another bite, and then thought better of it. "Of course she did. It's her job."

"I just know you don't like to talk much."

"I like to talk." Well, that sounded plenty defensive. Shit. "As much as anybody else, probably."

"You never told me any of it," she said. "About finding the body, and all."

"Why would I?" He stared at her. "Why would I tell anybody about that?"

She shrugged. "I don't know. The whole sharing thing, I guess."

"I didn't tell *her* about it, either," he said. "If that makes you feel better."

Sort of true. He'd hit the high points with Taylor Beckett, but not breathed a word about how bad that mess in the barrel smelled. Or how awful it looked, or how fast he'd run back up that hill like the hounds of hell were snapping at his ass, after he'd puked his guts up in last year's dead blackberry bushes. If not wanting to ever tell those things to another living soul meant he didn't like to talk much, then fine. She was right. He didn't.

Haley finally took a sip through her straw. "Jordan told Daddy he saw you in the truck with her."

Eric frowned. Jordan? Her Daddy? What was she talking about? Clear as mud, this conversation.

So he gave it some thought while she sat there and let ice melt in her cup.

Her brother Jordan—a nobody. Town cop in one of the county's smaller jurisdictions, barely out of the academy. Prick. Her Daddy owned about two thousand acres in The Flats, a trough between two mountain ranges that didn't have so much as an anthill to trip over. Their farm raised sheep and cattle. Her Mama worked in the County Administration Building. Wasn't sure about her job title, but it was nothing special. Secretary, or something like that. None of them cared much for Eric, but they'd never been petty about it. Now they were getting Haley all wound up because somebody saw him in the truck with a grown-ass woman riding around talking about county politics?

Oh, hell. Wait a minute. He looked at Haley hard. "What is it your mama does again, for the county?"

"She's a receptionist. Answers the phone for Bud Mabry's office."

Ah, yes. Bud Mabry, County Administrator.

Eric squeezed his eyes closed and bit back a smartass comment. But Haley still hadn't looked at him for more than point-five seconds, so it was doubtful she noticed.

"Daddy says you need to leave all that alone." Now she chewed the straw, grinding it between her teeth like it was Big Red. " 'Cause it ain't none of your business, and it's just going to cause trouble."

"Trouble for who?" A flash of temper boiled up that didn't quite take him by surprise. "You? Me? Your mama?"

"Oh God, Eric. Don't start."

"I'm not starting shit," he said. "Seems more like somebody's trying to start shit with *me.*"

"Nobody's starting shit with you." She pushed herself off the picnic table and stood, movements jerky and tense. "You just don't need to be talking to strange folks about what happens around here.

It's none of anybody's business. Seems like you got vet school on the brain and lost your mind."

"What?" He shoved the foil back around his burger. "What does vet school have to do with anything?"

For the first time, she looked at him. Cool blue eyes appraising and distant, chin up, hair blowing wild. "What was I supposed to do while you were off at Tech, huh? Wait back home while you shoved your arm up cows' asses for eight years? I was glad you got hurt. Meant I didn't have to worry about that shit any more. You'd be here and just be a normal guy. But sometimes you act like you don't have a lick of sense—running around talking to some big city reporter like you're all that. Sometimes I see exactly what Mama and Daddy are saying. I just don't know what to do about it right now."

She might as well have slapped him, judging by the sudden spike of adrenaline that burned his cheeks. He stood bolt upright, bracing into her onslaught rather than backing away from it. He slammed his hamburger back into the bag and didn't care that the whole thing fell off the table and rolled all the way down the hill to the caboose.

"First of all," he said, holding up one index finger. "I wouldn't have been shoving my arm up cows' asses for *eight years*. "Second—" Another finger joined the first. "You're glad I got hurt? God damn it, Haley—fuck you, too. And third—" One more finger. "I don't even fucking know … what the hell do you mean, you see what your Mama and Daddy are saying?"

"Don't yell at me, Eric." She threw her cup on the ground. Squares of ice went everywhere. "You're the one living in a dream world—walk around with your head up your ass thinking everything's all peachy. Well, everything hasn't been 'peachy' for a while." She opened her car door, got inside, and slammed it behind her. "Don't call me tonight," she said through her lowered window. "Give me some freaking space." Then she cranked her car and screeched out of the parking lot while Eric just stood there shaking.

He growled and kicked her cup. Then glanced around to see if anyone had seen him do it. Nope. Park was empty. Utterly, completely void of people or activity, just like the rest of this goddamned town. He scooped the cup out of the grass and went hunting the bag full of uneaten hamburgers.

What a clusterfuck.

High maintenance bitch. Made him wonder if any pussy in the world was worth putting up with that kind of bullshit.

Hours later, Eric could still taste the Baconator in the bile that rose in his throat every time he thought about Haley—which had been pretty much nonstop since lunch. He'd calmed down a little, braced himself to start missing her like he always did. Not happening yet. Maybe she was right—maybe this had been building for a while. He'd never thought things between them were "peachy." He just wasn't the one with all the complaints.

He'd been in his room since he got home from work, trying to watch one movie or another on Netflix and not able to concentrate on anything he started. Down at the barn, sounds of yips and howls and Grandpap's occasional gruff voice. The new Redbone had whelped back in February, and now her pups were old enough to be holy terrors—all ten of them. Big litter.

Eric had lost interest in Grandpap's breeding operation about the time he found out how many dogs rotted every year in their county landfill. Pitbulls and hounds—not exactly in demand. What do you do with them if they weren't raised for pets? Couple of boys working for animal control had figured out they could turn a buck on the hounds that would hunt. They tested their drive by putting cats in trees out back of the pound and seeing which dogs knew what to do. The ones who didn't tended to disappear. The ones who did would turn up in somebody's dog box a few nights later, on their way to the woods.

Other memories circled around those, as well. Cats. Always a bone of contention around the Blevins house. Gram wanted some in the barn to stay after mice. Grandpap would sometimes call those boys from animal control and see if they had any feral cats come in. If they did, Grandpap would buy them five dollars a head to train his dogs on. Eric was around ten when he finally worked up enough nerve to tell his Grandpap that was a fine idea—if they wanted their dogs to hunt cats. Grandpap didn't like being told his business by a kid, especially if that business had earned him cash and a loyal customer base for the last forty years. But he never brought any more cats home.

Eric closed his laptop and stared out the window. Not much to see—sun going down behind a ridge, groundhog getting brave in the field next to the house. There'd been a day when Popper exterminated every rodent and pest within a half-mile radius. Those days were gone. Eric wasn't even sure Popper would give chase if the old whistlepig poked his head under the chicken hutch and blew raspberries.

His room held a lot of memories. Sitting there now, he really couldn't remember ever waking up staring at a different ceiling. Well, not entirely true. He'd been to see Gram's folks in Kentucky, took a couple trips with Upward Bound, but that was about it for his globetrotting.

Some of the memories were good. The night he got in after homecoming, after being with Haley at The Farm—he hadn't known what to do with himself afterward, once he was alone again. She'd been his first. He'd paced and puttered for a while before he finally stripped down and climbed between the sheets. His body had still smelled like hers. Still felt a little electrified, charged with currents of everything that sparked between them.

Other memories he could do without. Twelve years old, and Grandpap thought it would be a good idea for Eric to help those boys at the pound since he liked dogs so much. And talking about it, it seemed like a lot of fun. He showed up on a Thursday that summer, rubber boots two sizes too big and a bagged lunch. He shoveled shit, dumped some food, and helped clean out the dogcatcher truck.

"How many we got today?" Big Darrell Pace had raised the garage bay door and stood there for a minute, looking out over the landfill.

Twelve-year-old Eric couldn't answer. He didn't know what Big Darrell meant.

"Eighteen cats," Darrell's son Eddie said, from somewhere inside the bay. "Six dogs."

"Let's get to it." Darrell disappeared into the bay and Eric followed.

"Do the cats first," Eddie said, dragging a wire cage from somewhere inside the shelter. It was full. Mostly kittens, yowling and climbing the sides, eyes wide with fear.

Darrell walked to a storage area near the back of the bay. He puttered with something for a few minutes while the cats in the cage mewled and swarmed all over each other.

When Darrell came back, he carried a tray with a lot of needles on it, blue liquid pulled up in the plastic parts. Giving the cats their shots? Eric had helped Grandpap give puppy shots. Heck, he could do it himself. This ought to be easy.

"What do you want me to do?" Eric asked.

"Just put 'em back in the cage when we're through," Big Darrell said. "They'll be clawing and scratching too much before. Let me and Eddie handle that."

Eric watched a glove-wearing Eddie take one of the smaller kittens out and hold it by the scruff. Sure enough, lots of clawing and scratching. Eddie stretched the kitten's body, arching it backward, gloved fingers wrapped around the kitten's back legs. It squirmed and squalled, but Darrell moved fast. He stuck the needle in the kitten's chest and pushed all the liquid inside.

The kitten went limp. Kicked a few times, and grew quiet. Still holding it by the scruff, Eddie handed it to Eric. "Take this and throw it back in the cage. I'll get another one."

Stunned, Eric reached for it. The kitten flopped over his hand, tongue protruding. This wasn't anything at all like giving puppy shots.

He looked up at Darrell. "You killed it."

"Yep," Darrell said. "That's the idea. One down, seventeen to go."

Eric didn't know what to do. He just stood there, numb. Nauseated. With a dead cat in his hand.

"Get a move on, boy," Darrell said. "We'll have another one for you in just a minute."

What could he do? How could he stop this? If he fussed, they'd tell Grandpap. He didn't care that he'd never be able to come back and help at the shelter. He never wanted to do that anyway. Not now. But Grandpap would tan his hide. Probably use the belt. And that buckle hurt, digging into his bare backside. Eric swallowed hard and put the kitten's body in the cage.

All the other cats went crazy when the dead one dropped on top of them. One almost got out. Eric shoved it back inside, instantly sorry. That's one he could have saved. Maybe he'd save them all. He reached to open the cage back up, but there came Eddie, reaching in for another. Eric took several steps back and just tried to breathe.

This time, the kitten screamed. Big needle going right into its heart—Eric would have screamed, too. He closed his eyes and tried to keep tears from pooling up. If he cried, he'd never hear the end of it. Might get his ass beat for that, too.

Eighteen times he watched Darrell Pace stick a needle in a cat's heart and press the plunger. Eighteen times Eric carried a warm, limp body back to the cage, until there were no surviving kittens to terrify. Eric couldn't feel his arms or his legs. Couldn't feel his own heartbeat. Just wanted this to end.

And then, they walked a dog into the room.

She was black, with hair like a Gordon Setter. Except she probably didn't weigh thirty pounds. She wagged her tail, smiling up at Eric with a big, lolling tongue. His brain couldn't put it together. This dog? They were going to kill *this dog?* He had to at least ask, belt be damned.

"What's wrong with her?"

Eddie looked at him and gave a little grin. Tall and thin, light brown hair and a scruffy beard, Eddie could have been any good old boy from the holler. But here he was, helping his daddy kill dogs and kittens. Eric had never despised another human being more.

"Nothing's wrong with her," Eddie said. "Except she shits all over the kennel and we're tired of cleaning it up ten times a day." He looked at his daddy. "You gonna hit a vein on this one?"

Darrell nodded. "Yeah. Should be able to."

Eddie held up her front end so her paws were off the floor. The black dog still panted, still smiled. She looked at Eric and wagged her tail.

Darrell grabbed her paw and poked the needle into a vein, first try. He pressed the plunger. The black dog whimpered and tried to stand up, on her back legs. She looked at Eric, and she wasn't smiling anymore. Then she collapsed, a black puddle on the floor that never moved again.

Eddie was back with another one before Eric could take a step in any direction. This was a big dog, probably a chow mix. He took one look at the pile of death on the floor and lunged backward, taking Eddie with him.

"Get the catchpole," Eddie said, fighting to keep the dog from twisting out of the kennel lead. "Quick."

Darrell came back with a long stick that had a loop of cable on one end. He put the loop over the dog's head and pulled it tight. The dog kept fighting, but he was no match for Big Darrell and the catchpole. The two men wrestled the dog back to the center of the floor and Eddie straddled him.

Crack! The wooden handle of the catchpole snapped in half. Darrell stumbled backward, and Eddie yelped as the dog locked its jaws around his forearm. Darrell grabbed the half of the stick still attached to the loop and started twisting it, tighter and tighter, until the dog choked out and let go of Eddie's arm. They threw the dog onto the floor, and Eddie pinned him there with one booted foot across his neck. Darrell kicked the exposed white belly. Kicked it again. Stomped the dog's head until he didn't have to control the handle anymore.

Eric was no longer in his body. No longer on the ground. No longer afraid of that goddamned belt. He ran. Out the open garage bay door, down the road to the landfill. Didn't look back. They'd have to shoot him to stop him.

In his bedroom, all those years later, Eric retched into his trash can. Good thing he kept it handy. Damn, he'd forgotten almost every bit of that. Not that it happened—didn't lose sight of the reason he'd never set foot in that goddamned animal shelter again—but the details. Those had been buried way down, under as much mental clutter as his brain could rake over them. Self-preservation. What a horrible fucking memory.

He sat on the edge of his bed and tried to get his breathing under control. What brought all that up, he'd never know.

Maybe it was all those pictures he saw in Taylor Beckett's hotel room.

Maybe it was just one of them.

(Key of A^b)
Walking home late and I stop to breathe
I think about you, I think about me
Can't tell you why we took the higher road
Bet that low road's got some benefits, yeah.
So here I am and there you are
Wherever that is, it's too far
I keep you close in case you are
In case you try, in case you change your mind.

Walk me home tonight, find me in the lonely
We'll make it work out right, we'll make it worth the fight
Make it more than nothing, in the lonely, tonight.
---Erik Evans, 2004

CHAPTER SIXTEEN

Taylor stood in her loft, dead center of the main living area, and stared at the spot where her coffee table used to sit.

Man, she'd made short work out of that one. Probably hadn't had it a year.

The week before her trip back to Randall County, she'd dragged what was left of her table downstairs to the curb. It disappeared before the trash truck ran. Somebody recognized the cash it would bring in metal scrap, no doubt. She'd considered doing that, but had no means of hauling it. Her Audi didn't make a good pickup truck.

Funny, how much she missed that big Dodge rental. Couldn't drive it worth a damn, but Eric Blevins more than made up for that. Such a great kid—what the hell was wrong with his parents? How could anyone not be proud of a son like him, and want to be part of his life? Best she could tell, both mother and father were absent, and had been absent for years. She'd actually spent time researching the phenomenon of grandparent caregiving after she got back to Richmond. One study claimed that grandparents in Central Appalachia were twice as likely to raise their grandkids as grandparents in other parts of the U.S. So where were all the parents? An entire generation lost to drugs, poverty, and the general failure to give a shit?

Find something positive. Right, Charles. *You* find something positive. And document that motherfucker well, otherwise you're talking about the same kind of urban legend as Nessie or Sasquatch.

Taylor clapped both hands over her ears and a gave a mental scream.

Okay. Get it together.

Two trips to Southwest Virginia, and she still didn't have a story. Oh, she could do a segment and scrounge up a canned soundbite about the murders. But wasn't her refusal to go that route the very reason that Sheriff Hastings trusted her? And with such sensitive information? He knew she wouldn't rush to air with anything half-cooked. What else did he know? Plenty, evidently. One didn't attract awards for coverage about murders, even sensational ones. One attracted that kind of attention for stories that changed the world, or at least some corner of it.

She sat on the edge of one sofa cushion, which was pale cream again after Servpro unleashed their trauma and crime scene professionals on it. They'd saved her rug, too. She hadn't held much hope for that.

Hastings.

What did he know about journalism awards, anyway? He could have done ten minutes of online research and been able to hold an intelligent conversation with anyone about her career. Likely as not, he'd done exactly that and used it like a carrot on a stick to lead her where he wanted her to go.

But what if that's where she wanted to go anyway?

Shit.

He was a master manipulator. But also a pretty good guy. She felt sure of that. Taylor stared down at her arms, at the angry crosshatching already faded from red to pale pink. She'd been using his wife's pine sap concoction for almost a week, and damned if it didn't seem to be making a difference. From extensive inspection in the mirror, she knew her face showed the same improvement as her arms. She wouldn't have been disfigured anyway—thin little lines would fade and disappear completely under makeup. But the poultice seemed to expedite healing—increase blood flow, and all that. She'd had Perry help her with a screen test to see if any of the cuts showed up on camera. They didn't, at least not at standard resolution. High def? Meh-who cared. Not her. She was just glad she could report for duty soon without being mistaken for Jigsaw.

But Hastings—what did she know about him, or at least what did she suspect? First, he struck her as a decent cop. He had more on the ball than many of his small-town counterparts. Hands-on kind of guy, at least for the big stuff, and an uncanny knack of knowing the difference between "big stuff" and routine bullshit.

He had local press eating out of his hand. They asked exactly the questions he needed them to ask and didn't appear to suffer any confusion about where he might draw lines. A real dog and pony show, very well-rehearsed.

Board of Supervisors controls that paper. Eric Blevins had said that, outside the bed and breakfast.

Did they control Hastings, too? Is that why he made such a big show of shutting her down during the press conference, yet laid almost every card he held—or photograph, anyway—on the table for her in the privacy of his office? He was an elected official, just like the Supervisors. Whatever leverage they had wasn't about the chain of command.

My wife owns a business in town. What was Hastings really trying to say? *I have a girl at the high school and my son's in middle school.*

Implying what? Some harm would come to his family if he didn't play the game?

What game?

If the Board of Supervisors did not want the kind of media frenzy that would draw the attention of outside news agencies and invite federal scrutiny, what did that mean? And what organic leverage might they have over the county Sheriff, since none of them could actually pull rank?

Funding.

How much funding did the Sheriff's Office receive from the county every year? Did the Board of Supervisors control all of it? Taylor couldn't remember how all that worked exactly, but that kind of information should be public. She could find out how beholden Hastings was to the Supervisors for all that fancy technology he used and the late-model patrol cars his officers drove around in. But then she had to figure out why any of that mattered to her story.

The room seemed empty without her coffee table. Must buy a new one asap.

She remembered bits and pieces of that night, enough to be embarrassed about the condition Charles found her in. But what else had he found? Vaguely, she remembered crawling around at some point with photos of Erik scattered on the carpet. Had she put them all up before Charles got there? One way to find out—check for blood. On the storage box, storage envelopes, the photos themselves. She could do that without looking directly at the images. Maybe just by looking at the box and glancing inside.

Maybe.

On her knees again in front of the cabinetry, she reached far inside the bottom storage area and placed her hands on the big, familiar box. Pulled it halfway out, looked for blood. Nothing. In fact, everything inside was packaged neatly and in its place, the way she normally kept it stored. Her hands found a small leather binder, about the size of a large iPad, only much thicker. Taylor froze. Unmistakable, what that was.

No photos inside—she knew that with all certainty. Just words. Hundreds upon hundreds of words, arranged on dozens of pages, handwritten, typed, scribbled. Musical notations she didn't understand. She could barely read sheet music—forget guitar tabs. And what was that other thing? Oh yeah, the Nashville Number System. She understood how that worked, but it still seemed foreign, a language for people like Erik Evans, with minds like musical data processors.

Against her better judgment, she carried the binder back to the sofa with her. Lying across her knees, closed, with all its secrets tucked inside—it didn't seem very sinister. Yet Taylor knew how quickly it could send her spinning into the abyss. Erik's music—his songs—his words. They belonged to her now and would stay permanently hidden, where no one would ever come looking for them.

She tugged at the snap until it popped loose, then lay the binder open in her lap and stared at the pages folded inside.

It's like driving down a road that goes to nowhere
And I can't read a single goddamned sign
And I don't know if I've ever been real enough
Or if I was just a waste of time.

"I Know," from 2001, before she met him.

Well, I'm a boy who loved a girl
Who loved herself and loved the world

154

Who loved his love but didn't love him back.

"Switch Track," from 2002, about the ex-girlfriend.

Hey, this is me, and now I've got you in sight.
You're where I go from here, and it all starts tonight.
Where were you while I've been living my life
You're where I go from here, and it all starts tonight.

"Where I Go From Here," from 2003—the first song he wrote about her, and the night they met.

Also in the binder, "What If." "Gentle As The Rain." "Dangerous." "These Lies." "What My Heart Said." "Dreams Don't Lie." "Forward." "The Lonely." "God Help Me." "Make It Count." "Best For You." "Scars."

Taylor touched her face. *Scars.* Damn right.

Fuck you, Erik.

Taylor felt it coming. Knew to hit the deck. In this case, the sofa. She curled herself into a ball and let it wash over her in waves.

Yes. Fuck you. Fuck you, fuck you, fuck you.

Fuck you for being so goddamned clueless about how much we all had at stake.

"I'll be goddamned."

Well, she certainly hoped he wouldn't be, but the tone with which Erik Evans made that statement put Taylor's fears to rest. He remembered her. And with more than just passing interest.

Between sets, she intercepted him on his way to the bar or wherever he was headed when he came off the stage. Not Luiz's bar this time, but a bigger crowd, across town. She'd seen the flyers on campus, knew Mellow Jennie had gained a following and could take their pick of Chicago area venues these days. All this in a few months, and all due to a song that could have been written about her, but probably wasn't.

It's okay if we don't talk
If we just sit here and catch our breath
It ain't like we jump fences every day.

Maybe it was that "jump fences" line. He'd said something very similar to her when they stood facing each other on the sidewalk outside Luiz's bar. Possibly, it was one of his pet phrases, nothing to do with that night at all. But what if the song was a reference to her? To their missed connection? What if the airplay MJ got from Q101 had been his version of a Craiglist personal, since they never exchanged contact info and Karmen sure as hell wouldn't have told him how to find her?

Ugh. Karmen. Still roommates, but not really friends. At best, they tolerated each other. No romance ever blossomed between Erik Evans and Karmen. He never came to the dorm, never called Karmen again, best Taylor could tell. Taylor never mentioned him to her, and Mellow Jennie ceased being a shared interest—or an interest at all, at least one they talked about. Karmen had moved on.

And Taylor moved in for the kill.

He stood there, stopped in his tracks, looking at her with a crooked grin. "Taylor. You know—I never caught your last name."

"Maines," she said. "Now you have no excuse."

His grin got bigger. "I know, right?" He glanced around the crowded club. "Are you here with someone?"

Taylor pointed to the general area where she had a table with some friends from school. "No one in particular, but yeah. There's a pack of us."

He squinted. "Anybody that's going to deck me if I come over and talk to you?" A pause. "Karmen?"

"Nope." God, she hoped her smile didn't look as goofy as it felt. "Just some girls from English Lit. I might have to beat some of them off you."

Erik laughed out loud. "Surely not."

"In case you haven't noticed, you have quite a fan base these days."

"I'd like to think it's for the music," he said.

"I think it's the total package." Jesus—how many beers had she had? Not like her to be so bold. But hey—if it worked. "I'm a fan, too."

"Are you, now?"

Oh, God. This could go south really fast. Putting herself out there—liberating, exhilarating, but scary as hell, too.

Taylor's legs felt shaky. "We're in the back. That round table in the corner."

"Want me to bring you something from the bar?"

Oh, wow. This was happening.

She nodded. "Surprise me."

"Beer drinker, or do you need something with an umbrella?"

Her turn to laugh out loud. "Beer's fine."

"Okay. Save me a seat."

Her weak knees didn't improve on her way back to the table. Grateful to be off her feet, she slid onto the curved bench seat, wondering how he was going to fit. Everyone was talking, not paying her much attention. That changed when he walked up and handed Taylor her beer.

Silence. Every girl at the table gawked at him. Taylor thought she might get a laugh out of it later—the expressions on their faces—once she'd calmed down and didn't feel so damn nervous.

"You going to let me sit, or what?" He nudged Taylor's leg with his knee.

Instantly, everyone on the bench scooted left. Taylor did, too, and Erik took the spot they opened up for him on the end.

She looked at her beer. "Blue Moon?"

He leaned close to her ear, pressed against her from shoulder to hip to thigh. "Ever tried it?"

All she could do was shake her head. Words—just gone. Flown away like birds.

"It's good," he said. "A Belgian beer—Belgian recipe, anyway. It's my favorite."

Well, damn. Guess it was her favorite now, too. She tried a sip. Not bad.

One of her friends kicked her underneath the table. "Are you going to introduce us?"

"Uhmm—" She pointed to him. "This is Erik. Erik, this is—" Jesus, lord. She knew three of their names. Not four. Who was the fourth girl? They'd told her, but damned if she could remember. "Uhhh...."

They all supplied their own names, one right after the other, smiling big at the rock star who'd floated down from heaven and landed at their table.

I'd like to think it's for the music. Oh yes. She understood what he meant now.

"Something I want to show you." He leaned close again. "Come with me?"

Taylor nodded. Of course. And the sooner the better.

He stood and reached for her hand. Long fingers, a couple chunky pewter rings and the strand of wood beads looped around his wrist that he'd worn the first time she saw him—it was the same hand that mastered the frets of his guitar and gave it such a stunning voice. Now it folded around her own hand and tugged. And Taylor followed. Through the crowd, out the back door of the club, into a quiet alleyway where a few stars actually peeked through and winked at them from the sky.

"I really don't have anything to show you," he confessed. "That just wasn't working, in there."

"No." She shook her head. "It wasn't."

"I'm glad you came tonight."

"I didn't know if you'd remember me."

"I have a memory like an elephant. And you left an impression."

Taylor gulped. She might hate his answer to her next question, but she had to ask it anyway. "That song—the one about jumping fences—"

"Yeah," he nodded. "It's about you."

He set his beer on the back bumper of a van parked near the door. Mellow Jennie bumper stickers suggested it might belong to the band. Then he took her beer and set it beside his.

Breathe, Taylor.

So softly she thought she'd imagined it, he slipped an arm around her waist, placed a hand on her lower back. The touch became more confident, firm. And he pulled her to him.

"Okay?" he asked, almost a whisper.

She nodded. Better than okay.

He kissed her. Sweetly at first, just the brush of his lips against hers. He tasted like beer, and man. Taylor's entire body softened against his, melted. Nothing she had planned. Not a calculated response. Just agreement with everything his touch implied.

Maybe she was the one who deepened the kiss. Maybe it was him. Maybe it all happened at once, and neither struck the match. But in the space of a breath he consumed her, like flames licking up a dry branch. Shoulders against the van, arms around his neck, fingers threaded in that tousled blond hair—Taylor gave in to the fire and let herself burn.

After a moment he pulled back, breathing hard when he looked at her. "I have to play another set now," he whispered. "God help me."

"I'll wait for you," she said. "You just have to come find me."

"To hell with that." He folded her into his arms, held her close. His heartbeat thumped away, fast and steady. "You can come backstage. I'm not letting you out of my sight again."

She sighed and lowered her head to his shoulder.

Jump quietly, fall on me, gentle as the rain.

(Key of G)
Just wait, the best is yet to come, she sounds so certain
And I'm pretty sure she's right.
She walks across the room and closes all the curtains
To shut out all the light.
I never wanted to be the higher stakes
Or the reason that she puts on the brakes
And changes her direction.
But I'm glad she wanted me to stay
And not just look the other way
It just feels right.

God help me now
She's inside my head
She's tangled linens on my bed
She's everywhere I am.
God help me now
She's my limit
My everything, roulette wheel spinning
Now, I can't let her go
God help me now.

---Erik Evans, 2004

CHAPTER SEVENTEEN

Charles rang her doorbell before nine the next morning. Taylor let him in, sorely tempted to remind him that even God Almighty didn't wake up before ten. Yes, they'd planned a working breakfast, and she'd been expecting him. Just not before ten. Everybody knew not to speak to her before ten. Even Kavanagh and Perry gave her a wide berth until her second pot of coffee, which never happened before ten. But Charles didn't seem to care. He breezed through her door with a satchel in one hand and a cardboard drink tray with two Starbucks cups in the other.

"Rise and shine, Pocahontas," he said. "We got work to do."

She took the drink tray and set it on her kitchen counter. "I haven't even brushed my hair yet. Or my teeth."

"No worries, Fa Mulan. I've seen you slobbering drunk with spit bubbles running down your chin. I can handle it."

"Shut the fuck up." She glared at him. "Disney princesses? Really, Charles? Really?"

"Yes ma'am, Cinderella. Hand me my double shot espresso. Mine has an X on the lid."

"I'm going to X your lid, all right," she grumbled, giving him the cup with the proper marking. "Better be glad I don't sleep naked. At least I'm in pajamas."

He pulled the lid off his coffee and blew across the tan foam on top. "I think I'd like naked better."

She stared at him. "Men are disgusting."

"So does that mean Vanessa has a better chance than I do?"

Taylor grabbed a plastic soup bowl out of the drainer and threw it at his head. It was the closest thing handy that wouldn't splatter brains on her nice, clean sofa.

Charles ducked and laughed out loud. "Had to ask."

She tossed the drink tray in the garbage and stood there blowing on her own latte while Charles unpacked his satchel. Pictures, paper, multicolored Post-It pads. A Sharpie. He set them all on her dining room table and looked around.

"You said you had a corkboard." He scratched the back of his head. "Where might that be?"

"I didn't say I have a corkboard," she said. "I said I have something that will work." She pointed to her east wall, an expanse of flawless white paint. "Pushpins will stick just fine in that sheetrock."

"Taylor, you're crazy."

"You think they won't?"

"Oh, I know they will. But I don't want to screw up your wall."

"I'm going to repaint anyway. White's boring. They make a little putty-patch thing for nail holes. I've fixed plenty of them. Thumbtacks are nothing. So go for it. Whole wall. Whatever you want to hang up there."

"Okay," he said. "Your wish is my command, Princess Jasmine."

Taylor groaned. What a doofus. Then she headed down her short hallway toward the master bath. "I'm going to take a shower," she said over her shoulder. "Do your thing. Plaster my wall with jackasses. We'll play Pin The Tail when I get back."

She stepped out of the shower twenty minutes later feeling better, certainly smelling better, and hopefully looking better. No use drying her hair or putting on makeup—Charles got it right about seeing her at her worst. And still here he was, carrying on like none of that ever happened.

On her wall, he'd arranged photos—probably taken from the Internet since that was his bailiwick—and name tags of every "player" in Randall County, including Sheriff Hastings and Eric Blevins. They hung off to the left, presumably in the "friendly" camp. To the right were photos of Bud Mabry, County Administrator, and all the Supervisors in a row. Between them, a photo of Nate Bostick, Commonwealth's Attorney. Dead center of the collection were names—not the photos—of all four barrel victims, since they now knew the latest discovery was Jamie Ratliff.

"Wall's kind of empty right there under the victims," she said. "I assume that's where our suspects go."

Charles nodded but didn't say anything. He stood beside her dining room table, where her laptop sat open and running.

Taylor blinked. Not a doubt in her mind that when she left the room to take her shower, it had been closed, powered down.

"What are you doing?" she asked.

Jaw tight, face tense, Charles looked at her like he was studying a crime scene. "Something you need to tell me, Taylor?"

"No. Why?" Her own jaw clenched. "What are you doing with my laptop?"

He held up a flash drive. "I was going to transfer all this information to you, so you'll have the same things I do." He placed the tips of his fingers on the top edge of the laptop cover. "This is WRCH equipment. I didn't know I needed to give you a heads up before I used it."

Shit. What site had she been surfing last? The one about the grandparent caregivers?

No. Something after that. God damn it.

"It's station property," he said. "You know better than to hit certain sites with the default browser."

She stared at him, trying to slow her breathing. "It's not pornography."

"No? Maybe not. May be worse. Sites like this are wall to wall malware, and malicious code. What the fuck are you doing surfing around in that, anyway?"

Swallow hard. Choke down the panic. "I've never had any problems with that website."

"Right—and you would know. Looks like you've hit that URL at least three times a week since you last cleared your browsing history, which was over a month ago. You know every bit of this shit can be traced, right?'

Slowly, she nodded. "It's not a big deal. I could be working on a story about the Dark Web, for all anybody knows. But for God's sake—the site's legal. You don't even need Tor to access it."

"Legal," he echoed. He rubbed his lower face hard with one hand. "That's a video of a teenage kid, from the looks of it. Hard to tell, since his hands are chopped off and his face peeled. And somebody's pinning his head to the floor with a steel rod through the back of his throat—" He took a breath. "While the other guy tries to saw his neck open with a box cutter. *Taylor*—"

She jumped at his loud use of her name.

"You watched that fucking thing six times last night."

Yes. At least.

He squinted. "That's Mexico, or some underdeveloped Spanish-speaking piece of shit country. You're not covering a story. I don't know what the fuck you're doing."

She didn't say anything. Couldn't.

"What the hell is the matter with you?" He pointed to the laptop. "This is evil. Sick, awful stuff. What could you possibly get from watching it?"

It took her a few seconds to form the words. Even when they came out, they sounded thin. "The knowledge." She tried to take a breath but it hitched in her throat. "That something's always worse."

He stood there for a moment, just looking at her. Then gave a small shake of his head. "Than what?"

A tear fell. Just one, but those were never good. They only meant more were coming. She swatted it away with the back of her hand.

And didn't answer him.

He held up both hands. "Worse than the pictures of those kids in the barrels?"

Oh God, Charles. Way off—

He lowered his arms. "Worse than Chicago?"

Her gaze snapped up. She glared at him. "You don't know a damn thing about Chicago."

"I know a little." He didn't blink. "That night, when you were so drunk—you said your last name isn't Beckett. You don't get to say things like that and not expect me to dig until I know what you're talking about."

"Get out."

"Come on, Taylor. You can't just chase everybody off who tries to give a shit."

"Get out." She took a step toward him, both hands clenched into fists.

"Fine." He grabbed his satchel from the sofa, took a quick glance at the wall covered in pictures, but made no move to grab anything hanging on it. "I'll go. But you got a problem. And it's going to eat you alive if you don't get yourself some help."

She picked up a hardback book from one of her end tables. Something about seventeenth century frescoes—who cared. Flea market special. It felt heavy in her hand, just the right weight to throw. *"Out."*

"I'm going." He walked fast toward the door. "But remember what I said."

After the door slammed behind him, Taylor stood staring at it, holding the book, holding herself together. Somehow.

"I did get help," she said after a minute, though Charles wasn't there to hear. "But just keep digging, Slick. You'll find out all about it."

"Why are you hanging my Chagall prints on your wall?" Taylor watched Erik drive another nail into his previously pristine sheetrock.

He took two more nails out of his mouth where he'd been holding them. "Because maybe your shit nailed to my shit means you're staying a while."

Taylor grinned, but she shook her head at the same time. "It's Expressionism. Not your taste at all."

He shot her a look underneath a ledge of dark blond brow. "You don't know squat about my taste in modern art."

Her laughter bubbled up. "No, but I see how you decorate."

"What's wrong with how I decorate?"

"Nothing, if you like post-grunge in the visual sense."

"You." The hammer thunked onto the coffee table with nails clattering after it. He stalked her in three strides and wrapped both long arms around her, walking them backward until her back hit the wall. "Need to learn some manners. You don't insult a man's house, especially if he's giving you the door keys."

"It's not a house," she said, breathing in the same air he'd just exhaled, taking in the essence of him that was more than scent, more than warmth. "It's a greystone, and only half of it. You and your neighbor share a wall."

"Yeah … and?" He brought his face even closer, melded his body to hers until he had pressed her flush against said wall, from shoulders to hips.

He kissed her, deeply, mouth tender and wet and hot. She pressed into him, too, having to reach up, way up, to lock her arms around his neck.

"And—" she whispered against the side of his face. "I love it."

She felt his smile more than she saw it, against the side of her face. Scratchy stubble, not even a day's worth—the little golden birthmark underneath one cheekbone, visible only at close range. Very close range.

"I'm glad Karmen threw you out," he said softly. "Took her long enough."

"I should have left my cell phone sitting there for her to snoop through a long time ago."

More smile, against her neck this time as he nuzzled her. "Did she find the dirty pictures?"

"Wait—what?" She grabbed his shoulders and made him stop. "There weren't any dirty pictures."

"I know." He pulled back, his grin for her to see this time, not just feel. "But it's fun to imagine."

"Ha ha," she said, and slid a threatening knee between his thighs.

But he was cat-quick, scary strong—hooked a hand behind her knee and the other arm around the small of her back, and down they went, onto the sofa, scattering throw pillows in every direction.

"Why do you even have these," she complained as one tumbled across her face. "So many of them."

"The girl who loved herself and loved the world loved pillows, too."

"Burn them," Taylor said, settling beneath him in the softness of the cushions. "Burn this damn couch, too. Everything she touched."

"That means you'd have to burn me."

"No, not you." She frowned. "Don't be ridiculous."

"Hush," he said. "I don't want to talk about her ever again. Just you."

"Fine." She wrapped her legs around him and held him against her as tightly as she could. "I just want you to prove to me that you're real. That this is real. That I'm not dreaming."

Bracing on one elbow, he pushed a strand of hair out of her face and traced the outline of her mouth with the tip of one finger. "I can do that," he said, so softly she almost couldn't hear him. "Thank God you came to Reggie's that night. I had no idea if I'd ever see you again."

"I'm here now," she breathed into the little hollow beneath his ear.

He shivered. "Me, too," he said. "And I'm not going anywhere. Count on that."

(Key of F)
You and me on the edge
On the line, downhearted
We are stung
We're scared we can't go back.
I agree, it's a mess
But if we're strong like we started
Hearts will lead and I'm not scared of that.

What if the truth is everything that it seems
What if we trust and let it just be?

This is me
This is real and this is how it could be
I'm just a man
I'm just what you see
This is me.

You get more of my heart
Than anything, anyone
Ever has
You are the strength I need.
So let me be here for you
Let me know your heart
Like you know mine though you don't believe.
                              ---Erik Evans, 2004

CHAPTER EIGHTEEN

Taylor stared at Charles' murder wall until she had memorized every face, every bio. Every jotted note and suspicion. She had nothing else to do with the passing hours. Charles hadn't called or texted since she kicked him out yesterday. And she hadn't slept. Hard to imagine she'd ever sleep again.

She'd had a good run there in Richmond. Lasted a lot longer than she expected before one of her colleagues thought to do a background check. Hennessey had always known. Not about Chicago, but about the fact that she used a stage name. Most of the executives at WRCH knew as well, but thought little of it. A fairly common practice in that line of work. A Google search of "Taylor Maines" would turn up some fairly unsavory information, so it was in the station's best interest as well as hers that she used her mother's maiden name, "Beckett." Maybe everyone at WRCH knew that. Maybe they didn't. Taylor didn't much care.

Damn Charles. He'd been nothing but a friend to her. Yet he crossed a line she'd drawn in the sand years ago, and there was no going back from that. And the bitch of it was, he hadn't betrayed her, hadn't violated trust. He'd simply wandered too close to the monster. Close enough to feel its breath. Taylor couldn't let that happen. Not now.

Not ever.

"I'm so sorry." Taylor couldn't face him, couldn't look him in the eye. Erik hadn't deserved any of that, didn't ask to be the target of her father's ridicule. "Dad's a decent person when he isn't drinking."

"Why do you think you have to apologize?" In the driver's seat of his Impreza, Erik squeezed the steering wheel hard with both hands until his knuckles turned white. "I get it—how crazy parents can be. Got two of my own. There's a reason Christmas only comes once a year."

"Quit being nice." She stared out the window at miles of fresh snow. The view hadn't changed in minutes, not since he pulled over and parked in a rest area just east of Des Moines. "I'd feel better if you were pissed."

"At your Dad, yeah," he said. "I am, a little. He was out of line. But I'm not pissed at you. Why would I be?"

"Because I took you home with me. I know damn well how he gets, and I led you right into it."

"Is it every Christmas?" He relaxed his grip on the wheel and rested his palms on his thighs. "Every holiday?"

Taylor looked at his hands. Strong, straight fingers, callouses at the tips. Give them anything with strings—or give them her body— and they made music. "No. Just random times when he can't put the bottle down. I don't even know what triggers it."

"Maybe things like, 'hey Dad. I've been shacking up with this guy for about eight months now, and I'm bringing him home for Christmas.' I don't know, Taylor. Some dads don't take that sort of thing too well."

She sighed. "He can be pretty protective."

"See? Maybe it's our fault, in a way. We should have broken it to him more gradually. Let him get used to the idea that his little girl's not so little anymore."

"Still, he didn't have to talk to you that way." She scowled out the window, at all the flat nothingness. "Like you're just some loser I found in a bar."

His features twisted, a hybrid expression between smile and grimace. "Well…sorta."

"In a bar, yes. But you were at *work*. Paying gig. Not to mention…oh, you know. That other job. The one where you have your own office with your name on the door?"

He grinned. "Yeah, I guess there's that." His grin softened, faded. "You know, at least he's there for you to go home to. My Dad's in London. I haven't seen him in five years."

Taylor didn't know how to answer. Erik had never seemed like it bothered him, the emotional and physical distance between him and his family. Now, how could she be sure?

"And Mom—" He shrugged. "She's so busy with her own life she doesn't even 'do' Christmas. At least that's what she told me last week. No time for it. Some merger or acquisition or something is always so much more important than spending time with people who annoy her."

Ouch. She reached for the closest of his hands.

He wrapped his fingers tightly around hers, then placed his other hand on top. "You have the family you're born with, and then the family you make. And you get a little bit of choice in that second one, there."

Her breath caught. Not just his words, but how he spoke them. The rhythm, the beats of his conversation—his inner poet, the songwriter.

She wanted to crawl inside his skin and live next to his heart, forever.

"Why don't we find a hotel?" He brought her hand to his mouth and kissed her fingers. "We're four hours from home, and we weren't planning to be back until tomorrow night anyway." His lips found the inside of her wrist.

"Sure." She smiled. "Christmas Eve at the Holiday Inn. Seems fitting."

An hour later, while Erik found a better parking spot, she got their things settled on the fifth floor of a chain hotel near the interstate with a view of snow, snow, and more snow. Not a bad room, especially for the price. Clean, with modern everything. The hotel even had room service and a decent menu. She rifled through Erik's duffle and found one of his old T-shirts, the one with a silhouette of Hendrix silk-screened on the front.

His clothing dwarfed her—he was every bit of six-feet-two, and what tucked in well for him hung almost to her knees. She took off everything else, wanting to feel nothing but the fabric of his clothing against her skin. She tugged the shirt over her head and just stood there for a minute, inhaling the scent of his fresh laundry from its collar.

The sound of the door lock responding to a key card, and Erik slipped back into the room, snow still clinging to the wool fibers of his coat.

"I think it's dropped ten more degrees out there," he said. Then he looked at her and blinked. "Going through my bags, I see."

She nodded. "Yep. Guilty."

He smiled. "Looks better on you than it does on me."

"I doubt that," she said.

Off came the coat, and he draped it over the back of a chair. "At least it's warm in here." He peeled his hoodie over his head. A second later, the T-shirt he'd worn under it.

Taylor stared. She couldn't help it. Eight months, and his body still left her speechless. Tall and rangy, muscles ripped from working out, a ribbon of script on his chest just below his collarbones— "When Words Fail, Music Speaks." A thin armband tattoo on his left bicep, the music staff, with the first few bars of "Imagine." And on the inside of his other bicep, where he could see it easily, his newest ink—her name, her exact signature, traced and duplicated by the tattoo artist.

Mr. Guitar—she'd called him that once, before she knew anything else about him. Never dreamed he'd be hers to touch any time she wanted, or that the hands capable of turning an acoustic guitar into pure emotion could do the same thing to her.

Erik crossed the room, held her in front of him, but turned her around so she could see them both in the room's large wall mirror. Slowly, with a feather touch, he gathered her hair into a ponytail and kissed the back of her neck. Then the soft skin between her shoulder blades, and over, to the left. His mouth found the exact spot where the autographed letters of his own name were still healing. Taylor held on to his arms for balance—dizzy and spun by the sensations only he could create. He dropped her hair, hands slipping underneath the T-shirt, warm against her skin. And slowly, he walked her backward until she bumped into the bed. He turned his shirt that she wore inside out as he lifted it over her head. He kicked out of his jeans until they stood together flesh on flesh—nothing between them now. Like always, his kiss took her breath—and took all possibility that she would deny Erik Evans access to any part of her, body or soul, until the end of time.

Thoughts of the past always hit her with the force of a Category Five hurricane, knocking Taylor's feet from beneath her and sending her head into a spin like a rotating updraft. She always regained her senses on the floor, or under a table, or under her bed, depending on the memory. It just didn't seem possible that all these years later, it could still hurt so damn much.

Taylor pulled herself upright, leaning heavily on the sofa. Once upon a time she'd been agile and limber, able to shrug off several hours on a cold, hard floor with little more than a few stretches and maybe a handful of ibuprofen. With every passing year, though, her bones and joints ached a little more after every episode. Hope to God one day it would all just stop, and either she wouldn't remember a damn thing at all, or she could remember it without having a fresh nervous breakdown each time.

Taylor sighed. So long ago—Jesus Christ, how could those memories stay so fresh. She placed a palm across her left shoulder, although she couldn't reach far enough to touch the ink with her fingers. More than just nine letters there now, not that anyone would ever see.

She'd just swallowed four Advil when the Avengers theme song nearly vibrated her Samsung off the end table. A quick check of the incoming number surprised her. She hadn't put him in her contacts, but she recognized the last four digits because the first two of them were zeroes, and that had always stood out for her. Eric Blevins, calling on his cell. Of all fucking times. No way she could answer that and have a sensible conversation. So she just let it ring, and finally it went to voice mail.

Ten minutes later, she checked it.

"Miss Beckett, this is Eric Blevins. I've been thinking about those pictures—well, that one picture with the guy's neck—I want to talk to you about that. Will you call me back?" And he left his number.

Yes. She would call him back. Once she remembered why she was supposed to care about anybody's neck except her own.

(Key of F)
There's no blame, don't forget why you're leaving
No regret, there's no shame in believing
Better things wait if only you don't back down.

How could I tell you this is the wrong thing
How could I say that? How could I mean that?
How could I stop you, this has been your dream
How could I keep you to myself.

Best for you, not best for me
Love is blind but I still see.
What's true for you's not true for me
Best for you, not best for me.

Walk every mile
Walk every mile
No regrets, don't forget why you're leaving.
                    ---Erik Evans, 2005

CHAPTER NINETEEN

Taylor didn't tell Hennessey she was going back to Randall County. She didn't tell anyone. Just packed enough off-camera clothes for several days, her laptop, and all the pictures and notes Charles had hung on her wall. She drove her own car, used her own credit card for gas. That way she answered to no one—not Hennessey, not the broadcasters' union, and not Charles. Especially not Charles.

The room she got this time at the hotel on the four-lane had a kitchenette, with a microwave and a mini-fridge. Locked inside after her five-hour drive, she took a few minutes to just sit and enjoy the change of scenery. Those four walls didn't look anything at all like her own four walls, and that was refreshing. She didn't plan to poke holes in these. She'd stopped at Walmart on her way in and bought a sticky, double-sided tape the manufacturer promised would do no harm to any surface it adhered to. Even wallpaper.

She spent the afternoon recreating the murder wall exactly as Charles had hung it in her loft. Certainly, guilt niggled. He'd done all the work—and she'd ripped it out from under him and taken off without a word. She hadn't even told him "thank you."

Eric Blevins had said he could be there after his shift, so she texted him her room number and waited. Tried to understand the headspace she'd fallen into, the resurgence of memories she usually kept so quiet, the stifling, overwhelming sadness that eclipsed everything else, even the urgency of those four murders. She understood depression, or at least as much as anyone could understand it. Embarrassing, that she could be weak enough to succumb after so much practice resisting. She should recognize the signs by now. She certainly knew how to duck out of it before it crippled her.

Or did she? Because it sure didn't seem like she'd done much ducking this time.

A sharp knock at her door startled Taylor so badly she jumped. She glanced at the bedside alarm clock. Four-fifteen. Really? Time had flown.

One quick glance through the peephole confirmed it was Eric, in the hallway, wearing jeans and a dark blue tee-shirt with "Randall County PSA" printed in white letters over the left front pocket.

She opened the door and let him in.

"Hey," he said.

"Hey, right back."

He stood there for a moment, awkward, and shifted his weight from one foot to the other.

Taylor knew the perfect ice breaker. "Want a beer?"

He stared at her, dark eyes round. "Really?"

She opened the mini-fridge and showed him—twelve bottles of Blue Moon.

"Just one," she said. "Because you have to drive home. But, sure. You could get drafted, shipped out, and shot by ISIS at your age, but you can't have a beer? Come on. Fuck that." She took one out and handed it to him.

"Hell yeah." He twisted off the cap.

"Besides," she said. "Judging from your tone of voice last night, you could use a little courage in a bottle."

He shrugged. "It's not that bad. Just a lot of shit going on."

Twenty-to-one odds that "lot of shit" was female and had cut him off, for whatever reason.

Holding his beer by the bottle neck, he walked over to her murder wall and stared at it. His eyes stopped scanning when they landed on his own photo, his profile pic from Facebook. "Why am I up there?"

Taylor let his question hang for a couple seconds, long enough for her words to carry some weight. "Because you're here, talking to me."

"What's that supposed to mean?"

"You're a big part of this," she said. "Have been from the beginning."

He turned back to the wall. "Pretty sad, if I'm all you've got."

"I disagree."

"At least you put me over there with Hastings." He pointed to the Board of Supervisors. "And not with them."

"What's the difference?" she asked.

His eyes cut to her. "Because if you were lumping me in with those jackasses, I'd be wondering how much rat poison you put in my beer."

Taylor laughed. "What do you think about the Sheriff? Do you know him?"

Eric nodded. "His daughter was a couple years behind me in high school."

"What do you think about him?"

He looked at her with a blank expression. "What does that matter?"

Jesus.

"You seem very comfortable with the idea that your opinions have no value." She watched him for a reaction.

"Huh?"

"Do people normally dismiss your ideas, like they aren't important?"

Something that looked a little like panic flashed across his face, but it was gone quickly, leaving only residual wariness. "I don't know. Don't think about it much."

"Bullshit, Eric. You know exactly what I'm talking about. And you have an opinion about that, too."

"Yeah," he said, his tone snappy. "It pisses me off."

"Good. I'm glad to hear it."

His wariness morphed into a look that said he thought she was nuts. "Hastings is okay." He took a swallow of beer and pointed once again to the Supervisors. "But he's had his balls cut off by these guys."

Taylor tipped her head to one side. "Would it make you feel better if I told you he may not be quite as neutered as you think?"

"Hmm." Beyond that, he didn't answer.

"So, tell me about a catchpole. What is it?"

The night before, when she'd finally called him back, he explained that the marks around Michael Dillow's neck looked like they could have been made with a catchpole. She'd Googled it while they were on the phone. Never mind what she found. She wanted to hear it from him directly.

He took another drink of beer, then held his hands apart to indicate length. "It's a long stick with a loop of coated airline cable at one end. You control the size of the loop and can lock it from the other end." He lowered his hands. "So if you catch an animal like a raccoon or a coyote—in a trap, usually—and you need to move it, you put that loop around its neck and hold it away from you with the pole."

"I see," she said. "It's an animal control device."

"Yeah." He nodded. "Few years back, I was going to help at the animal shelter, out there by the landfill. And they used one. I saw 'em pick a dog up with it. They were euthanizing that day—dog was fighting and kicking, so one of the animal control officers lifted him up where somebody else could stick him, and the pole broke. It was an older wood one, maybe homemade, or something."

"Wait." Taylor gave a quick shake of her head. "They had a cable around the dog's neck, and they picked him up with it? Like, choked him, and dangled him?"

"Yeah." Eric's expression looked tense, pained. "But I don't guess it mattered. Dog was going to die anyway."

Something whispered across Taylor's skin like a wraith—a horror, a feeling of total despair and nerve endings so raw they buzzed from pain more intense than synapses could process.

Like the kid in the video she'd watched, the one Charles found in her browsing history. Hands chopped away, skin of his face peeled off, head little more than a bloody skull with eyeballs and a snapping jaw. Yet he still cried out when the boxcutter went in. Tried to grab the stick in his throat with hands that no longer existed, bumped the ragged, bleeding stumps of his wrists against his neck in helpless desperation.

But it didn't matter. He was going to die anyway.

Stop.

No. Her thoughts would not travel one more step down that path.

"How old were you when you saw that?" she asked.

"About twelve, I guess."

"Twelve years old," she echoed. "What in the hell were they doing letting a little boy see all that?"

Eric gave a short, humorless laugh. "Miss Beckett, I don't know what world you live in, but around here, most boys in elementary school can gut a deer, clean a fish, skin squirrels and rabbits, and if they're like me, have watched dogs tear more coons in half than you could shake a stick at. That don't mean I like it. But that's how it is."

Good God. Maybe she should just let it go. Move on. Talk about Michael Dillow.

She walked closer and looked at the dead men's pictures, which she'd hung instead of the name tags Charles had used. Dillow's picture, in particular.

"So you think those lines of bruising around his neck could have been caused by a catchpole," she said.

"I don't know," Eric said. "Maybe. Crank it down real tight, and yeah. It makes sense." He pointed to the front of Dillow's throat, where the bruised lines ended. "See that? If somebody had him with a pole, and held him from the front, that's where the end of the pole would rest—just under his chin. So there wouldn't be any lines. But on the back of his neck, they'd probably be worse. Darker. More bruised, from all the pulling. Unless they had it on backwards. And then who knows."

"Wow." Taylor cleared her throat. Took a sip of her beer to wash down the lump trying to form. "That's a hell of a mental picture."

"Yeah," was all he said.

"Can we still go to the other two dump sites tomorrow?" she asked. "Where they found Dillow and Hess?"

"After lunch, maybe" he said. "I've got to help Grandpap haul off the trash tomorrow morning." He looked rueful. "We do that every Saturday."

"That's fine. Gives me a chance to sleep in."

Like she'd been trying to do for the past week, except insomnia had different ideas.

"Did you get that truck again?" he asked.

Taylor shook her head. "I drove this time. I have my car."

Eric frowned. "What kind of car is it?"

"Audi."

"Uhh—we're going to need that truck, if you want to drive to where they found Hess."

"That rough, huh?"

"Little bit."

"Okay." She wondered how much of that had to do with Eric just wanting to drive the Dodge, and not so much the difficult roads they needed to travel. "I'll see what I can do about that tomorrow morning."

Taylor had twenty minutes from the end of her American Legal History class until the start of Behavioral Neuroscience. The buildings were across campus from each other, which meant she had to hustle. She could make it on foot faster than she could make it to the parking lot, get her car unlocked and cranked, and fight traffic. She'd already been late twice that quarter, and the professor hated her. No sense provoking his wrath.

Halfway across the courtyard, Erik stepped into her path.

"Whoa." She stopped and stared at him. "What are you doing here?"

"Nice to see you, too."

He was smiling, so that ruled out her most alarming guesses about why he was there. Erik had visited her on campus a few times over the course of the past eighteen months, but never when he was supposed to be at work. And never in his three-piece from Lord & Taylor, looking as buttoned-up as any stuffed shirt on LaSalle.

She grabbed the lapels of his jacket and tugged. "What the hell, Erik? Is the Financial District on fire? They evacuated everyone?"

He laughed. "No. But I have something to tell you. Can you come with me? Grab a coffee, or something?"

She pointed to the Psychology Department. "I have—"

"Yeah, yeah—you have that neuroscience head-shrinking bullshit course in ten minutes. But this is important. Can you miss it today?"

"Uhhh—sure." Fuck it. "Let's go."

Erik took her off campus to a coffee bar that overlooked Lake Michigan. He seemed antsy, amped. Like the last thing he needed was caffeine. But she didn't say that to him. No point.

"So spill." She stirred her latte. "What is it?"

"Okay." He rubbed his hands together. Sleeves buttoned at the wrist, cuff links. Not even a hint of ink peeked out.

Oh, the secrets she knew about that man's body. Taylor smiled.

"Do you remember a few weeks ago, this dude came into Reggie's asking a lot of questions about the band?"

She nodded. "Yes. I do remember that. He wouldn't tell you who he was."

"Well, he told us his name, but not much else. Sat down and talked to us for about an hour after the show, real friendly."

Taylor nodded again. "You said he was interested in who did the songwriting."

"Yeah, but turned out he already knew—he knew most of the answers to everything before we told him. He was just feeling us out."

"Better than feeling you up, I guess."

Erik laughed. "I guess, yeah."

"So what's the deal?" she asked. "What's got you all in a twist?"

"Tillman called me this morning. Turned out this guy is from Atlantic Records. And he wants to talk to us about signing."

She just looked at him for a minute. Tried to put the pieces together in her head.

Signing. As in a real, honest-to-goodness label. As in, Atlantic-freaking-Records.

"Holy shit," was all she could say.

"Yeah, I know. Right? He didn't give Tillman many details, just said he wants to fly us all to New York day after tomorrow and have a meeting."

Taylor sat back in her chair, latte forgotten on the tabletop.

Marcus Tillman—he'd started the band back in 2000, just a couple of guys with guitars. Soon, they added a drummer and a keyboardist, and let Erik play whatever instrument he felt like playing when he agreed to join them in 2001. Here it was four years later, and this was a game-changer.

"Wow." Taylor drew a shaky breath, stunned. "You're going, right? To New York?"

Erik fidgeted for a second or two, then sat forward with his forearms on the table. "Of course I'm going."

She gave him a sideways look. "But?"

He rubbed his face, calloused fingertips scratching audibly over his mid-day stubble. "This is scary stuff, Tay."

"Scary?" She blinked, not sure what to do with that word. "I can think up a lot of adjectives to describe this, Erik, but scary? Not on the list."

"Seriously? It doesn't worry you—even just a little?"

"Worry me how?"

He rested his chin against a loose fist. "Us."

"What about 'us'? This is your dream. 'Us'—or 'we'—will figure it out as we go. We'll be fine." She just wished her heart felt as certain as her words. And it did, mostly. But what if? Always that damned "what if."

"It'll mean I'm gone a lot."

Inside, Taylor cringed. They'd talked about this—talked it to death—when getting the big break wasn't a realistic possibility. Then, it was safe to let the mind wander, to imagine. To hope. But now— Atlantic Record Group was real. The consequences of what Erik chose to do next would affect them forever.

"You have to do what's best for you, Erik. Not what's best for me. Maybe not even what's best for 'us.' You have to walk every mile of this until you know where it's going. I can't keep you to myself just because I'm afraid to share you with the world. So how could I tell you this is the wrong thing? How could I even say that? How could I mean it?"

He looked at her, dark blue eyes almost cobalt in the slanted light angling in over Lake Michigan. Ran a hand through his tamed, white-collar-professional hair until a lock of it went rogue and fell across his forehead. "If it makes you feel better, I'm not going to run from this. I'm going to see what Atlantic has to say. But the drive in me isn't the same as it is for Tillman. I don't know what I'm supposed to do."

She swallowed hard. "You follow your heart. That's what you do."

"But see, that's the problem," he said. "Music is just *in* me. It's effortless. All I have to do is let it out. I could leave M.J. tomorrow, hit open mike night in some little dive, and be just as happy."

"So what, then? I don't understand."

"It's never been about the big lifestyle for me," he told her. "Do I want to sell my songs? Hell, yeah. Thirty years from now, I want to be sitting somewhere with my toes in the sand collecting royalties and trawling YouTube for jackholes who use my tunes without a license. But I can't see me touring for half my life—burnt out, strung out, worn out—I've never wanted that. That's why I got my CPA when I damn well knew I had the chops to make it in the music business. I can have a family this way. Find a good woman, have some kids, teach 'em at least three chords before they can walk—" He let the sentence trail off, gaze locked on hers across the few inches of tabletop. "You can't tell me you're not thinking about it, too—settling down with me. Getting married. Babies, the whole nine yards. I can't imagine anybody else I'd ever want to be with."

She put her hand over her mouth, not surprised by anything he said, but leveled by it just the same.

Yes, she'd thought about all of that. At length. Repeatedly. But to hear those words come out of his mouth, just roll of his tongue like he talked about marrying her every day—

Life didn't get any more real than this.

"Listen," she said, wrapping both hands around her latte. "I would follow you to the moon. If you're a rock star, I'll be your groupie. If you're a nerdy CPA with glasses and a Donald Trump combover, I'll be the PTA mom driving our kids to soccer practice. It doesn't matter to me. I just want to be wherever you are."

He nodded. Took a deep breath, and blew it out slowly. "But then there's that whole Cambridge thing."

Yes. There was that.

He squeezed his eyes shut and pinched the bridge of his nose. "I know you want to spend your last year abroad, before you graduate. And everything just fell into place for that—my Dad living there in London, you being what the University wanted for the exchange program, your folks agreeing to pay the extra expenses—I'm not going to throw your dream under the bus, Tay. Not for all the record deals in the world. Now, there may be a way to make that work. M.J. will end up touring the U.K. at some point anyway, if we sign. But I'm just telling you where my head's at. Tillman would sell his grandmother's liver to make this happen. Me—" He flashed her a crooked smile. "You're always going to be my priority." His left hand moved back and forth between them. "*We* are always going to be my priority."

She grabbed his hand out of the air, captured it between both of hers. Brought it to her mouth, and kissed the fret-toughened skin of his fingertips. "I don't think I could live without you."

He frowned. "I don't think I could live without me, either. Be kinda hard, really."

Taylor shook her head and laughed. "You're an idiot."

"Then it's a good thing you like idiots," he said. "Or at least this idiot. Because this one loves you."

CHAPTER TWENTY

Before he even made the turn up the holler to go home, Eric's cell phone had already started beeping. He braked just after hitting the graveled section of his road and checked his messages. Two from Haley, and one from Bobby Cordle, his PSA co-worker. Haley was asking if he still planned to meet her at the mall, and Bobby wanted a callback. Cell service got spotty past the "End State Maintenance" sign, so Eric put his Escort in park and called Bobby back before he drove any further.

"Did you hit a deer?" Bobby asked after he answered on the second ring. "Or a tree?"

Eric scowled. "What?"

"The truck. What did you hit?"

"I didn't hit anything. What the hell you talking about?"

"Talking about the busted headlight and crack in the bumper. I just took it over to maintenance. They have it up on the rack right now looking to see if you fucked anything up underneath."

"I didn't fuck anything up anywhere." A brief flare of temper, but he blew a breath out slowly and let some of his anger go with it. "What makes you think I did?"

"Cause the truck's got a big-ass dent in it, Blevins. And you were the last person to drive it."

Eric rubbed his forehead. "I'm telling you, man—I didn't hit a damn thing. It was fine when I parked it."

"What time was that?"

"Around four o'clock."

"Where'd you leave it?"

The surge of temper came back, stronger and darker this time. Eric made a fist, then he relaxed it slowly, stretching his fingers until they ached. "Who told you to call me?"

A moment of silence. "Nobody told me to call you. I figured you'd want to know what's going on."

"And everybody says I did it?"

"Well, yeah. That's your truck—the one you drive. Who else would have done it?"

"Bobby, how long have you known me?"

Bobby coughed, most likely into a closed fist based on how muffled it sounded. "I don't know—'bout a year, I guess. Since you started at the PSA."

"Have I ever struck you as the kind of person who'd wreck a fucking county vehicle and not say anything to anybody about it?"

"Well, that's not what I'm saying, Blevins. But I know sometimes you take your time getting back from lunch—maybe you had a little nip of something—hell, I don't know. I can think of some reasons you'd park it like that and not say anything."

Eric's temper flared again, firecracker red. "You think I was drinking?"

"I don't know. Maybe—"

Eric hung up on him and slung his phone into the passenger seat. Put the car in reverse and spun tires backing out to the hardtop. He whipped onto the nearest wide shoulder he could find and turned around. Drinking, on the job. Of all goddamned things. He'd show them. He'd drive straight to the goddamned maintenance shop and blow his breath in somebody's fucking face, if that's what it took.

Then he stopped. Foot on the brake, car idling.

Shit.

The beer from Beckett. He probably still smelled like it—wouldn't do much good to go storming up to anybody now and try to prove he hadn't had "a nip of something," as Bobby put it.

Eric smacked the steering wheel with his palm. Then again, and several more times in rapid succession. It hurt, and he slung his hand up and down to shake off the pain.

"Fuck." He spat out the window. "God damn it."

Okay, nothing would be accomplished this way. They couldn't prove he wrecked the truck—mainly because he didn't—so he had no idea what their next play might be. Might as well just go on home, shower and change, and meet Haley as planned. At least she was talking to him again.

It seemed important that he look his best for Haley that night. Eric spent extra time shaving, and wondering if his hair looked better smooth or messy. He combed it, ruffled it. Combed it again. Shit. He scowled at himself in the mirror. What a pussy—turning into a fucking girl—who would have guessed.

He left with his best shirt untucked and hair hanging in his eyes. Didn't tell Gram where he was going, didn't say what time he'd be back. Just got in his car and drove to town, wishing he could pick Haley up in that big Dodge instead of a rusty subcompact with ripped seats and a cracked dashboard. She might actually ride somewhere with him in a truck like that, and not always insist on driving herself wherever they planned to go.

Get your ass back in school, then.

Oh, God. Now that uppity reporter was living in his head. He turned on the radio to drown her out. Luke Bryan on the country station—not really in the mood for that. He found Aerosmith in the low numbers. More static than music, but he let it blare.

Haley was waiting for him under the entrance canopy of the mall, in front of Belk. She'd been sitting on one of the brick flower planters that held no flowers, but she stood when she saw him and finger-combed her hair.

So beautiful. He hoped he never got over that initial kick in the gut when seeing her for the first time in a while—the jump in his heart rate, tightness in his throat. He locked his car and walked toward her, reached for her when he was close enough, public displays be damned. Just the brush of fingers, the pressure of her hand on his back or shoulder or something—it would be enough. Until later, of course. Then, all bets were off.

She moved away before he made contact with any part of her. Slung her bag over her shoulder, and started walking toward the double doors leading into Belk.

"I'm hungry," she said. "We have time for a Stromboli before the movie starts."

Eric's hand dropped to his side and just hung there. He used the next few seconds to breathe and try to salvage a little bit of composure.

By the time he caught up with her, Haley had already crossed through the second set of doors and made it halfway through menswear. Eric didn't try to touch her again, just let her keep walking, no physical contact, no show of affection. Not so unusual, knowing her personality. But still—some warmth in her eyes would have been nice. A fleeting touch. Something. Anything other than this indifference.

They walked past the theater on their way to the pizzeria at the other end of the mall. Not too crowded, from the looks of things. Sometimes, depending on what was playing, the arcade and waiting area out front would be packed with kids from the high school. Not so this night. Good. They'd have their choice of seats and could actually hear the movie instead of a room full of teenagers talking. Hayley would probably soften toward him then, without so many eyes on her. He looked forward to that.

The pizzeria was set up to order and pay at a long counter with menu items chalked on a blackboard. One Stromboli would feed them both, especially since Eric wasn't starving. Maybe not even hungry. He took the receipt with their order number printed on it and followed Haley. Once they got their fountain drinks, she led them to a bench in the back of the pizzeria, with a half-wall surrounding it, topped by lattice threaded through with fake ivy. He sat and tossed their receipt on the tabletop. Haley typed something on her phone. He picked the receipt back up. Folded it longways. Unfolded it, folded it in half. Set it down beside the salt shaker, tented. Haley hadn't stopped typing.

"Are you still mad at me?" he asked. "Because it sort of seemed like we were getting past that."

She looked up from her phone, face wearing no readable expression. "What do you think, Eric?"

Eric stared at her. What *did* he think?

You seem very comfortable with the idea that your opinions have no value.

Fucking reporter bitch. If she didn't get out of his head, he was going to make her start paying rent.

"Do you care?" he asked.

Haley's blank expression took on a pinched look. "Huh?"

"Do you care what I think?"

After a too-long moment, she gave a faint, slow shake of her head. "Not really."

He picked up his cup and took a sip of pop through the straw. Set it back down, used a napkin to wipe a few beads of condensation off the tabletop.

"Well, that's damn nice to know," he said after a few seconds had passed.

She made a noise like a snort. "Yeah, well it was damn nice to know you didn't listen to a fucking thing I said."

Fighting to keep his expression neutral, he raised his eyes to meet hers. It took some effort. "About what?"

Haley's gaze dropped to her phone. She swiped a couple times, and turned it around so he could see her screen. "About this."

It took him a minute to make sense of the picture. At first glance, it just seemed like a bunch of cars on a road. He looked closer and recognized the stoplight at the top of the hill not too far from the spot where they were sitting. Idling at the stoplight, a black Dodge Ram.

Haley turned the phone back around and did an open finger swipe to enlarge the picture. Made motions of centering it and turned the screen to face him again.

Yep. Black Dodge Ram, with him at the wheel. Beside him, not quite lost in shadow, Taylor Beckett.

"Haley, that was before you and I talked. You knew about this. It's nothing new."

"No?" She pursed her mouth and nodded. "Then what about today? Mama saw your car up at the Holiday Inn when she got off work this afternoon—figured I might have been there with you or something. So she called Jordan."

Eric swallowed hard. "Okay."

"Go ahead, Eric. Tell me what you were doing."

Funny taste in his mouth. Metallic, almost like blood. But not. He took another sip of his pop to wash it down. "I wasn't fucking around on you. I can tell you that much."

She laughed. It was a brittle sound. "Like the thought even crossed my mind."

Something in his gut turned over. Changed gear. Switched off.

He looked her in the eye. "So you're going to be a bitch about this because I went back and talked to that reporter again?"

"Now you think I'm a bitch, huh?"

Maybe he'd always thought she was a bitch. And just kept lying to himself about it, because it was easier to pretend than face the truth.

"Haley, I'm the one who found Dylan Altizer. You remember that part, right? It was me and him out there in the woods that night, and I'll probably never really get over that. So, yeah. I'll do whatever the hell I need to do if I can help figure out who killed him."

Her blue eyes narrowed. "You talk like you knew him. And you didn't."

"So?" he snapped. "He was a person. A human being. And he mattered. Nobody around here acts like they care. I found him, there was a story in the local papers, and not one more goddamned thing was said about him. Then they found three more. But they weren't local boys, so nobody gave a shit. Just some trash that washed down off the mountain. There was a little story in this paper or that one, a sound bite at eleven, and we all go on with our lives like nothing happened. Well, I'm not okay with that. And the fact that you are makes me really wonder about you."

An employee behind the counter called their number. Neither of them moved.

Haley put her phone in her pocket. "Once Jordan figured out why you were at the Holiday Inn, he called Daddy. And Daddy said you get one more warning. After this, if you don't leave all that alone, I can't see you anymore."

Odd, how quickly Eric managed to not give a shit.

"You asked me what I think," he said quietly. "Well, I think you need to get your Stromboli and go the fuck on."

She blinked. "What?"

"You're not the only one who can give a goddamn ultimatum. So here's mine. Get your family under control—especially that cocksucker of a brother you have—or don't call me anymore. Don't text me, don't do shit. Because I'm done. I've loved you for a long time, but I don't love you enough to put up with this."

Abruptly, Haley stood. Grabbed her bag, and hooked it over her shoulder. "Fuck you, Eric." She grabbed her cup on her way past the table.

"Fuck you, too, Haley." Then he thought about it. "Actually—" He turned on the bench seat to look at her retreating back. "I probably won't ever fuck you again. But if the next guy needs some tips on how to make you squeal, have him call me. I'll tell him all about it."

She turned around. Two steps toward him, three, and the contents of her cup poured over his head, ice cubes sliding beneath his shirt collar and leaving trails of burning cold down his chest and back.

"Shit!" He stood as far as he could in the booth and shook out his shirttails. Ice cubes bounced across the carpet squares, and pop dribbled down the inside of his jeans. He sat back down. Knocked the salt shaker and parmesan cheese dispenser off the table with once punch. "Fuck."

Then he looked around.

Thank God the pizzeria wasn't crowded. Bad enough that the people at a table on the other side of the room had watched the whole thing, and the employees. If the place had been packed—Jesus Christ.

Eric took another sip of his pop. Shook his head. Smiled and waved at the people across the room, who hadn't stopped staring.

Left his pop on the table and went the fuck home.

(Key of E)
When the day comes to an end
And the night starts slowing down and folding in
And you're left here with your thoughts and dreams
And plans and all your secrets
And you have to face yourself.

So what does that mirror say
Cause you have to live with the stains you made today
They don't come out in the wash
You'll never be just like you were before
There's always one spot left.

You can strip the whole world down and make it show its bitter bones
You can look the other way and just leave well enough alone.

Make it count
Whatever you can live with, run it down
Just make it count
Keep it close and run your fear to ground.

So you tried to leave your mark
And you can't believe you're left here in the dark
It's worse by light of day
You can't erase the scribbled margins
But you can just turn the page.

That graffiti on your soul today
Is a work of art tomorrow

So make it count
Whatever you can live with, run it down
Just make it count
Keep it close and run your fear to ground.
                                        ---Erik Evans, 2005

CHAPTER TWENTY-ONE

Saturday morning, Taylor took advantage of the hotel's hot breakfast, tanking up on coffee and protein before heading to the car rental office. She didn't see the black Dodge on the lot, but surely they had more than one truck. She parked by the front entrance, but would move to the side lot once she had the keys to a rental. Probably going to raise some eyebrows, her sporty coupe parked among minivans, but hell—at least it had Virginia plates.

The office was small, tucked in a plain rectangle of a building with no waiting area. She went straight to the counter, recognizing the young man behind it from her previous trip.

"Hi," she said with her best friendly smile. "What are the chances you could put me in a truck today?"

"Pretty good, actually," he said. "Do you have an account with us?"

"Last time I was here, I used a corporate account. But this trip, it's all me."

"You have a major credit card, right?"

"Yes." Taylor took her Visa from her wallet and gave it to him.

He looked at the card and frowned. "I remember you. Black Dodge."

"Yes."

Manager-Of-The-Year handed her card back to her. "Miss Beckett, uhm—there's a problem."

Taylor glanced down at her card. Her name was embossed across the bottom. No mystery how he knew what to call her, but he hadn't even run the card. What kind of problem could there be? "Excuse me?"

He didn't back down from a direct stare. She had to give him that. He met her gaze without expression, eyes unreadable.

"We have a policy," he said. "Anyone who operates our vehicles has to bring in a copy of their license, and it's ten dollars per each additional driver that you put on a rental agreement." He hesitated. "And no drivers under twenty-one."

Holy hell. Was he talking about Eric?

"Okay," she said. "And?"

"And we have reason to believe you've let an underage person operate our vehicle."

"I don't understand," she said. "How would you even know if some unauthorized person drove your cars? Do you have cameras mounted in the vehicle somewhere?"

He shifted his weight from one foot to the other. Scratched the nape of his neck.

Hah. She made him uncomfortable. Good.

"No cameras." He shrugged. "But if someone reports that kind of thing to us, we take it seriously."

"Reports it?" It took sheer force of will to keep from yelling. "You mean, someone just walks in off the street and says children are driving your vehicles, and you believe it? Just like that?"

His gaze hardened. He quit shifting weight. "It was a town cop who told me."

Taylor gaped at him. "A cop?"

Manager-Of-The-Year reached underneath the counter. The sound of shuffling papers, then he lay a photo in front of her that had been printed on regular copy paper. The black Dodge at a stoplight, Eric Blevins behind the wheel.

"I know Eric," the manager said. "And I know he's not twenty-one. Because you were listed as the driver when this photo was taken, we can no longer rent anything to you at this location."

Surreal. Down-the-rabbithole kind of stuff. Twilight Zone, cue the creepy music.

Might be a case to argue. If she pressed it hard enough and went over enough heads, she could probably get her way. Maybe. But worth it? She generally reserved her tantrums for more deserving issues.

She smiled. "Okay. Sorry to waste your time."

The membrane between civility and mayhem could be very thin. So, quickly—get out the door. Get back in her own car. Before she did something she'd regret.

Ah, yes. Her own car. An Audi, no less. Late model, and loaded. Nothing on that paltry lot came close. Maybe a slow cruise past the rental office window would underscore the idiocy of what just happened and send a reminder about how much money she might have spent doing business at that location.

Back at the hotel, Taylor paced in her room for about half an hour before texting Eric. A little embarrassing, that she'd been turned down for a car rental. Policy, her ass. This felt different. Sinister. Deliberate. But why? It made no sense.

Half an hour went by, and nothing from Eric. She texted again. "Can't rent the truck. Is there another way?"

Fifteen more minutes, and a reply finally came. "Got hung up with Gpap. Can't make it today. Sorry."

Taylor stared at her phone. Well, this was just bullshit.

Okay—so what *could* she do—in a sport luxury car, with no spirit guide?

She fired up her laptop and looked for touristy things. Not much. An exhibition coal mine across the West Virginia line. An ATV trail. Riiight. A museum. That might be cool—if she could focus long enough to understand anything she was looking at. What else? How to kill time in this godforsaken place, without killing every brain cell in the process?

Damn it, Eric. Talk about letting a girl down.

She could go to the mall. Nope, been to the mall. It was a vault, a mausoleum. Not even anyone pushing a floor waxer down the rows of tile. Just one long empty corridor with an out-of-business K-Mart on one end, Belk on the other, run-down theater in the middle, and acres of unused retail space between.

Taylor flopped onto the bed, on her back, crossed her legs at the ankles and stared up at the ceiling.

So just think for a minute. Think about what Eric had told her. A catchpole, for animal control. Possible? Actually, yes. It made sense. She'd watched a few YouTube videos on proper use of a catchpole—on animals and not humans, of course—and could see exactly how it might cause bruises just like those on Dillow's neck. Surely to goodness the medical examiner had reached the same conclusion. Just because authorities didn't talk about something served as no indicator that they didn't know about it.

Wait a minute. *Animal control.* Why was that registering? What had she read about that?

Taylor sat straight up on the bed.

Oh, shit.

Lawsuit. Sexual harassment. Filed by a former animal shelter employee.

She couldn't get to her laptop fast enough.

Ah, yes. There it was—"Randall County Board Of Supervisors Named In Sexual Harassment Lawsuit Filed In U.S. District Court."

What? Board of Supervisors? Why the hell hadn't that jumped off the page and slapped her when she first read it? What in God's name would the Board of Supervisors have to do with a sexual harassment case at the animal shelter?

"The suit was brought by former Randall County Animal Control Officer Elaina Sheppard, who claims that over the course of a two-year period, Darrell Pace, her supervisor, and his son Eddie, a co-worker, repeatedly made inappropriate sexual remarks and touched various parts of her body."

She read those lines again. Great journalism? Nope. Not even close. But it did tell a story.

"Attorneys for Sheppard allege that Eddie Pace falsified official documents after a September 2015 inspection done by the Virginia Department of Agriculture and Consumer Services that found nineteen instances of non-compliance and eight critical violations. Sheppard was terminated from her position in November of 2015. Attorneys for Sheppard do not confirm or deny that Sheppard reported unfit conditions at the shelter prior to the state inspection."

Taylor sat back, hand over her mouth.

Fucking hell.

Disgruntled former employee? Maybe. But given the bias and inadequate scope of local press, Taylor figured she was pretty safe assuming there was more to the story than what that article reported.

She Googled the shelter itself. Facebook page, shelter. Facebook page, "Friends Of," run by volunteers. Yellow Pages. Mapquest. Yelp. Then, further down the list, a petition. "Stop The Murder and Abuse At Randall County Animal Shelter."

Taylor froze.

"Murder" and "abuse" were strong words.

Page two of Google search returns—"Randall County Officials Contesting State Shelter Inspection Report."

So the upper levels of county administration had stepped in.

Damn, she needed Charles on this.

Taylor stormed up from her chair, prowling around the hotel room like a madwoman. Chewed her nails. Twisted her hair. Stared at herself in the mirror. She looked pale. Drawn. A little crazy.

She'd picked a hell of a time to have a fight with her best friend.

"God damn it!" She covered her face with her hands, peeping at her reflection between spread fingers.

She picked up her cell phone and initialized speech-to-text. "Are you still mad at me? Because I really need you right now." Not "need your help." Not "need help." No. "Need *you.*" Her finger hovered to edit, then she just hit send and threw her phone on the bed.

Within thirty seconds, Charles had replied with his own text. "I was never mad at you, Cinderella. Just worried."

Oh, Charles.

She allowed herself a moment to almost tear up, but shook it off before she embarrassed herself.

Suck it up, Buttercup.

She fired up speech-to-text again and asked him to call her.

When he held his guitar, Erik's hands became magic. The connection between the sounds in his mind and the sound in the strings was instant and absolute, like the reflex to duck a flying object before it struck. Instinctive, and hard-wired. Taylor could watch him play for hours and never lose interest.

When he wrote "Best For You," using the words she said to him that day at the coffee bar, he'd composed it on the piano. But tonight, he sat on the balcony outside his Dad's flat in Blackheath with his red acoustic cradled in his arms, working on a different kind of song. Taylor sat in the patio chair beside him, breathing the London air, marveling that a place could be so foreign, yet so undeniably familiar to the soul. Hard to believe she'd be living here in a few months. Her, a Londoner. Imagine that.

On the frets, his fingers held a steady chord while he found a riff on the strings. He played it a while, over and over, eyes closed, no doubt feeling it more than he heard it. When he did move to a different chord, the change of position was swift and certain. Except right now, when the guitar honked like a goose plowed over by a tram.

"Hah," he said with a grin. "Fat-fingered the hell out of that one."

Taylor laughed. "You think?"

"Well, I keep trying to go here—" He demonstrated, and it sounded nothing like a goose. "And I should be going here." He changed chords. Still no goose. "So what ends up happening is that I catch myself right in the middle of fucking it up and do this."

Ah, yes. The goose was back. She laughed again.

He played the same chord progression several times in a row, training his fingers, training his mind. He mixed it up, did some arpeggios, then some kind of crazy thing that sounded like a Flamenco. She watched, listened, scooted her chair closer so she faced him, leaning forward until she sat almost between his knees.

Summer had come to London, and the air blowing across the balcony felt warm and smelled of freesias. Erik looked comfortable in a loose tee and cargo shorts, his bare legs golden tan and covered with dark blond hair. She put her hands on his knees and threaded her fingers through the soft wisps, running her palms up the outside of his thighs.

"That's very distracting," he said without missing a note. "Just so you know."

She grinned. That had been the point.

"Do you regret not taking the deal with Atlantic?" she asked.

"Not really," he said, playing through the chord progression and moving on to another measure of the song. "I regret they only wanted to sign me and not the band."

The hurt on Tillman's face when he'd realized—Taylor would never forget it. The immediate look of betrayal he cast in Erik's direction, barely tempered by the fact that Erik rejected the idea on the spot, without having to consider it.

"I would only do it for the guys anyway," he said. "So no guys, no do it."

He went back to the home chord, hung out for a while, then moved into the opening riff.

"When the day comes to an end," he sang. "And the night starts slowing down and folding in. And you're left here with your thoughts and dreams and plans and all your secrets, and you have to face yourself."

Taylor's breath caught. Just beautiful—the words—his voice....

Next stanza. "So what does that mirror say? Cause you have to live with the mess you made today." He stopped playing. "I don't like that."

Taylor blinked in surprise. "What don't you like?"

"The word 'mess.' It doesn't fit."

She thought for a minute. "Okay—so, maybe we don't make messes every day. I mean, some of my days I could have written in pen and been just fine. Other days were pencil days all day long, and made we wish I had an eraser as big as my head."

He laughed. "So indelible versus washable mistakes."

"Washable mistakes," she echoed. "Stains. Sometimes they're indelible."

He drummed his fingers on the pickguard. "Interesting." Slowly, he started playing again, first just full chords, then he worked his way back into the riff. "So what does that mirror say? Cause you have to live with the stains you made today."

"Oh!" She sat up straight. "That's good."

He kept playing. "They don't come out in the wash, you'll never be just like you were before. Blah, blah, blah, blah, blah, blah, blah."

And he muted the strings.

"So what's your rhyme?" she asked.

He pulled a spiral note pad from the table beside him and wrote the newest lines, then sat staring at all of them with a frown. "Yourself," he said. "That's the rhyme."

"Elf?" she suggested. "Shelf? Elf on a shelf?"

He didn't laugh. "Doesn't have to be a perfect rhyme. Just a similar vowel sound."

"Okay, then. Back to stains. You never get most of them out, right? Always a shadow of them left."

His head snapped up and he stared at her. "That's it."

"What's it?"

"Left. That's the rhyme."

He started playing again, from the beginning. Sang through the first stanza with just the riff, then started keeping time by slapping his hand against the body of the guitar. It almost sounded like he'd added a percussion track.

"So what does that mirror say? Cause you have to live with the stains you made today. They don't come out in the wash, you'll never be just like you were before. There's always one spot left—"

In Randall County—three o'clock in the morning—Taylor sat straight up in bed, the chords from Erik Evans' red guitar still ringing in her head. She tried to breathe through the panic, tried to slow her heart rate, tried to calm herself. It didn't work. She kicked the covers off and barely made it to the hotel's tiny bathroom before she threw up every bite of everything she'd eaten all day and hung retching over the toilet, no more fight left in her.

(Key of A)
Starting over
How I wish that was a choice to make
How I'd love to just re-do the take
That led us here and left me incomplete.

It's a cycle
First you're up and then you're at the bottom
Second thoughts and hindsights, yeah I've got 'em
The worst is that I brought you down with me.

I don't want this to be a wedge between
I just don't believe I'm ever going to make it work
All these pieces I'm never gonna put together
I just don't know how to stop the worry and the hurt.

So this is where it's gonna lead
You're going to ask me what I need
And I have no words left to say.
I know where it's gonna lead
When you tell me what you need
I have no words left to say
Just no words left to say.

---Erik Evans, 2005

CHAPTER TWENTY-TWO

They'd been back from their London trip almost four months when Taylor first noticed the dust on Erik's guitar.

Winter had come again, their second together as a couple. She'd be leaving for Cambridge in the spring, and everything in their stars seemed to align. But that dust—when had he stopped playing? Taylor wasn't sure if it bothered her more that he'd quit, or that she hadn't even noticed.

If she thought about it, maybe he had seemed moody lately. Distant. Distracted. She could attribute it to stress, a heavy workload at the office. But things were still good between them. Weren't they?

He got home late that evening, not unusual anymore. Traded his suit for a hoodie and jeans, shook his hair loose, and zoned out in front of the TV with a beer. He'd gotten a Netflix account and had a never-ending supply of DVDs, but for the first time, it occurred to Taylor just how desperate he seemed to escape, to shut everything off—to disappear into a 42-inch flat-screen world that excluded everything, even her.

But not tonight.

She made one of their favorite junk food meals, a crock pot full of cheesy nacho dip filled with jalapenos. When it was ready, she took the whole pot into the den, along with a bag of chips, and set everything on the coffee table. That got his attention, and he paused the movie.

"Oh hell," he said. "Good woman."

She grinned. "Good woman not much of cook, but can melt cheese and render meat safe for consumption."

He laughed out loud. "Shit."

They watched the rest of the movie together, something with Adam Sandler that was actually pretty funny. It felt good to see Eric smile, and for a moment, she almost convinced herself that trouble lived only in her imagination.

Then his phone buzzed. He glanced at the display and set it down again, unanswered.

"Work?" she asked.

He'd started rubbing his eyes, but stopped and nodded. "Yeah. But they can take care of their own damn problems tonight. I'm off the grid."

"Hmm," she said. Then, a moment later, asked, "Are you ever going to tell me about it?"

His brow furrowed. Barely, but enough to notice. "About what?"

"Whatever it is that has you wound so tight."

He didn't reply right away. Instead, he watched a couple more minutes of the movie before he paused it a second time. Once he did, he sat forward and rested his elbows on his knees. "I can't really talk about it, you know? It's Backstrom shit."

She nodded. "Client confidentiality."

Again, the hesitation before he answered went on a beat too long. "Something like that."

His phone buzzed again. Like before, Erik looked at the display. But this time, he turned the phone off completely.

"If it's important, maybe you need to answer it," she said.

"I don't fucking need to answer it."

With no warning, he hurled the phone across the room. It hit the opposite wall, inches from the TV, and knocked a wireless speaker off the entertainment stand on its way to the floor.

Taylor stared at him.

Good lord.

She got up and retrieved his phone from behind the entertainment stand. Big crack down the screen, smaller cracks radiating in every direction.

She showed it to him. "Well, that solved everything."

Erik glanced at his phone, but didn't reach for it. He shook his head. "Been wanting a new one anyway."

Puzzled by his behavior, Taylor set the phone on the coffee table. Erik took extraordinarily good care of his things. To see him purposefully damage something like a cell phone—3G capable, no less—it didn't track.

"Are you okay?" she asked.

He shook his head. "There are times when I could kick the hell out of myself for not signing with Atlantic."

Ooooh, boy.

He kept talking. "I mean, I had some sort of fucked up sense of loyalty to the guys, but here we are less than a year later, no band at all now, and I haven't talked to Tillman since July."

Taylor sighed. True, all of it.

"He was never right after all that happened," Erik said. "One of those damned if you do, damned if you don't situations." He laced his fingers and leaned his forehead against them. "I don't think he's playing music at all anymore. None of them are."

"You, either," she said quietly.

He didn't say anything. Just stared at the TV screen with its frozen closeup of Adam Sandler.

"Your guitar has a layer of dust on it deep enough to plant string beans."

He gave her a sideways look. "To plant what?"

"String beans. I'm an Iowa farm girl, remember? I know my legumes."

"Ah, you're just talking shit," he said. Funny words, but he didn't smile. "You're from Des Moines. Grew up on concrete just like me."

Another minute passed, but he didn't restart the movie. Just sat there, staring at nothing.

"I regret it." His voice came out so low she had to strain to hear him. "Not taking that record deal. Tomorrow and every tomorrow after that would be entirely different for both of us, if I had."

Sunday. Day Two in the hotel accomplishing nothing. She hadn't heard back from Charles. Not a peep from Eric Blevins. Taylor couldn't take another day of this. She had to get out of there, or she'd start climbing the walls.

Even if they couldn't rent a truck and four-wheel out to the dump site, she still needed to talk to Eric. Didn't he say he'd volunteered at the animal shelter a few years ago? He might have some interesting things to say about Darrell and Eddie Pace.

So she texted him. "Hey. Would like to talk with you. Have questions. Available today?"

Fifteen minutes later, her phone buzzed with a reply message. "Want me to come there?"

Hallelujah!

She typed back, "Sure. If you want. Or I can meet you somewhere."

"There's fine. Give me an hour or so."

Forty-five minutes later, Eric knocked on her door. She let him in, noticing right away some differences since the last time she saw him. Weekend casual for him meant better-fitting Levis instead of his baggy work jeans, and a tighter t-shirt. Sneakers instead of boots. Hair hanging in his eyes, and a couple days of growth on his chin. Such a cute kid. Taylor smiled. His mother should be so proud—her boy on the cusp of being a man—should be the job-well-done of a good parent, but where was the parent?

Just sad. Pathetic, and heartbreaking. Nothing she could do would make up for that hole in his life. But maybe just being nice to him would help.

"I drank all the beer," she said. "But I have some bottled water and a Dr. Pepper in the fridge if you want anything."

He raised an eyebrow. "You drank all that beer? By yourself?"

"I've been here for two fucking days. Of course I did."

"Wow." He almost laughed, but sobered quickly. "I guess if you're thirsty."

"Or bored."

He shrugged, and it seemed like more of a commiseration than a show of disinterest.

He sat in one of the room's two chairs, fingers tapping the wooden armrests. "You said you had more questions? What about?"

Taylor watched him for a few seconds before she answered. More than just his clothing choices struck her as different today. Something about his eyes—more guarded, older somehow. "We'll get to that. Because I have to ask—are you okay? You don't seem like yourself."

She expected a stock answer of "yeah, I'm fine," or something along those lines. Instead he took a deep breath and let it out slowly.

"Why couldn't you rent the truck?" he asked.

Taylor chewed on her bottom lip. He'd asked one of those questions that wasn't just a question, and she didn't know quite how she should answer.

"Well," she said, trying to keep a grimace out of her expression. "Somehow they found out you were driving it."

He nodded. Not one hint of surprise. "Jordan-fucking-Asbury."

"Who?"

Eric pulled his phone out of his pocket and tapped on it a couple times. He gave it to her so she could see what he'd pulled up.

Facebook post by this Jordan Asbury person—the same photo she'd seen at the car rental office, but much clearer on the phone. A tag for someone named Brent Daniels in a comment by Asbury— *Isn't this one of yours?*

She looked at the profile picture of Brent Daniels. Mr. Manager-Of-The-Year.

"Okay, then." She handed the phone back to Eric. "I see."

"Jordan's a town cop," Eric said. "Total dickhead. I dated his sister Haley for about eighteen months. We broke up a couple days ago."

Ah. Now that explained a lot.

"I'm sorry," she said.

"Don't be." He didn't look at her, just tapped his fingers some more on the armrests. "You know, I asked her the other night if it mattered to her what I thought. She actually told me no. That it didn't." He raised his eyes to meet Taylor's, and they were dark, almost black. "And all I kept hearing was you, in my head, talking about my opinions, and their value. I wanted to slap both of you right then. Haley, because everything about her was a lie, and you, because you fucking told me the truth."

Taylor nodded. She knew exactly how that particular brand of frustration felt.

"Can we ride out and look at some things anyway?" she asked. "Maybe not the dump sites, but just around. Off the beaten path. I would very much like for you to show me some parts of this country most people never get to see."

"Yeah." He almost smiled. "Hey, is that your Audi out front? The red one?"

"Good guess," she said. "That would be mine, yes."

"Can I drive?"

215

Taylor laughed. "You bet."

"I'll give you the fifty-cent tour first." Eric wheeled Taylor's Audi around a hairpin curve on top of a mountain. "We'll get to the celebrity homes and abandoned movie sets later."

Taylor laughed. "Okay. If you say so."

Outside her window, a sheer rock wall rose so high she couldn't see the top of it. Long, vertical scars marked the limestone, where once upon a time massive drills had made way for sticks of explosive, the highway department's solution to terraforming. "I guess with your job, you know most of the roads in the county."

He nodded. "Areas out where we don't have lines run—I don't know those as well. But anywhere we have meters or hydrants, yeah. I'm pretty familiar."

Through the windshield, Taylor watched for glimpses of the world below them through stands of hardwood growing thick on the mountain. The trees were rooted below the level of the road, their branches spread over the guardrail. Occasionally, a break in the canopy let her see for miles, across smaller hills that rolled away toward the horizon, to flat land and a river that disappeared into yet another mountain pass on the other side of the valley.

"It really is beautiful here," she said.

Eric glanced at her, but turned quickly back to the road. "From a distance."

Slowly, she nodded. "Yeah."

"It's when you look too close that you see the ugly." He guided the car around yet another tight turn.

"A lot of traditions here," she said. "Customs. Ideals that should be preserved."

"Really?" He gave a short laugh. " 'Bout the only tradition I know passed down from one generation to the next is how to get your crazy check."

"Your what?"

"Disability. Some people need it—I'm not saying they don't—but there's an art to hiring a lawyer and a couple of doctors to say you have anxiety, or headaches, or bi-polar disease, and just live on the draw for the rest of your life."

"That's insane," she said.

"Where else around here are you going to make enough money to live on? Ringing up cigarettes down at the Fast Mart?"

"But what about crafts, and things like herbal medicines? Organics? I know the Sheriff's wife has a shop in town—she sells those things. Where did she learn how to do all that? Her mother? Grandmother?"

Eric burst out laughing. "Debbie Hastings? Are you serious?"

Taylor frowned. "Yes. I am. Why?"

"Good lord. She's from Boston."

"Boston?"

He was still chuckling. "You've never heard her talk?"

"I've never met her." Taylor sighed. "She gave me some stuff to put on all those cuts I had, but she sent it through him. I just assumed—"

"Well, you know what they say about that."

Yes, Taylor did know. Ass out of you and me. Old one. She sighed again, more deeply this time, and with feeling.

"Miss Beckett, all those cute little stories about Appalachian culture and fiddles and moonshine and homemade quilts—that world is gone. We lost our heritage two generations ago. These days the only tradition we pass down to our kids is dependency. We're addicted to drugs, alcohol, welfare, and coal. Sad, but it's the truth."

"Please," she said, hoping she didn't sound as peevish as she felt. "Just call me Taylor. We're both adults here."

They'd twisted and wound their way to the base of the mountain, and now the road flattened, ran straight through the heart of a small town with houses and storefronts only the width of a sidewalk from the driving lane. Everything looked tired, dusty. Desaturated.

"Gosh, look at the soil," she said, grateful for a reason to perk up. "How dark it is. I'll bet you could grow tomatoes big as grapefruits in that."

Eric snorted. "I'll bet you couldn't."

She tore her eyes from the ground passing by outside her window and stared at him. "Why not?"

"Ever heard that saying—sun comes up at ten in the morning and goes down at three in the afternoon?" He pointed in a circle around them. "Look at these mountains. Think about the shadow. Bet these houses don't get four hours of direct sunlight a day.

Besides—" He laughed. "That black stuff? It ain't rich dirt. It's coal dust."

"Coal dust?" She blinked in surprise. "On the ground?"

"You'll see right up here—big-ass mining outfit takes up half the mountain. One of the oldest in the region. Tipple sitting next to the road. Used to be coal trucks up and down through here nonstop. Nowadays they're supposed to tarp, but back in the day, they hauled open. Coal dust blew up off the dump wagons and covered everything. Probably won't ever go away."

Only a mile or so past the last row house, they drove underneath a massive metal structure that looked like part conveyor belt, part silo a hundred feet in the air. It crossed the road overhead, lined with halogens that must have lit the place up like broad daylight after the sun went down. Taylor studied it, turned in her seat to look behind them after they passed. It looked like something from another world, another planet, another time.

"So what I wanted to ask you—" She faced forward in the seat again. "You said you worked at the animal shelter a few years back, or volunteered, or something. Can you tell me about that?"

He shot her a quick sideways look. "Why?"

"Because I want to know, Eric. I want to know about Darrell and Eddie Pace."

He shifted in his seat. "What about them?"

She went for broke. "Tell me the part you've never told anybody else. What you saw. What they did. Why it bothered you so much."

His foot came off the accelerator. The car coasted, and before they headed into the next curve, he pulled to the shoulder and put it in park. Sat there for a minute, hands loose on the steering wheel, but fingers twitching.

"If you want me to tell you about that," he said. "Then you're going to have to drive."

(Key of E^m)
Just got in from a long day
And I'm too tired to move.
You push me hard for information
But I try to ignore the truth.
I don't want to go back
But I can't move on
And I don't know if I
Am more here than gone
Can you give me time to breathe?

And I can't stop you from leaving
But I could never be the one
Who put you on your own when I don't
Know the next step I can take
And when my back's against the wall
And you're just lying there asleep
And I don't know if we'll
Go the distance
Damn this heartache
And damn the distance.

Damn this heartache
And damn the distance.

---Erik Evans, 2005

CHAPTER TWENTY-THREE

Certain spots in town were nice. Like the one Taylor found to grab a quick bite of lunch in her car—a tiny park with a pretty view of a lake and a bright red caboose. Yet just across the street, a trailer park with old aluminum-shell singlewides, none in good repair. Beside them, a few houses with clapboard siding and dangling shutters, sagging outbuildings and overgrown grass. Right here in town, where curb appeal should be a priority. Maybe the county supervisors drove past this every day, saw it how visitors might see it, and came up with the "zoning mess," as Eric called it, as a means of reversing the trend.

Could it be that simple? Taylor doubted it. Eric's theory about a land grab was probably closer to the truth. But still—was anyone looking for community improvement grants? Doing any kind of outreach to property owners, offering incentives to clean up their neighborhoods? No way to know unless she asked those questions, and she might just do that, since in a peripheral way they seemed relevant to her story.

She looked down at the chicken sandwich in her hand. Not quite a double quarter pounder with cheese, but close. Eric had said this was a community addicted to drugs, alcohol, welfare, and coal. Taylor thought one could add "junk food" to that list. Almost every fast food chain was represented within a five-mile radius, but not a single branded restaurant with a healthy menu. How long would anyone last there without scarfing down a 2,000 calorie lunch? She hadn't even made it a week.

Her eye caught movement beside one of the houses. A dog, stocky and dark, dragged himself from beneath a porch and stretched. He ambled over to a battered plastic bowl and lapped up some water, then flopped down in a patch of dirt where no grass grew. Around his neck hung a wide collar, and clipped to that, a heavy chain.

On impulse, Taylor Google-mapped her location and switched to satellite view. Last update for those coordinates was two years earlier. She found the caboose, the trailer park, and the house across the street, and muttered a curse. That poor dog's misery was visible from space. A perfectly round dirt patch marred the green carpet, proving that he—or some other dog—had been tethered in that same spot for at least two years, without enough respite to even let the ground scar heal.

Last winter, a story from Accomack County had made the rounds through both mainstream and social media—a man let his dog freeze to death on one of the coldest nights of the year, and the photos were gruesome. Neighbors said they'd heard her barking long into the night, but then she went silent. Most assumed the owner had taken her inside. After what Eric had shown her yesterday, Taylor wondered how many dozens—hundreds—of animals in Southwest Virginia had suffered the same fate, with no media voice at all to speak for them.

In all her adult life, she had never owned a pet. Growing up in the Midwest, she learned that animals had a purpose, and it was to serve the needs of man. Food or fur—you either ate them or wore them. Dogs herded livestock. Cats killed mice. But a good man took care of his creatures. Even the Bible said so: "A righteous man regardeth the life of his beast."

Yesterday, Eric Blevins had shown her scenes that would be indelible in her mind forever. Stains on the world made by others that would always be that "one spot left." Housedogs—tiny, Maltese and Scottish Terrier types—chained behind homes in a busy neighborhood, with little plastic boxes for shelter. Covered in mud, long, luxurious coats matted and snarled beyond salvage. Hundreds of people passed by them every day and apparently thought nothing of it.

A big dog, chained to what looked like an old cargo container, able to chase cars around a full quarter of his dirt circle, getting so close to theirs she could have thrown a wadded napkin and struck him. And sure enough, the ground on that side of his limited territory was covered in missiles—paper cups, pop cans, beer bottles. Eric had pointed out that chained dogs of any breed tend to become aggressive. He'd said the owners made the effort to contain their animal with a ten-foot chain, but obviously never gave a thought to the cats and small dogs and children who might wander into his territory unawares.

Taylor finished half her chicken sandwich before her appetite disappeared. She looked at the meat on her bun and for the first time wondered what kind of life the chicken had led. She watched the dog across the street, imagining the hundreds and thousands of drivers that passed him every day without giving a thought to his boredom. His loneliness. The heat he felt in the summer, the bitter cold he endured in the winter.

Every community had those—the forgotten pets, forgotten children. But the ratio in Southwest Virginia just seemed staggering. Poor living conditions for animals was the general rule from what she had seen, not the exception. And it struck her that perhaps the solution to making a community care about itself again didn't lie in zoning restrictions or even improvement grants. Maybe it started with teaching a basic respect for life. If dogs and cats were disposable, it didn't seem such a great stretch that children would be disposable, too. Like Eric as a baby, when both his mother and father had better things to do than raise him, or even love him. And then the elderly— ten percent of the nation's nursing home population—how many of them were legitimately in need of skilled professional care, and how many had just been dumped by their families like puppies on the side of the road?

And the kids in the barrels—Jesus, lord. The brutality of their murders was bad enough. But the dispassion of local media, the apathy of the community—just too much. Those young men had been real, as real as Eric Blevins. As real as her own Erik, from so long ago.

Taylor slammed the door on those thoughts before her chicken sandwich came back. She forced herself to breathe, forced herself to sit quietly, wondering if anything, anywhere, would ever lay a trail that did not lead her thoughts straight back to Chicago.

Even later than usual, Erik's key in the lock told Taylor he was home. She'd waited up, beginning to feel something very close to worry. Six o'clock, seven—those hours had become the norm. But nine? Pushing it a little, although she wouldn't dare say that to him. At least not yet.

He dropped his keys and his broken phone on the hallway table, shrugged out of his jacket, and hung it over the back of a kitchen chair. Went to the refrigerator and took out a beer.

Taylor leaned against the kitchen doorframe. "Have you eaten?"

He nodded. "Yeah. Got something earlier."

"There's some stir-fry in the fridge, if you want it."

He shot her a look, scowling. "I said I'm not hungry."

Taylor blinked. Fine, but did he have to be so surly about it?

"Erik, what's wrong? I wish you'd talk to me."

"Not now." Same snappy tone. "Just back off, Taylor. I've had a shit day as it is. I don't need you breathing down my neck."

"Excuse the hell out of me." She pushed herself off the doorframe and went into the den. "Sorry I cared."

He followed her. "Don't give me attitude right now. All I need is a little bit of space. For just a minute. God damn it."

"Sure," she said. "Whatever."

"I fucking walked out, okay?"

She stopped. Stood there for a few seconds without moving, then turned to look at him. "What?"

"I quit. Told 'em to kiss my ass. I'm done."

Taylor squinted at him. "Quit what? The Backstrom account?" A hesitation while she watched his face for clues. He gave none. "Or work, as in—altogether?"

"As in unemployed. Jobless. A bum, just like your Daddy said I am."

"Oh God, Erik. What happened?"

"I got crossways with the mighty Heinburg & Associates. I'll never work as a CPA again."

"That's no answer," she said. "What do you mean, 'got crossways?' Give me some specifics, here."

He jerked his tie loose, stripped out of his vest, and kicked off his shoes. Left them scattered about, hung over furniture or lying on the floor. "The specifics are—I have no job, no prospects, no allies in the business, and a resume that isn't worth shit after today." He turned the beer up and took a hard pull. "I told Atlantic Records to go fuck themselves, pissed off everybody in the band, and shit all over a future I could have given you and me and our kids without ever breaking the law. I took the level path. Did the responsible thing. And look where it got me."

"Where it got you?" Taylor shook her head, completely flummoxed. "Without breaking the law? What the hell are you talking about?"

But he had nothing else to say. He disappeared into the guest room with his dusty guitar and keyboard that hadn't been played in months and slammed the door in her face.

By five that evening, Taylor had spent all the mental energy she could spare on Southwest Virginia social dysfunction. Problems with no solutions could exhaust her faster than shoveling snow. What had she been thinking all those years ago? Sociology? Was she nuts? She wouldn't have lasted a year in that field. Now, she looked forward to a night alone in the hotel room, just her and the walls and whatever was on HBO.

She turned into the parking lot and found her favorite spot near the main entrance. The only thing she had to carry was her handbag, so she grabbed it and headed through the front doors.

Charles unfolded himself from one of the padded chairs in the lobby and stood to greet her.

Taylor stopped walking. Seeing him there felt incongruous, like finding a giraffe on the twenty-ninth floor of the James Monroe Building. She just stared at him for a moment, utterly incapable of doing anything else.

"Hey there, Rapunzel," he said. "I was about to give up."

"What the hell are you doing here?"

In typical Charles fashion, he grinned big. Lit up the whole room with his high-wattage smile. "Good to see you, too, Sunshine."

Odd, the way he looked in jeans and a t-shirt, baseball cap instead of carefully shaved head, familiar leather satchel hooked over his shoulder. Yet somehow, despite the casual clothes and playful banter, he was still all business. Focused. Poised.

Perfect. Beautiful. Everything good in the world. He grounded her soul.

"I'm sorry," she said, and squeezed her eyes shut. "I was just surprised. I don't know why you're here, but I'm really glad you are."

When she blinked them open again, she found him staring at her with something that looked very much like concern on his face.

"Wow," he said. "That may be the nicest thing you've ever said to me."

"Then I'm sorry for that, too—for never being nice." She pointed toward the elevator. "Come on. Whatever it is, we probably don't need to talk about it out here."

She took him to her room on the third floor, where the murder wall he'd created in Richmond now hung, replete with gruesome photos that watched over her every night while she slept. He barely glanced at it when they walked through the door.

"Got beer?" He pointed to the mini-fridge.

"Sadly, no. I think I've forgotten how to shop."

He laughed. Then he tilted his head and looked at her with a shrewd expression. "So what made you focus on the animal shelter as a tie-in to this case?"

"Eric Blevins. He said the bruising around Dillow's neck looks like someone used a catchpole on him. That's an animal control device, so wondering about the shelter was a natural next step."

"Yeah." Charles nodded. "Well—I have some things to show you, but I didn't want to email any of it. That sexual harassment case? Pretty tame reading, compared to some of the shit I found." He reached into his satchel and brought out a stack of papers, clipped together in the top left corner. "I think I'm going to run out and grab us something with a kick. You start reading. I'll be back before you need the anesthetic."

She took the papers from him and glanced at the cover sheet.

Report On Chronic Animal Abuse At The Randall County Animal Shelter From The Period 1997 to 2015.

It was at least twenty-five pages long.

"What's this?" she asked.

At the door, he stopped and smiled, but it was tense, tight-lipped. "Just read it, Cinderella. I'll be back in fifteen."

(Key of D^m)

For what it's worth, I hate this too
A simple word does so much hurt.
So take a step back, maybe two
Just take your time
And speak your mind
Not sure how much I can take
I can bend but I don't want to break.

Wherever you are, I am too
I'll be there in heart and I'll be there for you
But know, just know
I'm wherever you are.

So watch me crash and watch me burn
Fear or flame, both the same.
They eat you up and take you down
Just leave ashes
 Scattered on the ground
Chalk it up to lessons learned
A page I did not want to turn.

                                        ---Erik Evans, 2005

CHAPTER TWENTY-FOUR

"My name is Mary Beth Donovan and I live in Culpepper, Virginia. I have degrees in Social Work and Criminal Justice and have experience interviewing witnesses, clients, and patients. In 1995 I saw a horrific media story on conditions at the City of Richmond, VA, animal shelter and became involved, with others, in helping to remedy the problems."

Arranging hotel pillows behind her back, Taylor settled onto the bed to read.

"This experience led me to look at other shelters in the Commonwealth, and I was shocked to see the deplorable conditions in so many of them, including the Randall County Shelter in 1997, then supervised by ACO Darrell Pace. With impunity and disdain, Pace repeatedly ignored orders given to him by State Vet Inspector Dr. Ray Masters. Thousands of animals have been cruelly treated by Darrell Pace, as you will read in the following pages, and by his son ACO Eddie Pace, after he was hired. The fact that neither Darrell nor Eddie Pace was charged criminally for any of the documented violations, and that both are still employed by Randall County and have daily contact with animals is both egregious and unconscionable."

Taylor curled her legs beneath her and flipped a few pages. Credentials, legal language, definitions. A chart that showed the number of animals killed by euthanasia at the shelter by year, and a percentage breakdown. "Kill rate" had gone as high as 66% in 2013.

She sat still for a moment and tried to imagine how many dogs that really was. A staggering number, especially if considered alongside the meager population. 882 dogs, according to the report.

How big would a pile of 882 dead dogs be? How much landfill space would that require, since apparently, that was the county's method of disposal?

Reading on, she learned about the euthanasia of a horse off shelter property, with drugs requiring certification that both Darrell and Eddie had allowed to expire.

"ACO Darrell Pace maintained a key to the drug cabinet after being instructed by State Shelter Inspector Teresa Hamlin to surrender it to ACO Elaina Sheppard."

Taylor stopped reading for a moment. *Elaina Sheppard.* She sprang off the bed, rushed to her paperwork on the table underneath the murder wall. She dug through, found the sexual harassment lawsuit. Yep—a match. Elaina Sheppard.

Oooh, boy. All the little puzzle pieces, fitting and clicking together at last.

She curled up with the report again.

"Darrell continued to access and take drugs from the cabinet until at least 2015. This caused a shortage that grew to 300cc's. Darrell removed drugs to provide euthanasia services off site to the public's animals. ACO Sheppard was unaware that Darrell continued to remove drugs from the cabinet. Darrell did not make a record of the drugs he took from the cabinet."

Taylor took a notepad from the bedside table and made a note to contact the closest DEA field office as soon as possible.

"On 8-25-15, State Police Special Agent Dave Reston found drugs in Eddie's animal control vehicle and the key to the drug cabinet on Darrell. Both admitted to Reston that they had taken drugs from the shelter to euthanize a horse."

Shit. The State Police. Taylor thought back to Hastings' press conference, and the State Police officers who flanked him.

Just how high did the good old boy network go in Southwest Virginia?

She read on.

"Intracardiac injection (heart sticking) of conscious animals was performed on dogs, puppies, cats and kittens. This is an illegal and very painful form of euthanasia. Animals must be completely unconscious before performing intracardiac euthanasia, not simply sedated and certainly not conscious. (3.2-6503; 3.2-6570(A) Animals would take 20-30 minutes to die. They would 'flop around' until they died and if they didn't die, they were heart stuck again. Note: Intracardiac and IV euthanasia should cause death within seconds. The length of time it took animals to die is evidence of the lung or diaphragm being painfully injected, not the heart.

At that point Taylor had to set the report aside. She rubbed her face, rubbed her upper arms. But the chill was internal, in her soul, and in her gut.

Yesterday, in the car, Eric had described most of these things firsthand. Granted, he hadn't seemed to know anything about the legal aspects of what he'd witnessed, but good lord. Why should he?

She picked the papers back up.

"Darrell would straight out heart stick fully conscious, fractious dogs, stating, 'That'll calm his ass down!' If the dog didn't die and was still breathing after 20 minutes, he'd heart stick the dog a second time. Dogs could be stuck 3-4 times before Darrell finally hit the heart and the animal died."

Where the hell was Charles? A beer would be nice, or maybe something a hundred proof, straight out of the still.

"Darrell and Eddie would get mad at dogs and cats they decided 'had a bad attitude.' Those animals always got a brutal death.

"They would take an aggressive dog out of the Quarantine Room on a catchpole. With the tightened catchpole around his/her neck, they would then close the door to the room tightly on the dog's abdomen so the animal was in a 2-point restraint. The dog would be euthanized in this position. If Eddie was not available, Darrell would use an untrained Community Service Worker to help him. Animals were euthanized in front of each other. Note: This is inhumane because of the great stress it causes on the observers when "stress pheromones" are released and the 'smell of death' is present at these times. Euthanized animals lose control of their bowels and bladder. Per ACO Sheppard, the whole environment was one of great odor, sound and stress.)

Taylor took a deep breath. Thank God for all those years of forced desensitization, the "trigger-training" that Charles hadn't understood when he found that trail of videos on her laptop. It was never, ever a matter of "getting something" from any of those atrocities she watched. It was a matter of emotional defense in a barbaric world where the monsters lived among the children, not just under the bed.

"Dogs who became frantic on a catchpole would be heart stuck. Darrell and Eddie would get very angry at these dogs. Eddie would hold them forcefully with the catchpole, take them down hard to the ground; and Darrell would stick them between their ribs just as he did feral cats. He would often pull catchpoles so tightly around some dogs' necks that they would be rendered unconscious. They would then euthanize them."

Jesus, lord. Taylor ran a hand through her hair, jerking at the tangles she found near the ends Anything to distract. Sitting calmly on the bed was no longer an option. Taylor got up and paced. Prowled. Longed for alcohol. Finally picked the report back up and forced herself to continue.

"Darrell's grandsons (as young as 5 y/o), have been in the garage and watched him euthanize animals. They came on 'snow days' and during the summer.

"Darrell's 15y/o grandson would 'help' by going to the kennels and getting dogs to bring to the garage for euthanasia. This untrained child would also 'hold animals' while Darrell euthanized them."

Enough. Taylor set the report on the table and walked to the murder wall. She looked at the photos of the victims, alive and dead. At the bruising on Michael Dillow's neck. No way—simply no way in hell—that it was coincidence.

A sharp rap on her door meant Charles had returned with the anesthetic. She let him in, glaring at him as he walked past.

"What the hell took you so long?" she asked.

He set the brown paper sack he carried on the table. "Had to drive all over town looking for your poison." He reached into the sack and handed her a Blue Moon.

"I could have saved you the time," she said. "Walmart's the only store here that carries it."

"Wrong," he said. "That little gas station near the mall has these."

She nodded and twisted off the cap.

"I take it you didn't get to the good part," he said, studying her with a squint.

"That shit doesn't have a good part," she grumbled. "It reads like 'How To Train Your Local Creep To Murder In Five Days Or Less.' "

"Oh yes, it does have a good part." He picked the papers up and flipped through a few pages. Folded them back, and handed the report to her. "Read, Pocahontas."

Taylor scowled down at the report. But she did what he asked.

"Wildlife was inhumanely trapped alive and forced into a 2' x 6" PVC cylinder tube. The tube was placed on the Animal Control truck and left capped until the animal in it perished. These animals experienced a long, slow, agonizing death until they suffocated.

"The tubes were already in use by the Darrell and Eddie Pace when ACO Sheppard was hired in 7-2011 and continued to be used at least until they were discovered by State Vet Inspector Hamlin on 9-14-15. The necropsy done on the skunk discovered in a tube by Hamlin at the time of her inspection on 9-14-15 showed no trauma or disease. Cause of death was determined to be asphyxiation."

Like the wildlife in the report, Taylor couldn't breathe. She panted quietly for a few seconds, then slowly raised her eyes to meet Charles'.

"This woman," she said, barely able to speak above a whisper. "Mary Beth Donovan—did you happen to run across any contact information for her at all?"

Charles smiled and reached into his satchel. He produced one of his own WRCH business cards, with a phone number and Culpepper address written on the back. "You know it, Sunshine." He gave her the card. "She's waiting to hear from you."

The night he quit his job, Erik had asked for space. So Taylor gave it to him. As badly as she longed to knock on the door of their spare room and beg him to talk to her, she didn't. She finally went to bed—alone—around two a.m. Sometime between then and the following morning when her alarm went off at six, he had lain down beside her and gone to sleep.

She had classes all morning, but wasted no time going home afterward. He was still there, napping on the sofa. He'd showered and changed, even shaved. He just didn't seem interested in doing anything except shutting out the world.

Finally, around three o'clock, he got up and started moving around, first the bathroom, then the kitchen for a beer. He barely looked at her. Taylor closed her eyes and breathed in the scent of him when he walked past, longing to touch him, longing for some way—any way—to connect.

"That stir-fry is still in the fridge," she said. "I can heat it up for you."

He gave a curt shake of his head. "I'm not hungry."

"Have you eaten anything at all today?"

"Lay off, Taylor." He shot her a warning look. "If I want food, I know how to get it."

"Jesus, Erik—do you really have to be such an ass to me? I haven't done anything to you."

He stared at her for a long moment. "I'm sorry."

She sighed. "I know you're worried. I'm worried, too. You said some things that scared me last night. What did you mean—if you took the record deal you could have given us a future without breaking the law?"

He ran a hand through his hair and left it standing on end. "See? This is why sometimes I just don't want to fucking talk to you. You can't let anything go. I've told you I can't discuss Backstrom business. Even now. So back off."

"Well, don't talk about Backstrom. Talk about Atlantic. There's no reason to think they're going to slam the door in your face if you go back and ask for a meeting. You have all those songs—how many did you tell me? Upwards of a hundred that you've written, just sitting there waiting for somebody to pick them up? You don't want to be a performer? Fine. Sell the songs. You know they're good enough."

He stared at her for several heartbeats, unmoving. Then he spun around, went into their spare room, and emerged a few seconds later carrying his leather binder. It was stuffed with loose papers, different shades of white and cream and yellow, even a napkin or two that contained scribbled lyrics. He slammed it onto the breakfast bar in front of her.

"Here you go," he said. "Sell them. They're all yours."

"Erik, for God's sake. That's not what I meant."

He grabbed a zippered hoodie from the hall closet and put it on. "You want to know about Backstrom?"

"What are you doing?"

He grabbed his sneakers from beside the sofa and put them on, too. "I'll tell you about Backstrom. They're a bunch of crooks getting over on half their clients, and using dumb fucks like me to help them do it."

"Please," she said. "Just stop. You don't have to leave."

"I want off the account, so I go to Heinberg, right? I tell him what's going on—but guess what? He's going to fucking burn me if I leave. It's my signature on all that paperwork. I try to say I didn't know what was going on—you really think anybody's going to believe me?"

Taylor's hand flew to cover her mouth. "Oh my God, Erik—you're in trouble. Like … real trouble."

"No shit." He grabbed his car keys and headed toward the door. "Gonna see if I can straighten any of this mess out. Give me a few days. Give me some breathing room. I just can't deal with you on top of everything else right now."

And he slammed the door behind him.

CHAPTER TWENTY-FIVE

Monday morning turned Eric's weekday routine on its head. Instead of climbing in his truck at five minutes before eight and heading out for morning readings, he followed instructions and drove his own car to the PSA administration office. An ass-chewing was certainly on the agenda. He'd wracked his brain over the weekend trying to figure out how the truck might have been damaged, and still came up with nothing. That short, screwed-up conversation with Bobby Cordle had been the only thing he'd heard about it until he got the text from Mack Bowling last night.

Which seemed odd, once he thought about it. Mack Bowling was maintenance. What business did he have summoning employees, like he was keeper of the goddamned gate? No doubt, Big Mack knew everything that went on at the PSA. More reliable than CNN, at least for county bullshit. But it sure seemed to Eric that if Ted Whitt wanted him at the administration office first thing, then Ted Whitt should have got his ass on the phone and made the call himself.

Big Mack wasn't the problem. Eric liked him just fine. He couldn't think of anybody who didn't. Big Mack got himself in trouble a lot because he didn't know how to tell anybody no. Wouldn't do a bit of good to be pissed off at him, or Bobby Cordle, either, really. Save it for whoever really wrecked the truck and had the big idea to pin it on somebody else.

Turned out, he beat Ted Whitt to the office. So he sat there for a while with the front-end girls, who'd always been nice to him even when he first started and didn't know anybody. Maybe it was his imagination, but today they seemed a little less talkative. So he quit trying to make conversation after the second time he said something and got only a terse smile in reply.

Hell, they could have at least offered him a cup of coffee.

"Eric." Ted Whitt must have come in the back door, because he appeared in the little hallway that connected the front room of bill pay windows with the administrative offices in the back. "Come with me."

Eric stood and followed him, wincing every time the man's shock of white hair almost clipped a light fixture. How tall was Ted Whitt, anyway? Six-six? Six-nine? Tall. Just ... tall.

He ushered Eric into his office and shut the door behind them. "Please—sit."

Eric did, waiting with his elbows on his knees, trying to not look anxious even though he was, and trying not to *be* anxious because he hadn't done anything wrong.

Whitt folded his long frame into the chair behind his desk. "Employees are supposed to report accidents right away, Eric. You know that."

Eric nodded. "Yeah, I do know that. If I'd done it, I would have reported it."

"Come on, now. Nobody else drives that truck but you." Ted moved a paperweight from one side of his cluttered desk to the other. "What time did you park it on Friday?"

"Four o'clock. Just like I always do."

"Where did you park it?"

Eric hesitated before he answered. Seemed like maybe Bobby had asked that question, too. "Same spot as always—beside the generator."

"Well, by five o'clock on Friday, it was down the hill parked beside the pump station. Have you seen it?"

"No. Of course I haven't seen it. I didn't work this weekend."

"A little over two thousand dollars' worth of damage, and that's without repainting. Gotta replace the whole headlight assembly and the bumper. The hood may be okay, but somebody's going to have to knock a bunch of dents out of it if it's ever going to shut right again."

"I don't know what to tell you," Eric said. "It was fine when I left it."

"You're going to have to go by the clinic and pee in a cup."

"Sure." Eric shrugged. "I don't have a problem with that."

"I'm taking you off meters. Gonna put you in maintenance—you can ride around with Big Mack for the next little while. It's about a fifty-cent decrease on the hour."

"Wait." Eric sat up straight. "What? You're cutting my pay?"

"It's that or terminate you."

"God damn it, Ted. I didn't do it. I didn't wreck that truck." Eric looked at Ted hard. "So what's this really about?"

"Settle down, Eric. You still have a job. But I can't let you drive a county vehicle right now. I don't know what our insurance is going to need to get this straightened out."

Eric braced his hands on his knees. "This is bullshit and you know it."

"It may be, but it's bullshit I don't have a choice about."

Eric blinked. Subtext, or his imagination?

"Big Mack said he'd run you by the clinic." Ted reached for his phone. "I'll tell him you're ready."

"Are there cameras mounted anywhere?" Eric asked. "Security? Traffic—out on the road that would see who came and left Friday afternoon?"

Ted shook his head. "There are no cameras, Eric. It is what it is. Now go wait out front and Mack will pick you up."

It took a lot of focus and discipline to stand and walk quietly out of Ted's office. But Eric managed. Out front, in one of the vinyl-covered aluminum chairs that served as reception furniture, his right knee kept bouncing. He'd force it to stop, think about something else, and it went right back to bouncing. His cheeks burned. And he wished to hell Big Mack would hurry up so the girls in the front could go ahead and talk shit about him after he left.

Mack rolled up about five minutes later in the F250. "How'd it go?" he asked once Eric had climbed in.

Eric scowled at him. "Like you don't know. Hell, you knew before I did."

Mack didn't say anything, just drove out of the parking lot and across the bridge leading to town.

"I didn't wreck that goddamn truck." Eric was starting to feel like a CD stuck on repeat. "But I'll bet you know who did."

"Hey," Mack held up one hand, beefy fingers spread. "Don't bring me into it. This ain't got nothing to do with me."

Really? Then why had he been so happy to send that text? No doubt Whitt put him up to it. But nothing would have forced Mack to comply.

"What the hell, Mack? Who wanted me off the meters?"

"Ain't got nothing to do with the meters."

"Then what?"

"The truck, Blevins. The truck. The big-ass dent in the front."

"Except I didn't put it there."

"Well, they think you did."

Eric's knee started bouncing again. He pressed the tips of his fingers into the top of his thigh to stop it.

From the corner of his eye, he watched Mack sneak a glance in his direction.

"You just gotta keep your head down," Mack said. "Do your job, and don't worry about anything else."

"Meaning what?"

"Meaning just what it sounds like I meant."

"I have a feeling," Eric said. "That somebody's not happy with me talking to that reporter."

Mack rolled through a stop sign and kept going up the hill to the clinic. "I don't know about any of that. Go ring your cup. I'll wait out here."

It took less than ten minutes for Eric to donate a sample for drug testing and hand the full cup to a girl he went to high school with. It still felt warm, the temperature of his body. He cringed when she took it, even though she wore a glove. Who would have thought the girl he borrowed Earth Science notes from would be playing with his piss one day? It seemed too intimate somehow, awkward, and wrong.

In the truck, Big Mack waited, staring out the window at deer grazing in a field across the road. He didn't say anything when Eric climbed in and shut the door, just cranked the engine and headed out of the parking lot.

"So tell me this," Eric said after a mile or two. "Was I right? About the reporter?"

Mack drove with one hand, the other propped on his hip underneath the paunch. He shrugged without changing position. "Nobody wants her here. She needs to take her ass back to

Richmond and worry about what happens on that side of the state. Plenty of murders to cover in D.C."

"What's everybody so afraid she'll find out—who did the killing? Maybe I'm off base, but seems to me like that might be a good thing."

"Well, here's how I see it—none of the people in those barrels are from Randall County. They could have been killed anywhere and dumped here. Law's investigating. They had the state mobile crime lab out on every one of them. Damn reporter comes messing around, making everybody nervous—how the hell's that supposed to help?"

"Maybe by holding everybody's feet to the fire? Making them actually do their jobs?" Eric shook his head, frustration rising inside him like slow floodwater. "I've met her. Talked to her. She's smart. She sees shit happen and isn't afraid to say something about it. Around here, people don't even care enough to come in out of the rain half the time. Much less drag a friend in with them."

Mack scowled. "I don't even know what the fuck you're talking about."

Of course he didn't. Eric rubbed his face hard.

Behind the wheel, Mack sighed and shifted positions, changed hands on the steering wheel and propped his left elbow on the window ledge. "Sometimes you try to drag folks in outta the rain, and all they do is sit over there and bitch about it."

Eric stared at him, wondering what the hell he'd missed.

"You think somebody set you up over that truck deal?" Big Mack asked. "I don't know a damn thing about that. But if it's true, it came from higher up than Ted Whitt."

Startled, Eric blinked. "From higher up what?"

"Just thinking out loud, Blevins. Don't read nothing into it."

Right.

Eric sat back, tried to calm his breathing, and watched things pass outside his window. Cows in a pasture, a nice brick home with lots of old trees around it, a mining supply company with big rolls of black conveyor belt parked like oversized hay bales in front of their building. Rosewood, the county's great project of nothing. Small green signs for the animal shelter and the landfill, both at the end of the same road the maintenance building sat on. Said a lot about priorities—wonder what the hell it meant if that's where he'd be reporting to work every morning from now on.

The bright side? At least he'd get home around the same time every day as before. If not earlier. Half those boys in maintenance had even less interest in hitting an honest lick than Bobby Cordle. Fifteen minutes until four, and they were already heading out with car keys in hand, ready to congregate in the parking lot until the minute hand went vertical.

It could have been a worse day, but should have been better. Getting things right, doing things right—being the responsible one, the smart one—Eric had never been the fuck-up, didn't know quite how to wear that particular hat. Good-natured ribbing about his wrecked truck felt anything but good. The battered Ford sat shamefully in the main bay, there to remind him of all the mistakes he didn't make, but ended up paying for anyway. Eric took his lumps, but inside he felt shredded. Just didn't seem fair that it came down to this, being the target of offhand jokes and the lowest man on the PSA totem pole after almost a year of giving them nothing but his best.

Shit like that made a man not even want to try.

He'd parked his Escort and spent a minute with Popper before he heard voices from the house—Gram saying something he couldn't quite make out, then a few seconds later Grandpap, yelling for her.

"Vella!"

Fuck.

"Veeeellla!"

He knew what that slur meant from halfway across the yard.

Eric almost got back in his car and left. Almost pretended like he didn't hear anything, didn't know anything, or just plain didn't care. Either one of those excuses would have worked. But then Gram's voice rose again, begging. Pleading.

"Hoyt, please get up. I can't help you if you don't get up."

Passed out drunk again, no doubt. Piled up in a doorway, or in front of the stove, or wherever he went down. Eric closed his eyes. Opened them again. Gritted his teeth. Kept walking to the porch, and waded in.

"Oh, Eric, thank the Lord," Gram said, stooped over Grandpap with blood all over the front of her blouse.

He stopped and stood still for a minute. Took inventory, and thought he knew what had happened. Gram was fine. He'd seen Grandpap take a swing at her a few times when he'd been drinking, but nothing to draw blood. No, looked like Grandpap fell and busted his head on the doorframe. Big cut, right over his eye, bleeding like a sonofabitch.

"Grandpap," he said, voice raised like he was talking to somebody half deaf. "Look here, Grandpap. Let me see your head there, where you busted it."

"Aaaah, you donnneedta see my head. Veeeellla!"

"I'm right here, Hoyt," Gram said, leaning forward with a dishtowel already bloody from her attempts to blot. "Now be still. Let Eric look at that."

From what Eric could tell, the gash didn't look all that serious. Might need a stitch or two, not like Grandpap would get them. Old fart would close it himself with fishing line before he'd go to the clinic.

"Let's get him up," Eric said. "Get him in a chair or something. It's gonna kill my back, leaning over like this."

"Your back," Grandpap slurred. "Your baaaaaack. Ain't never worked a day in your life. Don't know what it feels like, your back to hurt."

Eric stood over him, looking down, tasting bile and smelling the tang of blood—all he could do to not just turn around and walk out like none of it mattered. To hear Gram tell it, Grandpap had been a drinker his whole life, before Eric was born, before Eric's daddy was born. He could handle his liquor most of the time. But when he couldn't—Eric's daddy had grown up watching this shit. First DUI at sixteen. And all those talking heads in Washington thought pot was a gateway drug. Well, Eric had news for them. Pot didn't have a thing on ninety-proof.

"All right, old man," Eric said, bracing his feet with the intention of lifting Grandpap by the armpits. "Help me out a little here."

"Ain't your goddamned old man." Grandpap shrugged away. "Get your hands off me or I'mma whoop your aaaass."

Eric tried again to reach and lift. "You ain't gonna do nothing to me in that shape. So shut your fucking mouth and help me out a little bit here."

"Eric!" Gram popped him with the bloody towel. "Watch your mouth."

Hello? Watch *his* mouth? Eric didn't think so.

"I'mma whoop your aaaass." Grandpap took a sloppy roundhouse at Eric's face and missed.

Whack. The solid thud of Eric's palm connecting with Grandpap's forearm—Eric squeezed his fingers tight around it and shoved it back, down, toward the floor. He let go and grabbed the old man by the collar, bunched-up shirt and maybe a little bit of saggy skin, and hauled him up against the wall.

"You ever lay a hand on me again," Eric said, his face inches from Grandpap's. "And I will beat you to fucking death."

"Eric!" This time Gram screamed his name, took him by the arm and tried to pull him loose. She tugged a couple times, fingers digging into Eric's bicep. "Let him go! Eric!"

So Eric did. Just opened his fingers, and let go. Grandpap staggered, reached for the wall, staggered again. But he stayed upright, swaying. Blood poured from the cut on his head.

"I swear!" she cried. "Your daddy never done anything like this. He knew how to show some respect. He wouldn't dare take a hand to either one of us—"

"Well maybe if he had," Eric said, pinning her with as direct a stare as he had in him. "He wouldn't have spent half his grown life in prison and wouldn't have turned out to be just another piece of shit meth-head who doesn't belong anywhere else."

"Oh, I can't believe you're doing this." She wept openly now, hands wadded in the bloody hem of her shirt. "Eric, I'm so ashamed of you."

"Maybe you ought to be ashamed of yourself," he said. "Letting a little boy like my daddy—and like me—grow up thinking this is the way everybody lives. That this is somehow okay, because it's how you were raised, and how Grandpap was raised, and everybody all the way back to the beginning of time was raised. You're so full of shit, both of you. If you were such great goddamned parents, you might have raised a daddy who would have stuck around for me. I don't know what the hell you call the mess you made out of his life. But I'll tell you what I call mine—*over it.* I'm fucking *done.* Because I finally figured out that the only way I'll ever turn out right is to do the exact goddamned opposite of everything you ever told me to do."

He didn't even bother to see if she was still crying. He just walked out of the house, got in his car, and left.

CHAPTER TWENTY-SIX

Five hours to Culpepper—oh, the irony. Taylor had set up base camp in Randall County to be near the story, and her story ended up being an hour and a half from her loft in Richmond. Go figure.

Charles made the drive with her, happily navigating from the passenger seat of her Audi. He doubled as D.J., bluetoothing songs from his iPhone, blues and jazz, and a little Motown. Not a chance she'd run into a song from her college years on his playlist. Thank God.

North of Charlottesville, he turned the music down and paid more attention to the landscape. After passing a particularly long stretch of five-board double horse fence, he took his cap off and rubbed his shiny head.

"Hard to believe this is the same state we just left over there in the southwest corner." He put his cap back on and tugged the brim.

Taylor couldn't agree more. "Different world."

"What is it, though? What's the difference? I mean, there are nice homes in Randall County. Right there on the four-lane, not hidden. But it doesn't look like this."

"Trash, for one thing," she said. "You don't see it here. You don't see junk cars, you don't see boarded-up windows. Signs aren't hand-made. Things are hung straight and don't droop. I don't know—stuff like that."

"Hmm." He scrolled through his phone, distracted by the playlist or the map or whatever he was looking at.

"So you never told me—" She watched him from the corner of her eye. "Are you here on your own time like me? Or did you get right with Hennessey before you left?"

He didn't look up. "Oh, I'm always right with Hennessey. But, yeah. I took some personal days."

Taylor smiled, but said nothing.

"I think we got a turn coming up." He looked at his phone. "Yep. Make a right at this next intersection."

The directions took them another few miles through farming countryside and thousands of acres of natural woodland. They finally reached a gravel road that led through a stand of pines, framed on both sides by wire cattle fence. No cows in sight yet, but Taylor could smell them—a dense, organic miasma of hay, leather, and manure that wasn't altogether offensive. She drove slowly over a cattle gate, a gaping hole topped with steel bars that livestock wouldn't cross. At the end of the lane, a one-story home sprawled among the trees, inhabiting a patch of sunshine carved out of the forest like a fairy glade.

"Wow." Taylor parked and shut the car off. "I could live here."

"Me, too," Charles agreed. Then he pointed to the field behind the house, at least fifty acres of prime grazing. "But who's going to mow all that grass?"

"That's what the cows are for."

"Nope, no cows. You have to get up at the ass-crack of dawn to feed a farm, in all kinds of weather—negatory. I'm not down for that. We could raise hay. Hire one of those outfits with a baler to come harvest it a couple times a year. Buy a tractor and do hay rides at Halloween for the kids."

"Or we could just get a condo in the city and let building maintenance handle everything."

He gave her a sideways look. "We moving in together now? Like, for real? Or are you just punking me?"

Taylor cracked up. It felt good to laugh, to completely drop her guard and not have to edit every word that came out of her mouth. "Sure, but it has to be Westham, Highland Road area. I'm very high maintenance."

"Girl, you're so full of shit, ain't no damn wonder your eyes are brown." He opened the car door. "Come on. Let's go do this."

Mary Beth Donovan met them at the door. Taylor recognized her from an Internet search she'd launched after reading the report. Not quite as tall as Taylor expected, with auburn hair cut short and camera-ready makeup.

Mary Beth looked behind them, like someone might be hiding in their shadows. "Just you two?"

Taylor nodded. "Yes, for now." Then she took another look at Mary Beth's flawless makeup and felt a pang of guilt, "We may be back, though, with a crew, if things go well today and you agree."

Something in Mary Beth seemed to deflate. "Okay." She held the door open wide. "Come inside, then. Would either of you like some tea? Coffee?"

The air inside her home hung heavy with the scent of some exotic dark roast, freshly brewed and sumptuous. Taylor breathed it in. "Coffee, if you don't mind. That smells wonderful."

"Yeah," Charles agreed. "I'll take some, too."

The main living area was open, much like Taylor's loft, but more organic and earthy. Rough-hewn beams supported a ceiling that was at least fifteen feet, and natural stone tile created a sea of warm tones on the floor. Two dogs padded across it with wagging tails and curious noses, toenails clicking on the travertine.

Ordinarily, Taylor might have ignored them. This time she put all her other thoughts on pause and gave them her full attention. Not purebreds—types, mostly—one a probable black lab mix, short and squat, with white hair around her muzzle, and the other a terrier with a wiry, iron-colored coat. Taylor petted them both, amazed by their steady, trusting gazes. They seemed to look right into her and just *know*—everything.

"Meet Lucy and Grayson," Mary Beth said, returning with two mugs of coffee. "Lucy was from Appomatox when it was still a very high kill shelter, and Grayson came from Fairfax County. Both were on death row—would have been destroyed within hours."

"High kill?" Taylor took one steaming mug from Mary Beth's hand. "Meaning the shelter had a high rate of euthanasia?"

"Euthanasia?" Mary Beth handed the other mug to Charles. "That's a medically-justified procedure to end suffering, whether physical or mental. When you stop a healthy heart inside a healthy body because the individual as a whole has become an inconvenience, that's killing. Plain and simple. We should get our phraseology clear right off the bat."

Charles had moved slightly behind Mary Beth, to the side, and out of her line of sight. He caught Taylor's eye and mouthed the word, "wow."

"That being said—" Mary Beth motioned toward the furniture in her living room. "There are worse things for an animal than death. Would you both have a seat?"

Taylor took one end of the sofa and Charles took the other. Mary Beth sat in one of the three chairs scattered in a semicircle around the room. Lucy and Grayson flopped on the floor at her feet and lay there like canine sphinxes.

"I think I should tell you up front that my main interest is not animal welfare," Taylor said. "I'm investigating political corruption for a news documentary series about Southwest Virginia."

"Then you've come to the right place," Mary Beth said. "Because you can't separate the two, at least not in this case. You have two psychopaths employed by a government municipality, with overwhelming evidence and admission of felony crimes, and a large-scale coverup to protect them and keep them in place. If that's not political corruption, then I don't know what is."

Good point. Taylor would let it stand undisputed.

But not Mary Beth's report. It needed a solid testing by fire. She reached into her briefcase and pulled out a copy.

"I want to talk to you about this report. You state that one of its purposes is to—" Taylor read aloud. " 'put eyewitness and former Randall County Animal Control Officer Elaina Sheppard's words into print about crimes committed at the animal shelter.' Sheppard is also involved in a sexual harassment lawsuit against Darrell and Eddie Pace, correct?"

"Yes. I have a copy of that, too, if you'd like to see it."

"Thank you, but I have a copy. Randall County administration has gone on record stating that the lawsuit is retaliatory after Sheppard was fired from her job in 2015."

"Retaliatory?" Mary Beth's dark eyes grew flinty. "If we're talking about retaliation, let's talk about the fact that they fired her in the first place. She blew the whistle. Spoke up. Talked about what she saw go on in that shelter. Next thing she knows, they've accused her of leaving the drug cabinet unlocked. She was the only one supposed to have the keys, but everybody knew Darrell and Eddie kept a spare set in the truck."

"Who is 'everybody?' "

"Maybe I should just say it was common knowledge."

The words hung for a moment, but Taylor waited. More was coming—she'd bet a year's salary on it.

Sure enough, Mary Beth continued. "When the Moutain Mafia wants you gone, you don't have to do anything wrong. They'll get you gone. They'll make you unhireable. They'll go after your family, your career—everything that matters. And they won't stop until there's just nothing left."

"Mountain Mafia?"

"The Good Old Boys. Whatever you want to call them."

Apt names for what Taylor had seen in action. Mountain Mafia indeed—jackass town cops, car rental offices. Crooked as a back road, the whole slimy lot.

"Elaina told me a lot of things about Darrell and Eddie," Mary Beth said. "It wasn't just animals—the neglect, and abuse. They're predators. They'd say disgusting things about women who'd come into the shelter looking to adopt a pet. Bring girlfriends into the building and have sex with them right there in the garage bay where they do all the killing. It's like they got off on it, all the death. They started in on Elaina, too—grabbed her breasts, her buttocks—talked about what they wanted to do to her. Inexcusable behavior, just sickening."

Taylor took a deep breath and steadied herself. Nobody liked hearing those sorts of things, not even her, and she'd heard it all.

"Sheppard filed a complaint about the shelter directly with the state inspector, right?" she asked. "Rather than through the online reporting process set up on the Department of Agriculture's website?"

"Elaina and the shelter inspector had known each other professionally for several years. But Elaina did file the right paperwork to lodge an official complaint, and she filed it anonymously."

"So how did the county find out she was the one who reported the abuse?"

"Easy. The information she gave could have only come from one person, and even anonymous complaints are public record. Elaina was terrified of repercussions—scared to death that Bostick would plant drugs in her car so they could get her on a bogus charge and throw her in prison."

"Was that a legitimate concern?"

"Are you kidding me?" Mary Beth had been composed until that point, but anger was starting to leach through, and her words had an edge. "Yes, it was a legitimate concern. They threatened her."

"Threatened her? How?"

"Some backhand comment on Facebook, I think. Enough to get the point across."

"Did she get a screen shot?"

Mary Beth gave a short laugh, filled with vitriol. "Let me explain something to you. Elaina Sheppard is a product of Southwest Virginia. You don't speak up, you don't fight back. You second-guess yourself about everything—maybe it really *is* my fault. If I would have just stayed quiet. If I would've just shut up. If I would've minded my own goddamned business. Her first thought was not to take a screen shot, Miss Beckett. It was oh lord, look what I've done. Look what a mess I've made. Look what I'm putting my family through. How can I fix this and just make it stop."

Taylor exchanged a look with Charles. He'd been listening quietly the whole time, on the other end of the sofa. The expression on his face didn't change, but she could have read the message in his dark eyes from across the room. *These details matter.*

"You get trained, after a while," Mary Beth said. "When you live in that kind of environment. You go along to get along. If you're stuck in that world and can't leave, it's the only way to survive. Elaina and her family finally moved to a different county. Even then, when she first came forward as a witness it took nearly a year of cajoling, comforting, talking to her until she even believed she had a case. She didn't think she could ever find the courage to go public. And when she did, the pushback nearly ruined her."

"Where does the sexual harassment lawsuit stand now?"

"Continuation after continuation. I'm sure the lawyers hope she'll just give up."

Yep. Tried and true tactic, effective more often than not.

"Okay," Taylor said, steering the conversation back on track. "Looking at the bigger picture—The Huffington Post recently published an article that states two different statistics about animal abuse. First, that animal abusers are five times as likely to commit violent acts against humans. Secondly, the article states that a child who witnesses animal abuse in the home is *eight times* as likely to engage in abusive behavior as an adult. Do you agree with this?"

Mary Beth didn't hesitate. "Oh, absolutely. It's a predictor of crime—of violent crime—a social issue, not a 'dog problem.' Even the FBI is tracking animal abuse now. The correlation is undeniable."

"If that's the case, why would the Commonwealth's Attorney in Randall County fail to act in such a clear-cut case of abuse and cruelty? It's all documented by the State Shelter Inspector," Taylor said. "A matter of record. People can FOIA the report."

"Because the CA doesn't have to do a damn thing that he doesn't want to do," Mary Beth said. "He answers to no one. He's an elected official, not an employee. And there is no oversight of his office at the state level."

Taylor jotted down a note to contact the Virginia State Attorney General's Office for clarity on that point.

"It's very hard to make people who are not from Southwest Virginia understand the dynamic over there," Mary Beth said. "The priorities of a good old boy society are not the priorities you and I are used to dealing with in a civilized world. Mountain communities are a closed culture. They all know each other's dirty little secrets and it's been that way for hundreds of years."

"So—what's the leverage? Blackmail? Extortion?"

Mary Beth gave a small, cynical laugh. "*Would* they blackmail each other? I have no doubt. But it's much simpler than that. Okay, let me see if I can explain this. The State Police rent their offices in the same building as the County Administrator. They all go to lunch together. They grew up together—played high school football together. The owner of the local television station is one of Nate Bostick's hunting buddies. Bostick's wife is the executive assistant to the state delegate right there in Randall county."

"Bostick—the Commonwealth's Attorney."

"Yes. It's all very incestuous. And let me tell you something else. Darrell and Eddie Pace have been harvesting ginseng out of season for years. I've heard they have barns full of it. This is big money we're talking about—upwards of a thousand dollars a pound. You take more than two-hundred-dollars-worth off someone else's property without their permission, and it's felony grand larceny. Jail time. You think the local State Police don't know what's going on? Come on. They all hunt coon together. Probably poach ginseng together, too. And none of them will rat on each other. Apply any pressure at all, and they'll just circle the wagons."

Taylor rubbed her forehead. Jesus, lord. "Couldn't the State Vet's Office do something about the shelter, though? Because that's within their purview."

"According to the law they could. They could contact law enforcement and ask for an investigation. Instead, they hash it out with civil penalties. Felony cruelty charges in Randall County? Just levy fines against the jurisdiction. Randall County ponies up a couple thousand dollars, and the ACOs who could tell everybody's dirty secrets just keep right on keeping on with no consequence whatsoever. And nobody's the wiser for any of it."

"Have animal rights organizations like the ASPCA, the Humane Society of the U.S., and PETA gotten involved?"

"Oh, please. Major national welfare groups like that have no authority at all, contrary to what all their donors and sponsors believe. They help when a jurisdiction reaches out. If a jurisdiction slams the door in their face, forget it." Mary Beth's expression hardened. "And PETA—why would anyone ask the highest kill private shelter in Virginia to do something about the highest kill municipal shelter in Virginia? That's completely counterintuitive."

Taylor blinked. "PETA runs a high kill shelter?"

"Oh, for God's sake—where have you been?" Mary Beth gave Taylor a long look. "PETA's kill rate has been as high as 95% in recent years. It's all right there on the VDACS online reporting website—you can go look for yourself. Anyone can."

"Vee Dacks?"

"Virginia Department of Agriculture and Consumer Services."

Taylor had to take a moment. Had to just stop, rub her eyes, and try a sip of coffee. And another. Stalling, giving herself a chance to think, consulting her notes. "So what about the Board of Supervisors meeting—the one where all the protestors showed up carrying signs? That didn't make an impression?"

"Of course it didn't." Mary Beth laughed. "Mabry's too damn arrogant to think opinions of the people matter."

"Bud Mabry—the County Administrator?"

"Yes."

"And he's the one who insists the shelter is now no-kill, therefore the county has responded appropriately?"

"Yes." Mary Beth nodded. "Because here's the thing—Mabry's a sleaze, but he's not stupid. He did manage to realize that Randall

County being the highest kill shelter in Virginia would invite scrutiny. And it *was* the highest kill municipal shelter in 2015. So he brings in the cavalry—a group of advocates from Eastern Virginia, who take over day-to-day shelter operations. And they're doing a fine job—for no pay. Rather than firing Darrell and Eddie and hiring competent staff, Mabry put the workload on volunteers who are looking to make a name for themselves, and kept Darrell and Eddie on as ACOs."

"Isn't that a good thing, though?" Throwing kerosene on a fire, but Taylor didn't care. She wanted to see how hot those flames would burn. "They solved the problem. Russell County now has one of the lowest kill rates in the state."

Mary Beth's eyes flashed. "Are you serious? What problem did it solve? Animals are still being victimized by those men, every day in Randall County. And think about the precedent—if you're an Animal Control Officer in the Commonwealth of Virginia, you can torture animals as a routine part of your job with complete impunity, because Darrell and Eddie Pace just proved that nobody's going to say a damn word to you about it."

Abruptly, Mary Beth rose from her chair, strode into the kitchen and set her coffee cup in the sink with a clatter. Came back, and faced Taylor with her arms crossed. "What's this really about? You told me on the phone you were working on a story. Then you show up with no crew, no cameras—I've seen you write one thing down since you've been here. If I didn't recognize both of you from WRCH broadcasts, I'd be starting to wonder what the hell you're playing at."

Taylor nodded. This was it—the breaking point she'd been waiting for, when Mary Beth dropped the pretense and just got real.

"Mary Beth, do you think Darrell and Eddie Pace are capable of violence against humans?"

"Of course I do," Mary Beth snapped. "Have you not listened to a damn word I've said?"

Okay, then. Taylor smiled.

She dug in her briefcase for a small collection of newspaper clippings about the murders. Once she found them, she placed them in Mary Beth's hand. "What do you think about this?"

Mary Beth looked at the clippings. Held them up one by one, studied them with a frown. Went back to her chair, found a pair of glasses on the end table beside it, then took a seat and read each one.

She handed the clippings back to Taylor. "Seal it up just right, and a big poly drum like that would work just as well as a PVC tube."

Taylor put the clippings back in her briefcase. "Do you understand why I'm here now?"

Mary Beth pulled her glasses off and folded the arms. "Maybe. Keep talking."

"That Supervisor's meeting," Taylor asked. "Was it recorded, by any chance? Does video exist?"

"One of our volunteers said a camera was on a tripod during the whole meeting," Mary Beth said. "And footage is supposed to be online somewhere. I haven't seen it, though."

"Do you think Mabry would give me the same spiel he gave for the Supervisors at that meeting? On camera?"

Mary Beth placed her glasses back on the end table. "I can't imagine why he wouldn't. Just one more chance to gloat. Stroke his ego. He'll tell you anything if you do that."

"If it turns out that Darrell and Eddie had something to do with those murders," Taylor said. "Can you see how video evidence of the County Administrator admitting he knew about the abuse and cruelty at the shelter—and doing nothing about it—could make one hell of a hand grenade in a civil case?"

Mary Beth said nothing for a long moment. She tapped her fingers on her mouth, stared out the window. When she looked at Taylor again, a whole new gleam shone in her dark eyes. "You could burn down the whole corner of the state with that."

Taylor held her gaze. "Yep."

Mary Beth sat forward in her chair. "What can I do to help?"

In the car, it took several miles of riding in complete silence before Charles said a word.

"Remind me to never get on your bad side," he said.

Taylor didn't take her eyes from the road. "Just don't kill innocent people and chop them into tiny pieces, and we'll probably be okay."

He didn't respond. But she could feel his gaze burning into the side of her face.

"Can you call Hennessey?" she asked. "We're going to need Kavanagh and Perry. And I have to swing back through Richmond to get some clothes to wear on camera. It'll add some drive time, but since we're on this side of the state ...."

"Fine with me," he said. "I'm along for the ride."

She glanced in his direction. He was poking at his phone, probably looking for Hennessey's number. "Bullshit." Might as well call him on it. "This has been your story from the beginning, as much as it was mine. You did all the heavy lifting, while I was in the weeds. Think I don't know that?"

He stopped poking the phone. "I tracked down information for you, Taylor, when you asked me to. I'm good at that. I helped you talk things through. I brought what I had to the table. But you're the one who wouldn't settle for the obvious. You took all the risks—with Hennessey, with the sources—you knew to sit on this thing, and I probably wouldn't have. It's all about the instinct. Knowing when to push, and when to pull back. Knowing when a story is not just a story. That's the difference between a reporter and a journalist. That's what *you* bring to the table."

Well, if he put it *that* way.

Taylor smiled. "In other words, Chuck—we make a damn good team."

CHAPTER TWENTY-SEVEN

"I want you to look me in the eye and tell me you didn't know about this." Taylor slammed the Donovan Report onto the desk in front of Sheriff Hastings and pinned it with a fingertip. "Because it's all there. Right—" Jab with the finger. "Fucking—" Another jab. "There."

Behind his desk, Hastings hadn't had time to stand after Taylor and Charles barged in. He looked up at her, reading glasses perched on his nose. Said nothing at first, just picked up the document and frowned.

"Yeah, I did see this," he said after he'd flipped a couple pages. "Couple years ago. I didn't read it all."

Taylor took a step back and folded her arms. "Well, you'd better read it now."

Hastings moved the papers already on his desk to make room for the report. He glanced at the open door.

"Want me to close this?" Charles asked, pointing.

"Yes, please." Over his glasses, Hastings watched Charles ease the door shut. "Thank you."

Charles took one of the wingbacks in front of Hastings' desk and Taylor took the other. They sat. And waited.

After a few minutes, Hastings thumped the pages lightly with the backs of his fingers. "What is it you want me to do with this?"

"Flip to the sticky tab," Charles said.

Hastings did. And started reading again.

It started with a slow loss of color, the moment understanding dawned for Sheriff Hastings. Taylor watched, rapt, afraid to blink. Muscles in his face began to go slack, tiny ones at first, then his hairline crept up and back as his forehead lost all its creases. From watching his eyes, Taylor could tell he'd stopped reading. He was just sitting there, staring at the page they had marked with a sticky tab— the page that talked about suffocation tubes.

After another several seconds, he stretched his jaw down, touched a finger to the side of his neck like his ears were popping. Taylor knew why. Sometimes the shock of seeing what you didn't want to know could feel almost physical.

He looked at her, shallow breaths causing his shoulders to rise and fall with a subtle but quick tempo. "I still don't know what you want me to do with this."

"Come the fuck on," she said. "Really?"

Hastings laid the report on his desk and took off his glasses. He rubbed his eyes, rubbed his jaw, and his forehead, too, while he was at it.

"You know what word I'm about to use, don't you?" he asked.

Of course she knew. Circumstantial. "I'm way ahead of you on that. But this gives you your first real person of interest and you know it."

Hastings rested his forehead against his hands and just sat there. For a while.

Finally, he sighed and looked up. "We have the DNA recovered from Hess." He pointed to the report. "This isn't enough to get a warrant for a swab. Not by the stretch of anybody's imagination. But we could always just ask and see what hits the fan."

Taylor nodded. "I need you to give me twenty-four hours first, before you approach anyone about a swab."

His eyes narrowed. "What?"

"I have some things I need to do," she said. "Balls I need to put in play. You're just going to have to trust me."

"If you think Darrell and Eddie had something to do with killing those boys," Hastings said. "Twenty-four hours is enough time for a lot of things to happen."

"That's why you put eyes on them," she said. "Round the clock." She took a deep breath, held it a few seconds, and released it slowly. "And don't tell the State Police any of this."

He pinched the bridge of his nose between a thumb and forefinger. "Shit."

Another pause. Time to be really careful what she said, and what she asked. "So tell me—have Darrell and Eddie's names ever come up? At all?"

"No," he said with no hesitation, no uncertainty. "Not that I've heard."

"But everybody from Nate Bostick all the way to the SAG's office in Richmond knew what was going on at that shelter."

"I can't comment about that, Taylor." Hastings grimaced. "The Sheriff's Office has nothing to do with animal control, or the shelter, or those allegations. We never investigated."

"All those crazy animal rights people, huh?" She said it with a half-smile. "So easy to just lump them all in the nut basket and toss it overboard."

The look on his face said it all.

Taylor stood. Beside her, Charles did the same.

"If I were a betting woman," she said. "I'd lay a bundle on the odds that the next victim you find won't have any mechanism of death at all, other than finally just running out of air. Whichever Pace did this didn't have the guts at first to just seal them up and throw them over the mountain. But he was working up to it. And thanks to everybody ignoring that report, four men are dead, four families are ripped apart, four futures gone to hell. God knows how many more are out there that nobody's found yet. Right now it's looking like you're okay in all this, Hastings, but get your house in order. Because scorched earth is nothing compared to what I'm capable of. Trust me on that one."

Charles had started to complain about the lack of decent takeout meals, so after they left Hastings' office, they stopped by a Chinese buffet where he could pick and choose between preservatives. It was late afternoon by the time they finally got back to the hotel. Bellies full, they settled in for a long evening with all the documentation and photocopies Mary Beth had sent back with them.

"So what's the story with this veterinarian?" Charles asked, holding a copy of an invoice. "There's just so much—hell, I can't keep track."

Taylor kicked off her shoes and padded barefoot to the bed, where her briefcase sat. "She's the one who stood up at the

Supervisors meeting last year with Bud Mabry and refuted the State Shelter Inspector's report from September of 2015." Taylor opened her briefcase and took out an enlarged photo. "She said the dog that was lying there paddling in its own feces had only been down for one day when Hamlin took the photo. The eyewitness disagrees. Sheppard says the dog lay there for eight days like that, on concrete, unable to get up, unable to eat or drink. No veterinary care or comfort provided."

Charles took the photo from her. "Well, ain't this just cozy."

The image showed Dr. Gretchen Morehouse sitting beside Darrell Pace at the Supervisor's meeting. The wall behind them was lined with sign-carrying protestors, several of them holding a gruesome, pitiful image of the dog in question.

"Want me to hang this up?" he asked.

"Yeah—" Taylor frowned. "I'm just not sure where yet." She pointed to the rows of Supervisors. "Put it here. We have another one of Darrell we can put under the victims."

"Humor me, Sunshine." Charles pointed to the veterinarian. "What's her deal again?"

"Her uncle's a District Court judge. She went to vet school, came home, opened a practice, and bam. Suddenly she's the county go-to. Mary Beth FOIAed the RFP—Request For Proposal—that should exist when a job in the county comes up for bid. No such document exists. No contract, nothing. So Mary Beth FOIAed the paper trail that would show every other vet in the county declining to accept shelter and animal control patients, which is the only way the contract should be defaulted to Morehouse without an RFP."

From her briefcase, she pulled a photocopy of a lined notepad page covered in handwriting. "This is supposedly the log of phone calls made to each veterinarian practicing in the county and their response about treating shelter or animal control patients. This—" She waved the photocopy. "Is not acceptable. The county needs signatures from each and every veterinarian who opted out of that agreement. Not just some notes scribbled in the margin by a county employee."

Taylor put the photocopy back in her briefcase. "Then, Mary Beth called each of these veterinarians herself to confirm they'd actually declined. Two of them said yes, that they'd spoken with the county and the notes in the margin were correct. Two others said they'd never received a phone call at all. One of those vets actually has his office staff keep physical records of all messages on their machine complete with time and date. That veterinarian pulled those old message books out of archives, and there was no record whatsoever of a message when the county employee's notes specified they left one."

Charles nodded. "So basically, the county shoehorned Morehouse right into their contract for county vet, to the exclusion of all other vets in the area."

"Exactly."

"Because her uncle's a District Judge."

"And because her family owns land. Lots and lots and lots of land. They're old guard—several generations."

"Aha." Charles nodded.

"It looks good at a glance. Morehouse does low cost spay and neuter for animals adopted from the shelter—the name of her clinic is even in the adoption contract. She's not making any money off those surgeries. In fact, she's probably going in the hole. But what all that amounts to is that the county is setting her up with a nice little loss leader, funneling all new pet owners who adopt from the shelter to her clinic exclusively. Some may have their own vets, but there's no low-cost option if they use them. So she's gaining clients from shelter adoptions. And other vets in the area just get shut out."

"Because of who her family is."

"Bingo." Taylor pulled another stack of papers from her briefcase. "All of this is illegal as hell. It's collusion. But the dollar amounts for each individual little honey hole that I'm finding in this county are not significant enough to interest the feds. If the community weren't happily snoring away, some well-placed votes could end all of this. But then again—nobody but old guard gets to run for office."

Charles nodded. "The Facebook thing."

"Yep."

"Okay, you're going to have to start from scratch on that one," he said. "I think I was in the bathroom."

Taylor laughed. "I think you were, actually." From the papers in her hand, she pulled a screenshot of a Facebook post, dated October of the previous year. She handed it to him. "Some hotshot whippersnapper transplanted here from Texas. He had big ideas about running on the Republican ticket for CA. He wanted to unseat Nate Bostick, the Democratic incumbent. Now, some evidence exists that Mr. Texas may not have been the best candidate either, but that doesn't matter in the context of this story. From out of nowhere springs a smear campaign. Front page of Sonny Heflin's Supervisor-controlled weekly rag—a mug shot of Mr. Texas from 2004, before he got his law degree—drunk driving and disorderly conduct. He was twenty-two at the time."

She gave the photocopy to Charles. He held that in one hand, the Facebook screenshot in the other. Then she gave him an inkjet-printed photo of a hot dog stand that he held together with the newspaper picture. "A young couple from North Carolina opened this in the spring of 2014. They renovated an old Joy gas station and were doing a pretty good business. It was in a great location, right in town. They offered use of their facility to Mr. Texas so he could do his stump speeches. It was a good day for local Republicans. Big turnout.

"The next day—" She pointed to the Facebook screenshot he held. "That appears. It's a post by Tommy Pratt, Chairman of the Board of Supervisors. 'Business folk better be careful who they support.' Within twelve hours, every Democrat in town, including the family of the incumbent Clerk of Court up for re-election, was on social media calling for a boycott of the hot dog stand. It nearly put them out of business, Charles. They hung on, but not too long afterward, the husband gave up and went home to North Carolina. Marital problems or did he just get tired of the bullshit? Hard to say. But Bostick won the election. Call it another win for the Mountain Mafia."

Charles lay all the papers he held on the table and leaned back against it. "Jesus Christ. This is partisan bullshit?"

"Not really. Not by our standards, anyway. I doubt either Convention would claim any of them. It's just the Good Old Boys Club." She frowned. "Most of this isn't criminal. Nothing to interest the feds. But all this goes to show how the political bullying happens, and how the whole disorganized crime network here gets away with it time and again."

"Out in the open, too," Charles said. "They're bold."

"But before you start feeling too sorry for the poor downtrodden, I want to show you something else I found myself, just Googling around."

Charles laughed out loud. "Flog that search engine," he said. "I'm proud of you."

She showed him the last piece of paper she held in her hand. It was a printout of a Topix post, dated 2016.

"A little backstory," she said. "Are you familiar with an NFL wide receiver named Travis Stiltner?"

"Oh, yeah." Charles grinned, rubbing his chin. "Seahawks, Packers, Bears…."

"That would be him, yes. Well, he was born and raised in Randall County."

"No shit." The chin-rubbing stopped and Charles' hand floated there for a few seconds before dropping to his side. "Really?"

"In 2010, he opened a non-profit learning center here for kids. Put almost two million dollars of his own money in it. The program showed steady growth, and kids were getting involved. They had a concert every year to raise money—had some pretty big names on stage. Eventually Stiltner approached several leaders in the community about help with funding. They shot him down cold."

Charles didn't say anything. Just looked at her, brows raised.

"No outcry, nothing in the media. But here, in the Topix forum, we get an idea what the community was thinking."

Rather than hand the paper to him, Taylor read the short paragraph out loud. " 'I don't remember this whole learning center being something that our towns would eventually have to fund. I remember Mr. Stiltner starting these programs, but I do not ever remember hearing that eventually taxpayers would have to help with the funding of these programs. I think it's shameful to ask for money when our towns didn't know we were responsible for doing so in the first place.' "

Charles rolled his eyes. "Oh, for the love of God."

"It gets worse." She read the next portion of highlighted text. " 'Travis Stiltner's earnings are like, ninety million. He should just fund the thing and quit begging for money.' "

"Trolls," Charles said. "Fucking trolls."

"Maybe. One or two people spoke up complaining about those comments. But at the end of the day, the learning center disappeared.

The county just let it go. It meant nothing to anyone here. At least not enough to fight for."

Charles shook his head slowly.

"How do you help that kind of ignorance?" she asked. "What do you do for a whole community full of philanthropic cripples?"

He raised both hands, palms facing upward. "Hell if I know. Is it even worth digging through all this shit? You've scratched the surface, enough to see what's underneath. Just kick some dirt back over it and keep moving."

"I don't think I can do that," she said. "Ethically, I'm obligated."

"Okay, then. So let's talk about this. Bring it home for me—what are we looking at here?"

"Are you asking because you don't know, or because you want to hear me say it?"

"I want to hear you say it. I want to know how you've sifted all this down."

She sighed. "Well, we're looking at two completely separate problems. And they're going to have two completely separate solutions." She held one hand out to the side, cupping air. "Here, you have criminal." She mirrored the action with her other hand. "Here, civil. The criminal issues don't have a through-line. They're a hundred little brush fires burning just below the threshold. It's not organized. There's no leader, no kingpin. Just a way of doing things that probably goes back several generations. It's a Gordian's Knot, and it's going to take a long time and a lot of commitment to untangle it."

He nodded. "Go on."

"But the murders—not so much the actual homicides, but the fact that you have a serial killer honing his skills in full purview of the local government … that's a problem. That's a class action suit with the potential to bankrupt this county. That's where my focus keeps going. Let the feds have a crack at the other stuff, like they did with Operation Big Coon Dog in Buchanan County. We'll find a way to get them interested. But this other part—the civil side of it—this is huge. This is my story."

He grinned, and chuckled. Then it blossomed into a full-blown laugh. "That's my girl." His smile lasted another few heartbeats before it faded. "Fairly common 'tell'—politicians balk at paying for something with a proven track record, you can usually find a conflict of interest between how the public's money is supposed to be used, and how they're actually spending it."

"Right. So, next step—I need to bait a few traps. Get some things on camera. I have some ideas, but—"

A sharp knock at the door chased her next words so far away she couldn't even remember what she'd been about to say.

She looked at Charles. "Expecting anyone?"

He shook his head. "I was about to ask you the same thing."

Taylor padded across the room and looked through the peephole. Eric Blevins, and he didn't look happy.

She opened the door.

Two days' worth of beard on his chin, rumpled clothes. Hair standing on end and dark rings under his eyes. So dirty he looked like he'd been dragged behind a tractor.

"I don't have anywhere else to go," he said. "Can I come in?"

CHAPTER TWENTY-EIGHT

The sound of the dryer thumping and bumping behind her had almost lulled Taylor to sleep on her feet when Charles walked into the hotel's coin laundry with two Styrofoam coffee cups in his hands. He offered her one.

"This close to bed time?" she asked.

"It's decaf."

She took the one he offered and blew on it. "This from the coffeemaker by the office?"

"Yeah. They got the whole lobby smelling like Starbucks." He leaned back against the dryer next to the one tumbling the last bit of moisture from Eric's clothes and took a careful sip. "Hoo—not tasting like it, though."

Taylor smiled. "He asleep?"

Charles nodded. "Out as soon as his head hit the pillow. Good thing my room's a double."

"Poor kid. This is all my fault."

"Don't start blaming yourself, Sunshine. His life was fucked up a long time before you ever rolled into town."

"Yeah, Chuck, but he wouldn't be digging up sewer lines and sleeping in his car if he hadn't talked to me."

Charles looked at her for a couple beats, corners of his eyes crinkling with a smirk that didn't fully materialize. "Think his grandparents will let him come back home?"

She nodded. "Of course they will. They're all co-dependent. Well, maybe not Eric—yet. But we're all a product of our environment. He doesn't have a chance."

"Yes, he does."

Taylor looked at him sideways. "How?"

"You."

"Me?"

"Who did he come to when he needed somebody? You sat in there tonight and listened to him for three and a half hours. I've never seen this side of you. Taylor. I like it."

She didn't say anything. Just stared into her coffee cup.

"Kid's got a lot of anger," Charles said. "Said he threatened to kill his grandfather. And I don't know—you get a boy all twisted around like he is right now, hard to say what he'll do."

Taylor shook her head and then squeezed her eyes shut. Stood there with the world blocked out for a moment, breathing in the scent of dryer sheets and hot lint.

Eventually she forced herself to rejoin the conversation. "I'm just glad he's getting it all *out*. I've been working on that, helping him to not be so shut down—to talk—I mean, we can't expect him to get it right the first time he says what he thinks. There's a learning curve."

Charles shot her a look with his brows raised. "You're one to talk about being shut down."

"I know." She didn't even bother with denial. "And that means I know how much damage all that rage can do bouncing around inside with no way out. He's just a kid. And I gotta say this—part of me thinks his grandmother needed to hear every word he said to her. More, maybe. Yeah, he should apologize, but goddamn. They owe him an apology, too."

"He grew up in a toxic environment," Charles said. "No doubt about that. I understand these mountain people have a heritage they want to romanticize, like it's an American pearl. But if your way of life is destroying your children, you don't get to treasure it, and you don't get to hang on to it. You figure out where the hell you went wrong, and you fix it."

Taylor took a slow sip of coffee and thought for a minute.

"So, were you taking notes?" she asked after a bit. "All that stuff he said about the PSA? Because I wasn't."

"Yeah. I wrote a lot of it down."

She glanced at the timer on the dryer to see how long they had to discuss it. Fifteen minutes.

"From memory," she said. "What I got about nonpayment cut-offs is that somewhere in Virginia legal code, there's language about giving a written notice ten days before termination of service. But the county attorney here has told the PSA Administrator that printing a generic message on their water bills about cut-offs being the last Tuesday of the month is all they need to do."

"Right." Charles took another sip of coffee.

"The PSA doesn't have online account access, so there's no way for customers to check their balance. They can call, but may not think to do that until they don't have water. And cut-offs are quick— exactly thirty-one days from the bill that's unpaid, service is subject to be interrupted. No grace period, no warning, nothing."

She set her coffee on top of the dryer. "Think about how many of the people here live on a government check. It's a disproportionate number—almost thirty percent of the population. If payout is first of the month, and cut-offs are at the end of the month, that increases the likelihood that a customer can't come up with the money to prevent the interruption of service. And that seems deliberate to me."

"Pretty shitty."

"When customers complain that they got no notice, they're told the warning about cut-offs is printed on every bill. But here's the thing—does that satisfy the language in Virginia code? Or has Randall County been doing illegal cut-offs for years and racking up on the reconnect fees?"

"That's a question for a lawyer," Charles said. "And I'd damn sure ask it."

"I'm going to send a FOIA request for the total amount of reconnect fees they've collected over the past five years. And I'm also going to request the total of new service deposits for the same time period. Because apparently, another section of Virginia code stipulates they have to return all deposits after service has been established for a year. Eric seems to think they haven't refunded a dime of any deposit to anyone—ever."

He folded one arm under the other holding his coffee cup. "You may run into the fact that with the PSA being a service authority and not a utility company, that code may not be enforceable."

"Yes." Taylor nodded. "Again, a question for a lawyer. But even if the county attorney has been clever enough to find them a legal loophole so they can ass-fuck their customers, that doesn't make it right. It's perfectly legal to pull all the wings off houseflies and leave them crawling around on the windowsill, but what does it say about you as a human being if you do that? Laws don't get the final word. Not always."

"No," Charles said. "The voters do."

"But if the voters have no choices—" Taylor picked her coffee back up and slugged it. "What the hell are they supposed to do?"

Eric left for work the next morning before she woke up. Charles told her he'd seemed in better spirits, not great, but rested and coherent. He'd made sure Eric had a hot breakfast from the spread downstairs and sent him on his way with a friendly smile. Underrated, those friendly smiles. They could set the tone for a whole day, dial optimism up to life-changing levels. And nobody could give one better than Charles.

Kavanagh and Perry rolled up in front of the hotel at ten minutes after nine. As per Taylor's instructions, they drove an unmarked WRCH van and brought two cameras. They took a while getting checked in and settled in their rooms, which was fine. It gave Taylor a chance to read over her notes one last time and square up with herself in the mirror about the ethics of completely misleading an interview subject.

County Administrator Bud Mabry had agreed to talk to her with no conditions. Surprising, until she remembered how cocky he'd been in all his recorded interviews, and how confident he seemed about the animal shelter's recent performance. Would he give her the same song and dance he'd given everyone at the Board of Supervisor's meeting, when animal rights protestors had lined the walls and demanded action against Darrell and Eddie Pace? Please God, let him. She didn't need footage of him discussing veterinarians or RFPs or PSA water cut-offs. She needed him talking about the shelter, only the shelter, and all the reasons that September 2015 State Shelter Inspector's report wasn't worth the paper it was printed on.

Bud Mabry's office was in a low-slung brick and stucco complex that sprawled at the base of a steep mountainside. It might have been a strip mall at one time, or some type of big retail venture. Now commandeered for office space and outfitted accordingly, it pleased the senses with cute little planters of geraniums and a breezy entrance where old sepia photos of the area hung in a well-conceived display.

Hey, at least somebody was trying.

He met them in the large reception lobby with his right hand extended. "Hi," he said. "Bud Mabry. Pleased to meet you, Miss Beckett."

She shook his hand and made appropriate pleasantries, then introduced her crew. Didn't identify Charles as a fellow reporter, just a cameraman.

Mabry was a strapping fellow, with broad shoulders and large, strong hands. Farming background? His youth spent slinging hay bales and footballs? Thinning brown hair, moustache. Features—even his eyes—that seemed pulled to the center, like someone had taken his nose while his face was forming and given it a good, hard tug. He was a native. That much she'd learned. Alumnus of a local community college, with online post-graduate studies and an MBA. Best she could tell, he'd never lived anywhere but Randall County.

He led them to a meeting room directly off the lobby. Perry busied himself setting up both cameras, squinting at the overhead lights and tweaking the blinds on the window. White walls, all the way around. Taylor couldn't resist a grin, but she hid it behind her hand. Big difference between Mabry and Hastings. Before she'd gotten to know him a little better, Hastings had seemed presumptuous with his grey backdrop and clamshell lighting. Now, she saw it as just another small touch of professionalism, one more tiny detail that showed he actually gave a shit.

Taylor had no desire to be on camera at any point during the interview. She'd made sure Perry knew this well in advance. This was Mabry's moment to shine, and she'd let him talk until he had nothing left to say. But for show, she had Charles pretend to operate a second camera with the lens focused on her. That would make it seem they were after a feature story, not just a sound bite—or evidence.

"I'm interested," she said once Mabry was seated and miked. "In the big turnaround at your animal shelter. A 2014 Mayor's Study published by Boston University showed that many thriving American cities have a commitment to no-kill sheltering." She kept her diction elevated, almost formal. "In the survey, a cross-section of community leaders were asked what ideas they gleaned from those thriving cities, and of the forty-eight 'ideas' listed, one of them was a no-kill animal shelter. Randall County is the only municipality in Southwest Virginia showing such dedicated initiative. And that's what I want to talk to you about."

Booyah. Perfect delivery.

Mabry smiled. Ear to ear, the cat that ate the Peabody. "Oh, that's wonderful. Because I'd love to talk about that as well."

"Tell me about your kill rates." She adopted jargon she'd learned from Mary Beth Donovan's report. "Especially between 2015 and last year."

"Before we initiated no-kill strategies, our local shelter was euthanizing up to sixty-six percent of all animals in its care. Our last reporting cycle to the state, we submitted figures that demonstrate our kill rate has dropped to less than half of one percent. We euthanize so few animals at the Randall County Animal Shelter that we've surrendered our DEA license to possess those drugs and currently have no staff with current certification."

Good lord. Like he really thought people wouldn't know the real reason?

Taylor shook it off and smiled, a regular fan. Wide eyes, bat the lashes. "So how did you do it?"

"We met with a group of humane society volunteers from Eastern Virginia and hashed out a plan." He went on to describe their trap-neuter-release program for cats and intake counseling procedures, straight from the No-Kill Advocacy Handbook she'd read online. "Our volunteers frequently do adoption events out in the community, and they also run a separate Facebook page to promote community awareness and adoptions."

"The 'Friends Of Randall County Animal Shelter' page."

"Yes." He lowered his gaze and poked at a nonexistent spot on the table, aiming his aw-shucks grin at the floor. "If I'd thought about it, I could have had some of them meet with us today, so you could talk to them, too."

"That's okay," she said. "I can always meet with them individually. Maybe go to the shelter, do a feature there." *Bullshit.* Taylor hadn't the slightest bit of interest in those volunteers. She had no beef with them. To her, it sounded like they had their act together. Too bad the ones not getting paid were the ones doing all the work.

"We also transport dogs out of the area and out of state if necessary," he continued. "To no-kill shelters that can find homes for them. The county voted last year to purchase a van specifically for the animal shelter, and we can fit up to thirty dogs at a time on it for long trips."

"That's wonderful," she said. "And this is all done by volunteers—not employees?"

"Yes. We're very proud of our volunteer base. It's a sign of a healthy community, when people step up to help in these ways."

It took every bit of self-control she possessed to not share a glance with Charles. She felt his eyes on her, unspoken words burning up the air between them.

But willpower won, and she kept her gaze fixed firmly on Mabry. "What about paid staff?"

In his eyes, not a flicker of caution. Just pride, reckless and smug. "We have two animal control officers who do a wonderful job. They're out and about in the county, picking up strays and handling nuisance calls. They've both been employed with us for many years."

Time to bring it home.

"There was some scandal, wasn't there? Recently? About those two?" Lean toward him, just a little. Maintain eye contact. Reassure. "Would you like to say a word about that, for people who may have heard some things?"

Mabry frowned. "Unfortunately, there are always people who want to make trouble. Disgruntled employees, and whatnot. So, yes. I would like to say some things, actually." He reached toward the chair beside him and picked up a stack of papers and graphs and charts from the seat, and copies of the report Taylor recognized from the State Shelter Inspector. "It concerned us that we'd had an inspection only four weeks prior to the one in September of 2015 that showed no violations—no major deficiencies. We had learned of an existing relationship between the State Shelter Inspector and the former employee who lodged those complaints. To us, that casts suspicion on the whole inspection report."

He proceeded to show her copies of the report with blank signature lines circled, which according to his explanation, voided the entire document. "This report should never even have been a matter of record," he said. "Seeing as how it was filed improperly with the state to begin with."

Taylor listened. She didn't interrupt. She smiled on cue. Nodded encouragingly.

But what a crock of shit. A missing signature meant those poor animals didn't actually suffer? The fact that that Teresa Hamlin, State Shelter Inspector, and Elaina Sheppard, the whistleblower, had a friendship outside their professional capacity meant the skunks and opossums and raccoons that died in those tubes didn't actually suffocate?

Go there. She knew she had to.

"What about the suffocation tubes?" she asked. "That sounds so gruesome."

"There were no suffocation tubes," he said. "Those airtight PVC devices were to control odor from roadkill picked up by our animal control officers."

Taylor itched to remind him that no dead wildlife had been picked up at all by Darrell and Eddie Pace in the year 2015, at least according to the yearly report submitted to VDACS, the Virginia Department of Agriculture and Consumer Services. But she said nothing. Just let him talk.

When he ran out of steam about the tubes, she asked, "In light of all the allegations about abuse and torture, and the admission by those two animal control officers of having Schedule II drugs in their possession—" She took a breath for the next mouthful. "And verbal acknowledgment that animals in the shelter in need of veterinary care did not receive it, what would you say to people about the reasons they're still employed by Randall County?"

"I'd say that no criminal charges were ever filed." No smile now, and his words had an edge. "Had the State Police, or the Commonwealth's Attorney seen any evidence of illegal activity, we'd be talking about an entirely different ballgame here. The Randall County Circuit Court even appointed a special prosecutor from outside this jurisdiction. His report concluded that the matter of the Schedule II drugs was one of policy and technicality, not legality. And he said there was no way a jury of peers would convict even if they did bring charges."

She'd pushed him hard enough. Any more, and he'd get suspicious. So she cheerfully accepted his answer and moved on to the charts he'd placed on the table, line graphs that showed how Randall County ranked among other shelters in the state.

Bud Mabry rambled for another half hour before he finally exhausted his supply of canned spin. Taylor posed and smiled at all right times, kept him talking, kept winding him up. At the end of the interview, he shook her hand again, but this time placed his left hand on top and thanked her sincerely for her time.

It was everything she could do to walk calmly out of the building. But she did, head held high, barely glancing at Kavanagh and Perry as they all moved toward the van. Behind her, she could sense Charles in a similar state of agitation, but he said nothing.

Kavanagh slung his equipment bag in the back of the van with a little less care than normal. "What the hell was that about, Beckett?" he asked. "Felt a little bit like you went soft in there."

Taylor looked around, grateful that the body of the van blocked the view of anyone who might be looking out county administration windows. And then she let it out, a protracted growl of pent-up tension—and maybe just a little bit of predatory aggression, a lion celebrating the kill.

She ignored the slack-jawed stares coming at her from everybody at the van. "I promise you," she reassured Kavanagh. "We'll go to air with a story. And who knows—we may even use some of what we got just now. But today? I wasn't doing the news." She patted him on the bicep. "I was building a case for those families. And that cockeyed son of a bitch gave me everything I needed."

She set her own bag between the van seats and didn't look directly at Kavanagh. But she paid attention from the corner of her eye. He remained in place for several seconds, lips pursed. Thinking. She could almost hear the wheels turn.

Then he chuckled. Silently at first, but out loud as he finally realized what they'd just done. He spread his arms, palms facing forward. Tipped his head back, and laughed up at the sky.

CHAPTER TWENTY-NINE

When the fourth victim's parents agreed to see her, Taylor felt a surge of hope. Cody Hess had lived in Roanoke, light years removed from Randall County. To hear some tell it, Roanoke lay on the easternmost edge of Southwest Virginia. Geographically, perhaps. But culturally? Not a chance. Cody's people would have a completely different mindset about challenging the status quo and holding the system responsible. In fact, they seemed eager for a meeting. So eager that they invited her to visit that evening, and Taylor took them up on it.

"What about Blevins?" Charles asked, while he and Taylor waited in the van outside a Subway down the street from Mabry's office. "Think he'll be alright at the hotel by himself tonight?"

"He's nineteen," Taylor said, watching Kavanagh and Perry's progress in line through the plate glass storefront. Would they remember to get spinach greens instead of iceberg lettuce on her Club? She'd told them twice. "Not like he needs a babysitter."

"I'm not talking about that." Charles cracked his window, letting in a rush of warm air. "Just being alone—I don't think he's going to benefit from having spare time on his hands right now. Too much stuff rolling around in his head. Boy needs a distraction."

"Does he even have a keycard for the room?"

"Yeah. I got him one this morning before he left."

Taylor almost smiled. "He's getting to you, too, isn't he?"

Charles made a small noise like a grunt. "I'm not made of stone."

They exchanged a sideways look, held each other's gaze for a few seconds, and both looked away at the same time.

"If you don't need me on the Roanoke thing," Charles said. "I'll stay here and keep an eye on him."

"I can text him and see what his plans are."

"Tell him we can go to Bristol—or somewhere—do the guy thing. Seems like he could use some of that."

"I agree." Taylor typed a quick message to Eric. "Just feed him. A steak. Half a cow. All-you-can-eat buffet. Make sure the kid has a good dinner."

Charles laughed. "Aaaight, Mama. I will."

Taylor's turn to make a noise like a grunt.

"Hey," Charles said, and his tone sounded odd. "Look there. What's he doing here?"

Taylor followed his finger and saw a black Charger cruise slowly through the parking lot. It was unmarked, but even from where she sat, Taylor recognized law enforcement.

It pulled alongside the van and Sheriff Hastings looked up at her from behind the wheel. He made a circling motion with his finger indicating she should lower her window.

She did. "Well, hello. Fancy meeting you here."

"Development," he said simply.

"What happened?"

"I sent a car out looking for Darrell. Real casual, laid back—told him we were swabbing county employees to rule out a match for a case where there might have been cross-contamination. It was sketchy, but he bought it. Didn't hesitate. Came right in and had it done."

"Holy shit."

"I'm not sure what that means." He squinted at her. "Not the reaction I expected."

"Did he know about the DNA evidence from Hess?"

"I would imagine. It's been in the news."

Taylor rubbed her forehead. "Wow. Guess that rules him out."

"The Crime Lab's always backed up," he said. "So I sent it to a private lab I've worked with off and on since Knoxville. If you give them a good enough sample and are willing to pay for it, they'll expedite. These days they have the technology to turn it around in as little as forty-eight hours. Costs a chunk, and it'll probably bite me in the ass. But we need an answer."

"What about Eddie?"

"He's off today. Darrel said he's in Elizabethton with some girl."

"Thought you had a tail on him."

"We do—within the county," Hastings said. "Once he crosses that line, we don't follow. And hell, he went all the way to Tennessee."

Taylor sighed. "Well, please keep me posted. And thank you for letting me know."

"Sure thing." He raised a few fingers in the way of a goodbye and drove on.

Charles stared at her. "How in the hell did he know where to find you?"

Taylor shrugged and gave him a rueful smile. "They probably know where I am at any given minute."

"Until you go to Roanoke tonight. They won't cross that county line, remember."

"Right," she said. "And I'll bet Eddie knows that."

Cody Hess' parents lived in a neighborhood between Roanoke and Salem, where all the homes were made from industrial brick and shaped like boxes. Kids' toys lay scattered in the yards, colorful bicycles, trampolines, and the occasional bright blue above-ground pool—these were working-class people, but they still had hope. Lives and community in good repair. They'd not retreated into a haze of addictions—drugs, alcohol, welfare, or coal. It made an interesting study in contrasts with the southwest corner of the state, and the sociology major Taylor never became took note.

Sharon Hess opened the door, flanked by her husband, Greg, and a girl of about twelve who Taylor guessed was the baby sister, Caitie. The middle sibling, Connor, wasn't with them.

"Hi." Sharon waved them in. "Thank you all so much for coming."

Taylor waited until everyone was inside, including Perry with the camera, before she replied. "Mrs. Hess, it's me who needs to thank you. You just don't know how much this means, that you're willing to talk to us."

"Please call me Sharon." Cody's mom smiled, her features tired, but still attractive in a suburban housewife kind of way.

Except she wasn't a housewife. Taylor had learned everything she could about the family from news archives and social media. Good people, or so it seemed. Sharon worked in the office of a local Montessori school. Greg was a shift supervisor at a nearby tire manufacturing plant. Everyday folk who didn't deserve to be front and center of a gruesome crime story.

Nobody did.

Taylor blinked that thought away before it took root. Nope. Wasn't going there right now. Couldn't.

"I'm going to let my production crew get set up—maybe over there by that window? That's still good light and will be for another hour or so." Then Taylor pointed to the photos hanging on one wall of the living room, many of Cody, smiling with his whole life ahead of him. "Can you tell me about these pictures?"

Sharon took them through a lifetime of young boy, from Tonka trucks and trains in the dirt outside, to fishing on Claytor Lake, to high school wrestling and prom, and graduation. First car. First year of college. Her son had been a real cutie—brown hair and green eyes, not very tall but solid as a tree trunk. Well-muscled. Middleweight wrestler, All-State his last two years of high school. Taylor had never met Eddie Pace, but she'd seen plenty of photos. No way he could have overpowered this kid with his bare hands. Pace was tall and lanky but short on substance. She didn't even want to imagine the gear he must have needed to control his victim—*this* victim— physically.

But what would have brought them together in the first place? Why had they crossed paths, and what was it about Cody that triggered the killer?

Taylor went back to the photo of Cody at Claytor Lake, still a scrawny kid at the time, holding a largemouth bass that must have weighed at least ten pounds. "Was he into this kind of thing? Fishing? Outdoor stuff?"

Sharon nodded. "He loved it. Always wished we lived out in the country, where he'd have land to ramble."

Land.

Something Southwest Virginia had a nearly unlimited supply of.

Kavanagh beckoned from the living room. "We're ready if you are."

They all took their places where he instructed, and this time, Taylor had legitimately prepped to be on camera. This was real, no manipulation on any level. She was there to tell Cody Hess' story, to turn him from a half-rotted corpse in a barrel to a real, flesh and blood young man on the verge of a brilliant future. As an adult, he would have been productive in society, an influence on everything he touched, and left a mark on the world. Now, all that had been ripped away. Potentials untapped. A loss humanity would never understand or appreciate, unless somebody spelled it out for them. To hell with four inches of follow-up on page three. Cody Hess would finally get his moment.

She walked Sharon and Greg through moments of Cody's life as a child, through his school years, probing for tender spots, avoiding wounds that still bled. The last thing she wanted to do was destroy them on camera. Or at all. They talked about a precocious youngster, a kid always asking questions. An opinionated teenager, active in school debates and sometimes in trouble with the principal for arguing with a teacher. Under it all, a sweet, concerned human being who loved his family and never complained when they asked him to let his baby sister tag along. And the photos his parents gave them for use on air—Jesus, lord. Cody Hess had a smile that could break a person in half.

She wrapped the interview in less than half an hour. Any segment that went to air would be a fraction of that, so now it would be a matter of sifting down to the most evocative parts and editing for impact. She had software on her laptop to do that, but she also still worked with the video editing department back at WRCH for projects like this, when they had time to fine-tune the aesthetics. Taylor wanted those minutes of film to look good. Sound good. The details—like Hastings' clamshell lighting setup—those were critical, when the end goal was winning hearts and minds.

Kavanagh and Perry did the heavy lifting when it came to carrying equipment and packing the van, and Greg Hess helped. Taylor had only her briefcase to collect. Hard to drag that chore out, but she managed by shuffling a stack of handwritten notes a dozen times before she put them in. And eventually the living room cleared, except for Sharon Hess, who hovered and seemed to feel lost without some type of task to keep her busy.

Taylor smiled at her. "I have another question," she asked. Gently, because this was the big one.

Sharon perked up. "Sure." She took a few steps closer, arms folded, but face upturned and features relaxed.

Mixed signals. Hell—Taylor would take it over a total shutdown.

"I've talked with the Sheriff's Office quite a bit in Randall County." Taylor kept her voice low. "I do think they're running a good investigation. And they may have a lead or two."

Sharon's eyes grew wide. "Really?"

"So, here's my question. If it turns out that a negligent party enabled these crimes—not committed them, but had the opportunity to circumvent them and possibly prevent these deaths altogether—would you be interested in a civil action?"

Color drained noticeably from Sharon's face. One hand fluttered to her mouth. "Oh, my God."

"Please—" Taylor touched her arm. "Don't take this to heart just yet. But I have to know if any of the families would be willing to pursue this angle and stay with it until the end, or if it would just be too painful."

"What would they say about Cody? Would they drag him through the mud?"

"Is there mud?"

Sharon slowly shook her head. "Not that I know of. He was a good kid. But you know how lawyers are."

Yes, she certainly did. "I don't think so, in this case. Because if it ever got to that point, the trial would be over and someone would already be in prison. Any blame-the-victim mentality would probably backfire with a conviction on the books."

"Do you know who … enabled … these crimes?"

Taylor stood there for a moment, trying to think of a way to be honest without saying too much. "It depends on the identity of the killer. And we don't know that yet. But I think one scenario points to a degree of recklessness in the infrastructure of a certain local government that—if not criminal—is darn sure actionable."

Sharon drew in a quick breath and let it out slowly. "I'd have to talk to Greg, of course. But if somebody just stood by and let our boy get hurt …."

Taylor nodded. "I understand. And there's zero pressure to respond right now. This is all hypothetical at this point. I just wanted some idea how you felt about it."

Sharon nodded.

"I have one more question, though."

"Sure," Sharon said. "Anything."

"You said Cody liked outdoor things—fishing, and whatnot. Did he hunt?"

"Yes. Quite a bit. He could spend the whole fall season in the woods. We got him a rifle with a really nice scope for Christmas two years ago. He went out and bagged an eight-pointer the next day."

Taylor smiled with her, enjoying that memory vicariously. "So, it was deer, then. Anything else?"

"He hunted turkey sometimes," Sharon said. "I don't really know what all."

"What about coon?"

Sharon frowned. "I don't think so. Maybe. Don't you have to have dogs to do that? We never had any dogs."

"Did he ever hunt at night?" Taylor asked. "Because that's when coon hunters go."

Sharon looked thoughtful. "You know—seems maybe he did. Recently, though, like this past year."

Taylor steadied herself. She couldn't afford to react in any visible way.

"Greg would know more about that sort of thing," Sharon said before Taylor could speak. "Let me talk to him tonight. Can I call you tomorrow?"

"Yes," Taylor said. "Of course."

She'd made it almost to the door when she sensed Sharon directly behind her, approaching too closely to just be walking her out. Taylor stopped and turned around.

Sharon stood there wringing her hands, face crumpling with anguish and eyes ready to brim. She took a breath—or tried to—but it hitched in her throat, and she made a whimpering sound.

Taylor reached for the wall. Placed a palm on it, braced herself. This couldn't be good.

"You seem like you know a lot about the investigation," Sharon said after she recovered a bit.

Answer carefully. "Not too much, no. There isn't much *to* know."

"They wouldn't let me see him." Sharon wiped a tear. "I am his mother. I carried him inside my body for nine months. Raised him. Loved him. And when they finally found him, I couldn't even—" She broke into a sob, covering her mouth with her hands. "Why wouldn't they let me see him? What was wrong with him?"

Taylor leaned against the wall, pressing her shoulder hard into the sheetrock. The room tilted, spun. Her head felt like someone had shoved a big glass fishbowl over it.

"Uhm—" What could she say? Not the truth. Never the truth—not about that. "Sharon, I don't know why—"

"Bullshit. I can tell from looking at your face that you know."

Right. No—let me tell you what you see on my face. You see the absolutely certainty that you do NOT want answers to those questions.

Instead of saying that, Taylor sucked in as much oxygen as she could and stood up straight, holding Sharon by both upper arms. "Okay, Sharon. Listen. What they wouldn't let you see—that wasn't your son. You couldn't have connected with him at all, even if you touched him with your hands." True, that. Bloated, swollen tissue, peeling away from the bone in layers. Bulging and discolored eyeballs, protruding tongue. The mess in that barrel looked nothing like anything a parent would have recognized. "He wasn't there to say goodbye to. There was nothing of his personality left, nothing of his last moments. The parts of him they found had nothing to do with the kid you knew."

"Parts of him?"

Jesus. What the fuck made her say that? *Get it together, Beckett.*

"No, no—he was all there. It just wasn't—him. He was gone. Trust me about that."

Sharon caved in, folding herself forward with her arms around her waist. Taylor grabbed her, held her, so cold inside and out that she thought she might have died herself.

The heavy oak front door opened and Kavanagh stuck his head in. "Ready to roll?" Then he glanced sideways and spotted Taylor.

They locked eyes.

Taylor was still holding Sharon upright, but she managed to motion toward the outside. "Get her husband."

Kavanagh's head disappeared. A few seconds later, Greg barged through the door.

"Oh, Christ," he said, and took Sharon from her.

Kavanagh stared hard at Taylor. "What the hell did you do, Beckett?"

"She didn't do anything." Sharon pushed herself away from her husband's chest, but not out of his grip. "I just miss my boy. That's all." She grabbed Taylor's hand with both of hers. "Thank you. Thank you so much for everything you're doing to make him matter."

Taylor held herself together long enough to be pleasant. To be kind. She kept it together while she walked out of the house and climbed in the van. Kept it together while they drove away, Kavanagh and Perry in the front, leaving her in the back with her horrors.

Strands of disheveled hair hung in her face. She watched them shake as her body trembled, inches from her eyes, but she couldn't brush them away. She felt numb. Felt sick. Felt eviscerated. Like she'd left a trail of guts dragging behind her and they were unspooling a little more with every inch.

She tried to breathe and it didn't work. Got a little air in, but it got stuck going out. Took her voice along with it, from her insides, tearing her throat as it went. Taylor clapped both hands over her mouth to muffle the sound.

Too late. Perry whipped around in his seat, and Kavanagh slammed on the brakes.

"What the hell?" Perry unclipped his seat belt and launched himself between the seats. "Beckett? Beckett!"

But she could barely hear him. All she could do was cry.

"Fuck." Kavanagh pulled the van to the side of the narrow little street, slammed it in park, and jumped out. A few seconds later, the side doors opened and he was there with Perry, in her face, eyes wide with panic.

"Beckett, what is it? What's wrong?" He tried to pull her hands away from her mouth, but gave up when she resisted.

Perry patted her on the back. "Please just breathe. You're going to pass out."

Taylor nodded. "I'm breathing," she whispered.

Kavanagh shot a look at Perry. "Get Carter on the phone."

"No." Taylor grabbed Perry by the arm. "Don't. I'm fine. Or, I'll be fine. Just give me a minute."

They sat with her until she calmed down. Neither said a word.

"It just really gets to me sometimes," was all she said in way of explanation. She tried to muster a glare for both of them. "Don't you tell a fucking soul about this."

"We won't," Kavanagh said. "We all have our moments."

Perry nodded. "When I have mine, I usually just get swamp donkey drunk so I can't remember the stupid shit I did."

Kavanagh scowled at him. "Not helpful."

Taylor laughed. "Yes, it is."

With a mutter of what sounded like relief, Kavanagh backed out of the side doors and stood. "Can we go now?"

"Yes," she said. "Please."

CHAPTER THIRTY

Eric parked in a spot near the garden center and shut off the engine. Shopping sucked, but he'd rather buy a whole new life than go home long enough to put his old one in a bag. He had his car, his wallet, and a couple changes of PSA shirts. Piddly shit like a toothbrush and boxer briefs were easy to replace. He could pick those up twenty-four-seven right there at Walmart.

He'd just gotten out and slammed the door when his cell buzzed. Who now? Damn thing hadn't quit squawking all day. Fifteen notifications from Facebook, a dozen texts—his voice mailbox was full. Most of the calls were from home. Then later in the day, from numbers he didn't recognize. Cousins and kin folk no doubt, put up to it by Gram. Old broad was persistent. At least he'd give her that much.

A glance at the display told him this was an incoming call from Big Mack. That was different. He swiped the screen and answered.

"You need to pick up your damn phone once in a while." Big Mack said. "Folks trying to get hold of you."

Fuck. Should he lie and say he'd been out of cell range? No, because all Big Mack had to do was find out where the maintenance crew had been working all day and he'd know it was bullshit.

"I've been busy." There. Nobody could argue with that.

"Look, man—it ain't none of my business, whatever you got sideways at home. But your Gram's in the hospital. They think it's a heart attack."

Eric sagged backward against his car. "What? When?"

"I don't know—earlier today. They called the office looking for you, but you'd already gone."

Something heavy and hot started climbing up Eric's throat. He swallowed hard, but it didn't budge. He managed to speak past it but didn't recognize his own voice. "Thanks for letting me know."

He ended the call without a goodbye and scrambled back into his car. The local hospital was close, only two miles away. Small towns with no industry didn't have rush hour traffic, so he made it there in minutes. Parked in the small lot and headed for the entrance.

One of his cousins once or twice removed stood under the front canopy smoking a cigarette.

"'Bout time you showed up." She flicked her ash into the barberry hedge beside the door.

He stopped walking. "Hey, Brenda. Where is she?"

Brenda nodded once toward the emergency entrance. "Still in the ER. They're moving her to Holston Valley."

"Moving her? Why?"

"She needs a heart cath, or something. They don't do that here."

Brenda finished her smoke and ground the butt under one toe. She might have been attractive once, when she still had teeth, before the lower half of her face collapsed. Now she just looked tired, a brittle, blond version of Gram, but thirty years younger.

Her dark eyes were small and mean when she turned them on Eric. "I hope you're happy."

His heart thumped. "What?"

"You just couldn't leave it alone, could you? If she dies, you'll have a lot of explaining to do to your Maker."

"It was a fuss, Brenda. Like all the others. Grandpap was drinking again—"

"I ain't heard nothing about a fuss. All I know is she went to work this morning and found out she don't have a job. She's been working that school lunchroom for thirty years, Eric. And now all of a sudden they up and don't need her anymore? You don't really think that's coincidence, do you?"

"Wait—what? She lost her job?"

"Is there an echo out here?" Brenda fumbled in the purse she'd plopped on one of the fat cement bollards underneath the canopy. Out came a cigarette pack, and she plucked a fresh one with trembling fingers. "Yeah, she lost her job. And you can't stand there and tell me it wasn't because of you running that yap."

"They fired her? What reason did they give?" Damn voice always jumped an octave when he got upset. Made him sound twelve. "They have to have a reason, Brenda."

"Do they?" She started at him with flinty black eyes for a long few seconds, then shoved the filter between her lips and flicked the lighter. "They just said she was laid off."

Eric stared at her hand. It shook as she scissored the cigarette between two fingers. "So what are you saying—she lost her job, and that made her have a heart attack?"

"Something sure as shit made her have a heart attack." Brenda took another long pull. "She made it all the way home and fell out in the kitchen floor."

Jesus. Eric could only imagine the scene. How long had Grandpap yelled at her to get up before he finally broke down and called for help?

"She's sixty-two fucking years old," Brenda said. "Who's gonna hire her? Even before this—" She gestured toward the ER. "All her health insurance is through the school. Gone now. At least she has her retirement, 'cause she and your Grandpap can't live off his check. So yeah, I hope you're proud of yourself. You and your damn big ideas."

Instantly, his thoughts flew back to Haley, ridiculing him over plans for vet school. Berating him for talking to strangers.

Sometimes you act like you don't have a lick of sense—running around talking to some big city reporter like you're all that.

"God damn it." Eric left Brenda smoking under the canopy and took off toward the ER.

He didn't have trouble finding Gram once he stepped inside. Community hospital, six-bed ER—three generations of his family stood huddled at the end of the hallway wearing grim expressions. Grandpap, Gram's sister Bertie, her daughter Alene, and Brenda's brother Clayton, still wearing blackface from his hoot owl shift at the mine. Conspicuously absent was Gram's own son. Eric had no idea where his father might be, or how to find him. Or even if anybody should try.

Grandpap broke away and stepped toward him. Shoulders hiked, arms away from his sides just enough to let Eric know to tread carefully. "Where you been, boy?"

"I was working."

"We called work. They said you'd left."

"Hoyt." Bertie broke away from the group and put her hand on Grandpap's arm. "Not now. Just let it alone."

It's going to be all right, Eric wanted to say. *I still have a job. I can take care of us.* But he kept his mouth shut, compelled into silence with a glare from his great-aunt.

The heavy curtain blocking the door of Gram's room snicked open and a nurse joined them in the hallway. "One of you can go back in with her now. But just one. She's resting."

Bertie was the first to move. "Me. I'll sit with her." She shook a finger at Grandpap. "You behave yourself."

Eric peeped past the edge of the curtain. The head of Grams' bed was raised, and she seemed alert, eyes open, tracking Bertie as she walked in. Wires protruded from under the blanket covering her, hooked to a machine that registered her heartbeats as squiggly green lines. Other than being slower than he would have expected, the heartbeats looked okay to him. Nice and strong, and her color was good.

She glanced up, toward the doorway where Eric stood.

"I thought you couldn't find him," she said to Bertie.

Bertie whirled and yanked the curtain closed. "Yeah, they found him, Vella. Now you just take it easy. Don't get yourself worked up."

With the backs of his fingers, Eric nudged the curtain open just enough for Gram to see him. "I'm right here, Gram."

The machine beside her bed started beeping.

"Keep that closed." Bertie jerked the curtain shut again. "Clayton, get him out of here."

Heat flooded Eric's cheeks. Really? They weren't going to let him speak to his own grandmother?

One of the nurses from behind the main desk rushed past him and silenced the alarm. "Mrs. Blevins, I need you to stay calm for me."

"Come on." Clayton put a hand on Eric's shoulder. "Let's go sit in the waiting room."

Eric stared at him. "You go sit in the waiting room. I'm fine right here."

In Gram's room, the nurse kept talking. "A transport is on its way. They're going to take you to a hospital over in Tennessee with advanced cardiac care. We want you good and stable for the ride, okay?"

Something rattled in the hall behind him. Rubber soles squeaked on the tile and new voices joined the quiet chatter. Eric ducked Clayton's grip and turned around. An ambulance crew wheeled a bright yellow stretcher to a stop in front of the main desk and started shuffling paperwork. Two men, brawny sorts, looking battle ready in black cargo pants and tactical boots. With transport, most likely. No way to tell if they knew what to do with an old woman's heart, but Eric felt sure they could protect her from most muggers.

"Eric." Clayton tugged at Eric's elbow. "Let's go, man. Let's get out of their way."

Eric jerked his arm loose. "Don't put your fucking hands on me."

Clayton took Eric by both biceps and tried to walk him backward. "I said let's go. Now."

Instead of backing up, Eric lunged forward and slung both arms wide, breaking Clayton's grip and shoving him against the wall. "I said keep your goddamned hands off me."

Clayton pushed back. Eric braced against him with his forearms and refused to give. Up close, Clayton smelled like sweat and gear lube. Eric stared him down, eye to eye, unblinking. No way in hell some greaseball like Clayton Sparks was going to wallow him around like that.

"Hey!" One of the ambulance crew hooked Eric by the elbows and pulled him back. "Easy there, big fella. No need for this."

The alarm from Gram's room started beeping again. Loudly.

Brenda burst through the swinging doors that led outside and walked fast in their direction. "What the fuck are you people doing? Why is her alarm going off?"

"Where's Eric?" Gram's voice wafted from the room, thin and reedy. "Let me talk to my boy."

"Eric, scram. Shoo. Get the hell out of here." Brenda grabbed the curtain and held it closed. "You ain't doing nothing but causing trouble."

The nurse wrestled the curtain from Brenda. "All of you. To the waiting room. Now. Or I'll get security."

"Oh, for fuck's sake." Alene, quiet until then, stormed off in the direction of the exit doors. "Stand there acting like idiots if you want to. I'm gonna go burn one."

Alene marched through the doors and disappeared. Clayton followed close behind.

Burn one what? Knowing that bunch, it could be anything.

Brenda pointed in the direction they'd gone. "You. Out."

He'd just drawn a breath to tell her what she could do with her pointer finger when Grandpap cleared his throat.

"I didn't feed the dogs before we left," Grandpap said. "I expect maybe you'll go to the house and do that for me."

Feed the dogs. Sure. Anything to get him gone. "Yeah, whatever."

Eric shot one last glance in the direction of Gram's doorway. The ambulance crew had pushed the stretcher part of the way through it, and he couldn't see anything past that. Brenda still stood nearby, bony arms folded, glaring at him. What a family. The Clampetts had nothing on them.

"Let me know when y'all get there," he told his Grandpap. "And what room she's in."

Grandpap nodded but didn't say anything else.

Eric backtracked through the main entrance in hopes he could avoid Alene and Clayton loitering in the ambulance bay. Under the front canopy, he paused for a few seconds to see if he could spot them. Nope. Whatever they came out to smoke evidently wasn't something they could do right there in front of God and everybody.

Damn his fucking knee and that scholarship. Damn all the missed opportunities. Was he really stuck here now, destined to become just like his cousins—worn out, strung out, and ready to fight the world? For the first time since their breakup, Eric felt a wave of relief that Haley hadn't trapped him there, that he could finally move on and maybe even move the hell away from all that mountain crazy. Maybe Beckett was right. Maybe he did need to enroll in some sort of degree program. He should apply for some grants. Student loans. Anything, everything that might be his ticket to a different kind of future than his sorry-ass family had.

The hounds Grandpap kept in the barn had finally gotten quiet, their bellies full of Old Roy. Popper lay stretched on the ground beside the porch steps, and every now and then, his deep breathing became a snore. Darkness had finally come, real darkness, not just the extended twilight that lasted for hours in the shadow of a mountain. Crickets sawed in the meadow past the chicken hutch, and fireflies danced above them.

The land could convince him to stay. Nights, just like this one with stars glittering and the air sweet with the scent of phlox, were in his blood, and he belonged here. Surely a world existed where nature could dwell as God intended, and people didn't throw their lives away for lack of greater vision.

In his pocket, his cell phone chirped. A text, because calls didn't come through out here. He glanced at the display and his throat tightened. Haley. He hadn't heard from her since their showdown at the pizzeria.

"I need to talk to you," she'd typed.

He stared at the words for a long moment, remembering the ice cubes tumbling down his shirt and the ice in her eyes. What had caused the sudden thaw?

Another chirp. "It's important."

He pulled up the touchscreen keyboard and pecked the words, "Bad time."

"It's never going to be a good time for this."

Good lord. What now? Her brother on the warpath again? No doubt the prick had seen him run that yellow light on the way to the hospital earlier and was making a federal case of it.

"I'm not fucking around, Eric. This is serious."

"Give me a hint," he typed in reply.

"I'd rather be face to face."

"That may not happen for a while."

"A while is too long. I need to see you now."

"Now is not an option. Just tell me whatever."

"Fine. Don't say I didn't try to do this a different way. I'm pregnant."

(Key of E)
It's been a long time coming
Yeah, it's me but I'm not the same
I spent a long time running
Where nobody knows your name.
But I can't move ahead 'til I go back
And face the truth I buried with our fade to black.

I'm not afraid of this now
Yeah, hurt means I'm still breathing.
I'd move on but I don't know how
To stop these wounds from bleeding.
And I don't know what I'm supposed to do
If I can't find my way back to the point where, where I find you.

Sorry doesn't have much worth
When it's just a token
Just a word
That you say when it's the only thing you can.
You're the one who made it work
You bottled up the pain
And hid the hurt.
And I couldn't see the scars you carry
But time is gone and now I understand.

---Erik Evans, 2005

CHAPTER THIRTY-ONE

A ringing doorbell in the greystone Taylor shared with Erik could have meant any number of things at nine o'clock in the morning. Mostly, she just hoped it meant he'd lost his keys and needed her to let him in.

She'd cried so much over the last two days that her eyes were nearly swollen shut. Finally around three a.m. that morning she'd given up her vigil and gone to bed. The sheets still smelled like him. But Erik himself hadn't been home since Thursday afternoon. Hadn't answered his phone, wouldn't return a text. Irritation that he'd walked out like he did had given way to anger sometime late Friday, morphed into near hysteria in the wee hours of Saturday morning. She had called everyone they knew as a couple, including his dad in London. No one had heard from him. Marcus Tillman told her to call Atlantic and see if he defected to New York.

Here it was Sunday morning, almost seventy-two hours since she'd had any contact with him. She was damn near ready to file a missing persons report. Only his pleas for her to give him space had stopped her from doing it yesterday.

The doorbell rang again.

Taylor moved the drapes aside for a better view of their front stoop. So completely had she expected to find Erik standing there that at first she couldn't make sense of the people she actually saw. She blinked and rubbed her eyes. They still stood there, a man and a woman she didn't recognize, dressed well, both looking like they'd rather be anywhere else in the world but at her door.

She opened up as far as the security chain would allow. "Yes?"

Both were ready with shields in hand, held low, not in her face like she'd seen on TV. "Chicago PD," the man said. "We're looking for Erik Evans. Is this his residence?"

Taylor blinked slowly, her swollen eyes aching. "Yes."

"Is he here?"

She shook her head.

The woman finished putting her shield away and smiled. Or tried to. It looked forced, unnatural. "May we ask who you are?"

"Taylor Maines," she said. "I live here with Erik."

The man again. "Can we come in?"

Surreal. All of it. Taylor pushed the door closed, unfastened the chain, and let them inside.

The man was thin, not very tall, with dark, buzz-cut hair and a well-trimmed moustache. He wore dress slacks and a white button-down with a wide tie. The woman wore a burgundy blazer over gray slacks and a lighter gray blouse. Her curly hair was short, above her shoulders. By their clothing and hair, Taylor pegged them for detectives. Miserable detectives. She wondered if she should offer them something to drink.

Before she could ask if they were thirsty, the man started talking again. "Miss Maines, I'm Detective Roger Kennan, and this is my partner, Detective Ann Sullivan. We're working a case with a small PD up near Sturgeon Bay. Mr. Evans' name has come up. When was the last time you spoke with him?"

"What do you mean his name came up?" Taylor's heart did a funny little skip. "What kind of case?"

"We'll get to that," Kennan said. "For right now, please just answer the question."

"The last time I talked to him was Thursday afternoon." A lump grew in Taylor's throat and she swallowed hard, but it didn't budge. "We had a—well, he was mad when he left. I haven't heard from him since."

"Are you in a relationship with him?" Sullivan asked.

"Yes."

Sullivan looked at her hard. "Would you know about his tattoos—any ink that ordinarily might be obscured with clothing?"

"What?" Taylor squinted, her head starting to pound. "Why would you ask me that?"

"Please just answer the question," Kennan said again. "It's important."

"Yes." She wrapped her arms around herself, chilled by the encounter. "He has four tattoos. They're all fairly discreet unless he wants you to see them."

"Where?" Kennan asked.

Taylor took as deep a breath as she could and pointed to each location on her own body as she named it. "Here, on his forearm." The James Dean quote. "And here." Her name, inside his bicep. "One here." The music staff circling the other bicep. "And here." She pointed to her chest, just under her collarbones.

"Miss Maines, do you have family nearby?" Sullivan's eyes looked dark, solemn. Unfathomable.

Taylor shook her head. "My parents live in Des Moines. I'm in Chicago for school—Northwestern."

"What about Erik's family?" Sullivan asked. "Anyone close?"

"Friends you can call?" Kennan, this time.

"What's this about?" Breathing—oh, lord. That was getting hard to do. Taylor couldn't move air past the tightness in her throat.

"Let's go sit," Sullivan said, and gently touched Taylor's elbow. "Come with me."

Taylor followed her to the sofa, which was devoid of throw pillows. They sat, knee to knee, on the edge of the cushions.

"We have to make an identification, Miss Maines, and it may be very difficult for you." Kennan stood near the arm of the sofa, flexing and curling his fingers. "I'd really prefer it if you had some family here."

No way she'd wait for them to drive all the way from Des Moines, not now. "Just tell me what the fuck's going on."

Sullivan's gaze stayed on her, dark eyes probing her soul in a way Taylor found entirely unacceptable. But she couldn't break away. Couldn't get up and leave. Just had to sit there and wait for them to tell her what had happened to Erik.

"Describe the tattoos," Sullivan said.

"Words," Taylor whispered. "Mostly. Left arm is a music staff. Right arm is my name. Left forearm says 'Dream as if you'll live forever.' The big one on his chest says, 'When words fail, music speaks.'"

Kennan pulled a phone from his belt, or out of his pocket, or from somewhere. A Motorola Razr, with an LCD screen. He fumbled with the keypad for a moment, until a picture appeared. Taylor couldn't tell what it was. Didn't want to look.

"Miss Maines, please tell me if you recognize this." He lowered the phone for her to see.

Plastic trash bag. That's what she saw. At first. Wrinkled, glossy black plastic. Then something lighter. Too light. Not golden, not at all. Pale. Gray. With writing on it.

Dream as if you'll live forever.

Very distinctive font, easy to read, with perfect kerning.

She couldn't say a word.

The phone moved. Image disappeared. She grabbed for it, fingers gripping Kennan's wrist so hard he winced.

"I don't understand," she said.

At least she hoped she didn't.

She took one more look. Only that section of his arm, hand buried in the trash bag, other end out of frame. Just that small expanse of skin, nothing else. It was enough. Taylor felt like someone had lifted a lid on top of her head and sucked everything that was *her* out through it, so she was still in the room, still aware, but nowhere near her own body.

Sullivan pried her fingers off Kennan's wrist. Taylor didn't feel it. Couldn't fight it.

"I think that's our answer," Kennan said to Sullivan, putting his phone away.

"Miss Maines?" Sullivan touched her on the arm. "Look at me, please. Miss Maines?"

Somehow, though she didn't feel connected to any part of her body at all, Taylor moved her eyes. Saw Detective Ann Sullivan inches from her face. Drew her knees together, propped her elbows on them. Knitted her hands together and rested her cheek against them. Numb. Brain buzzing. Every sound was muted, like someone had dropped a baffle over the world.

In front of her now, her own cell phone. In Sullivan's hand.

"Call your parents, Miss Maines. You need somebody here with you."

Taylor just stared at the phone. Couldn't move.

"See if they're in her contacts," Kennan suggested.

They were. Sullivan called them.

"I'll stay with her until you get here," Sullivan said into the phone.

Taylor hadn't heard any other part of the conversation.

Erik.

Oh, no.

Oh dear God.

No.

"I just don't understand why they couldn't come here," her mother said, navigating traffic on northbound 43. "It seems so cruel, making you go all the way up north of Sturgeon Bay to have a conversation."

Taylor didn't tell her mother the truth, that nobody had asked her to come. That she made that decision all on her own, wanting to see the place where Erik's body was found, and look the people in the eye who found him.

Erik's body.

Still not real. After Detective Kennan showed her the photo, Taylor hadn't moved for almost an hour. Then she walked only a few steps to the chair where Erik's jacket from Wednesday night still hung. She picked it up, buried her face in it, and curled up on the sofa breathing the scent of him off the collar.

How could he be dead if her world still smelled like him?

An endless stream of people showed up at her door as word got out, friends she didn't know she had. Old Mellow Jennie fans littered the sidewalk outside with flowers and cards, and candles. Naturally it rained and ruined almost everything.

Erik's mother flew in from Philadelphia. His dad was making arrangements to come from England. And Taylor still couldn't think of Erik Evans in past tense.

Had to be a mistake. All of it. Any minute now he'd walk through the door, give that little half-smile of his, and ask what the hell was going on. Any minute.

In the meanwhile, Taylor would try and remember to breathe.

Some fisherman in a little Wisconsin town called Danhope had pulled Erik up in his nets late Saturday afternoon. Taylor knew a few details, understood something very real had happened three hundred and fifty miles north of her. But she couldn't connect any of that to any person she knew. They'd sent a body to a crime lab or something—a medical examiner, maybe—but she couldn't touch that with her soul, couldn't make it seem real. She cried because she missed him. She didn't cry because he was dead. She needed him, and he wasn't there. That hurt more than anything. He just *wasn't there.*

So maybe, if she were a little closer to the body everyone seemed to think was Erik, she could finally figure it out. Maybe they'd let her see him. Maybe she could finally pull the two halves of reality back together, or maybe she'd take one look and realize the man in the morgue wasn't him at all. Maybe an answer like that would get his stone bitch of a mother out of their home and back on a plane to Philly. Maybe Taylor could actually get out of bed then, or at least change the linens because if Erik weren't dead, laundering his scent from the sheets would no longer mean putting an absolute end to him.

Danhope was a speck on the map. Such a tiny police force seemed woefully inadequate to handle a case like the one that had been dredged up with the fishing nets. Taylor heard people talking about that, saw it on the news, how the Chicago PD had sent people to help, and how the FBI was stepping in. Erik had been taken across a state line, after all, alive or dead when it happened—that was irrelevant. Every agency operated on the assumption that he hadn't gone on his own free will. Sometimes Taylor wasn't sure he'd gone at all.

The Danhope police station occupied a very flat half-acre near City Hall. It was a low-slung, stone-sided building with lots of space around it. Not many trees, and not many cars, either. Taylor's mom parked out front, and they just sat there for a moment, not looking at each other, and not talking.

Finally, Taylor grabbed the door handle and got out.

"Sweetie, wait." Her mom leapt out of the car and rushed around, taking Taylor by the hands. "Are you okay? Feel strong enough to do this?"

"Mom, I don't feel much of anything right now. Just let me go."

They'd never done this before—either Taylor or her mother. So whatever procedures and protocols one might expect during an official homicide investigation—well, those didn't even ping Taylor's radar. She didn't know or care how things were supposed to be done. She just wanted to find Erik, alive or dead, somewhere in the mess that had become her life. And this was the best place she could think to start looking for him.

She'd never seen a police station so deserted. Not that she was an expert on police stations, but a lone uniformed officer at the reception window and one or two milling around in the bullpen did not a police force make. Where was everybody?

"Hi," her mother said to the officer at the window. "We're here to speak with Sergeant Mueller. I think he was expecting us?"

No. Actually, he wasn't. But Taylor saw no need to clear up the misunderstanding.

"He's at a scene right now," the officer said. "You can wait for him over there." He pointed to a row of uncomfortable-looking straight back chairs lining the opposite wall.

Shit. Okay.

Beside her in the chairs, her mother wadded a tissue until tiny bits of white lint covered her dark slacks. Taylor rested her head against the wall behind her and closed her eyes.

It had to be a dream. The only explanation. Any second she would open her eyes to find herself snuggled in bed with Erik, pressed against his warm, solid body, pinned under the weight of his arm and possibly a leg. Such a cuddler—some part of him always had to be touching some part of her, and Taylor didn't mind a bit. Without him in it, the bed seemed big as a hockey rink, and just as cold. She missed him. Every molecule, every cell, and every atom of her body missed every molecule, every cell, and every atom of his. Death separated in ways she had never even thought to contemplate.

She couldn't sit still. The chair hurt the backs of her legs, hurt her tailbone. Maybe she had to pee. Maybe she didn't. She got up and left her coat lying on the chair.

"Where are you going?" her mother asked.

"Need a restroom," Taylor lied. She needed a lot more than a restroom, but how could she even begin to put that into words?

The cop behind the window had his back turned, busy with something on a computer screen. At least it looked official, not solitaire or something dumb like that. A quick glance around the lobby area didn't reveal a sign for facilities, so Taylor poked her head around the hall leading in front of the bullpen toward rooms in the back. There, at the end of the hall. She'd at least go splash some water on her face—or something.

In the single-stall restroom, Taylor studied herself in the mirror. She looked like hell. Hair straight and stringy. Dark smudges under her eyes. Why was she even there? Why had she dragged her mother three hundred and fifty miles on some false pretense of a debriefing—Sergeant Mueller no more wanted to talk to her than she wanted to talk to Karmen Fernandez. Erik's body wasn't even there. It was in some medical examiner's drawer, possibly hundreds of miles away. She had no idea where they sent murder victims in Wisconsin. This had to be the stupidest thing she'd ever done in her life.

She turned the restroom light off and headed back down the hall. Same as before, a few doors shut, a few doors open. But from this angle, she could see different things as she walked by. One room had a large whiteboard with lines and circles that looked like football plays.

And the name Evans scribbled in messy print at the top.

A fucking whiteboard. That's all he was to them. Taylor stood in the doorway and stared at it. Stepped closer, squinting at the words. All the way into the room now—the writing was barely legible. One circle said "torso." Another said "leg."

What?

What the hell were they doing? Carving him up like a roast?

Peripheral vision could be a bitch. Because surely she'd been seeing it in the corner of her eye since she walked in, but it just now registered. She turned and stared. A corkboard wall, covered in photos. Notes written on index cards, pinned here and there among them. And black. Shiny black, wrinkled plastic. Photos of garbage bags. Nine of them, some covered in mud and plant fragments that looked like seaweed.

Among them, pieces of something human. A leg, colorless against the plastic, still lightly furred with dark blond hair. Severed at the hip, a large flap of skin rolled down from the gash showing meat and bone. The arm she'd seen on Kennan's Razr, except this image wasn't cropped. Hand buried in the plastic, yes. But nothing above the bicep. Her name should have been there. Now, no "there" for it to be. Just a nub, bone protruding. A messy cut that left the edges of his tissue ragged and torn halfway down to his elbow.

The photo beside it—a hand, half of each finger gone. They'd been chopped off at the first digit. Left hand, too. His fret hand, amputated at the wrist. She could see little tendons and straight, white bones hanging from the mangled flesh. Erik's bones. The nerves and connective tissue that made such beautiful music, now mangled. Bloodless. Lifeless. Dead.

But that wasn't all. *When words fail, music speaks.* Still intact, each letter, each perfect curl of script. Erik's chest, with no arms. His hips, with no legs.

His neck, with no head.

"What the fuck is she doing in here?"

Voices in the hall, quite a commotion. The sound of running feet, chairs sliding across the floor.

"Goddamn it, Mueller, get her out of there!"

Familiar voice—female. Sullivan? What was she doing in Wisconsin?

Doors slamming. Her mother in the lobby, asking somebody what was going on. Someone yelling at the cop behind the window, calling him a worthless piece of shit. The room behind her filled with people. Where had they been? Out finding more pieces of Erik?

Taylor pointed to the photo of his chest. "Where's his head?"

A hand on her arm, pulling her around. But she wouldn't turn. Couldn't turn. Couldn't stop looking.

"Where is his head?"

"Get her *out* of here!"

Her mother, shrieking in the doorway. "Oh, my God! What the hell is wrong with you people?"

"Get her out! Move! Now!"

"Taylor, oh God, baby!"

Arms around her waist, pulling her backward. Taylor flailed, trying to jerk free. "Where's his face? You haven't found his *face?*"

Nothing left inside. Not now. Taylor folded in on herself, knees buckling. Good lord, what was that noise? Who was screaming? Jesus—it was her. But she couldn't see anymore, couldn't hear anything outside her own head. The room was dark. Who turned off the lights? Hands, all over her. Trying to pull her up, trying to pull her out of that room. She didn't care anymore. Let them. Let them drag her straight to hell with the rest of the world and everything in it. She no longer wanted to participate. She closed her eyes and let oblivion take her.

CHAPTER THIRTY-TWO

At the Holiday Inn Express, Charles held her while she poured it all out, every grisly detail. Surely he'd known—had known for ages, in the quiet way Charles had of knowing things without using them as leverage. It just seemed important to tell him herself, to actually speak the words. It had taken her almost twenty-four hours to find the courage, to explain why she reacted so viscerally to the Hess interview, a day and a very long night that she'd spent smoothing dirt back over the freshly opened grave in her heart. A grave she'd never been able to give Erik, since his family had insisted on burning his remains once the coroner was finished with them. Taylor didn't even know where they'd scattered his ashes.

"Some girl at the medical examiner's office was a Mellow Jennie fan," she said, face pressed into the fabric of Charles' t-shirt. "All the way in Wisconsin. Turns out, she'd gone to school for a while at Rush. She recognized the ink on his arms. That's the only way they knew who he was."

Charles made a sympathetic noise but didn't say anything else. Just petted her hair, a slow repetitive motion that gradually took effect on her runaway pulse. Her anxiety waned, heart rate slowed. For the first time in a few hours, Taylor could breathe without fighting for it.

"Those bastards took his fingertips so nobody could print him, and his face so nobody would know him. No teeth, no dental records. Everything that made him Erik—they hacked off and threw away."

"Jesus." For a moment, his hand stilled. But not for long. Right back to stroking her hair, gentle as the rain.

"Nobody ever found his head. His face—just gone. Currents can be strong in Lake Michigan. Pieces of him could have ended up anywhere."

"I can't even imagine." Charles drew a breath, a slow one. "Just cannot."

"The autopsy report said the wounds on his neck were perimortem. He was alive when they cut his throat. No way to know if he was conscious, but he wasn't dead before they started hacking on him. He may have felt every bit of it. He may have known exactly what was happening to him right up until the moment he couldn't know anything at all."

A small sound from Charles, but no words. A brief tightening of his arms, then he just waited for her to keep talking.

"The videos—that website—Charles, I had to understand that kind of awful. Had to see it for myself. And it doesn't help, but at the same time, maybe it does, just a little. I don't think I have the right to look away from those things. Erik went through every second of it in his flesh. That was his body—his nerve endings. His heart, his blood. His skin. His throat, and fingers. He endured all that. Didn't have a choice at all. The least I can do is force myself to face what he suffered."

"I hear you," Charles said softly into her hair. "I hear you, Sunshine."

"And there's always the question 'what if.' What if I hadn't pushed him so hard? What if I had just left him alone, like he asked me to? He left our greystone to get away from *me*. If he had just stayed there, maybe the rest of it would have never happened."

"Now, I can't say I agree with your theory about that." His dark fingers pushed a strand of hair from her eyes. "They would have come looking for him at home. And you may have gotten caught up in it yourself. Then—no more Cinderella. And this Prince Charming would be very sad."

She smiled against his shoulder. But it faded quickly, humor only good for so much levity at a moment like this. "You did a background on me," she said. "So I guess you know about Elgin."

He nodded. "Yes. The 'not guilty by reason of' verdict."

"It's okay. You can say the word—*insanity*. I spent two years at Elgin as a forensic inpatient. Even today I can't take issue with the judge's ruling about that. I would have killed somebody."

"But you figured out a better way."

"Yes. And before I was finished with Newell Backstrom, I'm pretty sure he wished he'd taken the first option I gave him."

Walking into their greystone with those images burned in her brain was the hardest thing Taylor had ever done. All that music, all those words, forever silenced. All of Erik's talent, his skill, his kindness, all his love—gone. Like he'd never even existed.

Taylor understood that a crack had opened in her psyche. She wasn't oblivious, nor was she ignorant about it. Broken. Her soul was broken. And her mind—for the first time in her life, she couldn't trust herself. Not her thoughts, not her perceived realities. She hesitated to speak, in case no one had spoken to her first. Maybe she'd only imagined their half of the conversation. She was afraid that any answers she gave wouldn't match the questions people asked, because she could barely understand anything anybody said to her at all.

The idea came to her deep in the night when everyone else in the greystone was sleeping. She lay wrapped in a dead man's sheets, feeling his whispers against her skin, seeing his flesh torn and brutalized and bloodless every time she closed her eyes. Somebody would pay for this. She knew who killed Erik. Maybe not the owner of the hands that severed his head, but the bastard who put money in them to do so. And that person—those people—would answer to her. They'd answer for taking away the brightest light that had ever shone in her life, the moral compass of her entire existence, her very reason for living. Oh, yes. They would pay. And pay dearly.

Amazing how easy being invisible really was if you just acted like you were supposed to be doing a thing—whatever that "thing" happened to be. Once the sun came up and traffic grew heavy on the streets, Taylor pulled on a plain black hoodie and grabbed one of Erik's biggest sweatshirts out of his dresser. She tossed it over the Louisville Slugger he kept propped in the corner of their bedroom closet and walked out the front door without anyone in the house paying her the slightest bit of attention.

She caught a taxi into the Loop and had the driver pull to the curb in front of the building where Backstrom Engineering and

Consultants occupied the top seven floors. She paid the fare, carrying the bat and the sweatshirt as naturally as she would have carried a handbag. Taylor entered the building with a throng of people arriving for work, men in three-piece suits and women in heels. She studied the directory, then stood in the elevator with twelve executives who never gave her a sideways glance. Rode up to the forty-third floor and stepped directly into the lobby of Backstrom Engineering's administrative suites.

That was where she encountered her first obstacle. The secretary in Newell Backstrom's outer office tried to stop her.

"Courier," Taylor said, smiling sweetly as she kept the sweatshirt and bat below the secretary's line of sight. "Picking up for Heinberg. From Newell Backstrom? He's supposed to have the package himself."

Her feint worked. The secretary pointed to a hallway on her left. "Last door on the right."

Taylor walked straight down it and into the office of Newell Backstrom, CEO of the entire crooked empire.

Funny, really, the low level of security a man like Newell Backstrom employed. He was no celebrity, no untouchable. The idea of thugs from the street walking into his office with a deadly weapon had apparently never occurred. He looked up from his desk with only annoyance, not one bit of alarm.

"Are you lost?" was all he said.

Taylor took about ten seconds to size up the room. Plate glass overlooking Madison Street, heavy oak desk, credenza with office things on it. Lots of breakables scattered about. Decanters. Lamps. Computer screens. A couple of nicely-framed mirrors on the wall. Chairs. Models of buildings and even one tabletop diorama of what looked like a major shopping complex.

Seemed like a fine place to start.

Taylor let Erik's sweatshirt fall and drove the bat straight through the top of the diorama.

"What the hell?" Backstrom leapt to his feet and bolted around the desk, crushing tiny pieces of miniature shopping complex under his shoes every time his feet landed.

Taylor took a swing at him. He jumped back, scrambling around her in a play for the door. She took another swing, and another, backing him toward his desk again.

"Security!" He yelled. "Somebody get security up here *now!*"

She shattered the lamps. Disintegrated the mirrors. Knocked computer screens across the room, turned a spindly wooden chair to splinters. Smashed a couple of decanters full of brandy or whiskey or whatever the hell he kept in them, slinging tiny shards of glass and brown droplets of pungent liquid all over the room.

Newell Backstrom stood pinned against his desk, hands raised like he thought a show of surrender would have any effect on her whatsoever. Seriously? The bastard had no ethical conflict with procuring someone's decapitation—well, let's see how he felt about having his own head removed.

Taylor stepped into the swing.

Hands grabbed her from behind. Lifted her clean off her feet, swung her around. She dropped the bat. Made a sound for the first time since she'd crossed the threshold of Backstrom's office door. She screamed, a wild, raw sound that ripped from her throat and rang in her ears, and she kept it going long after she should have run out of air. She barely winced when the security guard jerked her arms behind her back and zip-tied her wrists. He used her elbows like handles, lifting her up to move her until it felt like her arms were being torn from their sockets. She didn't complain. Just fixed a stare on Backstrom and leaned as close as she could before the security guard caught on and shoved her away.

She looked Backstrom straight in the eye and delivered a promise she was willing to die to keep.

"I will fucking destroy you."

Pounding on her hotel room door the next morning roused Taylor from deep sleep. She squinted at the clock. Eight-thirty. Shit. Really? Ten a.m.—everybody knew to leave her alone until ten a.m.

Well, clearly not *everybody*. Someone had missed the memo.

She'd gone to bed fully dressed—if one considered mismatched sweats to be "dressed." So it was just a matter of kicking off the covers and padding to the door. A quick glance at the sofa tucked between the bed and the kitchenette showed a neatly folded blanket with Charles' pillow on top. No doubt he'd set an early alarm to make sure Eric had breakfast before work. Last night, though, he'd refused to leave her. And Taylor didn't spend much energy arguing with him about it.

In the hallway, Sheriff Hastings met her eye through the peephole. Creepy, that he seemed to know the exact moment she looked at him.

She threw the safety latch and opened the door.

He didn't offer to step inside. "We got another one."

"Another …." She didn't finish the sentence.

He gave a curt nod. "Yeah."

Jesus. What a kick in the gut first thing in the morning. Another family, another set of parents. Another notification. "Oh, no."

"This one's different." Hastings held a pair of sunglasses, turned them around a time or two in his hands. Lines of worry etched his face. Tension drew half of it down, pulled his mouth tight. The eye on that side also seemed to droop, lid heavy and thick. "I'm on my way to the scene. Thought you might want to come."

"With you?"

"Unless you need to wait for your crew."

"I can text them the address." She glanced down at her clothes. "Can I change?"

"Make it fast."

He waited in the hall while she tugged on a pair of jeans and laced up her hiking boots. Hair in a ponytail, no makeup—this was no time for vanity. If she ended up on camera like this, oh well. She'd flaunt her scars with pride.

Inside the same Charger that had pulled alongside the news van just a couple days before, Taylor fired off messages to Charles, Kavanagh, Perry, and Hennessey. Hastings didn't run the lights or siren, but he let no grass grow. They were already on the other side of town and headed down the four-lane before she got the first reply.

Hastings adjusted his visor, blocking out the angled morning light. "By comparison, seems like he was just dumping the others, getting them gone, out of his hair. But he didn't mean for anybody to find this one. She's pretty recent. Probably some time back in February or early March."

"She?"

He nodded. "He broke pattern. This one's female." He shot her a quick look over his sunglasses. "And like you said—looks like he may have just sealed her up and let her run out of air."

"Oh, Jesus."

"The medical examiner'll have to make that call, but when you open a barrel and see bloody scratch marks all over the inside, and the body has fingernails broke off down to the quick—what are you supposed to think?'

Taylor watched the Sheriff drive, feeling frustration roll off him in waves.

"After this—hell, I don't know if we're ever going to be sure we found them all. They could be hid like goddamned Easter eggs all over Southwest Virginia. See those ridges?" He pointed to the mountain range running parallel to the four-lane. "Full of limestone caves. We have scientists in here from time to time. Spelunkers— exploring, mapping, surveying the cave systems." He gunned his cruiser past right lane traffic like the other cars were sitting still. "Problem is, a lot of the access points are on private land."

"Forget that, then."

"Yep. Pretty much. So basically, nobody knows what all we've got up there. What connects to what, or how." He switched driving hands and propped his left elbow on the window ledge. "Couple of fellas out there yesterday looking at this year's ginseng stand, one of them falls down a hole. They've grown wild 'seng on that hill for the last twenty years—never been a hole big enough to fall in before. So they got him out, started looking around, up under all the leaves, and saw where somebody had dug it out with a pickaxe. Marks in the rock, cut tree roots and stuff like that. So they shine a light down trying to figure out what's going on. And they see the barrel."

He turned off the four-lane onto a narrow road that went to gravel almost immediately. "All the stuff that's been in the news— didn't take a genius to recognize what they found. One of them called the non-emergency line this morning. My phone rang about seven o'clock. Couple of deputies opened her up and knew what they had."

Taylor thought for a minute. Shuffled the pieces around to see how they fit. February or early March, he'd said. Before she took the story. More than a year after Dylan Altizer, several months after Cody Hess. And female. Of all damn things.

"So, he buried this one in a cave?" she asked.

He shrugged. "If that's what you want to call it. Big hole under the ground. Drops about four feet to a ledge, then another ten feet down a narrow shaft that dead ends about twenty more feet to the west. A gap in the bedrock, more or less. One of my deputies told me this morning they used to run dogs on this hill, but quit when they started losing 'em down that hole. Old coon can get in there and crawl back out. Not a hound. The recovery team found a lot of animal bones down there this morning."

Taylor perked up. "Who was running dogs?"

"One of the hunting clubs, probably. Maybe just individuals. I don't know."

"How recently did they stop?"

"Well, my deputy's in his late twenties, and he remembers it, so ten years ago, maybe?"

"So a coon hunter would know about that hole."

"If he's ever hunted this hill, yeah. I'm sure he would."

She told Hastings about Cody Hess, his interest in hunting and love of the woods. And limited access to that kind of land—she didn't spell out her thoughts about what an easy target a young kid like that might have been for a sick bastard like Eddie Pace, but from the look on Hastings' face, he got it anyway.

"I can find out if the other boys hunted," he said. "Should be a fairly straightforward question." He eased the Charger to a stop on the edge of the road, behind a line of marked patrol cars and a massive white mobile crime scene unit. "But right now, we got some walking to do. I hope you ate your Wheaties."

CHAPTER THIRTY-THREE

"Brandi Deel," Sheriff Hastings said, returning from his second hike out to the cars with a metal clipboard box. "Twenty-two years old. She's local."

Under the canopy of mountain hardwoods, Taylor and Charles exchanged a look. Evidently sometime in the early spring of that year, the rules had changed for their killer. Big time.

"We have a want out on her from February." Hastings took a sheet of paper from inside the box and clipped it to the front. A mug shot of a young woman, hair pulled back severely from her face, too much black eyeliner and skin pocked with acne and sores. "Failure to appear, drug charges back in August of last year."

"I guess now you know why she failed to appear," Taylor said.

"Yeah." Hastings grimaced. "Right."

Charles shifted his footing on the steep incline. "And you made a positive I.D?"

Hastings made a waffling motion with one of his hands. "We'll let the medical examiner call it, but it's her. We know Brandi. She's been a regular through the system for about a year now. Went M.I.A. back in February. We put her picture on Facebook and never got a good tip. We just figured she took off back to Kentucky where her family's from."

Taylor glanced at the barrel sitting beside the entrance of the cave, left there by a team of rappelers who'd winched it to the surface. She hadn't seen the body—had no desire to see the body—but Perry certainly would if he kept inching closer with that camera. They were on a twenty-five-degree, heavily wooded slope half a mile from the road, the only press on scene so far, and nobody had strung barriers yet. Perry was close enough to be getting a good whiff and Taylor was surprised nobody had chased him off. She caught his eye and waved him back. He ignored her.

"Any chance it's a copycat?" Taylor asked. "Because so much is different this time."

"I don't know," Hastings said. He sounded tired. "Hell, I don't know anything at this point. Eddie's still in Tennessee. DNA results from Darrell could take several more days. All we can do is process the scene and send the body off. See what the M.E. finds."

"How'd he get her down there?" Charles asked. "That's a deep-ass hole. Did he just drop her in?"

Hastings shook his head. "Doesn't look like it." He pointed to a tree with branches hanging over the entrance to the cave. "Some bark's rubbed off one of those limbs—he might have used a pulley. Whatever the case, this seems a lot more deliberate than anything we've seen so far. It took a lot of work. Logistics. I'm not convinced our guy dragged a barrel with a human body in it all the way up this hill from the road. I'm a lot more likely to believe that this is the actual murder scene."

Taylor rubbed her upper arms. Hastings' last remark gave her a chill.

"Doubtful we'll find much on the surface here," Hastings cast a glance around the hillside. "We're months down the road, a couple blankets of snow, and spring rain. But underground, things keep. We may find latents on the barrel, maybe even some trace."

He looked hard at Taylor, mouth pressed into a thin line. Something going on in his head—she just had to wait for him to work it all out to the point he'd talk.

"I'm not comfortable," he said after a moment. "With the fact that Eddie Pace took off to Elizabethton the day we swabbed his daddy—*before* we swabbed his daddy. And he hasn't come back yet. May be coincidence, but I'm not a big believer in that."

Taylor said nothing. But no doubt the look on her face spoke volumes.

"I have a lot of friends in Tennessee," Hastings said. "We have eyes on him there, too. He doesn't act spooked, so I don't know. But I'll tell you what I *do* know—whoever killed this girl is going to shit his pants when he finds out we pulled her up. By the grace of God, I had my brain engaged when I got the call this morning. I kept this off the radio, off the scanners—completely dark. Landline communication only. No press. I'm not doing a news release. So tell your people—this stays quiet. Let your cameraman get all the footage he wants. It may come in handy at some point. But remember our deal."

Ah. So that's why nobody stopped Perry before he got so close to the barrel he could have thrown a pine cone and hit it.

"I'll tell them," she said. "But there's no need. This is the best crew I've ever worked with. These guys know how it works."

Again, Hastings looked like he was thinking hard about something. Eyes narrow, features asymmetrical as stress pulled on them hard. Finally he took a deep breath and stepped closer to Taylor and Charles.

"Between you and me," he said, leaning toward them. "This is going to be the same killer. Not a copycat. It's the motive that's different. The *why*. My guess? There won't be any evidence of sexual assault on this girl. The whole point was to just make her go away. This wasn't a joyride. This was business."

The chill Taylor had felt before came back. It was everything she could do not to wrap her arms around herself and just stand there shivering.

"I'm going to go get busy being a Sheriff." He stepped back, his demeanor and tone of voice back in cop mode. "You guys get what you need, just stay out of the crime unit's way. Taylor, I'll get up with you this afternoon."

She nodded. Even smiled a little. After he walked away, she let out a huge pent-up breath.

"What deal?" Charles asked the second Hastings moved out of earshot.

"Just the standard I-tell-you-everything-and-you-keep-your-mouth-shut operative clause."

"Taylor." The way Charles spoke her name, it was both a prod and a mild tongue-lashing.

"Fine," she said. "He will give me all-access to the investigation, exclusive. I just can't go to air with anything unless he signs off on it."

"Taylor." This time, the lashing had barbs.

"I don't want to hear it, Charles." She hit back with a barb of her own. "Look around. Look where we are. Look at all the other networks with people on the ground here. Feel me?" A brief pause to let it sink in. "I'm not going to air with anything anyway. I don't need two minutes at six o'clock. I'm not breaking a story about bodies in barrels. *Capiche?*"

Slowly, he nodded. "Hastings—you trust him?"

"Yeah." She didn't even have to think about it. "He's too vulnerable, too wide-open to be anything other than what he seems. I've rubbed up against a lot of rotten human beings in my day. It's rare that you don't walk away with some of their stink on you." Or worse. "Hastings just seems to make the world around him better. And I'm going with that."

Taylor studied her laptop screen, fingers knotted at her mouth. In truth, she hadn't expected a reply from the State Attorney General's Office so quickly. But there it was in her inbox, a brief message from the woman who headed up Virginia's Animal Law Unit, marked with the dark blue seal of the SAG.

Across the table topped with brightly colored Spanish tile, Charles dipped a tortilla chip in queso. Pale melted cheese dripped all the way to his mouth. He leaned forward before it could glop onto his shirt and stuffed the chip in his mouth.

"There was a time," he said once he finished crunching it. "When you and I could eat tacos together without your nose stuck in a damn computer."

Taylor frowned. "I'm not eating tacos."

"Yeah, well, taco salad or whatever you call that thing."

"Remember I told you I was reaching out to the SAG's office?"

Charles nodded, mouth too full of fajitas to reply.

"Here's what I asked." Taylor read from a section of the email text. " 'Neither the State Police nor the CA in Randall County pursued any charges against Darrell or Eddie Pace, despite urgings from the State Shelter Inspector. It appears that if local prosecutors fail to take action, there is no recourse despite the heinous nature of the crime. There is simply no agency in Virginia with the authority to override that decision. Correct?' "

She glanced up. Charles had stopped chewing.

"So here's the reply." Taylor scrolled down a bit. " 'That is correct. Criminal prosecutions can be initiated by and conducted through the Office of the Commonwealth's Attorney in each Virginia locality on behalf of that locality's citizens. These offices are established in Article 7, Part 4 of the Constitution of Virginia. The duties and authority of Commonwealth's Attorneys are outlined in Virginia Code § 15.2-1627. The ALU was formed to assist prosecutors in animal abuse cases, but the authority to take action in those cases remains vested in the local elected prosecutor.' "

"Wow," he said. "And that came from who?"

"Head of the Animal Law Unit." Taylor started to take another bite of her taco salad, but ended up just stirring the lettuce into the ground beef instead.

"Well, that's the horse's mouth. Like it or not."

"I was going to interview her," Taylor said. "But after seeing that, I don't know. Kind of pointless. The SAG's office is a total dead end, at least as far as having any jurisdiction to intervene."

"So once the CA makes a decision to not pursue a case, there's no way to appeal it. No way to go over his head. Right?"

"Some cases can be filed directly with the magistrate. But in a small community like this, the same CA who declined to make the case will get final say over whether or not to prosecute if charges are filed by a citizen. So it's a no-win. CAs are elected. Not appointed. They answer to nobody but the voters."

"So we're back to that again."

"It's inescapable. No one offering any real catalyst for change can get near the ballots. The county won't hire outside experience, won't pay enough to attract real talent, and the residents get no options. Factor in the generations of defeatism and poverty, and you end up with a feudal society. The only way to truly rise above that is to revolt, and people here get smacked down so hard for speaking up that there isn't a chance in hell that the community is ever going to organize cohesively enough to make a difference."

"Do they want to, though, Taylor? That's the thing. You can't force your ideology on people. This is a whole subculture of folks living how they choose. Conservationists see a bunch of lions, they don't step in and choose who leads the pride. They don't mess with the food chain so the hungry baby lions get enough dinner to grow up strong and take over. You feel me?"

Taylor pointed to herself. "Sociology major. Hello?"

"Hey, I'm just sayin'."

"I'm not on a mission to save Appalachia, Charles. I just think the situation here is underreported and the people are underrepresented. Whether they know or even care is irrelevant to my job as a journalist. This is a whole subset of the American population that is basically living off the information grid. I'm supposed to just pretend I don't see that?"

"Nope. Not what I said. I'm just suggesting that maybe you'll have a hard time making viewers care about a group of people who don't even care about themselves."

"Well, that's why I make the big bucks." She shut her laptop with a little too much force. "It's my job to sell it. So just watch and learn, big boy. Watch and learn."

At the hotel later that night, Taylor's room phone rang.

She stared at it. Who the hell would be calling her on that?

Landline communication only. Wasn't that what Hastings had said?

Taylor picked up the receiver. "Hello?"

"DNA came back," Hastings said. "Paternal match. I'm on my way to pick up the warrant now. We're bringing Eddie in for a swab."

CHAPTER THIRTY-FOUR

The monsters who cut Erik's throat and tossed him, bit by bit, into the waters of Lake Michigan were never identified. Never charged. Never prosecuted. Never convicted, and never punished for anything they'd done. As far as Taylor knew, they still lived in the Chicago area, going about their lives, so far removed from the rubble of the Backstrom empire that they were untouched by its implosion.

Taylor saw them in every killer, in every violent offender whose next step might be the taking of a life. She saw them tonight, in the eyes of Eddie Pace. Through the two-way mirror, she watched his hands toying with a can of Pepsi in the interview room. Not shackled, not even shaking. No arrest. Just questions. And as badly as she wanted to hear them, the answers might give her no peace at all.

Hastings walked into the interview room carrying a manila folder. He sat on a metal chair opposite Eddie and slid the folder to one side. Clasped his hands on the table and squared off.

"Eddie, thank you for cooperating with the swab." Hastings didn't blink. "Makes things easier on all of us."

Eddie shrugged. "Don't reckon I had much choice."

His voice—his speech—so much like Eric Blevins', with the same slow vowels and cadence. But there the similarity stopped. He slouched in the chair, long legs sprawled under the table. Blond hair snarled over his forehead, unwashed for at least a couple of days. Bedhead, with no indication that he'd tried to tame it.

Fingers still laced, Hastings propped his elbows on the table. "Do you understand why we asked you for a DNA sample?"

"Not really," Eddie said.

Pulling the folder closer to him with one finger, Hastings opened it and took out a photo that Taylor recognized even from where she sat. Cody Hess. Fresh out of the barrel, the photo his mother would fortunately never have to see.

Hastings placed it in front of Eddie.

Reaction. Yes. Good. Eddie twitched when he saw the picture, dark blond brows knitting for just a second, before his face went carefully blank.

He folded his arms. "What the fuck, man?" he said. "Showing me that shit."

Hastings pinned him with a stare, steady and cool. "Just wondering if you recognize him."

"Why would I recognize that?" Eddie wouldn't look at the picture. Kept his gaze averted, high. Over the table, fixed on Hastings. "Jesus."

"That's not how he looked when you saw him last?"

"I don't even know who the fuck that is."

"This is Cody Hess." Hastings put the tip of an index finger on the photo. "He had somebody's DNA on him that was a family match for your dad's."

Eddie's scowl grew darker. "What the hell are you talking about, Hastings?"

The door beside her creaked open. Taylor glanced that direction. She recognized the man who walked in, though she'd never met him. Nate Bostick, Commonwealth's Attorney. Well-dressed in an off-the-rack kind of way, he pulled one of the metal chairs from underneath the folding table that took up most of the room and sat. He didn't acknowledge her.

Hastings smiled, but it didn't reach his eyes. "Eddie, if you like boys, nobody's going to judge you for that."

The scowl became diabolical. "Fuck you, man."

There with Taylor behind the two-way mirror, Bostick crossed one ankle over the opposite knee. The way his chair was turned, he could prop an elbow on the table and brace his chin on his fingers.

Taylor studied him with a couple of discreet glances. Nice enough looking fellow. Bostick would have blended well in any large city. Dark curly hair cut short, so it lay in tight waves all over his head. Pale green eyes, the color of a shallow sea. Cold. Humorless.

Hastings dug another photo from the folder. From where she sat, Taylor couldn't see it well. But it looked like a picture of the hillside where Brandi Deel's body had been pulled from underneath the mountain. A patch of bright blue in the corner of the photo helped Taylor orient the scene. Yes. A shot of the cave opening, from about thirty feet away. The barrel sat just in frame, on a white dropcloth the crime unit had put down.

Eddie didn't so much as twitch. He didn't appear to even breathe. His eyes floated up to meet Hastings'. They faced off across the table, neither speaking, neither moving.

Bostick got up from the chair beside her and disappeared through the door.

A few seconds later, he walked into the interview room with Hastings and Eddie Pace.

"Sheriff, let him think about it for a minute." Bostick pushed the Deel photo closer to Eddie. "Let's go."

Both men walked out.

Alone, Eddie started breathing again. Taylor could see the rapid rise and fall of his shoulders. She glanced up at the camera in one corner of the interview room, red light steady. So was the light on the digital recorder mounted on a shelf near the two-way mirror. Everything was being recorded. Perfect. Maybe Hastings and Bostick were letting Eddie stew in his own juices, alone in a room with a photo of a crime scene he'd never expected them to know about. She watched him closely, looking for tells.

Eddie stayed in the same position. Didn't unfold his arms, didn't sit up straight. Slouched in the chair, but both knees started bouncing. He didn't look at the photo. Didn't let his gaze drop anywhere near the table. If he truly had no idea what the photo was about, he would probably inspect it, looking for clues. It certainly wasn't gruesome, not like the first picture Hastings showed him. Brandi's body wasn't visible in it. Thirty seconds passed, and he hadn't so much as glanced down.

The door beside her opened. Bostick barged in, Hastings close on his heels.

"You can't hold him," Bostick said. "Get the DNA back and see what that gives you. As it stands, you have nothing. The longer you keep him here without an attorney, without making an arrest—the harder it's going to be for me in front of a judge."

Hastings' droopy eyelid twitched. "He's going to run."

"Then let him run." Bostick shut the door behind them. "I'm telling you right now—you fuck up at this stage, you might as well just give him the keys to the county. Because he's going to own our ass."

Taylor looked at Eddie. He still hadn't moved. Wasn't looking at the picture.

"Then let's get him a lawyer in here," Hastings said. "All it takes is a phone call."

"That's not how this is going to work and you know it, Hastings."

The two men glared at each other.

Taylor cleared her throat. "What about the animal cruelty charges you wouldn't make in 2015? Make them now. It'd be enough to hold him."

Bostick did a double take, as if seeing her for the first time. He stared at her for a couple seconds, then pointed to her and looked back at Hastings. "Who the hell is that?"

Hastings closed his eyes and rubbed his forehead. "Beckett."

"That's *Beckett?*" Bostick nearly spat her name. "Hastings, have you lost your goddamned mind? Get her the fuck out of here." He took a step toward Taylor, jabbing a finger at the door. "Go."

Taylor didn't move. Didn't bother to stand up. "What about the cruelty charges?"

"Statute's a year on that," Bostick snapped. "Get up. Walk out. Now."

"In case you forgot," she said. "Those animals died as a result of his negligence. That makes it a felony. Multiple counts. So the statue is five years. Not one. Virginia code 19.2-8, the paragraph below the one about taxes."

Bostick and Hastings both stared at her.

"You have some leverage, Bostick. Use it."

He jerked the door open, paisley tie flapping. "Out." He grabbed one of the chairs between them and shoved it against the wall. Advanced another step. "Go!" Pushed another chair so close to where she sat it almost hit her.

Fine. Whatever. She got up and grabbed her bag, ducking between Bostick and Hastings as she fled through the door.

She'd almost made it to her car when Hastings caught up with her.

"Son of a fucking bitch." He spat the words out and then just stood there, eyes wide and wild. Like more words dangled on the tip of his tongue but couldn't manage to roll off.

"He's blowing smoke, Sheriff."

He held both hands palm-up in the air. "You think?"

"You didn't surprise Eddie one bit with that picture."

"Don't I fucking know it."

"What do you think that's all about?"

He just shook his head. Pressed his lips together. Said nothing else.

"You know how to find me," she said.

He nodded and went back into the building.

Taylor got in her Audi and sat there for a long time before she cranked it. Replayed the whole debacle in her mind, from Eddie's bizarre reaction to the photos, to the utterly inexplicable behavior of Nathan Bostick.

What in the hell had she just witnessed?

At the hotel, Taylor dragged one of the room's padded chairs to the table in front of the murder wall and sat for a long time, staring up at the photographs. Such a convoluted mess, everything she'd learned about this godforsaken place. Like a multi-headed hydra, tentacles everywhere.

So basically, nobody knows what all we've got up there. What connects to what, or how.

Hastings, talking about the area's cave systems. He might as well have been talking about the community itself.

Taylor reached her right hand as far across her left shoulder as possible, stretching her fingertips toward her back, toward the name forever branded on her skin. *Erik Evans*. His autograph, tattooed the same day he'd had her signature inked on the inside of his bicep.

After her release from Elgin, she went back to Erik's tattoo artist and had the year of Erik's birth and the year of his death added below his name. In the same beautiful font with the same precise kerning she'd once admired on Erik's forearm, she had the tattoo artist ink one more line. "Words Failed. The Music Is Silent. But I Will Never Be."

Someone knocked on her door. Charles, no doubt. Yep. He stood in the hallway carrying his laptop satchel. She let him in.

"So listen, I think I got something," he said.

Not like him, to jump right into it without a least a truncated preamble.

She sat back down. "Okay."

She hadn't told him about Nate Bostick. She'd give him all the sordid details eventually, just not now. The whole thing made her head hurt. Four ibuprofen and one leftover oxycontin later, she'd finally gotten her skull to stop pounding.

"Let me just set this up." He put the satchel on the bed and started unpacking.

"Have you heard from Eric?" she asked.

"Not a word."

"Shit."

"I'm worried, too, Cinderella." He set his laptop on the table in front of her and woke it from sleep. "But he's a big boy. He's got a lot of figuring out to do. He's smart, though. I think we need to give him some credit. Not expect the worst."

She nodded.

Charles dragged a second chair to the table and sat down beside Taylor. He pecked around on the laptop, inserted a flash drive, and opened Tor. The browser crawled, typical slow speed with multiple relay points. But eventually images filled the screen, and Taylor's jaw went slack.

"What the hell is this?" she asked.

"Look close," he said.

Emerging from somewhere on the Deep Web, rows of naked men paraded across the laptop screen. Not exactly pornography—these photos were artsy, beckoning. Young men lounging backward, buff bodies exposed, come-on smiles and attributes that almost made Taylor blush.

"You're fucking with my head," she said.

Charles pointed to one of the men he centered on the screen. "You're telling me you don't know who that is?"

Taylor looked again. And gasped. "Oh, shit. That's Dylan Altizer."

"Yep." Charles clicked the photo and opened a profile page.

More photos of Dylan, posing, some photos of him dressed, others—not.

She pointed. "How old is this site?"

"I don't know. Couple years. Obviously he hasn't updated his info in a while."

"Was he a prostitute?"

Charles shook his head. "I don't think so. This is a social site. Hookups for guys—"

"He was gay?"

"Looks like it, yeah."

"Oh, my God."

"But gay is one thing. Deviant is another. They don't go hand-in-glove." Charles clicked on the bio. "Read that shit."

Taylor did, fingers over her mouth.

Dylan Altizer was no boy next door. Liked it rough, promised a wild ride. Scary, actually. Into bondage. Into pain.

"He was aggressive," Charles said. "Look at the comments in the forums."

Username "HurtCocker" had posted and replied often over a six-month period. He could be a troll when he wanted, charming when it suited his purpose better. Then everything stopped in January of the previous year. What remained was a time capsule of his mental state and habits in the weeks and months leading up to his death.

Taylor rubbed her head. The pounding was back. "So how did you find all this?"

"Looking for black market coonhound sales, any kind of underground hunting guide service—it was a crazy long shot and I didn't find much. Until I found this." He clicked again, and opened yet another photo album in Dylan's collection.

"Oh, dear God."

All the years of forcing herself to stare at butchered humans, at beheadings and executions and gang retaliations, and it was the animals that proved more than she could bear. Taylor simply could not look past the initial glimpse of whatever artwork Dylan Altizer had painted in blood. He hunted, all right—everything from deer to coon to the neighbors' cats. Gutted them. Skinned them. Took photos and bragged about it. All part of the show—"HurtCocker" acting out, torturing and abusing anything more vulnerable than himself.

"Jesus Christ," she said. "He was a fucking psychopath."

"Sure seems that way."

"So you think Eddie was surfing around on the Dark Web and found this guy?"

Charles laughed. "I doubt it. Eddie doesn't even have a Facebook page. I'd say they ran into each other on a hunt somewhere. One thing led to another, and they ended up in the woods together."

"Eddie met Eddie."

"And I'll bet it was a hell of a scene."

Taylor pressed her fingertips against her temples. "Apparently he's a real womanizer—Eddie, I mean—somebody on Facebook said they catch him up back roads all the time in the Animal Control truck with one woman or another."

"When he met this guy, he had something up a back road, all right, but it wasn't the Animal Control truck."

It took her a moment, but Taylor finally got it. She hooted with laughter. "That is so not funny," she said between snorts. "Stop it, Charles."

He smiled but otherwise didn't acknowledge her laughter. "Eddie got the best of him before it was over," he said. "But it was probably a close match. And if I had to put money on it, I'd bet the foreign DNA was probably on Eddie that time, and not on Altizer."

"Shit." She dug the heel of her hand into her forehead. Pound, pound, pound. She fucking hated headaches. "I did not see this coming. Eddie serves up so much better as predator, not prey."

"I don't know how much any of this would matter in a trial," Charles said. "Because even if a jury found him guilty of overkill rather than capital murder in Altizer's case, you still have to reconcile that with the others. So yeah—something happened with Altizer that pushed Eddie over the edge. But then he just didn't come back from it. Guess he figured out he liked it. And once he started, he couldn't stop."

"He was probably a sweet kid, once," Taylor said. "Until Darrell exposed him to so much brutality and forced him to participate. Probably thought he was making a man out of him. And the whole time he was just making a stone-cold killer."

"Darrell's going to have to live with this now, for the rest of his life."

Taylor rubbed the back of her neck. "He'll probably never connect those dots, Charles. The ability to understand one's own role in this type of dysfunction is limited. I mean—look at Altizer's parents. They still won't talk to me. Won't let me have his autopsy findings. I'm going to do beautiful pieces on Cody and Michael and Jamie—maybe on Brandi, depending on some things. But for Dylan? Just a picture and some basic facts. I doubt his family even knew the truth about him. So it's not like they're trying to keep that quiet. It's because of where they're from, and the way they were all raised—keeping it all private is more important than honoring the memory of their child, maybe even more important than holding his killer responsible."

Charles watched her with a frown. "Taylor, does your head hurt?"

She closed her eyes and nodded. "Yeah. So bad I almost can't think straight."

He got up and walked behind her chair. Moved her hand, and placed both his warm palms on her shoulders.

God, it felt good.

Taylor hung her head forward and let his fingers work, taking the tension and pain out of muscles that hadn't been touched by another human hand in over ten years. She felt warm all over, sleepy. And realized she was drooling.

"Oh, shit," she said, and wiped her mouth with the back of her hand.

He laughed. That big, booming laugh of his that filled a room and made everybody in it smile.

She pushed his hands away and stood. "Charles, I think I'm just going to bed. I'll sleep it off and feel better in the morning."

His arms fell to his sides. Face registered nothing, just careful neutrality. "Okay."

While he packed his laptop, she retreated to the bathroom and composed herself. Forehead against the cool tile, some took deep breaths and gave herself a silent pep talk.

He was still there when she came out, lingering by the door.

"I just have one question," he said. "And I think I know the answer. I promise you I will never ask it again, no matter what you tell me tonight."

She froze. *Shit. Not now, Charles. Please don't do this.*

But he did. "I don't think it's all in my head, Taylor—us. But you're like quicksilver. The harder I try to grab hold, the faster you move away. Is it because I'm black?"

She stared at him, her eyes bugged and her face twisted, completely unable to fix her expression. She couldn't breathe, so ridiculous his question had been, and so not any of the ones she had expected. But when she finally got air into her lungs, she started laughing, and then laughed so hard it made her cough.

When she recovered from that, she stepped into him, full body press, and placed one hand on each side of his face. "For God's sake, Charles—no." She traced his cheekbones with her thumbs. "It's because you're alive." Her voice dropped to a whisper. "And he's dead."

Slowly, he nodded. And after a moment, almost smiled. "Sounds like I have the advantage, then." He kissed her forehead and backed away, out the door, and waved at her from the hallway. "Goodnight, Sunshine. See you tomorrow."

CHAPTER THIRTY-FIVE

Eric circled the lake, driving slowly. Maybe he'd missed her. Maybe she changed her mind about talking to him. Through his open window, the sound of crows in a pine overhead drowned out the quiet murmur of his tires on the fresh asphalt. The county had only paved that loop the previous fall, just one more attempt to put lipstick on a pig. It did make for a nice, private spot to meet, though, since Haley insisted it not be in public.

There—through the trees, a flash of yellow. Her Cobalt, pulled to a wide spot on the shoulder. He rolled to a stop behind it and turned off the engine. No sign of her in the car. Still, just the sight of it caused something to flip-flop underneath his ribs. So familiar—so *Haley*—not another almost-her-but-not-quite, like all those yellow Cobalts he'd glimpsed across a parking lot that turned out to be somebody else's, or the blonde girls who nearly paralyzed him until they turned around.

He spotted her close to the lake, sitting on a large outcrop of limestone scarred with blasting marks. She looked softer somehow, without so many edges. Could his DNA growing inside her body actually have that much effect on her already, changing her biophysiology beyond the cellular level and turning her into a mother? They'd made a tiny human together. Him plus her. All those generations of Cherokee and Scotch Irish blood, along with her hodgepodge of Anglo-Saxon genes—their baby would be a true blend of Appalachian heritage. Not a small him or a small her, but someone completely unique.

She looked up. Her face seemed puffy, and her eyes swollen. So yeah, she'd been crying. No surprise. This would affect them both her most dramatically, at least for the next nine months. Say goodbye to those Wranglers for a while. Eric smiled. The thought of her plump and round with his child didn't turn him off one bit.

"Hey," he said, and slid onto the rock beside her.

"Hey."

His first instinct was to touch her, maybe place a hand on her leg or rub gently between her shoulder blades. Some gesture of comfort, anything to let her know she wasn't alone.

Ever so slightly, she leaned away from him. Okay. Maybe some things never change.

"You doing okay?" he asked.

Haley nodded.

"I'm sorry I acted like a douche on the phone." He grimaced. "You caught me by surprise."

"You?" She gave a short laugh. "*You* were caught by surprise? What about me? I'm not ready for this, Eric. I don't want a baby right now."

For the first few seconds he couldn't say anything. Then he found words that fit the situation, even though they felt like rhetoric. "I don't think anybody ever really thinks they're ready to grow up and be a parent. You just have to get your mind around it, is all."

"Oh, so you've got your mind around it already." Typical Haley. Such acid in her tone. "Figures."

Eric scowled. "I didn't say that, Haley. Don't go putting words in my mouth."

"Yeah, great parents we'd be. Can't say jack shit to each other without arguing."

He stared at her. Thought about stating the obvious, then resigned himself to the futility of it.

"Okay," he said after letting the sting subside. "We'll figure out what to do. We're both smart people. You're not in this by yourself, you know. It took both of us to wind up in this situation."

She said nothing. Just closed her eyes and lost a little color in her face.

"You all right?" He half-turned, watching tiny beads of sweat break out on her forehead.

"No," she snapped. "I'm not all right. I'm sick as shit. Been sick for about two weeks. It's how I knew something was wrong. I can't eat. I'm so tired all I want to do is sleep. We have finals coming up at school and I can't stay awake long enough to study."

Jesus. Why hadn't she called him sooner? If she knew something was wrong—

"When I didn't get my period, I knew." She leaned back against a ledge of rock, eyes still closed. "I got a pregnancy test from CVS and boom. There it was."

"You been to the doctor yet?"

"Doctor?" Her eyes flew open. "Are you kidding? I'm seventeen. I need a parent to authorize that. Besides, how am I going to pay for it? It's not like they'll see me for free."

"Your folks have insurance, right? If not, I can—"

"Eric, are you dense? I can't tell them about this."

"Well, they're going to know sooner or later."

"Jordan and my Dad would kill you."

He took a deep breath. "Listen to me. We're going to be okay. I'm here. I'm not leaving you to deal with this on your own. I'm not that guy. I will marry you tomorrow if that makes things any better. If you'd rather wait—"

"Whoa. Hang on a minute. What?"

"Hell, we were talking about it as far back as last year. It's not like we don't have the history together."

"I'm not going to marry you, Eric."

She might as well have slapped him. He sucked in a breath, blinked, and spent the next few seconds trying to keep her from seeing how bad that hurt.

"Fine," he said after a moment. "We don't have to get married. I'll still be here for you and this kid. That's one thing you won't have to worry about."

"No," she said. "You don't get it. I'm not having this baby. You don't have to 'be here' for either one of us. I just need help paying a clinic to make this go away."

The bottom dropped out of the world. Eric floated there for a moment, strung somewhere between the limestone rock beneath his ass and the infinity between him and the person sitting beside him. Blood rushed to his face, pounded in his ears, throbbed in his temples. Then it receded so fast he saw black spots and nearly lost sight of everything except a whole new kind of darkness.

"What the fuck, Haley? You're bullshitting, right? You wouldn't seriously consider—"

"Seriously consider what? Throwing my whole life away for a mistake we made? We never should have been together, Eric. I don't know what I was thinking. There's no way I'm having a kid with you. I found a family planning clinic that doesn't notify parents. It's out of state, but I'll drive as far as I have to. I just need to come up with a few hundred bucks to get it done. Gas and stuff, too. I'm thinking it's the least you could do, if you really want to help me."

He sat back, putting more space between them. His cheeks burned. "I'm not going to help you kill our kid."

"It's not a kid yet." She rolled her eyes. "For fuck's sake."

He scrambled off the rock and stared at her, barely able to breathe past the pressure in his chest. "God damn it, Haley."

"So you're not going to do it? You're not going to give me any money?"

"What the fuck is wrong with you?" He sucked hard for air, forearms and hands tingling. He could barely feel his legs. "How could you think I'd go along with something like that?"

"Yeah, because you're so righteous and all, with a drunk for a granddaddy and God only knows what happened to your own folks—talked to your mama lately, Eric? I heard the last time anybody saw her, she was walking down Mercer Street with a Mount-n-Do bottle in her hand."

The tingling moved upward, past his elbows. The black spots in his vision started to cluster. "You—" At first he struggled with words. Then they flooded out before he could stop them. "You are a miserable human being. You'd be a terrible mother. You *are* a terrible mother. I don't know what I ever saw in you."

"Really? Well, it's pretty funny that you'd think I would ever want to raise a Blevins. Your whole family is trash. And you're turning out just like your daddy—can't even pass a fucking drug test. Best job you could want right out of high school and you go and lose it. You think I didn't hear about that? Oh yeah—everybody's talking about it. It's all over Facebook."

"What? I didn't lose my job. I transferred to maintenance—"

"Dude, you better check your voice mail. I think you missed a message or two."

He fought the urge to snatch his phone out of his pocket and look.

"Actually," he said. "I think you're batshit crazy. And you're not killing my kid. I'll be damned if you're going to raise him, but you're not going through with this shit." He started backing away, in the direction of his car. "You haven't heard the last from me. Mark my fucking words on that."

CHAPTER THIRTY-SIX

Two years in state custody— "dissociative depersonalization/derealization disorder" was the official diagnosis, along with that little thing about homicidal ideations. Took a while to get past that, even after Taylor finally connected with her own psyche again.

Her mom picked her up the last day of her hospital incarceration. Her dad couldn't bring himself to make the trip. Taylor didn't hold it against him. Especially now, after the days and weeks of intensive psychotherapy that helped her understand all the factors that led to her breakdown, not just the obvious ones. She would try to move on now—really try, not just go through the motions. Erik would have expected more from her than total defeat, and she owed it to him to be a productive part of society. She could honor his memory with her life, and wherever he was, hopefully he would be proud of her for carrying on.

Several routes would have taken them directly from Elgin to Des Moines and not sent them through Chicago. But Taylor asked to see it one last time, the home she had shared with Erik. His bitch mother had handled the cancellation of his lease, and her own mother had gathered all of Taylor's personal effects from the greystone before the property owner put it back on the rental market. Surreal, knowing someone else lived and ate and drank and loved inside those walls now, people who had probably never heard the name "Erik Evans," people who would never know any part of the history that unfolded there, or hear any note of the music that had once filled every nook and corner of spaces they now occupied.

Music.

A flash of Erik—images from the past—superimposed themselves over the present, and she saw him as clearly as she'd seen him in the last moments she would ever see him at all, storming out of the guest room holding his binder filled with songs.

"Here you go," he'd said to her then, and in hindsight she could hear the desperation in his voice. *"Sell them. They're all yours."*

"Mom?" The apparition of Erik wafted away. "Didn't you say you brought my old handbag? The big Coach knock-off?"

Behind the wheel as their car idled at a curb outside Erik's old greystone, Taylor's mom nodded. "Yes, in case you asked for it. But when you didn't, I put it in the trunk with all your stuff from the hospital."

"Is everything in it just like it was before?"

Her mom smiled. "Yes, honey. I didn't get rid of a thing."

"Can I get it out of the trunk?"

"Of course. Let me do it, though. You sit tight."

It took her mother only seconds to release the trunk from inside, step to the back of the car, and retrieve Taylor's handbag. She plopped it on the console as she sank behind the wheel again, and Taylor pulled it into her lap.

"Thanks, Mom."

"Any time, sweetie."

Taylor unsnapped the fake buckle that held it closed. Inside, all of her things felt instantly familiar, as if no time had passed at all. Her wallet. Her cell phone. Keys. A leather binder stuffed with random bits of paper covered in Erik's handwriting.

She pulled it out.

All of Erik's words, his thoughts, his feelings and moods—there in tangible form, the essence of him, the proof that his mind and heart had existed and impacted the world around him—she held it her hands, forever safe from his awful, unsentimental family, and from Tillman, and from anyone anywhere who ever wished him less than the best. Taking away his fingers had silenced his music but could never destroy the words he'd penned. They were hers now, more enduring than flesh and bone.

She opened the binder. Touched the pages he'd folded and tucked and pressed against each other in storage. No doubt his fingerprints still existed on them. She rifled through with utmost care, not wanting to disturb the order or method he'd used to index them.

Her fingers landed on something different. A heavier weight of paper than almost everything else in the binder, several sheets stacked and folded together. She carefully tugged them from between two sheets of loose-leaf planner paper covered front and back with scribbled lyrics and hand-drawn guitar tabs.

She unfolded the grid paper and stared at the penciled notes it contained.

And quit breathing.

Account numbers. Names. Personal data. Sketched flowcharts of money distribution. A roadmap to white collar crimes? Certainly what it looked like.

Shouldn't be too hard, figuring out what Erik's notes meant. And after two years, Newell Backstrom had probably started to feel comfortable again, confident that he'd gotten away with everything.

She could change her major. No big deal. She had to repeat at least one semester, anyway. A law enforcement path would limit her. Too many rules. But journalism—she thought about all the reporters swarming the courthouse during her trial for the assault, interested mostly because she was the girlfriend of the man in the garbage bags—reporters could get away with a lot of shit. She had the face for it. The brains. And thanks to the control she learned from Vaccai, she could speak well. Why not? She could get a lot closer to Backstrom's evil with a camera than she had with the Louisville Slugger.

And he would never see her coming.

A knock at her hotel room door jarred Taylor from the memory.

Please be Eric. She hadn't seen him since he stormed out after the phone call about his grandmother. The one text she'd sent asking if he was okay had gone unanswered.

"Oh, thank God," she breathed as she looked through the peephole and saw him in the hallway.

When she opened the door, he didn't walk in. Just stood there, head down, barely looking at her.

"Get in here," she said, the words tough but her tone gentle.

He stepped into the room, paced at the foot of her bed for a moment, then went to the padded chair beside the sofa. He sat, slouched at first, but almost immediately he sat up and braced his elbows on his knees.

Taylor dragged the other chair from across the room and placed it in front of him.

"You okay?" She sat and mirrored his posture.

"I don't know," he said.

Uh-oh.

Taylor looked at the sneakers he wore and frowned. "You're not working today?"

He shook his head. "Nope."

"So are you going to tell me or do I have to drag it out of you?"

He rubbed his face with both hands. "Apparently I gave them a contaminated sample for a drug screen."

"Huh?" Taylor gaped at him. "So? You just re-test."

"It won't do any good. They wanted me gone, so I'm gone."

The journalist in her started to bombard him with questions. Who wanted him gone? Why? She stopped herself before asking anything. Truth was, she knew the answers as well as he did.

"Shit. I'm so sorry, Eric. I sent that FOIA request for the cut-off numbers. I should have known what that would cause."

Eric gave a bitter laugh. "They were all in an uproar about it yesterday, let me tell ya. And of course I'm the only asshole who'd say anything about that to anyone, so there it is."

"Jesus." Taylor got up and walked to the window. She pushed the curtain back with one finger and looked out. "Goddamned small towns."

"How much of this do you really want to hear?" he asked.

She turned around and stared at him. "There's more?"

"Oh, I haven't even gotten started yet."

"Fuck." She left the window and sat down in front of him again. "Start with the contaminated drug screen. Did you give them a dirty sample?"

"Hell, no. I'm clean."

"I'm glad to hear that. But I think you should re-test, regardless. Use a different facility and lab."

"Why? It won't matter. I won't ever get my job back. Too much shit went down. And now Gram—it's all just too much. My whole family is done."

"Wait. Your Gram. What about her?"

He told her a chilling story about his grandmother losing her job, then going home to have a heart attack on the kitchen floor. He talked about family members fighting at the ER, ninety-percent blockages, and stents. Even worse, his Gram's and his insurance had been through the school system, and now they'd lost it along with the family's main source of income.

"Then yesterday Grandpap got a letter in the mail saying he was being investigated for Medicare fraud. Somebody took pictures of him carrying a fifty-pound bag of dog food out of Walmart." Eric pinched the skin between his eyes. "He's disabled because of his back. He knows he's not supposed to pick up anything over twenty pounds. But he's hardheaded and you can't tell him nothing."

"Shit."

He nodded. "That pretty much sums it up."

Taylor sat in silence for a moment, digesting everything he'd told her. What a mess. "So—" She offered a wry smile. "Is there any good news in any of that?"

He sat back and spread his arms wide, palms up. His mouth smiled, but his eyes did not. "Hey, at least I know for a fact I'm not shooting blanks."

"What?" She squinted at him. "Shooting what? *Oh.*"

Oh, God. This, she hadn't expected.

No, Eric. Please say you're joking.

"Haley's pregnant."

Damn it all to hell. Just what he needed—something else to trap him here. A pregnant, teenaged girlfriend and way too many ideals. "Oh, no."

"She's going to terminate," he said. "My kid. My flesh and blood. And apparently there is not one damn thing I can do to stop her."

Taylor reminded herself to breathe. Not easy, given the fact that her heart had lodged itself somewhere just under her chin. "Maybe that's for the best. I don't know."

"I hunted clear to Roanoke, trying to find a lawyer who'd take my case. Couldn't even get anybody to return my calls."

"I'm so sorry." Jeesh. If only an apology could fix this.

"I never took one side or the other of that whole debate," he said. "I don't have an opinion about it, generally speaking. But this is *my* baby. *My* child. I sure as hell have an opinion about *that.*"

Taylor had covered enough stories about the subject to know why he couldn't get a callback from any attorneys. Haley had all the rights as long as it was a fetus inside her body. Eric had none. It was a losing case. Nobody wanted it.

"What did I ever do to anybody?" He dropped his head between his knees. "What have I ever done that's so bad I deserve any of this?"

Tentatively, she reached out and put a hand on his shoulder. Tense. God, he was tense.

How to answer that question? How to explain this truth? That it's not what you do in this life that burns you. It's where you happen to be standing when the lightning strikes.

"If you look at life that way," she said finally. "It'll never add up to more than Pavlov's dog—do this in order to get that. But it's a shitty reward system. If that's what you count on to give you purpose, everything you do will be a disappointment. Life isn't cause and effect. It's random as hell. The only thing you can ever blame yourself for are the choices you make. Never anybody else's."

The private lab Sheriff Hastings used delivered another forty-eight turnaround, this time on Eddie Pace's cheek swab. It came back a probable match for the DNA found on Cody Hess. It was enough to make an arrest. But Eddie Pace had done exactly what Hastings predicted. He ran. The Randall County Sheriff's Office issued a BOLO, and the only thing left to do was hope and wait.

Swab samples went to the state crime lab, too, of course, just to undermine any future challenges about their accuracy, since fast turnarounds still raised a few forensic eyebrows. Hastings subpoenaed Eddie's cell phone records and his ISP and got a no-knock warrant for his residence. Taylor took him information about the website Charles had found with the photos and comment threads by Dylan Altizer. At that point, the option of simply hiding in their holler with the truth buried among them was no longer an option for the Altizer family. Hastings showed them no mercy. He confided in Taylor that after a single conversation with them about Dylan's fetish behavior, he harbored no doubt that they'd known who killed their son all along.

Press conferences happened once a day for nearly a week. All major networks were now represented in Hastings' makeshift studio with its clamshell lighting. Taylor could have scooped them all, but didn't. She had her eye on the long game. Anybody could do a news-at-eleven segment about multiple homicides with a single suspect. She was the only reporter in that crowded room who could do a feature documentary about the whole community of people who stood by and let it happen.

Hennessey sent a satellite truck. Taylor hadn't asked for it, but she did a few live segments so WRCH wouldn't get shoved out of the ratings. Not like it was huge breaking news where people all over the nation stopped what they were doing and gathered around their TVs. Just one more crime story among thousands, covered only because someone else covered it, and forgotten before the next commercial break ended.

Hastings campaigned hard to release the name of their suspect with a photo and get it on the air. Taylor was willing, but Nate Bostick wouldn't hear of it. He arranged for several other be-on-the-lookouts to be issued within the same time frame, all with similar instructions. Only a matter of time before the BOLOs issued by the Sheriff's Office got picked up by the wire, but it was doubtful if anyone could tell which of those suspects they liked for the killings.

WRCH had two reporters on the story, a van with a cameraman and segment producer, and a satellite truck with its handful of technicians. What they didn't have was a runner. Tuesday afternoon, Taylor grabbed Eric by his beefy bicep and plunked him down in front of her laptop in the hotel room.

"Application." She pointed to the screen. "Fill it out. Let me look over it when you're done, and I'll send it to the right person."

He gave her a dark look. "Application for what?"

"Production runner. We need one."

"What is it, though? What would I be doing?"

"Everything nobody else wants to do," she said.

"So, general flunky, then."

"Pretty much."

"What's it pay?"

"Around ten an hour. All the overtime you want, benefits after ninety days." She knew this because she had asked. The station already had his new hire packet together.

He turned back to her laptop. "Where do I sign?"

Taylor grinned. "Put me down as a reference. I'm all you need."

From his seat on Taylor's hotel bed, long legs stretched out and crossed at the ankles, Charles spoke up. "Put me down, too."

"Me three," Perry said from the sofa.

Kavanagh raised a hand. Four.

"You'll have to pee in a cup," Charles said, focused on his own laptop that sat balanced across his thighs.

Eric turned in his chair and looked at him. "Not at this clinic."

"We'll get you set up in Abingdon." Charles pecked away on his keyboard. "I got your back."

Kavanagh reached for the empty coffee mug on the table beside his chair. He picked it up and held it toward Eric. "Black."

Eric stared at him. "What the fuck, man? I don't even have the application filled out yet."

The degree of stern on Kavanagh's face impressed even Taylor. "Do you want the job or not?" he asked.

"God damn it." Eric pushed back from the laptop and went to fill Kavanagh's cup from the coffeemaker two feet from where Kavanagh sat.

Taylor cracked up. Didn't even try to hide it. Kid would fit right in with that foul-mouthed, irreverent, once-in-a-lifetime crazy-talented bunch of Neanderthals.

CHAPTER THIRTY-SEVEN

The phone beside her hotel bed rang that night around ten-thirty. Taylor was alone—everyone else had cleared out to their own rooms a few hours earlier. Just her and the murder wall now, with a big photo of Eddie Pace added below the victims.

She picked up the receiver. "Hello?"

It was Hastings. "We found him."

"Oh, shit. Really? Where?"

"Holed up in Bland County, somebody's hunting cabin. State Police were doing aerial surveillance and saw his vehicle parked in a clearing. Recognized it from the BOLO."

"So you have him now?"

"Nope."

Taylor nearly dropped the phone. "What?"

"Guys were from VSP headquarters in Wytheville. They may have their own issues over there, but they aren't our issues. I got a direct phone call before anything went out over the radio. They put a team in the woods but aren't going to pick him up until tomorrow morning."

"What's the thinking?"

"The thinking," he said. "Is that Nate Bostick has court tomorrow. It's a homicide case and he'll be tied up all day."

"Another murder, huh? You guys are getting as bad as D.C."

"Lot of drugs flowing through this county," Hastings said. "They blaze a trail."

"Okay," she said. "I get it—about Bostick. For what it's worth, I like your style, Sheriff."

"Glad you approve."

"What's your plan?"

"They'll pick him up in the morning around nine, bring him here. Bostick'll hear about it, but he'll be stuck in court. You're welcome to sit behind the mirror. But come alone. My deal is with you, not with WRCH."

"Gotcha." She thought for a moment. "He'll actually be under arrest this time, right? Not just in for questioning?"

"Right. And if he wants to talk without counsel, we won't stop him. If he lawyers up, oh well. At least he'll be in custody. I feel like we can get the death penalty with what we already have. He doesn't need to say a word."

Jesus. Capital crimes. Plural. It would take one hell of a defense lawyer to get Eddie Pace out of this.

Or a CA with something to lose.

"I'm worried about Bostick," she said. "He's been the best defense attorney Pace could have had so far. I just don't see him being very effective for the people."

"Oh, there's no way he'll be lead on this. They'll bring in a special prosecutor. I just have to keep him out of the way until we get that far."

"Any ideas?"

"You bet. I burned this landline up tonight. Remember that scorched earth you were talking about a while back? You would have loved it. I lit the fucking match."

Taylor told Charles about the phone call, but no one else. She barely slept that night. Finally dozed off around three in the morning, but dreamed of prisoners in orange jumpsuits strapped to stainless steel tables. They awaited lethal injection, IV sites prepped. Taylor asked someone just before the alarm woke her if heart stick was an option.

Just after ten a.m., deputies brought Eddie into the county's biggest interrogation room wearing handcuffs. Shackled him to a ring on the table and left him alone.

Hastings joined Taylor in the observation room. Unlike Bostick the day he'd occupied the same room with her, Hastings didn't sit.

He went to the two-way mirror and stood there for a long while, watching Eddie.

Taylor watched alongside him.

"I'll never win another election in this county," he said quietly. "I'm done. You lose the backing of the political machine and you lose the votes. But I talked about it with my wife, and we discussed it with the kids as best we could without getting them too upset." He blew out a long breath. "You grow up here. You leave, you go out into the real world, and you find out half of everything you thought you knew is wrong. So you come back, and you want to change things. You want to repay a debt, for your raising." He shook his head. "But you just end up getting buried. The brightest kids graduate, go off to college, and never look back. Can you blame them?"

Taylor met his eye, and they shared a long look.

"Our greatest export is our children," he said. "They don't want this broken way of life. They try to challenge it and get the shit kicked out of them like that Blevins kid. So off they go, and all we're left with is defects like that right there." He pointed to Eddie. "No wonder our community is circling the drain."

He rubbed his forehead. "Okay. Guess it's show time." He checked the recorder while he was standing there. Apparently satisfied, he gave Taylor one last glance and walked out the door.

She settled in to watch.

Hastings walked into the interview room with a manila folder, just like before. This time, he removed photos of Dylan Altizer, taken from the website Charles had found. When she'd showed them to Hastings earlier that week, Taylor had no idea he'd use them to break Eddie. But now, behind the mirror, she smiled. Smart man.

He placed them on the table in a row, six photos of Dylan naked, semi-aroused, in suggestive poses. Sat back and folded his arms.

Eddie tugged on the handcuffs. "God damn it—what the fuck is wrong with you, Hastings?"

Hastings shook his head and wagged a finger. "See, you've got that backward. You're not the one asking questions here. I am. And right now, I'm asking about your relationship with Dylan Altizer. Were you lovers?"

"Jesus! Fuck, no." Agitated, Eddie jerked against the cuffs again, rising a few inches out of his chair with the effort. "You're a sick bastard, Hastings. Sick."

Eddie's clothes looked like they hadn't seen a good wash in days. Same with Eddie himself. Unkempt, his hair stuck out in every direction. His hands had dirt on them. Burying another body? Taylor had to wonder.

"Did he turn you on?" Hastings pointed to Dylan's near-erection in the photo. "Something had him going pretty good here. Was he thinking about you?"

Eddie spat in Hasting's face.

Oh, dear lord. Taylor recoiled in sympathy.

Hastings pulled a handkerchief from his pocket and slowly mopped his face. Took his time about it. Folded the handkerchief and put it back where he got it.

He reached into the manila envelope and pulled out photos of Dylan in the barrel, just the way Eric had found him. He lay them in a row above the others.

"Maybe you like him this way better," Hastings said. "Improvement?"

Eddie's face had started to blotch. Red on his cheeks, pale around his eyes. His features twisted, and he shook his head like that was going to make it all go away.

Hastings pursed his lips. Almost smiled. Didn't. Sat forward with his elbows on the table instead. "You know he was HIV positive, right?"

At first it looked like Eddie had hiccups. His body jerked, shoulders hitched up and down. Then he hung his head and just sat there crying.

"I want my daddy," he said.

Hastings laughed, a dry, cynical sound. "Your daddy ain't going to help you now, boy. He's gonna wash his hands of you. I mean, seriously—you think he's going to rush in here and save your sweet little ass? Now, he probably doesn't care that you killed all those fellas, as long as you didn't get caught. But you did—" Hastings sat back in the chair again, maybe to get out of range in case Eddie hocked another wad of spit. "And we have evidence of sexual assault. That part?" He shook his head. "I don't think he'll like."

Eddie sobbed and snotted and couldn't mop any of it up with his hands still shackled to the table. He bent over and rubbed his face on his sleeve.

Hastings gathered up the photos of Altizer and put them back in the folder. From it, he took an image Taylor had never seen. She squinted and leaned toward the glass, trying to get a better look. Ah. Brandi Deel. On the medical examiner's table, contorted in the same position she'd died trying to escape the barrel.

"Now this one," Hastings said, pointing to the photo. "Apparently she didn't interest you. She had DNA on her, but it wasn't yours. Thoughts?"

Eddie sat back up, but not straight. His shoulders slumped, chin dragged his chest. "I don't have a fucking clue," he almost whispered. Taylor had to strain to hear him. "She was one of Nate's girls."

The observation room door slammed open and a dervish blew in. Slightly built female in a blazer and slacks, curly hair pulled back from her face in a tight bun. Plainclothes, not street clothes. A cop—but why did she look familiar?

"Shut him up!" The woman yelled to someone behind her. "Shut him the fuck up *now.*" She stormed to the video recorder and ripped the feed from the back of it. Came around the edge of the table and beat a palm on the glass.

A fed?

Jesus, Hastings—what have you done?

The woman turned, and Taylor caught her in profile. And sat gaping, stunned by recognition. *No fucking way.*

A man in a dark suit entered the interview room and beckoned for Hastings. The Sheriff looked pale, but he got up and followed the man out the door.

The woman faced Taylor without a smile or a single trace of emotion. "Special Agent A.J. Sullivan. We've met."

Ann Sullivan. Chicago P.D.

Taylor reeled, and had to grab the edge of the table for balance.

"No, it's not a coincidence that I'm here," Sullivan said. "But we'll talk about that later."

Hastings ushered the other agent into the observation room. The four of them stood around the table, silent for a long moment. Then Sullivan spoke again.

"We need a meeting," she said. "We need it yesterday. So let's get it scheduled, then the two of you go wherever you need to go to get everything you have about this snakepit. Bring it with you. And clear your calendar for the evening. It'll take a while."

Taylor sat beside Anne Sullivan in an Abingdon hotel bar while they waited for the others to arrive.

"The Evans case fucked me up," Sullivan said. "Years went by, and I couldn't close my eyes without hearing you scream that day. I quit the force in 2006. Took some time off, thought I was done with law enforcement. But I'd stayed in touch with the agents in Wisconsin—they were my support group—and after you leveled Backstrom, I started putting out feelers. One thing led to another and here I am."

Taylor nodded, looking down at her drink. Johnnie Walker, neat. She thought about tossing it, then just took a sip instead.

"I check up on you twice a year," Sullivan said. "The anniversary of Evans' murder, and the anniversary of Backstrom's racketeering conviction. And that last one was just this past month. So I find you here, in this shithole, eyeball deep in Deliverance. I mean, if you hear banjos …."

Taylor laughed. "Paddle faster."

They shared a chuckle.

Odd, sitting here over drinks with Ann Sullivan. Taylor hadn't given that woman two minutes of thought in the intervening years since Chicago. Yet clearly she'd been on Sullivan's mind, and that touched her in a way she couldn't quite articulate.

Sullivan sat straighter, gaze fixed on the lobby outside the bar's main doorway. "There's Varner. He's got Hastings with him. Let's go."

They left their drinks on the bar with enough money to cover the tab and tips. The four of them rode an elevator to the fourth floor, where S.A. Varner led them to a room at the end of the corridor.

This was no Holiday Inn Express. Varner opened the door to a large suite, no beds visible. Just a large sofa in a large space, with closed doors on both lateral walls and a corkboard display on one side of the room.

Taylor walked closer to the corkboard and started tracking the flow of their investigation. Her fingers tightened on the handle of her briefcase.

Holy shit.

Most of the names she had pinned to her own murder wall also made an appearance on the FBI's. All of the county supervisors. Town leaders. Bud Mabry. And Nate Bostick.

Under the CA's photo, a picture of Brandi Deel, alive and looking much better than she had in the mug shot Hastings had showed her. But other photos accompanied it. Girls Taylor didn't recognize.

She pointed to them. "Are these more victims?"

Sullivan nodded. "Of a sort. But they're not dead. Yet." She took off her blazer and hung it over the back of a chair. "Sheriff, would you like to sit?"

Hastings shook his head. His color looked off. Way off.

"Okay," Sullivan said. "Beckett. Tell me what you have."

Taylor unpacked everything from her briefcase and lay it on a table sitting near the corkboard. "I don't know what I have, actually. A bunch of little pieces that don't add up. Piddly stuff, like a county vet doing contract work with no contract and no RFP. The PSA sticking it to their customers with cut-offs that are possibly illegal and failing to return new service deposits. That sort of thing."

"We want all of it," Sullivan said. "We need to look at it, see what puzzle pieces fit where. Hunt for patterns. In all honesty, it'll probably slide off the radar pretty fast. Those things may be crimes, may not be crimes. Mostly, they're symptoms of a broken society. If the citizens of Randall County don't give a shit, then neither do we. But we're looking for the money trail, and we have to know how it all works so we get there in good shape to follow it."

Sullivan walked over to the corkboard and pointed to a photo of Rosewood Industrial Park. Under it, two names—Parker and Emmalee Jackson, sellers. Five hundred acres. From those names, an arrow pointing to Bud Mabry.

"We've looked at this hard," Sullivan said. "This is a lot of money. We asked ourselves who profited the most from this whole deal. And this is where it gets interesting." She folded her arms and leaned against the table beside the corkboard. "Beckett, you know a lot about engineering firms. You know a lot about fraud. Has Rosewood come up for you yet?"

Taylor nodded. "Oh, yes. The engineering firm contracted for that project is out of Bristol—Jackson & Howell." She stopped talking and blinked. Looked at the corkboard. Looked at Sullivan. Looked back at the corkboard.

Parker and Emmalee Jackson.

"Oh, shit," she said.

Sullivan smiled, a closed-mouth, cat-munching-on-a-canary grin.

"It gets better," Sullivan said. She pointed to Bud Mabry's picture. "His wife is Caroline Jackson Mabry."

"Well, isn't that convenient." Taylor snuck a glance at Hastings. He'd leaned onto the table, braced on his hands.

"Jackson's a fairly common name." Sullivan folded her arms again. "But we didn't take anything for granted. Did some digging, and guess what? Same family."

Taylor let that sink in. "Wow."

"Now *that's* the kind of money that gets our attention." S.A. Varner finally spoke. He'd taken a seat at the table near Hastings, one leg crossed over the other knee, holding a pen longways in both hands and waggling it back and forth. "Which is why we're prepping a couple operatives. By mid-summer, they should be embedded."

Taylor's brows shot up. "As in, undercover?"

"Yes." Sullivan met her gaze, dark eyes as unfathomable as they'd been in Chicago, all those years ago. "Which is why we needed Pace to stop talking. There's a lot more to this. Some of it's connected, and some of it isn't. Until we get inside and figure out how it all lines out, we don't want to unseat any of the main players. And for that—" She looked at Hastings. "We're going to need your help, Sheriff."

He nodded, still braced on the table.

"I assume you wouldn't have called us if you didn't intend to follow through." Sullivan watched him.

He nodded again, a slower and smaller movement this time.

"Those girls," he said after a moment. "Under Nate's picture. I know all of them."

Sullivan glanced toward the corkboard. "I'm sure you do."

Hastings finally stood straight. "They're drug court participants."

"Yes, they are." Sullivan tapped one of the photos with a finger. "So, let's talk about that. Her, for example. Her sentence and her offense—on their merits, they could be totally unrelated. She was caught holding enough for felony distribution. She pled to less than half an ounce. Five-hundred-dollar fine, waived for community service. Have you noticed any kind of pattern to the leniency, Sheriff?"

Hastings said nothing, just rubbed his forehead.

Sullivan pointed to the others in the lineup. "These girls have all come forward at one point or another and talked about the deal they were offered. Bostick picks and chooses who he lets skate on the sole merit of whether or not he can make use of their talents. These girls are prostitutes. They're working it off on their backs. Every one of them was a felony arrest. He didn't pursue felony charges on any of them. This is what Eddie was talking about—they're 'Nate's Girls.' We have no fucking idea who the clients are at this time. But they exist. And we have to figure out how to bring this down without getting every single one of these girls killed."

"Good God Almighty." Hastings mopped his brow. Then he rubbed his chest.

"Sheriff, are you okay?" Taylor asked.

He nodded. "I am, but thank you for asking. I get chest pains—angina, and it's old news—I'm not having a heart attack. But the stress is killing me just the same." He looked at Sullivan. "You're telling me that Nate Bostick is running a prostitution ring right under my fucking nose. And that Eddie and Darrell know enough about it to bury him, and that's why he won't lift one damn finger to put them away." He paced a couple steps, then grabbed a chair and sat heavily. "And you want me to just keep working with that bastard, like I never heard any of this."

"Correct," Sullivan said. "Eddie Pace is going to prison. There's no squirreling out of that. But Bostick will find a way to keep him quiet. Pace won't last long in lockup. It'll look like a jailhouse beatdown and nobody will question it. And you'll have to treat it like one when it happens. Can you do that?"

Hastings put his elbows on his knees and hung his head. "God damn it." He sat there for a minute. "God damn it."

"Deel was a hit." Sullivan glanced at Taylor. "For sure. We don't know how Bostick arrived at Pace as the one to carry it out, but I'm willing to bet that Bostick had no clue about the other victims. He just wanted to shut Deel up. And Eddie saw the perfect opportunity to get himself a little leverage—make sure Bostick could go down for the same shit, so if Eddie ever started taking heat, he could count on Bostick wanting every bit of it to stay quiet."

"So what's my role in all this?" Taylor asked.

"You report the news," Sullivan said. "Do your thing. Whatever angle you're coming at this from—knock yourself out. Do your whole civil action thing. We'll applaud you. I'd like to think you'll be in communication with us before you go to air, though, just to make sure we're all on the same page. You're going to stay away from Bostick. But Rosewood? Fair game. And then—not a damn thing's going to happen. Nothing's going to change. And that's when they're going to get cocky. And careless. We'll already have our people in place, and we'll use their arrogance against them. Just like you did with Backstrom. It'll either work, or it won't. I intend to go down swinging on this one, like you and that Louisville Slugger."

Taylor and Hastings rode the elevator down together in silence.

On the ground floor, he finally brought it up. "What's she talking about—Louisville Slugger?"

Taylor shrugged. "Sullivan and I go way back. I took out some frustration once, with a baseball bat. She remembers."

For the first time in days—at least that Taylor had seen—Hastings laughed. Genuine, honest-to-goodness, and heartfelt.

"I'm glad we get along well," he said. "Because looks like we're going to be stuck with each other for a while." His smile faded. "Something I want you to know, though—it bothers me that you heard me go after Eddie today. I said some awful things."

"I get it, Sheriff." Taylor looked him in the eye. "You were just pushing his buttons."

"Yeah." He gave her a half-smile. "Still—the person I have to turn into to get this job done sometimes—I don't think I'm going to come out of this a better man."

"You will," Taylor said. "Even though at the end of the day we may never make a difference here. The people have to care first. They have to want better for themselves. There may come a time when you have to just take your family and walk away."

Hastings didn't answer, but the look in his eye said that idea wasn't a new one for him.

"I'm taking Blevins to Richmond with me," she said. "Him and his dog." Taylor smiled at the absurdity of that—a geriatric hound. In her loft. Of all things. "I got him a job at WRCH, entry level. He doesn't give a shit about broadcast journalism, but it's money. I'm going to make sure he gets some Gen Ed classes under his belt, even if I have to pay for them myself."

"Good." Hastings nodded. "I'm really glad to hear that."

"He feels an obligation to his grandparents," she said. "I don't think there's anybody else in line to take care of them. It'll be a lot to work out. But he'll never come back here. Randall County forfeited a national treasure when those petty-ass thugs treated his family the way they did. Personally—I couldn't care less if somebody dropped a nuke and blew this whole part of the state off the map. I know you have ties here, and I respect that. But just know where I stand so you won't be blindsided when I go to air."

"I appreciate the heads up," he said. "But for what it's worth, I understand. And part of me agrees with every goddamned word you say."

CHAPTER THIRTY-EIGHT

Sometimes so much flat land surrounding him made Eric want to take cover. Something to be said for all those mountains and ridgelines back home, like a fence for cows that kept the coyotes and bears out. You feel safe, when you think there's a wall between you and the things that want to hurt you.

But then somebody leaves the gate open, and you get out. You get lost. And you wander around for a minute, until you're standing on the other side of the fence, looking in. And that's when you see all the coyotes and bears were in there with you all along.

Life wasn't perfect this side of Appalachia. Eric didn't like his job. He didn't like that whole cutthroat, competitive, two-faced world of TV news, where even the production assistants were sniveling little bitches and nobody meant a goddamned word they said. But at least it was honest bullshit. Nobody pretended like they actually cared. You knew where you stood. He could have applied himself and made more money, gotten a better position. But seemed like applying himself to school instead made a lot more sense. He didn't like economics, either. Still, the class had a beginning, middle, and an end. You could mark it on a calendar. And then all the days that came after wouldn't have economics anywhere in them.

Every week he sent most of his paycheck back home to his grandparents. Grandpap was fighting to keep his disability. Good. Better to fight than just roll over and give up. Here in Richmond, Eric had it easy. Taylor gave him a place to stay, fed him, bought him a ten-year-old Dodge Ram to drive as long as he kept his grades up. Hard to believe she'd buy him anything after the way Popper pissed all over the inside of her loft. A walking sprinkler system with no off-switch, every vertical surface in there. Old dog wouldn't have survived another winter under the chicken hutch. But you'd think he'd show some gratitude. Eric put Popper in a crate. Popper hiked his leg and aimed outside the crate. Hit the side of Taylor's solid white sofa. Then the old hound sat on his dry, clean bed and howled like somebody was killing him.

Every now and then Eric let his mind touch Haley. She was a sore that never healed, wouldn't even scab over and start to itch. Just kept bleeding, a little bit of hurt seeping out every day. Eric didn't miss her, and he wasn't just telling himself that. He didn't dream about her, didn't have fantasies about her. Thoughts of her body left him cold. Wouldn't have been that way if she hadn't carried his baby inside, his DNA, his bloodline, and little cells of him that would have become little cells of a brand-new person, if only she'd given it enough time. He hated her for that. But maybe one day the wound would heal. Turn into a scar. He could live with that. Taylor lived just fine with hers. At least the ones on the outside.

He'd never fooled around much with Facebook when he lived back home. But here, so far removed from all the small-town drama, it turned into one of his guilty pleasures. He didn't talk to people, really. Just dropped a meme here and there, or a funny video, and ignored the hell out of Messenger. Last time he looked, he had fifty-six new notifications. Marked them as "read" and moved on.

But he'd figured out real quick that people watched his posts. So he gave them something to talk about. Who was it said living well was the best revenge? George Herbert? Well, old George might have been on to something there. Every good photo that Taylor took of him, like the ones in D.C. when they covered the White House for a story, and the Lincoln Memorial, and one of him behind the wheel of his truck—he made sure everybody back home saw those. Candid shots of him in the studio, working around high-dollar equipment and standing next to people who were household names, at least in that part of Virginia … folks might act like they didn't care about any of that, but he remembered his own pangs of longing and envy when others got to live real lives, and he was just stuck.

For several days, he'd known Taylor was planning a trip to Roanoke to meet with some of the attorneys mopping the courtroom floor with Randall County. He just didn't know why she made him ride along. Technically not work, yet not quite a day off—bullshit, more likely—Taylor just wanting a pack mule to carry her stuff. It was only when they blew right past 581 that he realized something else was up.

"Where you going?" He looked up from his Biology notes that he'd brought along to study.

"Thought we'd take a little detour," she said. "Something I want you to see."

Eric scowled at her. "I hate it when you do shit like this."

But Taylor just smiled. Hard to rattle that bitch.

"You'll thank me later," she said.

He closed his notes and watched the scenery flash by. Damn "safety corridor" on I-81—double fines. Just a speed trap. All the Salem exits, and then they hit the mountains. Slow grades. Not terribly familiar, this landscape, but getting there.

Eric's gut started to twist, and he shifted in the seat hoping a new position would make it stop. "We're going to be late for the appointment. You know that, right?"

"No, we won't," she said. "I know what I'm doing."

She took the main exit for Christiansburg and followed the bypass into Blacksburg. Pretty suspicious, where she was headed.

"Come on, Taylor," he said. "What the hell?"

The Tech campus sprawled on their right, off in the distance but still lording over the countryside. By the time Taylor hooked a right at the stoplight and rounded the traffic circle at Duck Pond Road, Eric no longer had to ask "where," but "what," and "why."

He hoisted his fat Biology textbook. "I'm going to throw this at you if you don't tell me why we're here."

She didn't even look at him, just burst out laughing. "Chill, Blevins. You're going to like it."

"You drive folks crazy," he griped. "Make people want to throttle the daylights out of you."

"Big talk, Blevins. I'd like to see you try."

"Pull over and it can be arranged."

She shook her head, still smiling. "God help me—I've created a monster."

"Maybe," he said. "But I'm a very cute monster. And you know it."

They passed a bronze, life-sized statue of a horse, a woman, and a dog. "Running Together—" he remembered it from Upward Bound, the day they let him tour the vet school.

And just that fast he had a lump in his throat the size of his fist.

He swallowed hard, all the smart-ass in him flown right out the window. "Taylor, what are we doing?"

She waited until she'd nosed her Audi into a parking space near the front entrance before she answered.

"There's a fourth-year vet student here named David Ingram," she said. "You're going to shadow him today. This will all be supervised by a staff veterinarian, of course, but you're going to get a taste of what it's like. You're going to remember what it felt like to have a dream. I won't let you give up on this, Eric. Not unless you spend your whole day here and decide it's not what you want to do after all. Then we'll have to back up ten yards and punt. But right now? We're running about five minutes late, so we need to go."

She opened her car door.

Eric did the same, stepped out onto the pavement and looked around. Cool green grass, towering pines, and a shade garden at the center of the parking lot. That lump in his throat just wasn't going away.

Taylor's cell phone beeped with a message.

"Shit." She shut her car door and pulled her phone from her handbag. "It's Charles. Give me a sec."

Eric waited while she sent a short speech-to-text reply— "We're here. Just going in now."

Hard not to smile, watching her around Charles. Even a stupid text message from him would stop her in her tracks.

What the hell. Might as well state the obvious. "You know he's in love with you, right?"

Taylor almost dropped her phone. She caught it in time and shoved it back in her handbag. "Yeah—I think maybe I noticed."

Dead serious now, no joke. "Are you going to break his heart?"

At first she avoided his gaze. Then, slowly, she raised her eyes to meet his. "Probably not."

Eric grinned so wide his face hurt, and he didn't even try to hide it. "Congratulations," he said. "Now let's go in here and get this done."

About the Author

Diane Ryan is Southern born and raised. Over the years, she has rescued and rehabilitated horses, dogs, and cats. She's an active blogger, cryptocurrency fancier, and author of two previous novels, *Talking to Luke* and *Wingspan*. These days, she lives on a mountain in Central Appalachia with a houseful of animals and enjoys the wildlife that regularly comes to visit.

Afterword from the Author

Writing this novel was a challenge for me on many levels. Aside from the alternating points of view and interwoven timelines, I also had to wrestle with the immediacy of the story and how close it hits to my own experiences in Central Appalachia. While violent murders are relatively commonplace here, they're mostly drug-related or the result of domestic dysfunction. We've yet to encounter an Eddie Pace, but I believe the environment is very nurturing for that sort of deviance and it's only a matter of time before it happens.

Although this is a work of fiction, I expect some backlash about this novel. Those who are oblivious to the social decay in our region may be appalled by my portrayal of modern Appalachian culture. Very few plot points in this novel are pure fabrication. I've taken great liberties with them, composited counties and crimes, and reached conclusions that may differ from those one could reach within the actual circumstances, all in an effort to ensure this creative work tells the story without indicting specific individuals.

That said, behind every twist and turn in this story is truth, none more poignant and heart-wrenching than my accounts of vicious animal abuse at the hands of county employees. A former animal control officer reviewed the scene in which Eric Blevins recalls an incident at a local shelter. She said it was so accurate based on her personal experiences that she could barely stand to read it.

This brings me to a final and most salient point. The characters in this novel are just that: characters. They are not depictions of real people. I took great care to avoid descriptions of physical appearance or personality that echoed those of actual human beings. I kept extensive documentation of the character creation process, including photographs and notes regarding celebrity personas I built profiles around. This is the first time I've ever done this while writing a novel, but I felt it was prudent in this case. Not a single character is based on a real person.